SEER

OF THE

STRAIT

SEER

OF THE

STRAIT

THE SEERS OF DAWN
BOOK ONE

Drea Talley

PERIAPTPRESS.COM

This is a work of fiction. Similarities to real people, places, or events are entirely coincidental.

SEER OF THE STRAIT
First Edition.
June 25, 2024

Periapt Press
PO Box 25693
Colorado Springs CO 80936
www.periaptpress.com

ISBN: 979-8-9903639-1-5

Chapter 1

CHIMES SOUNDED IN the small shop as the old, heavy wooden door opened. A telltale tittering accompanied the sound of multiple shoes shuffling past the door, which was met by a deep sigh from farther in the shop. Three young women—wealthy by the vibrant, bejeweled embroidery of their vests and the satin finish of their pantaloons—made their way into the very small shop toward the counter that filled the entire back wall.

"Carys," the young woman in front called out, clearly the leader of this little entourage. She looked as if she were not quite 20, with glossy caramel hair and bright eyes that nearly matched. "Carys, darling, I need you!"

There was another sigh, and movement beyond the curtained doorway behind the counter. A minute later the curtains parted, and the owner of the name Carys emerged from the back rooms. Carys was not old, but certainly older than any in the nervous trio before her, closer to her 30th year than her 20th. She pushed hair like buckwheat honey back from her face with hands stained by working with herbs and regarded the young women with a slight purse to her lips. Her eyes were veiled, a carefully embroidered bit of thin material that hid the upper half of her face, eyelash lace brushing the apples of her cheeks. Despite the veil, however, there was no question that the woman was glaring. Emiri came to Carys's shop for one thing, and one thing only.

"I do not give readings on the new moon, Emiri," Carys said without preamble or greeting. "You know this."

The young woman named Emiri stepped up to the counter, her eyes luminous and pleading. "Carys, please, you must help me," she said as her friends hung back, almost nervously. "Pasha Yazuv's son was said to have spent hours alone with Afet Doğan! Hours! I must know if I still have a chance with the pasha's son!"

Carys closed her eyes then reached up and rubbed her brow through the thin veil. She breathed deeply and did her best to school her features. This close, the veil didn't quite obscure her expression. At least, not enough to hide her exasperation.

"Calling on the spirits is tenuous at best during the new moon," Carys said wearily. This was not the first time young Emiri had made this request. "It will cost me, and therefore it will cost you."

Emiri looked sheepish and a bit uncomfortable. "Ah, yes, about that," the young lady said, shifting her weight from foot to foot. "I only have enough for your usual fee."

"Well then," Carys replied, turning to head back through the curtains. "Thank you for wasting my time and yours."

"Wait!"

Carys paused, a hand resting against the fabric of the heavy curtains, ready to move them, and looked back over her shoulder. "Yes?"

Hands on the counter, Emiri leaned forward, expression distraught and earnest. "I don't have more money, but I did bring something else to pay you with! I know the new moon is hard on you!"

Head tipped to the side, Carys considered. Emiri was foolish and obsessive like any other woman who had just crossed the bridge into adulthood. However, the young woman had a good heart. Carys had peered beyond for her many times and knew her to be one of the better examples of the merchant class. She also knew that Serhat Yavuz would be a very good match for Emiri, not only in temperament but also in elevating the aspiring young woman's status.

"Fine," Carys said at last, sighing again. She took her hand away from the curtain and motioned to the alcove at the far end of the counter.

"Please sit. Your friends can wait in the shop, provided they have the sense not to bother anything."

"Of course, Seer," one of the other girls answered quickly, wide-eyed and a little intimidated. "We would never!"

Emiri didn't quite scamper over to the alcove. It was a strange little room, added onto the small shop at some point. It did not close off, but the narrow doorway and domed ceiling helped make sure that the sound within did not travel outside very well. It had large windows of thick stained glass that filtered the light but made it hard to clearly see anything outside. In the alcove was a plush, curved bench that could easily fit two people and a sturdy wooden chair with a high back and a cushioned seat. The back of the chair was painstakingly carved with chasing vines, and on the crown of the high back was the crescent moon. Emiri settled into the bench and tried not to fidget as Carys took up the chair.

"Thank you so much for doing this," Emiri blurted out as Carys sat.

With a slight shake of the head, Carys held up her hand and Emiri grew quiet. Carys reached over and picked up a simple silken pouch, from which she removed a deck of cards. Emiri bit her lip as Carys shuffled the cards. Their backs were beautifully illustrated and accented with gold and silver leaf in the shape of vines, like those on the chair, twisting around a simple coronet. Once shuffled, Carys set the cards before Emiri. Emiri did not need to be instructed—they had done this many times. She cut the cards and waited for Carys to take them back.

The cards once more in hand, Carys flipped over the top three and set them on the table between the two women. The first was a crowned figure sitting on a throne. It was impossible to tell the gender of the figure, but it didn't really matter. The figure radiated strength and command. The second card was a woman, stretched out across what looked like a velvet bed, smiling and eyes closed as if awash with pleasure. The final card was simply the sun, golden and radiant, against a perfect sky.

"Well?" Emiri asked.

"Your patience has not improved," Carys said dryly, looking over the cards.

Silence fell at the table as the two women looked over the cards before them. They could hear the shuffling in the main room as Emiri's friends looked around but did their best not to touch anything. There really wasn't that much to look at in the small shop, just jars of tinctures and dried herbs, and then the counter, behind which were shelves filled with more herbs and also various powders. The silence at the table stretched, and finally Emiri exhaled sharply, frustrated.

"Now you're just tormenting me," the young woman said.

A smile quirked the corner of Carys's mouth. "Maybe. All right, little bird, don't ruffle your feathers at me. If you want Serhat Yazuv, you need to be more forthright in your intentions."

Emiri blinked. "What?"

With a snicker, Carys leaned forward and tapped the first card. "The Monarch represents your goal, which is the pasha's son. He is obviously not a prince, but he has a kingdom, even if it is simply trade routes and a manor. The Lover," Carys continued, tapping the second card, "represents what he wants. He doesn't want a good match; he wants you to be crazy about him. Emiri, my dove, you don't bring a lot to the table here other than yourself. Your father isn't as rich, and his connections aren't helpful to Pasha Yazuv's business ambitions. However, the pasha has allowed Serhat to choose his own bride, and Serhat is just enough of a romantic to pick you anyway. If, and only if, you can appeal to that.

"So that is my advice to you: Give Serhat a lover, not a business alliance, and then," Carys finished, tapping the Sun, "you will win."

"Oh," Emiri said quietly, cheeks pink, but with a hopeful smile on her face. "I… I can do that. He is very handsome, and we both love to read, and I do become enchanted when he starts telling me stories about where he's traveled. I just… I assumed… Well, nevermind." Emiri cleared her throat and sat up straighter, shoulders back. "Thank you, Seer, for the telling. Here is your payment."

As Carys gathered the cards and shuffled them back into the deck, Emiri emptied the contents of a small purse onto the table. Carys did not bother to count the pile of silver obols. Emiri was a frequent customer, and even if Carys wasn't sure of the girl's character it would be considered rude at this point in their relationship. The surprise came when Emiri also set down an envelope of heavy linen paper addressed to "The Friend of Emiri Bulut." Curious, Carys retrieved the envelope and examined it. The seal on the back was of the House of Özdemir. The Lord of the Strait. The ruler of Vasi.

Carys stared at the seal in shock. "Emiri," she began, looking back up at the young woman, "my dove, what is this?"

"It's an invitation to the Midsummer celebration in the royal gardens," Emiri said excitedly. The two girls in the main room apparently heard that part and looked into the alcove with a mixture of surprise and envy. "Father received invitations from the head of the Guild. I think all the Great Families did. Since I am not yet betrothed, my extra invitation is for a friend. I decided to offer it to you, to make up for inconveniencing you!"

Carys looked back down at the invitation in her hands. The Great Families were the top ten houses in the Merchant's Guild, and Emiri's family had just recently overtaken the tenth position. Emiri really was a precious thing. This was a rare and coveted gift, worth far more than the reading Carys had just given her.

"Are you sure?" Carys asked, arching an eyebrow.

Emiri nodded. "I am sure. I know you indulge me more than you should."

Well, that was true. Slowly, Carys smiled. "Very well, little bird. I will see you at the party. Now go soothe your friends who are prickling with jealousy. Oh, and wear something vibrant. Serhat likes women in flowers, reds, and pinks."

With an excited squeal, Emiri jumped up and rushed around the table to hug Carys before heading back into the shop and then toward the door with her friends. The chattering started before the door could close behind them. Shaking her head, Carys leaned back in the chair but smiled in the direction the girls had retreated. They were adorable, in their way.

"You are too kind to her," said a masculine voice. It came from inside the alcove, behind the bench where Emiri had been sitting.

Rolling her eyes, Carys looked over to where the voice had come from. There was a form, just starting to take shape in the dark corner. Wisps of purple and magenta smoke began to coalesce into the shape of a man. Well, not precisely a man. The eyes were too large, the features too sharp, and… well, the horns were certainly off-putting. The look Carys gave the figure was a touch weary but faintly amused.

"She's not so bad," Carys said, getting up. She slid the cards back into the pouch and moved back into the shop proper.

"Do you really think the pasha's son will take her?" the apparition asked, following behind and growing more solid with each step.

Heading toward the front door, Carys opened it long enough to flip the sign out front to "Closed" and then came back in, pulling it shut and locking it. "I am certain," Carys said after she turned the lock. "I could see the shape of him, how they are linked, and the strength of his desire. I'm sure Emiri was doing everything properly, but Sehrat wants a storybook romance. His father has been the first among the Great Families for decades; no one's going to overtake them. He doesn't feel the need for more power. Emiri can give him what he really wants. And when they've been married long enough to stop being besotted, she'll make a good partner."

The figure let out a short, sharp laugh. "It's pathetic what you waste your gift on," he said, looking back at the door. "The romantic aspirations of a rich girl."

Carys sighed and looked over at the spirit. He had grown as solid as he was capable at this point, though his edges blurred and wisped away in plumes of smoke. His face was the most clearly defined part of him, features sharp and clear, mouth set in a wry smirk, eyes brimming with judgment.

"What else would you have me spend my 'gift' doing?" Carys asked as she turned down the oil lanterns. "This is the shop my grandmother left me. Who will keep this practice if I do not?"

Another smirk. "Your grandmother would be disappointed."

Anger pulsed through Carys. Her gaze grew sharp, and her eyes began to glow, clearly visible through the thin veil. It was soft, but the light was growing. "Too far, Judex."

The apparition stepped back, his smug expression suddenly gone, and held up his hands. "I'm sorry, Carys. You're right, it was too far."

A deep breath, and the light faded from Carys's eyes. "You are horrifically insufferable," Carys remarked, glaring, "and you are welcome to move on at any time."

The smirk returned. "You can't get rid of me that easily."

"Oh, I am well aware," Carys snapped as she headed back behind the curtain again.

The back of the shop was about the same size as the front, though with no enormous counter taking up space. There was a tiny kitchen and a small table with a single chair. To the left was the bathing area and latrine. To the right, a set of stairs that was really more of a ladder, which led up to a bedroom that filled the entire second floor, though that really wasn't saying much given the modest size of the building.

Carys looked over the invitation in her hand. The paper was heavy linen, the texture smooth in her hand. She opened it this time, breaking the ornate wax seal of a hawk alighting on the top of a tree, wings unfurled. As the seal broke, she felt something. A tingle at the back of her perception. A shifting of potentials. She had a sudden very real sense that this event was important, and that it was also important that she attend. Lifting the flap, she removed the invitation and read it carefully. Midsummer's Eve was just three days away.

"So can you even attend this thing?" Judex asked, the smug tone fully returned to his voice. "Do you even have the right clothing for anything fancier than digging for roots?"

Another glare. "I think you will find my current ensemble is a step above what one would wear to dig for roots," Carys commented blandly, setting the invite down. "I have something. It wouldn't pass for a royal dinner, but it's enough for a garden party."

Silence fell, and when Carys looked up again Judex had gone. That was a relief. The capricious spirit would no doubt return when he was bored, but Carys would enjoy the break. She went about making a cup of tea and retrieved the invitation from the table before heading up the stairs, tea in hand.

The bedroom was cozy. The bed easily took up half the room, and it wasn't that large of a bed. There was also a soft chair, covered in a fleece throw with a side table. Carys went to the chair, setting her tea and the invitation down on the table. Alone, in the soft light of her room, she removed the veil from her face. She never liked wearing it, but the eyes of a seer tended to unnerve people and could be quite sensitive to light. Setting the veil down, she let herself collapse into the chair with a soft, contented exhale and picked up her tea.

"Three days," she mused to herself, and looked over at the invitation again. What had she felt? What was at this party?

Sipping her tea, Carys puzzled for a while then let the matter go. Her energy would be better spent preparing rather than ruminating. Right now, she was tired. She wasn't sure why seeings were so much harder under the new moon. Her grandmother had said that it was because the moon's light touched both their world and the plane of spirits, and without that light, guidance from the spirits became muddled. Whatever the case, Carys was going to finish her tea and take a nap before going in search of dinner.

☾ ☾ ☾

Three days later, just as the sun was dropping lower on the horizon and bathing the city in a golden late afternoon, Carys locked up her shop and made her way, on foot, through the winding streets of Vasi. There was not much rhyme or reason to the way Vasi was laid out. Oh, there were parts of the town that made more sense, that had clearly been planned at the time, but the different neighborhoods felt pieced together, as if someone had made a quilt of a city from different colors of fabric that were very similar but also definitely not the same. Carys liked that, though. Walking through the city was like a history lesson, if you knew what to look for. You could see the influences of past rulers in each expansion. The only two parts of the city that matched were the terraced, manicured homes of the rich and titled, and the sprawling port which filled the cove below before reaching farther out into the bay. They were built at the same time, carved from massive bleached stones, the same stone as the cliffs facing the ocean. The port was solid and brutal, but the gatehouses showed the artistry and eye for detail that was showcased in the noble quarter high on the hill above. The first Lord of the Strait had been determined to leave his mark, and he had succeeded.

Carys stepped lightly down streets cobbled with colorful stones, shadows growing longer around her on the pale buildings with their patinated copper roofs. Domes and spires of all sizes made up the skyline of Vasi, regularly interspersed with rooftop terraces and gardens. It was a beautiful place. As she moved through the different neighborhoods, the marks of their design became clearer. The glass in the windows, for example: in her neighborhood it was thick and often colored. As she approached the noble quarter, it became thinner, clearer, and easier to see through. Turrets were more frequent closer to the cliffs, rooftop gardens more common closer to the shore. The noble quarter, however, was largely domed ceilings and spires. And balconies! So many balconies. From a security standpoint, it didn't make a lot of sense. Perhaps that was also why the city guard was conspicuously present the closer one got to Watcher Castle.

Sitting almost at the precipice of the southern cliffs, Watcher Castle looked down across all of Vasi to the south, and Asuman Strait to the north. Distant Veli was visible on the other side of the strait, though there was no matching castle on the lower opposing cliff. Just a lone watchtower. Veli and Vasi were the wardens of Asuman Strait, but for reasons unknown to Carys, only Vasi ruled the waters. Veli's ruler was the Lord of the River, monitoring the travel and trade that left the bay and continued on deeper into the continent.

A guard stopped Carys as she reached the first gate of Watcher Castle. The young guard had been eyeing her suspiciously as she approached on foot rather than by carriage like most everyone else that had arrived. The cocky suspicion gave way to polite reverence when Carys was close enough for him to see the veil beneath her hood. He did not ask for the invitation; he merely looked at the remains of the broken seal and ushered her through.

Once past the main gates and into the courtyard, Carys slipped into the loose crowd of guests milling about before heading into the gardens proper. She found herself breathing a sigh of relief to discover she was not horrifically underdressed. Like many of the other women present, she wore full pants that caressed her hips before becoming voluminous and then cuffing at the ankle. The fabric of her blouse was just slightly sheer, as was the fashion. Her sash had fringed edges, and her short vest was sufficiently embroidered and beaded, even if the beads were glass and not precious stones. Unlike any other woman in the courtyard, however, Carys's vest also had an elaborately decorated hood. The hood was cut oddly, designed to come forward over her eyes but also cut away at the sides so that you could still see her face. Beneath the hood was another veil, with the same edge of eyelash lace as the veil she wore in her store. The final difference was her colors. It being the height of summer, most of the women were dressed in yellows and oranges, a few daring ones in red. From across the fountains, Carys smiled to see Emiri standing next to her father, in a golden vest over a pale rose blouse and vivid magenta pants, roses twined into her caramel hair. Carys, however, looked like she came up out of the sea. Her blouse was a faint misty gray, as was the veil over her eyes. Her hooded vest was the blue-green of the shallow waters, her pants the deeper blues of its depths. It complimented her unusual coloring, though, her more-golden hair and paler skin.

There was a chime, and people began to saunter toward the gardens, so Carys followed. Not everyone, she noted. She wondered what the chime meant. This was her first royal event. The spirits and her intuition would have to guide her.

There was another set of gates, and here guards were taking the invitations. In exchange, guests received a small golden brooch that looked like the sun, but with tiny blossoms making up the corona.

"I hope you see nothing but joy for us tonight, Seer," the guard taking her invite said, smiling as he presented the brooch to her.

Laughing softly, Carys pinned the brooch to her vest and smiled back. "I have not looked beyond this night, guardsman; I am merely a guest. I hope the spirits intend nothing but joy for us as well."

The guard nodded to Carys, then turned his attention to the next guest. Carys wandered past the tall garden wall, made all the taller by the lombard trees planted in a careful row all along the perimeter. The garden was delightfully private, or would have been were it not for all the people currently occupying it. There was a large area in the center divided by a long but narrow fountain, where water bubbled gently from spouts of various heights. Surrounding the fountain were flagstones, creating a broad, even terrace that could be set with tables and chairs. The side of the fountain closest to Carys was where the food had been staged, small tables laden with a variety of delights both sweet and savory, and servants darting about almost constantly to keep them filled. Other servants twisted deftly through the crowd with trays bearing glasses of wine, both white and rose. Carys delicately plucked one from a tray as it sailed past. The flavor was light and sweet, a perfect accompaniment to a summer evening.

"Oh, Seer Arslan," a voice called out, jubilantly. It belonged to a somewhat older gentleman who had clearly indulged in a number of glasses of wine already. "Carys! Sundrop! I didn't expect to find you here!"

Stifling a sigh, Carys turned with a smile toward the man addressing her. His name was Timur, he fancied himself a poet, and as one of the heads of the Great Families he made too much money for anyone to dissuade him of that notion. Rising up from a chair at the edge of the terrace, Timur weaved slightly as he approached Carys, smiling delightedly as his wife rolled her eyes and shook her head behind him.

"Sundrop, how delightful to see you," Timur said, reaching for Carys's hand. She relented, and he brought it to his lips to kiss and then hold affectionately. "I know it's been forever since I've sought your council; I do hope you forgive me."

"There is nothing to forgive," Carys said, giving Timur a squeeze in return then gently taking her hand back. "My shop is there if you have need of me. If you have not had need, I can only assume that you are doing well."

The older man smiled broadly. "Very well, Sundrop, very well," he not quite bellowed, forgetting himself in his drunken enthusiasm. "Things have been going wonderfully for us. What you saw in the cards, your advice; it led to great things, Sundrop, great things. Did your cards bring you here tonight? What brings the greatest seer in Vasi to the castle gardens?"

In a way, they did, but Carys was hardly going to say that. "I am hardly the greatest seer in Vasi. And I am a guest of Pasha Bulut this evening," Carys said, pausing to sip her wine. "Or rather, of his daughter. Young Emiri is often in my shop and offered me the invitation." Timur didn't need to know why.

"Ah, enchanted with you, is she?" Timur asked, still smiling, and still a little too loud. His wife was beginning to head their way, with a look of tired determination.

"Not in the way you might be implying," Carys answered with a small laugh. "Emiri is simply fond of my advice. As are a number of people. It is my profession, after all."

"Indeed, indeed," Timur rumbled with a huge burst of laughter, and a few people looked over in surprise. "But you are the greatest seer in Vasi! You have your grandmother's gift; may her rest be long. Perhaps that is why you are here, yes? To offer your services to the Lord of the Strait?"

Finally arriving, Timur's wife took her husband's arm and glared up at him. "I think they can hear you in the port, my love," she said wearily, then turned to Carys with an apologetic smile. "I should find him a coffee and a quiet corner. It is nice to finally meet you, Seer Arslan. I am Verda. Perhaps Timur and I will call upon you soon."

"I would be delighted to see you in my shop, madam," Carys said with warmth, and smiled as Verda led her husband away.

"The greatest seer in Vasi…" a voice behind her said, also masculine but younger and clear enough to imply sobriety. "That's a weighty claim."

Turning slowly, Carys had that feeling again: a stirring that had nothing to do with the light breeze floating through the garden. Behind her was a man around her age, maybe just a little younger. His thick, dark hair curled down just past his shoulders and framed his warmly olive face, and she had to tip her head up a touch to look into his cognac eyes. He was very handsome, and likely aware of it, given the careful manner of his dress and how perfectly trimmed he kept his short beard. Everything about him spoke of privilege and wealth, from his careful grooming to the silken fabric of his clothing to the fine leather of his boots. His eyes, however, were what most interested Carys. They were sharp, intelligent, and they searched her face curiously rather than sweeping down over her body.

"It's not a claim I made, sir," Carys said, subconsciously standing up a little straighter. "I won't deny that I have a talent, but I am sure there is an older and more-practiced seer who could teach me many things."

The response made him smile, and he took a step forward. "I like that you're not denying that you're good, just demurring to say you're the best," he said, and then he looked her over a little. It wasn't a leering gaze—he wasn't staring at her body, he was taking in the details of her appearance, and his eyes quickly came back to hers. "I've never met a seer. Unusual, I know, but my father thinks they're a superstitious lot. You're younger than I would have expected."

"I hear that a lot," Carys replied, canting her hip and shifting her weight. "Though I'm probably older than you think. You look familiar. Are you sure we have not met?"

A shake of the head. "Quite sure, though you may have seen me in passing," he said, taking another step closer. "But I know we have not met. Tell me, do seers dance?"

Blinking, Carys let out a surprised laugh. "I can't speak for all seers, but I do. When I know who I'm dancing with."

"Call me Hawk," he said, holding his hand out to Carys.

"Oh, that's creative," Judex muttered quietly from behind Carys. She managed not to jump.

Setting down the wine glass, Carys decided that she was absolutely not going to hide in a corner all night just to keep Judex quiet. "A pleasure, Hawk," Carys said, accepting the outstretched hand, and allowed herself to be pulled around the fountain to where, instead of food, there were musicians and people dancing.

The man calling himself Hawk turned out to be a fairly competent dancer. He led well and was able to quickly assess Carys's familiarity with the dance. She had to begrudgingly admit he probably made her look better than she was. He also wasn't being overly forward. Oh, certainly it was bold of him to ask for the dance, but he held her loosely and did not try to press himself against her, and for all that he stared at her as if she held some great secret, not once did she feel his gaze was lustful. She honestly wasn't sure if she was more relieved or disappointed.

"Do seers always wear a veil?" Hawk asked, as the music changed and slowed. He didn't let her go, though—it seemed they would be dancing to this one as well.

"Many of us, yes," Carys answered, comfortably following his lead. She knew this dance, was more familiar with the steps. "Our eyes are sensitive to light. The hoods and veils are as much to protect our eyes as they are to hide them from view. Those who do not have the gift find our gaze unsettling."

"Fascinating," Hawk said as they moved in a slow spin. "I would love to see your eyes, Carys."

That was a surprise. Either Hawk had been hovering long enough to hear Carys's name, or he had already known it. Either way, it implied that she'd had his attention for longer than she'd assumed.

"Perhaps, before the end of the night, I will indulge you,' Carys said, looking at him curiously. "Perhaps we can negotiate a trade."

A short, sharp laugh and Hawk grinned. "Excellent," he said, though it was hard to say if he was more delighted by the proffered deal or Carys's boldness. "And what would you require of me in return?"

Step, step, turn, and they separated for a moment for another turn before coming back together. "I would like to see what my cards think of you," Carys answered.

That got another laugh, and an even bigger smile. "I would be happy to," Hawk said as the song began to change again. This time, however, he led Carys back off the dance floor. "Let's find each other again after midnight. I have people to meet with, and I probably shouldn't just spend the party talking with you, though I would like to. This event will go until dawn, so we'll still have plenty of time. Until then?"

"Until then," Carys agreed, and then watched with some amusement as Hawk was swiftly lost in the crowd.

"What a strange man," Judex mused, sitting off to the side on an empty divan. Couches and divans had been placed all throughout the garden for guests to relax on.

"You should know I intend to ignore you as much as possible tonight," Carys muttered as she glanced over.

Judex laughed. "I would expect nothing less. Do you think Hawk is his real name?"

"Of course not," Carys snapped, favoring Judex with a withering glare. "And you don't either. You were just hoping I was naive enough to say yes."

The spirit laughed again, and Carys decided that was enough. The more she spoke with Judex, the more it would embolden him. Carys had no doubt that he would pop in occasionally through the rest of the night no matter what she did, but she didn't feel like being the crazy woman talking to herself at the party. Not yet, at least.

Moving back around the fountain, Carys got herself a fresh glass of wine and decided to peruse the food options. There was so much, it was a little ridiculous. Bacon-wrapped dates and grilled eggplant. Mussels stuffed with rice, nuts, and raisins. Nearly a dozen different savory pastries made with fish, grilled meats, and minced vegetables. The desserts were even more numerous in their variety. It seemed excessive, almost absurd. It was also delicious.

Chapter 2

GIGGLING FROM THE right alerted Carys to the approach of Emiri, and so Carys was ready when the young woman skipped up and excitedly hugged the seer. Carys smiled and shifted her wine to keep it from spilling.

"Oh, Carys, you came," Emiri exclaimed. The young woman was fairly glowing and looked quite lovely. "I'm so happy you're here! I wasn't sure if you were just humoring me when you accepted the invitation."

"I understood the worth of what you gave me, dove," Carys said and gave Emiri's arm a squeeze. "I was hardly going to throw it away. So! You look as if you're having a good evening."

Emiri fairly danced in place. "Yes! Yes, I'm having the best night," she gushed, then looked around, aware of herself. Leaning forward, she lowered her voice a little. "Carys, I know this won't surprise you, but you were right! Serhat loves what I'm wearing, and I've already danced with him four times!"

Carys felt an intense urge to giggle along with the exuberant young woman but managed to maintain her dignity. "I see," Carys said, simply smiling, and sipped her wine again. "Though what did you say to him that led him to dancing with you four times?"

Blushing, Emiri cast her eyes down. "I simply told him, truthfully, how happy I was to see him this evening," she said, almost shyly. "I am not usually so forthright, but that is what you said, isn't it? That I had to be honest with him, that I had to show him what I could offer as myself, not as my father's daughter."

Carys's smile softened, and she reached up to cup Emiri's face. "I am glad, little bird. He is a good match for you, and any man willing to follow his heart deserves the chance to do so."

Emiri blinked, seeming to find something profound in the words. "I will remember that, Seer," she said softly, then smiled again, the moment overwhelmed by her continued excitement. "He had to go to a meeting with the other pashas, their heirs, and the Lord of the Strait. I heard my father talk about it, it's some sort of tradition that happens at every event. He asked me to meet him at midnight, though! He said I should see the view from the northern balconies."

Thankfully, Emiri's excitement caused her to miss the curious twitch of Carys's mouth and the brief wrinkle of her brow. Hawk had said he needed to attend something and had also asked to meet again at midnight. So, Hawk was a pasha, or an heir.

"I am sure it will be lovely," was all Carys said. The music changed again, and Emiri gasped in delight.

"*The Rain on Water*," Emiri exclaimed as the chords of the popular dance played. Every girl learned *The Rain on Water* at some point. "Come on, Carys!"

Laughing and more than a little surprised, Carys let herself be pulled onto the dance floor for the second time that evening. *The Rain on Water* was a folk dance. One did not need a partner for it, and more women tended to know it than men. Carys danced along with Emiri through the song, and also through a few more as the quintet played a variety of folk dances. Carys let her hood fall away as she spun and clapped, her heavy braid flying out behind her. The two women then went back for more wine, and more sour cherry tarts with beaten cream.

"Carys," Emiri began as they dusted sugar and crumbs from their fingers, "I know I'm your client, and I know you put up with me because I pay you, but… well, do you think we might also be friends of a sort?"

"Oh, dove," Carys said, smiling again. Emiri was continuing to surprise her. "I am almost a decade older than you, so I assumed you would find me dreadful and boring. But I am willing to be your friend, Emiri."

The younger woman smiled again and bounced a little in her excitement. "Fantastic," she said, glowing and happy. "I know you're older, but you're interesting! And you're here! You can't be too old—you came to the party! And you danced with me, and I saw you dancing with that man earlier! Oh, who was he? He looks familiar, doesn't he, but I couldn't place him."

Carys giggled, suspecting that Emiri had maybe drunk a little more wine than usual. "I did; he was a lovely dancer," Carys responded. "And I had the very same experience. I feel like I should know him, but he says we haven't met."

"Oh, a mystery," Emiri said, eyes getting big. She was definitely a little drunk. "What was his name, did he say?"

A shake of the head. "No, he just said to call him Hawk," Carys replied, looking thoughtfully out across the garden. "He disappeared about when Serhat did, said he had people to meet with, and that he would be back around midnight. I think he might be an heir to one of the Great Families. Too young to be a pasha."

Emiri also looked thoughtful and chewed her bottom lip. "I'm not sure," she said after a moment. "I've met all of the heirs, or at least I think I have. Oh, he could be a noble!"

That was not a possibility Carys had considered, and now she felt naive for overlooking it. It would certainly explain the sumptuous clothing, and perhaps the desire not to reveal himself. There were three noble families in Vasi: Özdemir, Aydin, and Kilic. The three lords who founded Vasi, centuries before, or so the stories went. Özdemir had the vision and strength of will to rule, and so became the Lord of the Strait. Aydin cared more for wisdom and learning, and so founded the university and served as advisors to the crown. Kilic vowed that Vasi would always be safe, and took up the sword, founding the guard. And so it had remained ever since. The merchant houses had created their own court with the Great Families, because the nobles of Vasi refused to expand theirs.

With another shake of the head, Carys came out of her thoughts. "I suppose it's a possibility; it would fit, and the three houses are not short on descendants. Well, save Özdemir. Perhaps he is one of the younger Aydins. I imagine I'll get a chance to find out."

Emiri giggled and nodded, and the conversation was abandoned in favor of the newly-set-up food station where they were cracking and serving fresh urchins and oysters with a variety of sharp, flavorful sauces. Carys followed, trying to hide her amazement. This night would surely be burned into her memory for the rest of her days.

Midnight found Carys on her fifth glass of wine, warmly intoxicated, and perched on the balustrade that led to the northern terrace of the garden. The northern terrace was tiered, sloping towards the cliffs, which meant that she could see clearly over the heads of everyone sitting on various benches and chaises below her. There wasn't much to see, in truth—the slim crescent moon could only illuminate so far, and the lanterns all around the garden made seeing out over the water difficult.

"Do you think he'll come back?" Judex asked abruptly, materializing next to Carys on the marble.

"I don't know," Carys answered, swirling her wine in the glass. "I hope he does. He was interesting."

The snort of derision from Judex made Carys grin. Looking over at the spirit, Carys arched a brow.

"Jealous?"

Judex rolled his eyes. "Don't be ridiculous," he answered—practically sneered.

A giggle. "I'm just curious," Carys said softly, looking at the spirit with amusement. "You never seem to like the men I spend time with."

"I don't like anyone," Judex pointed out, "and you have horrible taste."

Carys snickered and sipped her wine. "I am delighted to say I am too drunk to be bothered by your assessment of my taste," she answered happily. Judex shook his head but smiled a little.

As if summoned by the conversation, Hawk appeared through the manicured archway, and stepped out onto the terrace, looking about. He looked like someone on a mission, and Carys wondered if the mission was her, or something unrelated. She took a moment to observe how the people near him responded to him. Reactions were mixed. Some observed him politely but did not act as if they properly knew him. More bowed their heads as he passed.

Turning around, brow furrowed, Hawk started back toward the gardens. He glanced in Carys's direction but continued on his way back through the arch. Not a breath later, however, he returned, now looking very pointedly at Carys, and smiling.

"I didn't immediately recognize you without your hood," Hawk said as he approached, and perched on the balustrade right where Judex had been sitting. Judex dispersed into smoke before he could be sat upon.

Carys giggled, mostly at Judex's expense. "And with my hair around my face, you didn't immediately spot the veil, yes? We're not obligated to go hooded; it just makes life more pleasant during the daylight."

"The lanterns don't bother you?" Hawk asked, looking as if he were planning something. Carys just shook her head, and Hawk grinned again. "Fantastic. Because I still want to see your eyes, and I promised to sit for a reading. Come with me?"

Standing, Hawk turned and extended his hand to Carys. There was such an earnest intensity to his manner. He had a goal, he was focused, and he assumed Carys would follow, but he had not once demanded it. Puzzled but still drunkenly happy, Carys took his hand and allowed him to pull her to her feet, then guided her back into the garden. He stayed slightly ahead, leading the way and avoiding clusters of people that might slow them down, but he never let go of her hand.

They made their way out of the garden and back into the courtyard. Hawk led them away from the castle, but instead of heading toward the gates, he turned down side steps into a lower garden, one that had not been made up for the event. There were still lanterns here, however, so it was easy enough to see. It was also quite empty of other people.

It was here that Hawk released Carys's hand and slowed his step, moving through the smaller garden. Carys looked about and realized this must be the kitchen garden. It was full of herbs, plus a handful of plants known for their medicinal qualities. Pausing by a planter full of small, pale-green plants bearing weeping white-blue flowers in a circle around a viny dark-green plant with palm-sized red blossoms, Carys tsked and completely uprooted the larger plant in the center.

"Are you always like this in gardens?" Hawk asked, looking back over his shoulder. "And don't you think the gardener is going to be unhappy about that?"

Carys brought the red blossomed vine to an empty planter and began to get it replanted. "It's not my fault the gardener doesn't know his plants," Carys returned. "This Red Sun would have choked out those Virgin Tears by the end of the season. I know it looks very pretty together, but Red Suns spread. Aggressively."

Standing back up, Carys dusted off her hands, then looked about. She wasn't about to wipe them on the pants of her one formal outfit, but maybe… There! A small fountain graced the corner of the garden, and Hawk continued to appear amused as Carys rinsed off her hands and dried them on the sturdier fabric of her sash.

"Not just a seer, then," Hawk observed.

"Are any of us just one thing?" Carys asked, smiling a little. "But I know what you're after. Yes, I'm also a witch. Like my grandmother and mother before me. It has been a family trade for generations, as I understand it."

Crossing his arms, Hawk looked Carys over again, something a little brooding in his gaze. "You really shouldn't be here," he said after a minute, though he didn't seem upset. "You are so outside the court and the merchants. It is… refreshing."

"Of course I should be here," Carys retorted, hands on her hips. "I was invited. And perhaps you were due to be refreshed."

Laughing, Hawk gestured to the far garden wall. There was a small terrace back here, perhaps a place where the cook took tea, simple but lovely. On it sat a carafe with two cups, and a plate with dried fruits and pieces of cheese.

"Let's get started, shall we?"

Once again surprised—the evening had been full of surprises—Carys made her way to the table and sat down. Hawk sat across from her and poured out the golden liquid from the carafe into the two cups, setting one before Carys. She took a curious sip—it was a wine of sorts, though heavy with the flavor of apple. She'd never had anything like it.

"So I think you should go first," Hawk said as Carys set down her cup. "After all, the reading will probably take longer."

"Very well," Carys said with a smirk, and began to unbraid her hair. She had put the veil on first, and then styled her hair around it.

Hawk watched appreciatively as Carys shook out her heavy, ruddy brass mane. "Your hair is magnificent," he said, sincerely. "Not a common color in Vasi, or Veli for that matter."

Shrugging, Carys began to untie the veil. "My father was a sailor, or so I understand it," she explained, eyes cast down for a moment as she removed the veil and carefully folded it. "I suppose he was from a place where it is more common."

The veil gone, Carys looked back up at Hawk, pushing her hair back so that it did not obscure or cast shadows across her face. The light from the lanterns was more than enough to see that her eyes were the gray of a heavy mist, the color so light that it almost didn't exist. The sharp black of her pupil and the thin, charcoal rim of the iris just made the bleached center all the clearer and more strange. Hawk stared into her eyes, utterly fascinated, and leaned forward onto the table.

"Do all seers have eyes such as yours?" he asked after a moment, still gazing into her eyes, almost as if enraptured.

"Yes," Carys answered simply. It was a little unnerving, the way he was looking at her, almost as unnerving as when people were afraid. "It is what marks all of us with the gift. When a child's eyes start to fade, you know it will be soon. In less than a month they will begin to see things, begin to have dreams that show them secrets they couldn't ever know. Our eyes are sensitive, and many of us go blind in old age, but we never lose our ability to see beyond."

"You're beautiful," Hawk said, smiling again, and Carys found herself blushing suddenly. "Different. Lovely. And honest. I feel like you wouldn't lie to me, or really anyone."

Leaning back, Carys looked away to pick up her cup. When she looked back again, the tension had ebbed, and Hawk leaned back as well, also picking up his cup.

"I try to be honest," Carys said after a sip of the apple wine. "I will omit things. I've learned that you can be honest without being blunt or cruel, and sometimes it's just safer to leave out details. But I don't imagine I'm incapable of lying. I just think it would take a particular circumstance."

Nodding slowly, Hawk drained his cup and filled it again, and hers as well. "Thank you for indulging me, Carys," he said, looking into her eyes once more, this time to make sure she understood his gratitude. "Will you leave it off, while we're here?"

"Happy to," Carys said, reaching for her belt and removing the satin pouch hidden beneath her sash that contained her cards. "Honestly, I'd rather not wear it, but necessity and all that. So then! Are you ready to reveal yourself to me now?"

The corner of Hawk's mouth quirked a little. He was nervous. The quirk was quickly replaced by a smile that didn't quite reach his eyes. "Of course."

That was interesting. Carys took a deeper drink of the apple wine and removed the cards from her pouch. Hawk leaned forward on the table, grasping a piece of cheese and nibbling as he watched. The cards slipped through her hands, the metallic leaf on their backs flashing in the light from the lanterns. She started to feel a stir again, and suddenly knew with prickling certainty that this moment was why she was there. This moment was what had been calling to her for three days.

Carys set the deck before Hawk. "Cut it. Only once."

There was that quirk again, but Hawk reached forward and cut the cards, then drew his hand away to rest at the edge of the table once more. He drank off the rest of his wine as he watched Carys take back the deck and flip over three cards. The first was The Monarch again, the androgynous but powerful figure on their throne. The second was a tall tower reaching into a cold gray sky, with a sharply pointed roof similar to the structures Carys had passed on her way to the party. The final card was simply the ocean, waves breaking with white foam. Carys set the deck down and her lips parted in surprise.

"Of course," she said softly, almost a murmur, then laughed and looked up at Hawk. "I should have pieced it together, but it just seemed so unlikely. You're familiar, but we've never met. Not from one of the Great Families, so the only possibility is one of the noble houses. I just never thought you would be the Heir of the Strait. Why the deception, Asil?"

Looking a touch sheepish, Hawk—or rather, Asil Özdemir—refilled his wine cup. "Asil, is it? Not 'my lord' or something else?"

"Would you prefer I call you lord?" Carys asked, with a raised brow, as she rather doubted it.

"By the waters, no," Asil said in a rush, and found himself smiling again. "It doesn't bother you at all, does it? I was afraid it would, but I wanted to meet you."

A shake of the head. "No, it doesn't bother me," Carys answered honestly. Surprising, certainly, but thankfully she hadn't said anything awful or done anything to embarrass herself.

Still smiling, Asil nodded to the cards. "Do you wish to continue?"

"Of course I do," Carys answered with a small laugh. "And you never leave a reading unfinished. Sets a bad precedent."

Gaze drifting back down to the cards, Carys's face grew still as she considered the second card. Her eyes started to glow, faintly, but enough that Asil looked up from the cards to stare in wonder at Carys's eyes once more.

"Something is coming," Carys said, the laughter gone from her voice as images flashed through her mind. "Change comes, an inevitable change. You cannot stop it—you can only shift its direction. You will want to shift it. It will try to alter the world you know; it will alter the world you know, but you must stop it from getting what it wants. You must control the change if you are able."

Carys didn't look up, her eyes drifting to the final card. "It will come from the sea," she murmured, and her voice and gaze eerily distant. "From across the waters, it rushes toward us. It will arrive in days. Not evil, but a tool for the hand that wields it. Unknowing and bound."

"What is coming?" Asil asked, concern etched in his features.

With a small gasp, Carys came back to herself, and looked up at Asil. Her eyes still glowed softly, and as she raised her head, she made a quiet sound of pain and brought her hands to her face, covering her eyes.

"Too much, too bright," she whimpered, pushing away from the table and getting clumsily to her feet. There were more lanterns by the table; she had to get away from them, at least until the sight left her. She stumbled blindly, and found herself enveloped in an embrace, her face pressed against a linen-clad chest, blocking out the light. She sighed in relief, leaning in against Asil.

"Carys, are you all right?" he asked, the concern clear in his voice.

Another sigh. "Yes, yes I'm all right," Carys murmured. She hesitated a moment, then slid her arms around Asil; if she was going to be here, she might as well hold on. "I wasn't expecting any of that, I wasn't expecting to connect to something, or I would have taken precautions. Though… Asil, I know I'm a bit drunk and so everything I say should be considered carefully. But something is coming."

"I understand," Asil said quietly. He ran his hands through her hair, which was both unexpected and lovely, then used the motion to sweep her hair to the side and pull her hood back up. "We'll have to try again tomorrow, I suppose, and see if things are different when we're both sober."

Carys nodded, and slowly pulled back. Asil let her, his hands falling away to rest at his sides.

"Can you fetch my cards?" Carys asked, a little embarrassed. "It's brighter by the table."

That got a small laugh. "Of course," Asil said, moving immediately to retrieve the cards and present them back to Carys.

Tucking the cards back under her sash, Carys sighed. "Well, I suppose I should find my way home now," she said with a rueful smile.

"You could stay here."

Carys blinked and looked up at Asil. The glow in her eyes had faded. It was still there, all the more obvious now that her face was shadowed by the peak of her hood, but when she swept her gaze over him Asil got the distinct impression she was seeing more than his appearance.

"You do not mean in the guest room," Carys said after a moment, smiling a little as she did. "Though you don't… this doesn't feel like a particularly romantic invitation."

Asil laughed. "Well, no. You're beautiful, and different, and I will enjoy exploring this mystery with you, but I was not intending to court you," he answered honestly. "Does that disappoint you?"

"Bit of a relief, actually," Carys remarked with a wider smile. "The difference in our stations would make that terribly awkward. So just hoping for a friendly tumble, then?"

Head tipped to the side, Asil looked at her carefully. "Yes."

"We're both too drunk," Carys answered, and Asil laughed again. She held up her hand. "However, I will stay here, and I am not against sharing kisses and affection, if you so desire. But should we decide to bed each other, we should be less drunk for it."

More laughter, and Asil stepped back up to Carys. "You really don't belong here," he said again, looking delighted as he said it, "but I am glad you are."

Pulling Carys in, Asil kissed her. It was neither gentle nor rough, but purposeful and exploring. Focused, but not passionate. It was just like the rest of him. And it was still very good. As they parted, Carys laughed a little.

"This will definitely be a night I remember," Carys said, taking Asil's hand. "All right, lead me somewhere with soft lighting, and have someone fetch us something refreshing and not alcoholic to drink. We will talk and kiss, and tomorrow we will determine what comes next."

With a smile and a laugh, Asil led Carys out of the gardens, away from the party, and toward the castle.

Chapter 3

THERE WAS A grumble from the pile of blankets as sunlight filtered in through the windows. Carys peeked her head up and blinked. It was so bright. Of course, the windows were clear and thin, so nothing filtered the light that came in. That seemed odd; this wasn't how most mornings went. Then Carys blinked again—those were not her windows. This bed, with its feather tick and its linen sheets and its deliciously snuggly blankets, was most certainly not her bed. She wasn't alone in the bed, either.

Snoring softly, Asil was sprawled out across the other side of the enormous mattress. He had kicked off the covers and appeared to be wearing a pair of light linen shorts and nothing else. Carys was in a man's sleep shirt, but still had her smallclothes on underneath. She remembered them talking long into the night about trivial things: their favorite constellations, which bakery had the best tarts in the merchant quarter, and a surprisingly heated discussion about floral arrangements (Asil thought they were stupid and wasteful, Carys thought they were lovely and brightened a room—though obviously live plants were better). There had also been many kisses, and while they had both likely longed for more at different points, neither pressed for it. It was fun. Possibly the most fun Carys had had in ages.

Asil shifted and opened his eyes, blinking at the sunlight and looking over to see Carys still in his bed. "Oh good," he said, then yawned. "You're still here. I won't have to go looking for you."

Rolling onto her side, Carys arched an eyebrow at him. "Did you think I would leave?"

"Honestly, I wasn't sure," Asil replied as he also rolled onto his side so he could look at her more easily. "I mean, I really don't know you; there are lots of reasons you might have run off. I'm glad you're here, though. And not just because it saves me the trouble of looking for you."

Carys laughed. "This is the most unconventional morning after I've ever had, I have to admit."

"I'll be more flattering if we actually have sex," Asil said with a grin as he started to climb out of bed.

"You know, somehow, I don't think you would be," Carys mused as she also moved to get up. "So, do I get breakfast? I assume we're going to pull the cards out again, and I would like to be fed first."

Asil paused to stretch, then made his way through the room toward a series of bell pulls by the door. Carys looked around with some wonder. The bed she was in probably would have fit three or four people quite comfortably. It had an enormous headboard that was as tall as she would be standing up, upholstered in embroidered silk. Plush rugs covered the wood and stone floors, and heavy velvet drapes framed the large windows. There was a rather large mahogany desk in one corner, littered in papers and books, and a mid-sized bookshelf next to it that was quite full, with a few stacked on top for good measure. Asil passed two heavy chests of drawers—both with small sculptures and various trinkets arranged on top—on his way to the bell pulls, and there were two more doors leading from this room that obviously did not lead to the hallway.

Carys padded over to the desk, still in Asil's nightshirt which hung down to her thighs. She did not go through his papers, but she did look over the different books. More than one volume on the stars. Several on natural sciences. Medicine also seemed to be of great interest.

"You were interested in my little library last night, too," Asil said as he walked back over to her. "Though I believe this is what kicked off the bouquet debacle."

"Oh, we are not starting that again," Carys asserted, and Asil laughed.

Before anything else could be said, however, the door opened, and a young man stepped in. "You called, my— Oh, miss I'm sorry," the boy said, covering his eyes as he turned scarlet. "I didn't know—my lord doesn't normally—I'm sorry!"

It took everything Carys had not to laugh at the poor young man. Asil hid a chuckle by clearing his throat, and moved so that he stood in between the servant and Carys, effectively shielding her from view.

"Nazim, please have some breakfast brought up and make sure the baths are ready," Asil said, his tone firm but not harsh. "And… see if there is a women's lounging robe available for my guest. Whatever the staff can find."

"Of course, my lord," Nazim said, eyes still covered as he backed out of the room, practice and long familiarity making it an easy feat. "I will—someone will be up shortly!"

The door closed, and Asil and Carys looked at each other, then burst out laughing.

"I feel so sorry for Nazim right now," Carys said, still giggling a little. "So you don't often entertain in your rooms? No regular trysts with eligible maidens?"

With a shrug, Asil shook his head and moved to his desk. "No, not really," he admitted. "Eligible maidens don't talk to me the way you do. If I need a physical outlet, there are plenty in the town."

That got a snicker. "No, I don't imagine they do," Carys said, picking up one of the volumes on Asil's desk. "They would be too afraid of ruining their chances. You're, what, the most sought-after bachelor in Vasi? Outside of the heirs of the Great Families, of course. No one has to prove pedigree to marry them."

Asil groaned. "Can we please not discuss this?" he asked, looking at her almost pleadingly.

"Tender subject," Carys commented, brows arching, "or does it make me sound like your father?"

"The second one," Asil shot back with a wry smile. "And as I'm still hoping we end up in bed together at some point, I'd prefer to avoid that association."

Snickering again, Carys flipped briefly through the book she was holding as Asil rooted around on his desk for a moment. It was a book about spirits, surprisingly, and a guide to phenomena in the wild that indicated places where the barrier between the planes was thinner. It was a very scientific approach to a subject that was typically relegated to oral traditions and the coveted notebooks of witches. Not something she expected on the shelf of a lord.

"Might I borrow this?" Carys asked, and Asil looked up in surprise, but nodded.

"I'll want it back, of course," Asil said, standing up from the desk again, "but I've already read it and am done with it for now. I'm surprised you're interested, given who and what you are."

Carys merely shrugged. "I find the new perspective interesting. I want to see what the author has to say."

Asil smiled at her as if she'd said something brilliant or clever. He looked ready to comment, but the door opened again and two older female servants, one of which looked like she could be Nazim's mother, came in with breakfast and clothing. Nazim followed, his gaze still cast down. Asil, still clad only in the soft linen shorts, seemed unbothered. The two women looked amused, and one set the tray and began to lay out breakfast while the other took the clothing through the door on the wall past the desk. That would be the dressing room, then. The woman returned, leaving the door open behind her, and smiled at Carys.

"Will you need assistance dressing, my lady?" the woman who resembled Nazim asked.

While not actually a lady, Carys felt it would be pedantic and rude to correct the woman, who surely knew that Carys was not a member of any of the noble houses. "No, I can manage, thank you."

The woman and the other servant bowed and took their leave, though the woman did pause to pat Nazim on the cheek, which caused the boy to just turn scarlet again. After they had left, Nazim stepped forward and cleared his throat, eyes ever cast down.

"The baths will be ready for you after your meal, my lord," Nazim said. "Will, ah, will your guest be… be joining you…?"

Turning toward Carys, Asil smirked and arched an eyebrow. "Well," he began, "will you be joining me?"

"Certainly not," Carys returned with an answering smirk. "I have to get back to my shop before people start to think I've been injured or something."

Nazim let out a breath and looked deeply relieved, then bowed quickly and took himself out. Carys giggled again after the door had closed and shook her head.

"How old is he?" Carys asked, looking at the door for a moment, before turning back to Asil.

"Thirteen or fourteen," Asil replied.

"Ah," was all Carys said in return. Just at the age where a woman not wearing much would be both an embarrassment and very intriguing. The boy's blush suddenly made more sense.

They both turned to breakfast, which had been set up on a table in front of those clear, enormous windows. Fruits, cheeses, sausages, and bread with honey and butter, as well as cups of sweet spiced coffee and a copper pot with more if they desired. Carys did not pretend a smaller appetite, and easily ate as much as Asil did. The food was delicious, just as it had been last night.

"And you just wake up to this every morning?" Carys said as she poured herself a second cup of the exceptional coffee.

"Well, not every morning," Asil said with a smile that said he knew he was being pedantic. "This is a bit more elaborate, since I have a guest. Most mornings it's just coffee, sausage, and bread. Maybe cheese. It depends on how I feel."

Carys shook her head. "I know it's just your life, but it's still strange to me," she said with a little shrug. "It's really a whole different world up here."

Shrugging back, Asil finished his own coffee. "So," he began, "are we going to discuss the incident with the cards, and the portents, and the part where you ran into my arms?"

"You can't make too big of a deal about that last part; you put yourself in the way," Carys said with a grin. "But yes. Do you remember where my clothes are? My cards will still be with them."

"Oh, yes, make me sound like a desperate lecher instead of a friend trying to help," Asil complained, though not convincingly. He gestured to the far door. "I believe you left them all in the dressing room when you changed last night."

Laughing, Carys headed into the other room. The dressing room was almost the size of Carys's shop. A vanity took up the wall on the far side, set with a basin and tools for shaving, and a number of various vials and jars that, mostly, appeared to be untouched. There were mannequins with suits of armor, one light and largely unused, one entirely ceremonial. Two chests of drawers, one tall and narrow dresser that Carys knew was mainly used for stowing things like jewelry, and two wardrobes. One of them had been left open, and in it hung a number of crisp, linen shirts next to finer silk ones. At the end of the wardrobe hung a woman's robe, a simple white dress, and a long tunic in a pewter color that went down to the knees but was open to the thighs on either side. The tunic was clearly intended to go over the dress, but it would easily match the pants she'd worn last night. Perfect.

Looking around again, Carys found her own clothing carefully draped over a chair in the corner. Her cards were on the seat of the chair in their pouch. Before dressing in a combination of her own clothing and the provided tunic, Carys took a moment to shamelessly examine the many jars on Asil's vanity. It appeared that, aside from one specific lotion and a number of beard oils, he didn't actually use any of it. She shook her head and sighed. Finding a comb, she tamed her hair and braided it back up. She also partook of the untouched lotions and perfume. Hair fixed, face washed, and smelling softly of orange and clove, Carys dressed and returned to the main chamber.

Asil was at his desk again, flipping through a letter that appeared to be several pages long, and frowning slightly as he did. He abandoned the letter the moment Carys came back out. Getting up from the desk, he smiled.

"Not bad," Asil commented, looking Carys over. "Bit loose in the shoulders, but they did a very admirable job of finding something approximately your size. And it looks good on you. I notice you haven't put the veil back on yet."

Carys shrugged. "You've seen my eyes, and they don't bother you," she explained. "And we are still inside. I will put it back when I leave. I really don't like wearing it, but it's… necessary."

Frowning a little again, Asil stroked his beard as if he were considering something, then shrugged and gestured back to the table. "I've cleared a spot and wiped it down, so that we may proceed. I imagine you don't want your cards soiled by the food."

"Indeed, I do not," Carys agreed.

Getting settled, Carys brought her cards back out of their pouch. As she had suspected, Asil had simply swept up the loose cards and placed them on top of the rest of the deck before putting them away. That was good; that meant he was still the last person to meaningfully interact with them and they should carry the energy and memory of last night's seeing. Asil came to the table with paper and pen, ready to take notes. Carys laid the cards out in the same order as last night: the Monarch, the Spire, and the Sea.

"Will you be overcome again, like you were last time?" Asil asked, watching her curiously.

Carys shook her head. "It's unlikely," she said, "though I can't say it's impossible. It's never happened before, but I will admit that these circumstances are a touch unique. I don't often revisit a seeing—this may only be the second time in my life that I have."

Settling in, Carys looked down at the cards and drew in a deep breath. Though the light of late morning made it harder to see, Carys's eyes began to visibly glow again, faintly at first. Her fingertips graced over the bottom edge of the cards as she looked them over. She wasn't drunk this time, but relaxed and calm.

"Heir of the Strait, to Watcher Castle," Carys murmured, almost trancelike, her eyes growing brighter, "but someone wants to take it from you. Someone comes from across the sea, from a place long forgotten. They are strangers, they don't know what awaits them, but the hand that guides them takes and takes and takes—"

With a sharp gasp, Carys blinked and looked up. The glow in her eyes faded but did not completely go away. She appeared somewhat startled, but calmed quickly, and finally closed her eyes with a sigh, reaching up to rub her brows. They felt warm, almost tingling, as if something had been laid across them. She rubbed her forehead as well, but her fingertips did not encounter anything different.

"Are you all right?" Asil asked, leaning forward.

Carys looked up at him. "Do you remember last night, when Timur Koc claimed I was the greatest seer in Vasi?" Carys asked, certain that Asil would say yes.

"Of course," Asil said, not disappointing her. "It is, I believe, the first thing I said to you. You were quick to correct me."

"I am… not the greatest," Carys said, looking down at the cards again, her eyes still persistently bright. "That was my grandmother. I have her gift, the strength of it, but not her training. She did her best with me, but 10 years was not enough time to hone this talent. She returned to the Cradle my twentieth year, and I haven't found a mentor in her place. I do not think one exists in Vasi."

Asil studied Carys quietly as she ran her fingers gently over the cards again. "I have the strength, but not the control," Carys continued. "She could have chased this thread over the ocean for your answers. I just know it's close. And I know that there isn't another seer in Vasi who could help you more. There aren't many of us to begin with; those who remain either do not have the reach, or are even younger and less trained than I."

"That means you are the best," Asil said, his voice careful and thoughtful, "and it means that even if you are uncertain, I and all of Vasi have need of you."

The glow faded completely as Carys looked at Asil skeptically. "That feels like a bit of an exaggeration, doesn't it?"

"I don't believe it is," Asil answered with a faint smile. "You can see something the rest of us cannot. You see a threat on the horizon from across the sea. Now, let's look at this realistically; your word alone will not move my father, nor any of the noble houses or great families, to action. But you can advise, and you can guide, and we have an advantage with you that we wouldn't have otherwise."

Carys still looked skeptical. "I suppose," she said, and she heard Judex laugh behind her. She did her best not to react—she didn't need the distraction right now. "If you think it is that important, I'm available to you when you have need of me."

Head tipped to the side, Asil looked at Carys for a moment. There was something very calculating in his gaze, like he was considering and weighing various options. It made her a little uncomfortable. Clients did not tend to study her the way Asil did. She gathered her cards and shuffled them to clear them of Asil's energy and the seeing. She would get nothing more from it. By the time Carys put the cards away, Asil's expression had relaxed. He looked pleased.

"You've come to a decision about something," she observed.

"I have," Asil agreed. "I promise we will speak of it soon. For now, I should free you to return to your home. I have a satchel for your clothes. And please, keep the tunic. The color is lovely on you, and I'm sure you can have it taken in a touch for a better fit."

Carys smirked. She felt a little like she was being dismissed, but also had to admit that she needed to get about her day. If nothing else, her shop should have opened hours ago.

"Very well," was all Carys said as she stood. "Thank you for your hospitality, Asil."

Grinning, Asil also stood. "Don't be like that," he said, coming around the table and embracing Carys. He kissed her forehead and stepped back. "I'll send for you soon. I have an idea, but I need to talk to some people first, and that I must do alone."

A smile twitched up the corners of Carys's mouth, almost in spite of herself. "All right, fine."

Asil headed to the bell pulls on the wall. "I'll get Nazim to arrange a carriage."

"You know I walked here," she said, arching an eyebrow.

"You had a long night."

Laughing, Carys held up her hands in surrender. "Very well, Asil, I'll take the carriage. Now fetch me that satchel and I will gather my things."

The grin only got bigger. "Of course, my lady."

Sighing, Carys rolled her eyes and Asil laughed.

☾☾☾

The arrangements took little time to line up. As Nazim, blushing, led Carys through Watcher Castle to the waiting carriage, Asil returned to his notes. He found the seer to be fascinating. She really was the first seer he had ever met. He had seen them before, of course, out in the city: the fake ones, with their flashy cloaks and speckled scarves over their faces, making coin off tourists and peasants; and the real ones, with their quieter demeanors and simpler veils. Carys's careful presentation and her vanity had made him uncertain. She wasn't gaudy like the charlatans in the port, but she wasn't drab like the older wise women he had seen serve the other noble houses. Younger, pretty, and just vain enough to care about what colors suited her and to edge her veils with lace.

Asil found himself smiling. He liked her. He liked that she called him Asil, that she had no aspirations toward him romantically, and did not see in him a means of social climbing. He found her very attractive and liked that she was willing to share affection with him without assuming it was a bargain that ended in marriage. He liked that she was honest about her skills and her shortcomings. That would be important.

Gathering the notes into a neat stack, Asil rose and proceeded to dress. By the time he returned to the main room, dressed and groomed, all traces of breakfast had been removed and the bed remade. Such as it always was. Picking up his notes, he headed out into the hall.

The pale stone that made up much of Watcher Castle lent it a brightness as the light from the lamps reflected back. The floors had been done over with wood at some point, a softer surface than the stone beneath, and then overlaid with brightly woven carpets to help muffle sound. The hallway leading to Asil's suite was hung with tapestries depicting mythical beasts. Along with his rooms, there were two other suites on this floor of the wing, both of which currently sat empty. The Lord of the Strait had no other sons, Asil's sisters had married and left with their husbands, and there was currently no visiting royalty in the castle.

As Asil turned the corner at the end of the hall, passing the southeast stairs, the tapestries gave way to artistic depictions of the Divine Mother, the Watcher of Souls. She was always depicted carrying babies, standing over cradles, or on rare occasions nursing infants. A woman of middling height in a simple blue dress, perfect in form and feature, her hair and the upper half of her face obscured by a long white veil. A frequent joke amongst the denizens of Watcher Castle was that you could tell which Lord of the Strait had commissioned each portrait by the size of the Divine Mother's breasts. Asil's great-grandfather had apparently been attracted to rather buxom women, while his grandfather preferred a more delicate form. He passed servants, who paused just long enough to bow, but everyone kept moving about their day. Asil's father expected his people to be respectful, but not to grovel.

Finally, Asil reached his goal, a large, ornately carved wooden door with two guards posted at the entrance. They both merely nodded to Asil as he approached and made no move to stop him. Beyond the door was an expansive office, a fireplace on the far left side, with comfortable chairs arranged before it. On the right was an enormous desk that had been carved in that room over a century ago and not moved since, made of a richly burled wood that had been stained a sooty gray, giving almost the impression of roiling smoke rather than a solid desk. Sitting behind the impressive piece was a man who bore a striking resemblance to Asil, though significantly older and with eyes that looked more like a stormy sky. But he had the same curling dark hair, the same impeccable beard, and the same analytical and piercing gaze.

"Good morning, Father," Asil said, pausing to bow before seating himself in one of the chairs before the desk.

"A moment." The Lord of the Strait continued to review the document in front of him. Asil did not mind the quiet. Finally, Egemon Özdemir set the papers down and leaned back, regarding his son.

"I understand you did not retire alone last night," Egemon said, with some amusement in his expression. "Dare I hope you've found a suitable girl?"

Shifting in the chair, Asil looked somewhat ruffled. "Father, please. I had the good fortune of meeting Seer Arslan at the garden party last night. I invited her to be my guest for the evening."

A strange expression filtered over Egemon's face. "Arslan? Really?"

Asil lifted an eyebrow. "Yes."

There was a pause, then Egemon laughed. "You mean the granddaughter. Beste Arslan held the city in her thrall for so long, I sometimes forget that she is no longer with us. She would have passed when you were a child. It's Carys, right?"

"Yes," Asil said again, surprised. "I am… how do you know her?"

Egemon gave a dismissive wave. "You don't ignore the most powerful seer in your kingdom."

"I'm surprised to hear you say that," Asil murmured.

"What, because I won't appoint one?" Egemon snorted. "My father didn't appoint a Lord's Seer because he saw how dependent some of the Great Families were on theirs. He felt we should not be looking to others for answers so often. I follow his example. But a seer like Beste Arslan… you could not stand near the woman without understanding she held power. Is her granddaughter the same?"

Asil considered for a moment, then nodded. "She is. I wasn't sure at first. She's pretty, and… well, vain, I suppose. I don't mean it poorly, but the seers I've seen, the real ones that weren't just fleecing people, always seemed to be…"

"Frumpy," Egemon filled in with a smile. "Unremarkable."

"Yes."

Laughter filled the office again, and Asil found himself smiling as well. His father did not laugh often. Asil didn't mind if it was just at his observations and assumptions.

"Still," Egemon said after a moment, "you are not one to bring some girl back to your quarters. Why did Seer Arslan enjoy the hospitality of Watcher Castle?" Egemon looked at his son carefully, curiously.

Sighing, Asil pushed his hair back. "She is attractive. Charming. Intelligent. Though she refused my advances, said we were both too intoxicated." Egemon's brows rose, and a look of surprised admiration crossed his face, but he waited for his son to continue. There was an uncomfortable pause, then Asil finally took a breath and got to the crux of it.

"I asked her to dance, and she asked me to sit for a reading," Asil said, looking up at the books lining his father's study. "Before I told her who I was. Though she knew when she flipped the first card. She… saw something. She said a threat comes from across the ocean. From the other side of the Sea of Falling Stars."

There was a sharp exhale, and Asil looked back at his father. Egemon's jaw was set, irritation in his expression. "As if we needed something else right now."

"You believe her?" Asil did not bother hiding his surprise.

"You do not ignore the most powerful seer in your kingdom," Egemon said again, a bit more sharply. He then sighed and leaned back in his chair. "All right. Tell me exactly what she said."

Asil did his best to recount Carys's words, referring back to the notes he had taken. His memory of her reading from the night before was slightly muddled due to how much they'd both had to drink, but this morning's was fresh and very present. Egemon stared ahead at the dark fireplace while Asil spoke, nodding from time to time. When Asil finished, Egemon was quiet for a moment.

"I wish it had been more clear," Egemon said after a moment. "To be able to see something coming across the sea… I think your seer doesn't have enough faith in her own abilities. I honestly don't know if Beste could have reached so far. Do you intend to see her again?"

"Well, yes." Asil shifted somewhat in his seat. "For both personal and diplomatic reasons."

Another laugh, though softer this time, and Egemon looked at his son with a wry smile. "You like her. Shame. The first woman to hold your interest for more than an hour, and she's a commoner."

Sighing, Asil rolled his eyes. "I have no interest in marrying her, Father."

"Or anyone else."

Asil suppressed a groan. "Can we not have the heir conversation right now? Can we focus on this matter?"

Leaning forward once more, Egemon picked up the report he had been reading and handed it to his son. "We can change subjects, but I'm afraid I have a more immediate concern. Another altercation at the Western Reach. Looks to be the same group as before. Two guards dead, and I'm not sure we even wounded them."

Brows furrowed, Asil reviewed the report. The skirmishes at the edge of the Western Reach had begun two years ago, spotty and intermittent, from late spring to the first snow. The attacks were always the same: guards patrolling would come across a small band wearing clothing and colors no one recognized, and there would be a light exchange of blows, but usually only long enough for the small party to make their escape. Which they always did. Once or twice one of the guards would suffer a greater injury, usually from being overzealous. The first death had happened last year, at the start of fall. Two more guards had died in the spring. Now two at once.

"Do we still not know what they're doing?" Asil asked, looking up from the report to see Egemon's face. His father just shook his head.

"Adnan says they were able to get one of the packs off the attackers this time," Egemon said, getting up from his chair. "Naturally, he didn't bother to tell me what was in it, because he wants me to come see him."

Asil arched an eyebrow. "I take it you're going there now, and I'm accompanying you?"

"I've always said you were a smart lad," Egemon said, smirking, and Asil rolled his eyes but rose to his feet and left the report on his father's desk.

They headed out of the study, the guards at the door falling in step behind the two of them as Egemon led the way through the Lord's Hall—the main thoroughfare that led to Egemon's study, the throne room, and the Salon, the place where the heads of the three noble families conferred over the future of Vasi. Then down the grand staircase, and through the Main Hall and the Vestibule, to a waiting carriage. Asil sighed.

"We're going down to the guard house, aren't we?" Asil glanced at his father, hoping he was wrong.

Smirking, Egemon looked back to his son. "Would Adnan Kilic be anywhere else?"

Another sigh. "No, I suppose not," Asil muttered, and climbed into the carriage.

They were well on their way before either of them spoke again, Asil looking up at his father. "About the seer?"

"You would like to call on her again, consult her further on this threat she brought up," Egemon said. There was a long silence as Egemon watched the streets go by, but at last he nodded. "You have my permission to pursue this. Should more information come to us, outside of her visions, we may need to discuss this again."

"Of course, Father," Asil said, and did his best not to smile.

Chapter 4

THE CARRIAGE FINALLY came to a halt before the brutalist structure that was the guard hall and garrison. It was the second-largest building in Vasi, after Watcher Castle. Standing outside, flanked by two captains, was Lord Captain Adnan Kilic. Asil was not particularly looking forward to speaking with Lord Kilic, whom his father described as an old warhorse. The older lord certainly looked the part—he was almost the size of a horse, though he had started to get fat in the last few years, and his hair was as thick and full as any horse's mane, kept long by Vasi standards and pulled back in a low tail. Both Adnan's hair and beard were mostly silver now, though one could still see strands of the original black, and his steel eyes were perpetually narrowed, as if he were suspicious of every person who approached. In Asil's experience, Lord Kilic was looking for one last war.

"My Highest Lord," Adnan said, bowing to Egemon. "Thank you for coming to see me. I assume you have read my latest report. I'm glad you have come as well, my Heir. While I would hope this problem does not continue into your reign, best you be aware. Please follow me."

They headed into the guard hall, and Asil felt his shoulders draw up tight. His senses were assaulted by the guards chattering, the ring of metal on metal from the courtyard as they trained, and a smell: the faint fragrance of steel, sweat, and whatever they were serving in the barracks wing. Vasi had no army, but it did have a guard. Asil had always hated the guard house, the noises and smells, the ill-concealed looks of envy and judgment. Egemon, as a youth, had been trained to the blade by Adnan, back when Adnan was just a captain, learning the guard before taking over as Lord Captain. Asil had preferred quiet study, and while he could wield a sword well enough, he had been taught by skilled duelists in the castle gardens, not by the Lord Captain down in the courtyard with the guard recruits. The guardsmen did not distrust Asil, but they also did not respect him the way they did Egemon.

He was relieved when they reached Adnan's office, and the doors closed behind them. "So, what are we here to see?" Egemon asked, glancing around.

Adnan motioned to a table, on which was a satchel with a broken strap, as well as its contents. The satchel appeared to be leather in make, and well worked. The leather itself was supple, the stitching precise, and the weaving patterns tooled into the strap and cover—the work of a master craftsman. The contents appeared to be a pretty-standard field lunch of bread and cured meat, bundles of plants from the forest—freshly gathered today, from the look of them—and several phials with cork stoppers containing different colored powders, as well as some liquids.

"Have we identified any of this?" Egemon asked, and Adnan nodded.

"Yes, though not as much as I'd like, and mostly just the plants. We have identified these two," Adnan pointed to one phial of yellow granules and another with yellow-green dust, "as collected from plants in the area, though to collect that much pollen must have taken some time. But the rest… I'm no witch, Ege, and I'm pretty sure that's the only person who could tell you."

Asil's head picked up, and he looked at his father. Egemon noticed but didn't respond to his son's sudden interest. Instead, he picked up a phial full of pink… crystals, it looked like, and rotated it a bit before setting it down again.

"Is this all they're doing?" Egemon said, a bit disbelieving. "Just gathering from the wood? Why attack if that's the case? And this," he picked up the bag. "I've never seen markings like this. They're not just bandits living out in the ruins; this is a community, a culture. Maybe a handful of leatherworkers down in the merchant quarter could render something like this."

Adnan grumbled. "There have always been rumors that people remained when the inland cities were abandoned. It was assumed they did not survive, but we need to acknowledge that they may be amassing resources and knowledge. These may be scouting parties."

Long practice kept Asil from making a face. He appreciated that it was Adnan's job to be wary of dangers to the Lord and Vasi, but this felt like a leap too far. Even Egemon had a gently skeptical expression on his face.

"Have one of your men bundle these up for travel," Egemon said, stepping away from the table. "I'll take them back with me, see that they are identified. And, of course, send back a full report."

With a nod, Adnan walked to the door and knocked on it. It opened almost immediately, and Adnan sent the guardsman who opened it to retrieve batting for packing the phials away. Egemon and Adnan discussed finer details about where the attack had taken place, as well as what was being done for the families of the guardsmen who had died, but Asil only half listened, his mind trying to piece together the true picture beneath Adnan's concern. He wasn't getting very far.

Another guard arrived with the requested padding, and in moments the satchel was repacked. Egemon nodded for Asil to take it.

"I'll let you know when we have answers, Adnan," Egemon said, turning toward the door. Adnan made to follow them back out of the building, but another guard came in with reports from the docks, and Adnan sighed and simply waved as they left.

"You want to take these to your seer," Egemon said as they climbed back into the carriage.

"I do, yes." Asil set the satchel next to his hip. It was heavy enough to stay put. "She is also a witch, and given your description of her grandmother, I assume she is a convenient expert. And... I trust her."

Egemon smirked. "I would say you're besotted with her, but you're not the type. And if you are to rule one day, I should trust you. Very well. After I am returned to the castle, you may take the carriage down to the merchant quarter and see what she thinks."

Asil bowed his head. "Thank you, Father."

ⅭⅭⅭ

The morning had been hectic. By the time Carys had returned to her shop, there was a small crowd gathered outside. She left them there long enough to change into something she wouldn't worry about staining, then got to it. She mixed tinctures, gave a handful of readings, and sold out of hangover remedy. That really wasn't surprising—many people had midsummer celebrations, not just the castle. Carys finally had a moment to breathe around midday and took stock while nibbling on cheese and nuts.

"I should not have stayed at the castle last night," she muttered to herself, counting out bottles and seeing if she had enough to make another full batch of hangover remedy.

"How fortuitous that you realize that now," Judex stated, materializing on the other side of the counter. "Perhaps you can avoid it in the future. Maybe even remember not to chase fickle noblemen who will forget you exist by this time tomorrow."

The pencil stilled, and Carys looked up at Judex with a weary sigh. "And, so what if he does? He was pleasant enough, but he doesn't owe me anything. We were honest with each other as to our goals and intentions."

The bells rang, and Carys glared at Judex before composing herself and turning to greet whoever had come in. She froze, however, when she found herself looking at Asil Özdemir, a guard just behind him. Asil grinned and stepped up to the counter.

"So, this is your shop?"

"It is," Carys said, recovering. She self-consciously dusted off the front of her tunic and pulled her sleeves back down. "I imagine this is where you look around with an air of jaded boredom and tell me it's 'quaint' or something?"

Laughing, Asil leaned on the counter. "It is quaint! Although I mean that more kindly than you're implying. I didn't expect it to be so small, but it's delightful and charming."

That got a smile. "Well, it really doesn't need to be bigger," Carys said, tipping her head to the side. "It's just me here. Gets a bit crowded at times, but customers generally know to be polite. And if I'm doing a lot of readings, they'll wait outside. Hence the bench out front."

Nodding, Asil looked around. "Have you had a busy day, then?"

"Rather, yes." Carys also leaned on the counter, folding her arms in front of her. "Mostly people seeking a cure for someone's hangover. It seems most of the city enjoyed the midsummer night. A few readings, but nothing important. You?"

Straightening up, Asil set the leather satchel he carried on the counter. "I have something I wanted you to look at. This was found by the guard, taken from a group that has been spotted several times at the edge of the Great Ruins."

With careful hands, Carys drew the satchel to her. "The Great Ruins… You mean the cities of the interior? Does our guard patrol that far?"

Asil just nodded as Carys opened the satchel and unpacked it. She lined up the phials and neatly twisted up the batting, putting it back in the satchel. "Very well. And what are you hoping I will do with this?"

"Tell us what it is," Asil said, simply.

"Us?"

Sighing, Asil leaned on the counter again. "Yes, us. In this case, myself, my father, and the Lord Captain."

Carys blinked and tilted her head to the side again. "Surely you must have a witch or at least an herbalist at the castle."

"An herbalist, yes, but I brought them to you," Asil said, with a weariness that implied his patience was starting to thin. "Or are you too busy to waste time on such matters?"

Carys felt both prickled and chastised. "You needn't take that tone; I was just confused. It seemed you were going out of your way for answers that might have been had closer to home."

"Your response implied that either you thought the task was beneath you," Asil said, a thread of irritation still in his tone, "or that you have so little faith in your own abilities that you couldn't understand why I would call on you. Neither says flattering things about you."

Glaring, Carys picked up the first phial, with the tiny golden nuggets. "Bee pollen," she said, and placed it in front of Asil. She picked up the next, with the pale green-yellow dust. "Pine pollen." She picked up the phial with the pink crystals. "Marsh pig blood salt."

Asil straightened. "I'm sorry, what?"

"Marsh pig blood salt," Carys repeated, setting the phial down in front of Asil.

"What on earth is a marsh pig? And why do you make salt out of their blood?!"

Carys found herself smiling a little, in spite of her irritation. "So, a marsh pig is not actually a pig. It's an amphibian. They start about the size of a fist. You find them in estuaries and other places where salt and freshwater mix. They extract salt from the water they live in and store it in a sort of cavity between their stomach wall and the rest of their body. It gives them huge, distended bellies. They have no way of purging the salt, so they just keep collecting it, eventually growing to the size of a melon. You catch marsh pigs, pop their stomachs, and drain out the liquid onto a table, leaving it to dry in the sun. This is what's left behind. Marsh pig blood salt. It kills the marsh pig, but once they're big enough to harvest, they're close to death anyway."

Asil's face was priceless. "That is disgusting," he said, looking down at the phial in front of him.

"I can guarantee you've eaten it," Carys continued, and had to fight not to laugh as Asil's disgust became more apparent. "It's shockingly nutritious, and less expensive than sea salt. It began as something the poor used, but the color made it unique and popular among the elite of Veli, and I know you've traveled there for state dinners multiple times."

"We can move on now," Asil said, then looked up at Carys. "You're enjoying this, aren't you?"

"It is making me feel better about you being difficult," Carys said with a smile, and picked up the next phial. This one held little shimmering blue flecks and was quite full. "Oh. Faeder scales. A lot of them."

Asil eyed Carys warily. "This isn't going to be like the marsh pigs, is it?"

"No," Carys said, snickering. "These are scraped from faeders, a type of fish. You don't even have to kill them if you're careful, and since faeders are somewhat rare, most people are careful. They're a popular ingredient in virility potions and aphrodisiacs. Jewelers will also grind them into paste and put them behind glass cabochons. It's quite pretty, provided the jeweler is honest about what they did and doesn't try to convince you it's some rare gem. Still, this represents weeks of harvest. It would be worth a lot of money on the right market."

That phial was set before Asil once more, and Carys looked over at the three that remained, filled with various liquids. "I can't tell you what these are just by looking. I'll have to open them."

Nodding, Asil motioned for Carys to go ahead. She picked up the first, full of something in a very unpleasant shade of yellow. She examined the phial for a moment, then uncorked it. The smell was immediate and noxious. Asil almost retched. Carys recorked it.

"Bile," Carys said after a moment, setting down the phial with the others. "Eel, I think."

"Truly, you live a charmed life," Asil said, pulling out a scented handkerchief and holding it to his nose and mouth.

Rolling her eyes, Carys picked up the next phial. This was a deep blue, the blue children's stories pretend oceans are. She uncorked it and sniffed, then brought the vial a little closer and sniffed again, waving toward her face to catch any potential fumes.

"Huh." Carys looked at the phial for a moment, then held it out to Asil. "Hold this."

There was that smile again, like the one Asil had last night when Carys ordered him about and used his name without titles or honorifics. "Yes, my lady."

She gave a tsking sound of disgust, but Carys turned around and gathered a handful of things from the shelves behind her, returning with a shallow dish and a couple of canisters. She took the phial back and poured a small amount in the dish before corking it and setting it down again. She then took the tiniest and most delicate little spoon and added a pinch of finely ground sapweed root to the dish. Using a small wooden whisk, she gave the mixture a quick stir. It turned a gorgeous, vibrant purple, and the shop was suddenly overwhelmed with a delightful floral fragrance.

"What is that?" he asked, curious, leaning forward and taking a deep breath.

"Don't do that too many times," Carys said, smiling. "Lily pearl extract. They're fruits that grow on certain species of water lilies. You have to pick them when they're overripe but not yet fermented. The powder I added is just the ground root of a sapweed, but it's a catalyst for many things. Anyway, this can't hurt you, but it will very literally intoxicate you. Lily pearl extract is one of the only aphrodisiacs proven to work. It's also good for clarity in an enfeebled mind. It's just a matter of what you combine it with."

Glancing up at Carys, Asil smiled. "Would that be so bad? You'd take care of me, wouldn't you?"

That got a giggle. "It's the middle of the day, and we're in my shop," Carys pointed out, setting the dish aside and reaching for the last phial. "Unless you have another guard keeping people out, we have no guarantee of privacy."

Asil sighed as Carys uncorked the last phial and gave it a sniff. "Oh," she said, and recorked it, handing it back. "Brine. Sea water, concentrated."

"That's it?"

"That's it."

As Carys cleaned up, Asil regarded the phials in front of him, arranging them in a row. "Does this mean anything to you? This combination of ingredients?"

Carys shook her head. "No, but other than the bee and pine pollen, they're all things gathered from a shore, and most of them take some time and distillation. If these are people coming from the ruins, as you put it, they probably bought them. That many faeder scales, extracting that many lily pearls, even evaporating and concentrating the sea water, these are all things that would take a lot of time. Someone's coming to the river to trade."

"Makes more sense than the scouting party of an invading force," Asil muttered, repacking the satchel. "Though... why attack the guards?"

"Who attacked first?"

Asil's head popped up, and he regarded Carys for a moment. "We're all a bunch of idiots," he said at last, and Carys furrowed her brow. "We attacked first. I'm sure of it. And you said they would have had to trade for these items, right? We only see them from spring to early fall, when travel is easy. They're not scouts at all; Adnan just assumed they had to be because they're better fighters than his guards!"

"There's a lot more to this situation, isn't there?" Carys asked, quirking an eyebrow.

Asil nodded. "There is, but not as much as we feared. Which is why I wanted to come to you. I trust you."

Something in Carys softened. "Oh, Asil, you barely know me!"

"But I know I can trust you." He reached out and set his fingertips on her hand as it rested on the counter.

"You can," she said, a gentle smile on her face.

They shared a quiet moment as they regarded each other, then Asil pulled away and picked up the satchel. "I should return with what I've learned. Though, could you make me a quick list with notes on their general use? It would be helpful for my report."

"Naturally." Carys walked over to where she had been taking inventory and pulled out the wrapped charcoal pencil and a fresh sheet of paper. She assembled the requested list: each item with where it could be found and its primary three uses. Handing it to Asil, she came out from behind the counter to walk him to the door.

"If you think of anything else, write to me," Asil said, smiling. He reached into his vest, and pulled out a small purse, offering it to Carys. "I will make sure any missive from your shop comes straight to me. Here, you should be compensated for your time."

"I will do my best not to abuse my newfound authority." She considered the purse for a moment, then nodded and took it.

Laughing, Asil headed out, the door closing behind him. Carys finished cleaning up, pouring the activated lily-pearl extract into a tiny squat pot and corking it. She had no idea what she'd use it for, but it was rare and seemed a waste to throw out. She felt a stirring again, and her gaze drifted over to the reading alcove.

"No," Carys murmured to herself, "I have things to do."

The next hour passed quietly, and the frantic morning seemed to have been replaced with a slow afternoon. She finished her inventory check and made up a list for when her runner came up from the markets in two days. She'd be able to make the hangover remedy and bottle half of it, but so long as the runner could get her more bottles, the rest would not go bad while it waited. Carys got the remedy brewing, cleaned the rest of the shop, swept the floors, and banked the embers in the oven so that the remedy would just simmer for a few hours, but still not a single person came into the shop.

"All right! You win," she said at last, heading over to the alcove and sitting down in the heavy wooden chair, then leaning back into it for a moment with a sigh. It felt as if the air around her vibrated, impatient for her to take action. She sat back up, picking up her cards.

It had been almost four years since Carys had done a reading without someone in the chair across from her. If she were being honest, reading for other people seemed to dilute the exchange. It was part of why the reading for Asil had surprised her so much with its strength. She picked up her pouch and pulled out the cards, letting them slip through her hands. The cards weren't really what connected a seer to the beyond; different seers used different tools. They were a focus, something to help the concentration. In theory Carys didn't need them, but they made the exercise easier.

Carys set the deck down on the table before her and looked at it for a moment. The shop was silent, save for the bubble of the cauldron. Even Judex was gone. Finally, she reached forward and cut the cards. She paused again and wondered why she hesitated so much. She didn't like to lose herself in the reading, but she was alone and safe in her home. Carys flipped over three cards. The first was a feminine form, not unlike the Divine Mother with their veiled eyes, though the hood they wore was not white, and soft curls framed their face. The second was an androgynous figure, weeping, as apparitions swirled around them. The last was a sprawl of towers and homes, with a single road winding through it.

The Seer. The Cursed. The City.

Hands set against the table, Carys took a deep breath, and opened herself to the possibilities, to what the tugging threads wanted so badly to show her. Her eyes began to glow, bright and brilliant through her veil, filling the alcove with light. Her head fell back, and she cried out. Her breath came faster. She didn't try to narrate what she saw. This vision was solely for her.

Carys saw herself, standing alone in her shop. Then the world around her shifted, and she stood in the great hall of Watcher Castle. Her hair was down, her eyes blazing, and hands reached for her. Then the vision spun around her, and she was looking at… soldiers. An army. No, not a whole army, just part of one. They marched forward across the ocean, every day a step closer, with a malevolent presence beating a drum that kept their steps in time. Then the sea below her gave way, and Carys fell through the ocean as the soldiers marched past her, over her, and landed at the shores of Vasi. Bright lines ran through the city, like an infinite web, the strands of connection and possibilities. They started to glow, and then to burn. Carys felt something ring her head, like a band of fire, and it coursed into her.

"Mother, it hurts!" Reality snapped back with a suddenness that had Carys gripping the table as if she might fall out of her chair. The burn in her veins receded, and she fell back against the smooth wood, panting, her hair plastered to her cheeks and neck by sweat. She reached up and ripped off her veil, tugging out hair in the process. She needed it off.

Whimpering, Carys stayed in the chair for a long time, eyes closed, until her heart finally calmed, and sweat had dried. Opening her eyes slowly, she looked down at the cards before her. The Seer, the Cursed, and the City.

Taking a deep breath, Carys leaned her head back against the chair. "I'm the Seer," she murmured to herself. "I sit at a nexus. The Seer is always at a nexus, for they see where the strands connect. The Cursed… this is the ones across the sea again. The Cursed represents outside forces, things you can't control. They're coming and I can't stop it. The City… connections to the city… The City is community, it's people, it's society and structure. I… Grandma, I wish you were here."

Alone, in the quiet, Carys let herself cry.

Finally, with trembling hands, Carys picked up the cards and put them back. She pushed herself out of her chair and stumbled to the door, locking everything up. She didn't bother to turn down the lights. Once behind the curtain, she tossed ash on the coals in the oven and covered the cauldron. It could cool overnight. She took one of her own tinctures, one for nerves and distress, and set the bottle aside to be cleaned and reused.

By the time Carys made it up to her loft, the tremble had left her hands. She was still so tired, but she was calmer and clear headed. She disrobed and, rather than climb into bed, she sat down and began to write Asil a letter.

Before the vision could leave her, Carys wrote down everything, including details that were becoming clearer as her mind calmed. It was not an army; it was a company. A company of soldiers, coming across the sea. They wielded swords of a heft and design Carys hadn't seen before, but she did her best to describe them. The malevolent presence that commanded them remained on the other side of the waters, but a… piece of them…? A representative was there with the soldiers, to keep them in line, to guide their task.

Carys's head was dropping by the time she finished. She set the letter down and climbed into bed. The comforting warmth of her blankets eased the remaining tension in her limbs, and she was asleep before she could think to turn out the bedside lamp.

Chapter 5

TWO DAYS LATER, Asil paced in his room. Carys's letter lay open on his desk, as it had since it arrived. He had written back right away, thanking her for it, but then floundered due to a lack of direction. He had already spent a long evening discussing the letter with his father; they'd explored many scenarios and possibilities, but ultimately the evening ended with the both of them looking grave but making no progress. Additional guards had been sent to the Southern Watchtower, though it was difficult to say if they would arrive in time. Carys's visions didn't narrow down the trajectory beyond "soon." And even if they did, what then?

"My lord?"

Asil startled and turned around, pivoting with the swift surety of a duelist. Nazim took a step back, properly intimidated. Sighing, Asil relaxed and straightened his vest.

"What is it?"

"I'm sorry, my lord," Nazim said, bowing. "I have been sent to inform you that your Lord Father requires your presence in his study."

That was interesting. "Thank you, Nazim," Asil murmured, and the boy bowed and left swiftly. Asil paused to check his reflection, wanting to be certain that there was no physical evidence of his agitation, then followed Nazim out the door.

As Asil headed down the hall to his father's study, he noticed there seemed to be a number of unfamiliar retainers in the Lord's Hall. While

Asil did not know all the names of the many individuals of varying rank that frequented Watcher Castle, he had a very good eye for faces, and an excellent grasp of patterns. The hours between lunch and tea were typically very quiet. The Lord's Hall would begin to fill shortly before dinner, reaching its peak capacity during court and then filtering to nothing a little before midnight. To see anyone other than servants (and the same handful of nobles who never seemed to leave) before teatime was unusual enough for Asil to slow his step and take notice of the new faces.

An older man, silver at his temples, reclined in a chair directly across from the guards who were perpetually stationed at the doors to Egemon's study. The man had broad shoulders, a thickness to his frame that implied muscle, not fat, and wore an ornamented blade comfortably. A young couple farther down the hall chatted amicably, both well dressed, the woman in a long dress that indicated she intended to attend court later, and the young man's embroidered vest said the same. They did not look at each other, despite facing one another. Instead, they looked over the other's shoulder as they talked. A woman sat in a chaise lounge at the far end of the hall reading a book, glancing up from its pages occasionally. Three young men walked the hall idly, as if waiting for something, all of them dressed well but not too well. Asil paused for a moment outside the door of his father's study, then went in.

Egemon was sitting on the settee by the cold fireplace as Asil came in and looked up at his son with a faint smile. Across from Egemon sat a slender woman about Egemen's age with auburn hair and sharp hazel eyes. Lady Meliha Aydin.

"Of course," Asil said, smirking a bit as he let the door close behind him. "So those are your people in the hall?"

The lady's eyes narrowed. "How many did you count?"

"Seven." Asil didn't hesitate.

"Damn," Meliha muttered, and Egemen's smile grew. "Correct. Well done as always, my Heir."

"Do you specifically do this just to see if Asil will notice?" Egemen asked, arching an eyebrow.

"Not only for that reason," Meliha said, still irritated, and Asil laughed as he sat down. Lady Aydin looked up at him. "What first tipped you?"

Asil shrugged. "Too many people for this time of day. There's no reason to be here if you don't have business. Too early for court, and my father prefers tea to be a quiet affair."

Nodding, Meliha considered for a moment, resting her chin in her hand as her gaze grew distant. It is said that Özdemir had the will to rule, Kilic the will to fight, and Aydin the will to learn. House Aydin had founded the university, after all. But knowledge could be found in many places, and House Aydin, as the keepers of all knowledge, also collected secrets. Meliha Aydin's network of spies stretched throughout the whole of the Kingdoms of Dawn. Egemon shook his head, still looking amused, and motioned for Asil to join them.

"Tea is on its way," Egemon said as Asil sank into the chair between the two settees.

"Are we going to discuss why Lady Aydin is here now, or wait until after the tea arrives?" Asil looked from Egemon to Meliha.

"A ship has been spotted by the Southern Watchtowers," Meliha said without preamble, and Asil's brows rose. "Our preliminary reports say that it seems to propel itself without sails and moves at a steady and even pace across the water. It will likely be here in days. And not very many of them."

Sighing, Egemon sat up in his chair. "When I said I wanted to distract Adnan from the bands on the northwest border, this is not what I had in mind."

Meliha smiled sympathetically. "Clearly no one wished for this, Ege," she murmured, then looked over at Asil. "But you knew this was coming. Because of Seer Arslan's convenient arrival at Watcher Castle. I will admit, when I first spoke with your father and learned of the seer's unexplained presence at the event, I was suspicious and looked into it. It seems, however, that the Divine Mother must have set events in motion."

"Meaning?" Asil shifted in his seat and wished Meliha had less of a tendency toward storytelling.

"Meaning that Carys Arslan was at the Midsummer party because she regularly advises Emiri Bulut," Meliha continued, "not because anyone was attempting to feed you information. The timing was, in fact, convenient."

Asil bristled a little, not enjoying the idea of anyone, even his father's spymaster, thinking that Carys had been planted there. "I suppose I'm glad you've been convinced," he said, shifting again.

"I told you he wouldn't like it," Egemon said, and Asil briefly glared at his father.

"However, this also makes what she has seen more dire," Meliha continued, the faint remains of her smile leaving as her voice and demeanor grew more serious. "Seer Arslan's reputation, as well as her lineage, make her someone whose visions one does not ignore. Which comes back to what I was discussing with my Highest Lord before you arrived." She turned back to Egemon. "We need her to be accessible. We need her here."

The servants chose that moment to arrive with tea, so Asil was forced to sit with his confusion as his father glowered at Meliha. The three were quiet as plates of finger sandwiches, cheese rolls, delicate tarts, and rose candies were placed on the table between them. Petals floated in the colored tea glasses that were being set down with increasing swiftness. The silence made the servants nervous. They acted as if they were interrupting something dire, something secret. Asil supposed that in a way they were.

As the door shut, Egemen sat forward and picked up his glass. "I still don't like it."

"You must like it more than an assassination attempt or coup," Meliha answered dryly.

"Don't like what?" Asil asked, his tone sharp. "What are we discussing, exactly?"

Meliha was silent, and arched her brows at Egemon, who sighed and leaned back with his tea. "The appointment of Carys Arslan to the position of the Lord's Seer."

There was a moment of silence at the table. Egemon nursed his tea; Meliha picked up a small tart and delicately ate it. Asil mulled this piece of information over for a long moment, then picked up his tea and took a careful sip before looking back at Meliha.

"Why?"

"Which is precisely what I said," Egemon said, sitting back up.

Lady Aydin sighed. "My Heir, are you really going to side with your father in his stubborn adherence to his father's fears?"

"No," Asil said, irritated, and Egemon looked surprised, "I want to hear why."

"Oh!" Meliha picked up her own tea and took a sip. "Well, as discussed, Carys Arslan is the most powerful seer on either side of the strait—"

"Even in Veli?" Egemon asked, curious.

Meliha glared. "My Highest Lord, don't interrupt. As I was saying: her ability to see beyond is the only reason we've had any warning this was coming. Because of that, an additional contingent of guards has been sent to the fort at Watcher's Step, as a precaution, and they will arrive in time to greet this strange ship. She has already helped us this much. Imagine what she will see once these strangers arrive?"

"But why the appointment?" Asil asked, still missing a piece of the puzzle. "Why not simply call her to the castle when we need her?"

"Aside from the fact that it would be grossly inconvenient?" Meliha looked at Asil as if he were being dull.

"Lady Aydin," Asil began, eyes narrowed, "if you are going to patronize me, I will leave."

"I apologize, my Heir," Meliha said, leaning back a bit. "The appointment is necessary because of her position."

Sighing, Asil reached up and rubbed his eyes. "Perhaps I am being dense. What position? As a seer?"

Egemon cleared his throat, calling for attention. "Her position as a common-born child of unknown parentage. Kiraz Arslan never wed; no one knows who the father is. The name 'Carys' is unique, and we assume it is from her father's people, but who they are is a mystery."

"She will need to be able to interact freely with the nobles, the Great Families, and whoever arrives on that ship," Meliha said, her tone earnest. "Being awarded the title of Lord's Seer does not make her a noble, but it puts her somewhere adjacent: a commoner of exceptional skill, who is worthy of that interaction."

That was it. The one thing about Carys that didn't matter to Asil was also the one thing that could make it impossible for her to advise someone like himself or the Lord of the Strait. She had to be more than just some girl. Respected as her gifts were, they would not be enough for many of the nobles or the Great Families to act on her behalf. Sighing, Asil poured himself more tea.

"So what is the problem, then, if the solution is so simple?" Asil sat back with his cup, looking from Egemon to Meliha.

"Well, Adnan hates the idea," Meliha said with a wry smile, "which of course makes me like it even more."

Egemen grumbled. "Should I not listen to the commander of my guard?"

"Not when his entire argument is 'but she's a low-born bastard,'" Meliha shot back, and Asil seethed a little. "He doesn't have a tactical reason."

Groaning, Egemon closed his eyes and rubbed them. "How soon would you like this to happen?"

Meliha set her glass down. "Immediately."

A defeated-looking Egemon turned to Asil. "If I consent to this, she will be your responsibility. She will answer to you, and only you. If there are any problems with the nobility or the merchant families, you will take care of them. Are you willing to accept this?"

"I am," Asil said, without hesitation. Egemon looked surprised. Surprised and also… proud.

"Very well," Egemon said, pouring himself some more tea. "I will have the papers and the letter drawn up this evening. You may deliver the letter tomorrow. Meliha, since this was your idea, I expect you to prepare the necessary announcements. But no more than necessary. I will speak with the castellan to have her room prepared. We haven't had anyone in the Garden Wing since your sisters left; I have no doubt the rooms will need to be aired." Asil had just enough sense not to ask why Carys wouldn't be placed in his wing.

"She's going to need more than just a room, Ege," Meliha pointed out.

"And Baris will see to it." There was a finality to Egemon's answer. He was done talking about the matter.

"Of course, my Highest Lord," Meliha said, a smile playing at the corners of her mouth.

"Asil, you may return to your own activities whenever you are done with tea," Egemon said with a small sigh. "Enjoy your evening. I suspect that once that ship arrives, we will all be very busy for some time."

ℭ ℭ ℭ

The day had been unbearably warm. Carys twisted her thick hair up into a bun to get it off the back of her neck and hiked up her skirts as she hid behind the counter. She had opened every window and even propped open the door (though not all the way) for any hint of a breeze coming up from the bay. Summer days in Vasi were often warm, but the wind usually kept air flowing. Not today. To make matters worse, business had been slow. Exactly one person had come into the shop early that morning, and not another since. It somehow made the entire situation more insulting—here she was, positively roasting behind her counter, and no one even had the decency to come make a purchase.

"You look like an old woman ready to wade in the river," Judex observed from his perch on the end of the counter, where he sat with his legs crossed. "You would frighten children in your current state."

"Leave me alone," Carys said as she fanned herself with her ledger. She tried to say it firmly, but it came out as a whine. "Why do you always pester me when I'm unhappy?"

Judex smirked. "Because agitated emotional states make you an easier target," he answered, almost cheerfully. "Which you already know. You're such a child sometimes."

Glaring, Carys continued to fan herself. The heat was draining her. She was hot, and sweaty, and she wanted to strip off her clothing and take a nap, not stand there and argue with a spirit of judgment. Furthermore, a spirit whose antics she had been forced to endure for nearly a decade. She turned away from Judex and looked around her shop. There was really nothing in here to alleviate the problem.

Just as Carys was about to head into the back and just pour water over her legs, the bells jingled as the door opened. She stepped up close to the counter so her customer wouldn't be able to see her legs, and set the ledger down, pulling up a fake smile. As she raised her head to see who was there, however, the smile was replaced with shock.

"Asil," she began as she watched the Heir walk toward her, somewhat mortified, "why are you here?"

"Can't I just come to see you?" Asil grinned, and the grin got bigger as he took in Carys's appearance.

Carys sighed. "You can, though I feel like nothing in your schedule would put you in my neighborhood without reason."

Finally reaching the counter, Asil leaned against it, brow furrowed. "I thought you would be happier to see me."

"Aw, you hurt his little feelings," Judex said mockingly.

Standing up a bit straighter, Carys brushed a lock of hair from her face and managed an apologetic smile. "I am happy to see you. It's been a tiring day."

"Have you been very busy lately?" Asil asked and seemed more than politely interested in the answer.

Carys shook her head. "No," she said, "summer tends to be fairly slow, as it were. People are generally in better health, so they don't come for salves or tinctures. Well, other than for sunburn. They still need advice, but summer is also the best time to travel, be out in the water, do pretty much anything other than sit closed up in my shop." She shrugged.

"It is warm in here," Asil pointed out with a smile, and Carys shrugged again, agreeing. His smile grew larger. "That's good, though. That means I can steal you away."

Carys blinked. "Oh?"

Standing up straight, Asil smoothed his vest and reached in to pull out an envelope, which he handed over to Carys. It reminded her of the invitation that Emiri had given her, heavy paper with the seal of House Özdemir stamped into the wax. Arching an eyebrow, Carys cracked the seal and opened the envelope.

"So, what is this for?" she asked as she withdrew a letter inside.

Asil smirked. "You're going to meet my father."

Pausing, Carys looked at Asil with wide eyes. "I thought you said you were not courting me," Carys said after a moment, the corner of her mouth quirking a little. "And even if you were, it would be far too early in the courtship for a formal introduction to our parents."

"I am still not courting you," Asil assured her, clearly amused. "I told my father about your seeing and the conversations we've had. I also shared with him the letter you sent. Then this morning we received a messenger bird from the Southern Watchtower. A ship has been spotted, coming up from the south. It is unlike anything we have seen."

A tingle rushed through Carys's skin, up her neck, and through her scalp. She had been right. Not that she thought she was wrong, but the confirmation was exciting. Her eyes looked down at the paper in her hands, and she skimmed the words, mumbling to herself as she read.

"…will accept the appointment to," Carys read, then paused, almost dropping the letter in her shock, "the position of Lord's Seer? The Lord of the Strait hasn't appointed a seer since your great-grandfather's time! And you want me to just… just accept this position?!"

Leaning on the counter again, Asil's brow creased as he looked at Carys. "Well, yes," he said, clearly surprised at her reaction. And perhaps a touch irritated. "I expect you to accept it, and also possibly feel honored. Because, as you said, the Lord of the Strait has not appointed a seer in a very long time. Though technically you will not answer to my father, you will answer to me. But I answer to my father, so really, it's an academic difference."

"But," Carys protested, her shoulders drawing back tightly as she looked from Asil to the letter and back again, "but my customers, my shop! I can't just… just leave!"

That flicker of irritation was there again, and Asil drummed his fingers on the counter. "Why not?" he asked, his tone growing sharper. "Carys, your shop is charming, and I am sure your customers love you, but you just told me you're not busy. You are not the only seer in Vasi, but you are the most gifted, and what are you doing with it? Helping girls chase husbands? Soothing sunburns and upset stomachs?"

"I still don't like him, but he's probably the most sensible man you've spent time with," Judex said, leaning back against the wall, the shelf jutting through his chest. Carys bit her tongue to keep from responding to the spirit and took a deep breath.

"Maybe I like doing those things," Carys said, her voice also becoming sharp. "Maybe I like keeping my grandmother's practice because it's all I have left. Maybe I have a life that I spent time creating, and it may not seem important to you in your castle, but it is still my life!"

Sighing, Asil pushed off the counter and stepped back. "This is stupid," he said, dismissively. "I am going to leave. I will return this evening after dinner to ask you again. I hope you will be ready to go. If you are not, clearly I was wrong about this. About you."

Carys was surprised by how much those words hurt. She watched in stunned silence as Asil left the shop, feeling almost like she had been slapped. The door closed behind him, and she stood at the counter until Judex's derisive laughter made her look in his direction.

"You really are pathetic sometimes," the spirit said. His legs unfolded and he slid off the counter, walking around it to stand in front of Carys. "The opportunity of a lifetime falls into your lap, and you're whining about clinging to mediocrity. If your grandmother were here, she would be aghast."

Carys glared at him. "If you had anything resembling the ability to care," she spat at him, "you might know that it would be hard to abandon your life at a noble's whim!"

"Yes, because you're going so far away," Judex said dryly, leaning against the counter where Asil had stood just a moment ago, mimicking the Heir's posture. "Far, far up the hill. To never see your city or the friends you don't really have again. Such a challenge."

"By the waters, I wish I could banish you," Carys said, seething.

Judex just laughed and dissipated into nothing. Somehow that made it worse, like someone leaving before the argument was over. Twice in one fight.

Carys shrieked and stomped into the back room, climbing up the narrow stairs to the bedroom and then out the window into the garden. Still angry, she proceeded to weed with a vengeance, tearing up small plants and shaking the dirt from them before throwing them in a basket. She not only did her own plots but those of her neighbor who owned the flower shop next door. An hour later, angrily throwing the weeds into the compost bin, Carys's actions slowed, and she finally set down her empty basket and dusted off her soil-covered hands with a sigh.

"I hate that they might be right," she muttered, looking over the garden, her eyes finally falling on a chair in the corner. Resting against the chair was her grandmother's cane, painstakingly carved with the same chasing-ivy pattern as on the chair downstairs in the alcove. It was made from a dark wood and had been soaked in dyes until it resembled the inky purple and blue darkness of the night sky. The cane was in her grandmother's hand every day that Carys could remember. When it had come time to return her grandmother to the Cradle, Carys had not been able to set the cane on the pyre with her.

"You would have left with him, no questions," Carys murmured, as she walked to the chair and ran her fingertips over the smooth, polished wood of the cane's handle. "It always galled you that both his grandfather and his father refused to appoint a seer. It really should have been you."

Sighing, Carys headed over to the basin and washed her hands, then went back into the shop. She was a little unnerved at how easy it was to pack up clothing, close and latch the windows, and make up a sign advising people to go seek out Seer Kaya in the merchant district. Carys changed into the outfit she had first met Asil in, placing her veil with care and putting a little more effort into braiding back her hair around it. She had long grown out of any formal dresses she had ever owned. This was the nicest thing she had.

Finally, Carys went to the flower shop next door. The shop itself was shuttered and closed by this point, but Carys went to the smaller side door and knocked lightly. An excited little girl opened the door, bouncing when she saw who was on the other side.

"Hi, Miss Carys," the little girl said, and turned to shout into the house, "Mama! Miss Carys is here!"

A moment later, a dusky woman with midnight hair who could most accurately be described as being very pregnant shuffled to the door. She smiled at Carys and looked the seer over. "Fair evening to you, Seer Arslan. What brings you over?"

"Hello, Oya," Carys said, bowing her head. "I'm sorry to bother you, but I have a favor to ask. I'll be gone for a few days, perhaps a week. Would you be willing to watch my plants? I leave tonight. I'm sorry it's last minute."

"Everything all right?" Oya asked, reaching out and setting a hand on Carys's arm. "You don't really take trips, and usually give a little more notice if you'll be away."

Smiling, Carys nodded. "I'm fine. This was unexpected, but everything is all right. I just need you to watch the garden for a bit. The shop is closed up, and I've left a sign telling people to go see Kaya by the markets if they need a seer."

Oya looked at Carys searchingly as her daughter hid behind her skirts, then nodded, letting her hand fall away. "Of course I'll be happy to. I'm up there most every day anyway."

"Thank you, Oya," Carys said, and took a step back, giving a small bow of her head again before heading back to her shop.

When Asil returned at dusk, Carys was sitting on the bench outside the shop, her satchel and travel bag next to her. Both items were old, having once been her mother's, and their appearance would make one think that Carys traveled far more than she actually did.

Asil approached and took everything in. "So you're coming?" he asked, hopeful.

"I am," Carys said as she stood, glaring a little at Asil as she did, "even though you were horrifically rude earlier, and it would not have cost you anything to try to have some compassion. You will find, princeling, that completely altering one's life can be difficult and require some time to accept."

"I am sorry, Carys," Asil said genuinely, placing his hand over his heart and giving her a small bow. "Change can be difficult, but it can also be good. I sincerely believe that this change will benefit us all. And please don't ever call me princeling again."

Carys arched a brow. "Try not being rude, and maybe I won't."

With a grin, Asil stepped over and took Carys's bag. "I will do my best," he said, and motioned toward the carriage. "Seer Arslan, if you please."

Chapter 6

CARYS TWISTED HER scarf around her hand as the carriage made its way through the city. The spires of the noble quarter seemed almost ominous as the sky around them slowly darkened with the onset of night. Asil's hand closed over hers, and she jumped, head turning sharply to look at him. He looked confused.

"You don't need to be afraid, Carys," he said, eyes full of concern.

Sighing, Carys looked down at the hand that held hers, but didn't pull away. "That is very easy for you to say," she muttered, and looked out the window of the carriage once more. "Asil, other than that party, which you pointed out several times I did not belong at, I have never been to Watcher Castle. I am not of high enough birth to enter through the main doors."

Still confused, Asil picked up Carys's hand and unwound the scarf from around it. "I don't understand," he said, his thumb gently brushing her skin. "You don't care at all about my rank. Why are you so concerned about yours?"

Carys shook her head. "I don't know how to make you understand. The reasons you admire me… Asil, do you know why I don't have more clients among the Great Families?"

"I have known you for less than a week," Asil pointed out, smiling wryly. "I have no idea what your client list looks like."

For a moment Carys just stared at him. Then she laughed. It was as if she could feel something unwinding in her as she did. There was a certain absurdity in the situation.

"Better?" Asil continued to hold her hand.

"A bit," Carys said, smiling at him. "Asil, I don't have clients among the Great Families because I'm not good at placating them. The few that do come to me are either young enough that they don't yet expect everyone to talk to them with reverence, or they admire my abilities enough to put up with my lack of decorum."

"I think it's incredibly charming," Asil pointed out, and Carys laughed again.

"But you're the only one!"

Asil looked at her with a skeptical half smile. "Timur Koc thinks you're charming."

"Timur Koc is an old drunk who thinks he's a poet," Carys countered obstinately. "I don't disagree with him, so of course he thinks I'm charming. But I don't grovel."

"Nor should you," Asil said, with a firmness that surprised Carys. "You are concerned about the opinions of people who do not matter. Yes, it would probably make things easier if everyone loved you, but they won't. They don't love me, but they have to listen to me because of who I am. Carys, you are about to become the Lord's Seer. They will have to listen to you because of who you are." Asil released her hand and sat back. "We are going to meet my father. After that... I know you're not going to like this, but you will have to be presented at court. You'll stand before the throne, be announced as the new seer, and bow, and then I'll be by your side for the rest of the night until we're both allowed to run away."

Being presented at court sounded terrible, but Carys nodded. She bit back her worried response and chastised herself. She was a seer! The threads of destiny were visible to her! If she didn't fear the other nobles enough to court their favor, why was she so afraid now?

The carriage rolled to a stop, and the door opened. Asil stepped out first and offered Carys a hand. Valets came and left with her luggage. Taking a deep breath, she accepted the hand down and, feeling every inch the pretender, followed Asil up the polished white marble steps into the vestibule of Watcher Castle.

Carys was grateful that the veil hid her eyes, and she made a conscious effort to keep her mouth tightly together as they paused in the vestibule long enough for a groom to take Asil's long vest. (It was summer, and hot, so most men traded their coats for a long vest with skirted tails.) The room seemed enormous for what it was. Some of the younger nobility and members of the Great Families milled about the vestibule, waiting for something, chatting amicably among themselves. They paused, however, as Asil led Carys up another set of stairs into the Grand Hall. Conversations dropped off as the two passed, then picked up again, twice as animated as before.

It was like walking into a story, something mothers read to their children to get them to sleep. They walked through the Grand Hall to a broad, gleaming staircase, and Asil headed straight up the center as if it were any other day. Carys followed after a beat of hesitation. It was the type of staircase would-be princesses lost their jeweled slippers on. Where rivals dueled until they both collapsed in defeat, dying together.

"I shouldn't be here," Carys murmured, her steps slowing.

Turning, Asil stepped back down and held out his hand. "And that is precisely why you need to be here," he said, smiling. "The people who should be here can't do what you can do."

Sighing, Carys looked up at Asil. "You're going to mock me for this later, aren't you?" She took his hand.

"Mock is a strong word. Tease, almost certainly." Asil held her hand and escorted her up the stairs, giving her hand a light squeeze before letting it go once they reached the Lord's Hall. Asil turned left and Carys followed, heading to the heavy wooden door with two guards posted outside.

As Carys followed Asil through the door, she immediately noted how much darker it was in here. That was not to say the room wasn't well lit, particularly near the imposing monolith of a desk on the far side. But it lacked windows and natural light, making it immediately darker than the hallways that were still gently illuminated by twilight. There were two people in the study waiting for them. One was an elegant-looking woman, perhaps the age Carys's mother would be had she not returned to the Cradle. The other was unmistakably Egemon Özdemir.

Carys found it interesting how much Asil resembled his father. They kept their hair at a similar length. Egemon's beard was longer, a touch more full, but it wasn't fashionable for older men to keep their beards too short. They had the same shoulders and the same shape to the eyes, though the warm cognac color of Asil's eyes must have come from his mother. Egemon had a slightly more square look to his jaw, his features what one might call rugged. Asil, however, was better described as chiseled. His mother's blood honed his father's more-blunt features.

"Lord Father," Asil said, an air of formality to his voice that was typically absent. He bowed his head. "May I present Seer Carys Arslan."

Carys bowed deeply and held it for a beat, her braid falling over her shoulder. As she rose back up, she was once again grateful for the veil. She didn't know if she was supposed to keep her gaze down, but masked she didn't have to.

"I am happy to meet you, Seer Arslan," the Lord of the Strait said, looking her over with a gaze that was critical but not unkind. "I have heard much about you these last few days. Are you prepared to accept the appointment we have offered you?"

Hands clasped before her, Carys took a shaky breath. "If it is necessary, my Highest Lord, I am prepared to do what I must for Vasi."

Both Egemon and the woman beside him looked very amused by this response. "I am Lady Meliha Aydin, Seer Carys," the woman said. "Am I to understand that you are accepting this position as a necessity? Is it not a great honor? You will be the first Lord's Seer in almost fifty years."

Carys felt her stomach twist. "It is of course a great honor, and I did not mean to imply otherwise, my lady."

"Meliha, stop," Egemon said with a faint smile. "I would much rather have someone accept this role out of a sense of duty rather than ambition."

Pink suffused Carys's cheeks, and Meliha bowed her head to Egemon. "As would we all, my lord."

Turning back to Carys, Egemon smiled apologetically. "I would very much like to speak with you longer, Seer Arslan, but I'm afraid we do not have the time. Court begins shortly. You will be presented to the assembly as the new seer, after which Asil will bring you to the castellan, who will show you your rooms and inform you as to what your next few days will look like. Hopefully you will have time to acclimate before we have need of you."

Carys bowed her head. "I hope to be so fortunate, my lord."

Egemon nodded and made his way out of the study. Meliha paused and turned toward Carys, smiling gently.

"I did not mean to alarm you, Seer Arslan," the lady said, regarding Carys with a steady gaze. "Your response was surprising. I wasn't expecting your reluctance. You are here, however. And Vasi does need you. I hope you understand that."

"I am working to, my lady," Carys said, flustered. Meliha smiled and nodded and also left the room.

Asil turned to Carys and set his hands on her shoulders. "It will be all right," he said. "I wish I could see your eyes right now, but our voices will have to do. I promise I will get us out of court as quickly as possible. I don't like being there either."

A very small laugh bubbled out of Carys. Her stomach still felt like it was tying itself in a knot. Asil released her shoulders and headed toward the door, motioning for Carys to follow. As they exited the study, one of the guards drew the door closed behind them but remained at their post.

Carys followed Asil back down the hallway and through the tall double doors that lead to the throne room. She continued to find it just astounding how large each of these rooms were. Carys understood objectively that Watcher Castle was a large building, the largest in Vasi, but actually walking its halls brought that knowledge home. She felt the tension spread to her shoulders, drawing them in. The room was less than half full, various nobility and members of the Great Families milling about and chatting as Egemon sat on his throne. Meliha stood next to the throne, conversing quietly with Egemon when someone from the crowd was not addressing or petitioning him. Asil made his way through the room at an unhurried pace. He responded to people who greeted him but did not linger, and Carys noted how not everyone appreciated his brevity. They all looked at her with curiosity. A few regarded her with ill-concealed distaste.

"Lord Asil Özdemir, Heir of the Strait, and Seer Carys Arslan," a herald announced as Asil drew close to the throne with Carys following close behind. Egemon rose from his throne, which sat on a dais up nine broad, shallow steps. Asil stopped at the foot of the stairs. Carys stopped just a step behind him.

"Seer Arslan," Egemon began, and it surprised Carys how his voice cut through the room. Conversations hushed, though did not disappear. "You have come before the nobles and elite of Vasi to pledge yourself to its service. It has been half a century since the lords of this castle last sought the guidance of a seer. Seer Arslan, are you prepared to accept this position?"

There was a collective gasp, and Carys bowed. "Humbly, my Highest Lord."

"Then let it be announced," Egemon said, his voice clear and resonant through the room, "that on this day, Seer Carys Arslan has risen to the position of the Lord's Seer."

There was a round of polite applause, followed by a rise in chattering conversations. Carys bowed once more, then allowed Asil to guide her back through the room. A handful of people rushed forward to congratulate her, mostly younger nobles, even one or two clients. The older nobles were unmoved. The heads of the Great Families, however, watched Carys's exit with something sharp and unhappy in their gaze.

Back out in the hall, Carys took a shuddering breath and pressed her hands to her cheeks. Her heart was hammering, and she took a deeper breath, trying to calm herself.

"It's awful, isn't it?" Asil asked, smiling sympathetically. Carys nodded.

"Seer Arslan."

The two of them looked up at a man of middling years with a stern expression who had approached. "I am Baris Akbas, castellan to Lord Egemon Özdemir and Watcher Castle. I will be showing you to your quarters and reviewing your schedule for tomorrow."

"Thank you, Sir Akbas," Carys said, her voice uncertain. The stern expression of the castellan softened.

"Baris will do, child," he said in a gentler tone. "My Heir, your father would like you to return to the court to answer questions as they arise. I will see to making sure our new Lord's Seer is settled."

Asil visibly bristled but nodded. "Of course. Thank you, Baris."

Unconcerned with Asil's opinions on the matter, Baris motioned for Carys to follow him down the hall. She looked back at Asil, faintly amused, and he sighed and shrugged before waving for her to go ahead. Asil headed back into the throne room, and Carys followed Baris through the Lord's Hall, moving away from the study and the grand stair, and turned down a wing decorated with paintings of great heroes and figures from legends.

"It is understandable if you are nervous," Baris said once they were a ways down the hall. "I know this will be hard for you."

"I… yes," Carys said, looking around. "My shop could probably fit in one of the privy chambers here."

Baris laughed quietly. "It is intimidating. My family has served House Özdemir for generations. I remember the first time my uncle brought me into the castle. It terrified me. And I knew I might be here someday. I assume you did not imagine this future for yourself."

"No," Carys said, with a touch of a laugh. "No, I certainly did not."

Nodding, Baris paused in front of a door. "Behind this door is your home for as long as you will be in the castle. Inside waits your maid."

"My what?!" Carys was so startled her voice twanged with surprise.

Baris just smiled. "Your maid. This is not your house, Seer Arslan. If you need a bath drawn, if you need food, if you need messages sent, you will not be able to do it yourself. Your courier doesn't come here. The cook would take you to task if you tried to just walk into the kitchens."

"I see your point," Carys said sheepishly.

"Additionally," Baris said, looking at Carys sternly once more, "you do not know how to be among the nobility. The Great Families, in their way, are even worse. In their attempts to prove that they are worth as much as the noble houses of Vasi, they have adopted a level of exclusivity that even House Kilic does not ascribe to. You will need her."

"Thank you, Baris," Carys said, feeling properly chastised.

The castellan nodded and opened the door.

The room inside was not as large as Asil's, but still easily larger than any place Carys had lived. A large bed was the centerpiece of the room. There was a small seating area, an empty bookcase, and a door to what Carys assumed was the dressing room. In front of the bed was a young woman, who stopped pacing as she noticed the door opening. She looked to be in her early teens, petite, with dark curls and large eyes. As Baris and Carys came fully into the room, she bowed as if they were the Lord of the Strait.

"My name is Aylin, my lady," the girl said, the words tumbling out too fast. "I am so honored to be assigned to your service! I promise to be the best maid you've ever had!"

Carys couldn't help but smile at the eager young woman. "You're the only maid I've ever had, Aylin; I have no doubt you'll be the best. And I am not a lady."

Straightening up, Aylin faltered. "Oh! Um… how… how should I address you?"

"Carys will do," Carys said.

"Oh!" Aylin's eyes grew wide. "My la—ah… um… I… I don't think I could…"

Baris cleared his throat. It sounded suspiciously like he was trying not to laugh. "How about seer," he suggested. Carys sighed but nodded.

Aylin's eyes lit up and she smiled. "Yes! Thank you, sir!" The young woman looked back to Carys. "Do you need anything this evening, my seer?"

"No, I—"

"Perhaps tea," Baris interjected. Aylin bowed and was out the door before Carys could begin to protest.

After the door closed, Baris turned to Carys. "Forgive me, but I think you'll find the tea relaxing, and I suspect you could use it."

Carys just nodded, and moved into the room, looking around. "It's lovely," she said, gently pushing on the bed. "Enormous. It will take time to get used to the space."

"I suspect you will be tired enough to ease your adjustment," Baris said, and Carys looked at him warily. "You have an early morning tomorrow. Aylin will bring you breakfast, after which you will go to the baths. Once you are done there, you will see the seamstresses. I have looked at the clothing you brought with you, and none of it is appropriate for affairs of state. What you are wearing is lovely, but it is also not appropriate."

Carys winced. "That makes sense, and was also surprisingly hard to hear," she muttered.

Reaching over, Baris patted her shoulder. "It is not a reflection of your character, Seer Arslan. You have moved into a different world. Like an actor who has taken a new role, you require a change of costume."

The words were reassuring, and Carys smiled softly. "I will remind myself of that."

"Good," Baris said. "Now for the rest of your day: Once the seamstresses are done with you, you will meet with Lady Aydin, who will review her expectations of your role with you. Finally, you will have dinner with the Heir. I will warn you now that you will be expected to attend court regularly, but not tomorrow."

Aylin returned with tea, taking it over to the sitting area and setting everything up. Baris watched Aylin for a moment, then nodded, satisfied.

"I hope you have a restful evening, Seer Arslan," Baris said, heading toward the door.

"Thank you for everything, Baris," Carys said, doing her best to smile. Baris nodded and left the room.

"Will you need anything else this evening, my seer?" Aylin smiled brightly.

Carys shook her head. "No, thank you. You… can you come back for the tray in the morning? I need a quiet evening."

Aylin just blinked for a moment and processed what Carys said. "Um… of course, my seer. Though… won't you need my help to prepare for bed?"

"Not tonight," Carys said, her fake smile wearing. "That will be all, Aylin."

"Oh," Aylin said, wilting a little. "Yes, my seer." She bowed and took herself out.

For a moment, Carys didn't move. She stood in the strange room, listening to the quiet. It was very quiet. No movement from the street. No one on the other side of the walls. Sighing, she walked to the dressing room. It was a wonder her footsteps didn't echo in a room this large. She unbraided her hair and set down her veil, then returned to the main room to have her tea. Baris had been correct in his instincts. The tea was comforting. By the time she finally climbed into her new bed, soft and laden with feather blankets and pillows, the knot in her stomach was gone, but the tension in her shoulders still hadn't quite let go.

☾ ☾ ☾

The morning went exactly as Baris had described it. Aylin came in early, trading out the previous night's tea for a lovely breakfast with that delightful coffee Carys had enjoyed when she stayed with Asil. Then it was off to the seamstresses. She was measured for underclothes, dresses, festival clothing, every imaginable situation. Several half-finished dresses were taken in and hemmed so that Carys would have something immediately.

By the time she was delivered to Lady Aydin for a late lunch, Carys was exhausted. Their food had been set up in the kitchen garden where Carys had first read the cards for Asil. The lady wore a verdant green dress with red and pink touches that fit with the garden around her. She smiled at Carys and motioned to the seat across from her.

"I thought you might appreciate the garden, Seer Arslan," Meliha said as Carys sat. "How was your first night in the castle?"

"Very comfortable," Carys said, carefully.

Meliha smiled wryly. "But you didn't sleep."

"No," Carys admitted, leaning back. "Not very well."

"Too quiet, too soft?" Meliha asked, and Carys nodded. "You are not the first person I've heard say as much. I know it's an odd transition.

I don't wish to add to your stress, but I feel like I need to make you understand what you have signed on for. The Heir is… an idealist, and his vision can be narrow and focused."

"Yes, it can," Carys said dryly, and Meliha laughed. "So, what do I need to understand that Asil doesn't?"

"To start, you should be mindful of who you are in front of when you so casually refer to the Heir." Picking up a glass of light wine, Meliha took a sip and looked thoughtful. "You will be called upon for far more than simply sitting down with Asil or Egemon occasionally to read the cards. The Lord's Seer is also a very public figure. I know Baris told you that you will have to attend court. You will be at every event that Asil attends unless it precludes you. You will be expected to be available for consultation at all times. This is why being the Lord's Seer is a position of privilege with a suite in the castle. Any time they need you, you must be there."

Silence reigned as Carys rolled these thoughts around in her head and Meliha took the opportunity to eat. It made sense. Of course it made sense. Though until that moment, Carys had not understood how restrictive the position was. How bound she was by it.

"I'm… not going home in a few days, am I?" Carys asked, looking up at Meliha.

Meliha regarded Carys sadly. "Oh, my dear… did you really think you would?"

"A bit," Carys admitted, gazing out at the garden. "I thought… I don't know. I knew change was coming. I saw myself in the castle, but I still hoped that… that perhaps I would give Asil the guidance he desired, and then he would allow me to return to my life."

"You can always retire," Meliha pointed out, picking up her wine again. "But you won't, will you?"

Carys closed her eyes, and took a deep breath, considering. "No," she said at last. "No, I won't."

Meliha nodded. "Finish your lunch, dear. I'll make sure to clear the rest of your day. Take your time with it."

Carys nodded. "Thank you, my lady."

Chapter 7

ASIL WANTED TO run down the hall, but instead he walked as swiftly as his legs would carry him. He could have sent someone to wake Carys, but he wasn't sure a servant would understand the depth of the situation or explain why she needed to be there. Reaching her door, Asil knocked lightly, then again, and let himself in. The room was quiet and dark, the curtains still drawn, and Carys was very much asleep on the bed. Asil walked over and pulled the curtains back, letting in the light. The bundle hidden in the bed didn't move. He cleared his throat. Still nothing.

"Carys!"

Startling up out of sleep, Carys flailed, briefly caught in the enormous feather comforter, but finally freed herself and hopped out of bed in her panic. Her hair was a tousled mess, though in an odd way it was appealing. She was panting and still clearly disoriented as her gaze came to focus on Asil. She looked like she was going to kill him, which was not something Asil had ever expected to see from Carys.

"I swear by the Mother that I will throw you off that balcony if you did this because you were bored," Carys snarled, and Asil held up his hands defensively.

"I am very sorry," Asil said, feeling properly intimidated, "I thought you would be awake already. But I was woken up early, so that was probably a stupid assumption. This was not a prank; this is important.

The ship arrived in the harbor before dawn. They have sent a landing vessel with a small contingent."

Breath now steady, Carys nodded and smoothed back her wild hair. "All right," she said, adjusting her rather abbreviated nightgown and standing up straighter in an effort to regain her composure. "What do you need from me?"

Asil blinked and tried not to get distracted by how little Carys was wearing, how her legs had a creaminess to them, like tea with too much milk. "As the Heir, I will be heading down to greet whoever is on the boat and find out what happens next. They have been peaceful and cooperative so far. If they continue to be so, I will bring them to my father. I would like you with me, to see if anything stirs you."

It took Carys a moment to consider Asil's words, and he took the opportunity to avert his gaze. The undershirt that Carys was currently utilizing as a nightgown barely grazed her thighs, and she didn't particularly look like she had anything underneath it. Seeing as Carys was an attractive woman and Asil could not say that his interest in her was strictly intellectual, he looked around the rest of the room. It was almost precisely as it had been when Baris had first presented it to her. Of course, that was not surprising; it had only been days. But other than setting a handful of objects on the bookshelf, the room was unchanged. Perhaps he should talk to the gardener about bringing in some plants for her, something that would make her feel more at home.

"I hope you sent for breakfast," Carys said as she moved past Asil toward the dressing room.

"I did," he replied cheerfully. He started to follow her, and then thought the action through and instead just sat at the small table by the window. "It should be up shortly. I asked them for something light and quick, as we are in a bit of a hurry."

There were sounds of shuffling from the other room. "Are they just waiting at the docks, then?" Carys called out, slightly muffled.

"Yes," Asil said, picking a bit of dust off the table. "Specifically, the guard is keeping them at the docks until we arrive, and they have been very pleasant and agreeable about it, apparently."

More shuffling, and Carys's maid chose that moment to arrive, laden with a tray. She curtsied to Asil and set the food down on the table, shy and pink cheeked, then poured out coffee and made sure everything was properly set.

"What on earth am I wearing for this?" Carys called out, and Asil snickered.

"Young lady," he said to the maid, and the girl paused, looking up, "Aylin, isn't it? Could you please assist Seer Arslan in choosing something for a matter of state?"

"Of course, my lord," Aylin said brightly, and set down the cheese she had been slicing to rush to the dressing room. The girl seemed excited at the prospect.

Shaking his head, Asil finished arranging the breakfast as he heard Carys not quite arguing with Aylin. Based on the tone of their voices, however, he suspected Aylin won. Soon enough, Carys emerged from the dressing area in a dress and sash in all the shades of tea roses, with a cream-colored shawl over one arm to match the veil over her eyes.

"Pink suits you," Asil said, smiling. "Particularly with your hair. Why don't you wear it more often?"

Carys sighed. "Because I don't work with anything that stains my clothes pink."

Stepping out just behind Carys, Aylin checked breakfast, but upon seeing that it was ready, she bobbed a curtsey and left. Asil looked at Carys quizzically as the woman sat down and began to add sugar to her tea.

"What do you mean by that?" Asil asked.

With a quick stir, Carys set the spoon aside and took a sip before answering. "I work with plants fairly often," Carys explained, and reached for one of the small cheese pastries. "Most of my clothes are browns or greens or darker reds, because that's what I get on myself when I'm working."

Asil arched an eyebrow. "You looked like a sea nymph when I met you."

Looking up, Carys blushed and smiled. "Well, yes. It was a party."

Asil smiled back, and then went about the business of eating. It took very little time before they were heading to the waiting carriage. Carys wrapped the shawl around her shoulders as they stepped outside, bringing it up over her head to shadow her face. It was an open carriage, it being summer, and the sun was bright and brilliant.

It was a beautiful summer day, and people were out and about, in gardens and at tea shops, and just walking around. Windows were open to let the breeze from the ocean in. People paused to watch the carriage go by, some waving cheerfully to Asil, who smiled and waved back. Mostly, however, the crowd just watched curiously as they passed. The closer they got to the docks, the more it seemed people were actually waiting for the carriage, anticipating its arrival.

Finally, they reached the pier where the landing craft was waiting. There was a troop of guards where the pier joined the docks, and from the carriage Asil could see that two captains as well as Lord Captain Kilic stood at the end of the pier before the stairwell that led down to the dock for smaller vessels.

Stepping down from the carriage, Asil paused to assist Carys, who followed quietly and curiously as they headed down the pier. The guards parted for them without a word, though many looked curiously at the seer who accompanied the Heir of the Strait. Asil wondered briefly if that bothered Carys. He would have to talk to her more about it later.

"Ah, my Heir, you're here," Lord Adnan Kilic said as they drew close. Lord Kilic's eyes flicked over to Carys, and there was a slight frown. "You brought your pet fortune teller, I see. Well, no matter. Come with me, my Heir." Adnan started to turn down the stairs, ready to get on with it.

"Yes, I brought the Lord's Seer," Asil said, unmoving, his tone making it clear that Adnan had crossed a line. "Seeing as it was her grasp of the threads of Fate that warned us to be ready for the arrival of these strangers, I hoped that bringing her here might allow further insight. More to the point, my Lord Father insisted on it."

The old captain paused and turned back around, his gaze moving from Asil to Carys and back again. Adnan Kilic had been the only representative of the Three Families that had offered a protest to Carys's appointment as Lord's Seer. After another moment, Adnan sighed.

"Forgive me, my Heir," Adnan said, bowing his head, "and Seer Arslan. Please follow me."

Asil didn't care for how Carys was added almost as an afterthought, but let it go for the moment. Carys remained silent behind him, her face still, and the combination of the veil and the shawl made her eyes completely unreadable in this light. At the bottom of the stair, on the end of the dock, stood a man with pale skin and unremarkable brown hair that absolutely reeked of ambition and sycophantic tendencies. His hair fell past his shoulders, yet he was clean-shaven, which was odd for someone who appeared to be somewhere in his 30s. The clothing he wore was downright tight compared to Vasi fashions, the pants following the lines of the legs instead of being more full and the doublet reminded Asil of paintings he had seen from the far west. The materials spoke of position and wealth. Overall, he was not unpleasant to look upon, but something from his weak chin to his sloped shoulders to the way his eyes lit up with excitement as Asil approached reminded the Heir of every wheedling third cousin who had ever shown up at court begging favors.

Behind the man, however, were four soldiers who were immediately more interesting. They stood in formation, at ease at first but stepping to attention as Asil and his small party approached. They wore hats with wide brims in a dark charcoal that were pinned to the crown on one side, displaying an elegant crest: a kite shield with a hammer in the center, wrought with fine knotwork and filigree. All four of them had a pauldron on the right arm and armored bracers, but they weren't heavy. Rather, they seemed carefully crafted to provide some protection while matching with the rest of their uniforms, which were mostly leather in that same charcoal, with slashes of color at the shoulders that likely indicated company and rank. The foremost soldier was a tall man with dark hair that fell down around his shoulders and remarkable bright blue eyes. Clean-shaven again, with a strong jaw and a faint creasing around the mouth—someone used to smiling.

"Strangers," Lord Kilic bellowed as they grew close, jarring Asil out of his observations. "I am the High Captain of Vasi's Guard, Adnan Kilic, and I thank you for cooperating with us this far. May I present the Heir of the Strait, Lord Özdemir, who has come to greet you and determine if you will be allowed into the city!"

The man in front bowed deeply, and the soldiers behind him followed suit, although their bow was not as long or as florid. "My lord, it is the greatest of honors to meet you," the man gushed, and Asil arched an eyebrow. It seemed they spoke the same language, though the man's accent and pronunciation was decidedly different; there was a clipped quality, and over-enunciation of the consonants. "We have traveled very far, not being certain what we would find, and are overjoyed to encounter such a bustling port. I am Ambassador Peadar Criddubh of Caernfell, on a mission of exploration and friendship, from the Empire of Ealdorlang. I represent the interests of the Council; may they continue to guide us toward our destiny."

There was the slightest sound, a "tch" that came from just over Asil's shoulder, quiet enough not to travel. It came from Carys. Asil very much looked forward to her thoughts on all of this later.

"Welcome to Vasi, Ambassador Criddubh," he said, smiling his court smile. His father regularly said it was too tight, not believable, but it was the best Asil could manage. "You say you are on a mission of exploration and friendship. Could you expand on that, if you please?"

"Of course, my lord," the ambassador answered enthusiastically, and Asil suspected expanding on a subject was Peadar's favorite activity. "It has been centuries since the Great Storm, which destroyed our ships and altered our lands. I am certain these realms felt its effects as well!"

"Indeed," Lord Kilic interjected, nodding.

"All lands needed to be rebuilt," Asil agreed. "Our histories as well as the ruins farther inland tell us much about what was lost."

The sycophantic ambassador bowed his head. "Yes, you are most wise, my lord," Peadar said with feeling. "It took many long years for the kingdoms of the south to recover, and there were years of ignoble bickering over resources and lands. Then, the Council was formed, and we began to unite, rising up to a greatness that had not been possible before our shared calamity. Now, strengthened by our unity and guided by the Council's wisdom, this ship has been sent to explore the northern lands, establish the contacts we once had, and see how the rest of the world has recovered."

"A noble endeavor," Asil said genuinely, and he looked past the ambassador to the ship in the bay. "You come in an impressive vessel; I have never seen anything like it. Tell me, the waterwheel on the back, is that what propelled you across the Sea of Falling Stars?"

"Ah, yes, the paddle engine," Peadar returned, smiling. "It was the only way to cross the Great Sea."

Asil nodded slowly. "How many men are on your ship, Ambassador?"

"Oh, I couldn't say exactly; there is the crew and a company of soldiers," Ambassador Peadar said, and Asil heard Carys tch again in response.

"One hundred and fifty soldiers, five ambassadorial staff, and sixty-five crewmen," the soldier behind the ambassador said, speaking for the first time. His voice was clear and authoritative, but not harsh. Carys took in a sharp breath, but neither Peadar nor the commander seemed to notice.

"Ah, yes, thank you, Commander," Peadar said, not particularly sounding like he meant it. "My lords, this is Commander Tadhg Bharda, Champion of Sunsreach."

The commander bowed, and Asil nodded, the corner of his mouth turning up. "Thank you, Commander. Ambassador, what are your intentions here in Vasi? For what I feel are obvious reasons, I am not certain we could permit that many foreign soldiers onto our soil."

"Oh, of course, of course," Peadar said swiftly, stepping forward and bowing again. "I understand traveling with such a large force appears threatening, but we did not know what to expect, you see. We have had some trouble with raiders on our shores, and the council simply wished to make sure we would all survive to make our report. The men are content on the ship for now—there is room enough for them—and we hope to purchase provisions while we are here. We do not come empty-handed to your shores, my lord."

"I see," Asil said, and glanced over at Adnan for a moment. The older man nodded, knowing what Asil was going to say next. "Ambassador Criddubh, I believe your mission and news of the south would be of interest to the Lord of the Strait. I would like to invite you and the men accompanying you to Watcher Castle to speak with the Lord of the Strait and the heads of the Three Houses."

The ambassador bowed again. "We are at your command, my lord."

The ambassador really was a touch too much, and Asil was beginning to find him distasteful. Is this what everyone was like in the Empire? Surely not, based on the manner of the commander. But then, he was a soldier, and that might make the difference. Nodding, Asil turned and led the way back up to the pier, heading to where the soldiers still stood waiting. Carys stepped up next to him as they walked.

"One of the knights is a woman," Carys remarked, her tone intrigued, and Asil looked at Carys in shock.

"Which one?" he asked, glancing back.

"The pale one in the back, with the hair like sunlight on snow."

Pausing at the line of guards, Asil looked back over. Sure enough, now that he was looking for it, the knight in the back was, in fact, a woman. A rather attractive one too, Asil couldn't help but notice. Tall and slender, with flawless pale skin, though cold in coloring and demeanor. Her icy blue eyes could freeze the sea in summer with the gaze she turned toward Asil. The knight standing just ahead of her was her opposite in every way, an exuberant man with hair like copper in the sun and flashing eyes that almost glowed like embers. Everything about the knight seemed open and friendly. The last knight was a touch older, not by much but enough that silver had just begun to touch his temples. He was also the only one among their number with a beard, and it was a great deal longer than what was considered fashionable in Vasi, but carefully combed and braided. His hair was the color of wheat, his eyes the gray-blue of an overcast day, and it was unnerving how much of a resemblance he bore to Carys.

Lord Kilic caught up with them and called over one of the guards. "Go and send for a coach," Adnan said to the guard, "covered, if possible, though it's more important that it be quick. Large enough to carry the five of them together. Go!"

"Yes, sir!"

The guard ran off, and Lord Kilic turned back to Asil. "If you wish, my lord, I will stay here with them and await the coach. You could return to your father and prepare him for our arrival."

Asil glanced from Adnan back to the party of foreigners, and then nodded. Whatever Adnan Kilic might think of Carys and her appointment, he had always been a steadfast and staunch defender of the Lord of the Strait, and took his position of High Captain seriously, spending many nights down in the barracks rather than at his lavish estate. Asil reached up and set his hand on Adnan's shoulder, and the old lord looked at him for a moment in surprise but smiled.

"I will see you at Watcher Castle, High Captain," Asil said.

"We will not keep you waiting, my lord," Adnan replied.

Chapter 8

THE CARRIAGE HAD left the port, passed Old Town, and begun to thread its way through the Merchant District when Asil turned to Carys and tapped her lightly on the knee. "All right," he said, "I was waiting for you to say something, but now I'm impatient. What are your impressions?"

Blinking, Carys pulled herself away from her musings and looked over at Asil. "It was… interesting," Carys said slowly, considering her words. "I understood what you were hoping for, and so I did my best to let the spirits guide me. I've never done it out in the open like that, and more practice will help."

"I feel like you're putting a lot of effort into tempering my expectations," Asil said, grinning. "I know you don't read minds, Carys. I asked for your impressions."

"The Ambassador is a weasel," Carys said firmly, and Asil laughed. She wrinkled up her nose in distaste. "Everything about him is… aggravating. I can't imagine how he came to his line of work, other than assuming that this southern empire has vastly different ideas of what makes for a good diplomat."

"You made a sound earlier," Asil remarked, his voice carrying his amusement at Carys's clear disgust. "That sucking of the teeth noise that my aunt makes when she's arguing with my father."

Tapping a finger against her bottom lip, Carys thought for a moment. "Oh, yes, when he spoke of destiny," Carys said, remembering. "That is not a word that the ambassador takes lightly. He genuinely believes that destiny brought him here. It is… something you should worry about. Also, he absolutely lied when he said he didn't know how many soldiers were on the ship. I don't… my gift doesn't let me know when people are lying, exactly, but sometimes, when the truth is so glaringly apparent, it… imposes itself? I'm not sure how else to say it. It's not that I know when someone is lying, it's just that sometimes I know the truth even if they're lying about it."

Asil arched an eyebrow. "Interesting, though I think we all knew he was lying," he said, looking away from Carys and across the city as they passed. "Whether the ambassador knows it or not, the commander salvaged that situation. Though speaking of the commander, what did you think of Commander Bharda? I heard you gasp. I suppose he is a handsome man. Had you just not looked yet?"

Carys snickered, and favored Asil with a wry smile when he looked back in her direction. "Well, that rumor about you liking men is definitely not true," Carys commented, "because if you found men at all attractive, you would know that the commander is a handsome man, not just suppose it."

"There's a rumor that I like men?" Asil asked, curious, and Carys nodded. He considered for a moment. "I suppose I can see how they got there. We're getting off subject, though."

"I did not gasp because I was overcome," Carys said with the same smile. "The gasp was actually because… well, the Commander is cursed. So are his knights."

Brows furrowed, Asil looked at Carys in confusion. "I'm missing something here," he said, shifting to face her more fully. "I thought curses were bad, but you said that so nonchalantly."

There was quiet for a moment as Carys considered what to say. Leaning forward, she tapped her bottom lip again, and had Asil been able to see her eyes at that time he would have noticed that they looked very far away. Most people who were not seers had a very rudimentary understanding of curses. Carys's experience with curses was even more immediate than that of most seers. Her eyes flicked around the carriage briefly—she half expected the talk of curses to summon Judex and was relieved when he did not appear.

"You are not entirely wrong," Carys said at last, her voice measured, the words coming slowly at first. "It is true that, more often than not, a curse is cast as a punishment or as a way to make a promise more binding. That isn't always true, however. Curses can be cast protectively, some even to the benefit of the cursed, though that is infrequent."

The carriage drew up to the castle grounds, and Asil shook his head. "Now I am completely confused," he said. "I suppose what you're saying, however, is that you are currently unworried because you didn't immediately get the impression that the curse was bad?"

"Something like that," Carys said with a smile, and then turned to leave the carriage, allowing the footman to offer her a hand down. "At least nothing malevolent. Suffice to say, it is something I will need to study more. When your father is not expecting us, I will be happy to give you a more in-depth description of curses."

Asil seemed to accept that answer, and Carys was relieved. It would take a lot of explaining, a lot of delving into the nature of spirits and their differences. While Carys was happy to do it, she wasn't sure Asil understood how much time it might take. He wouldn't be satisfied with the short answer. And… she would have to explain her own situation. Now did not feel like the time to explore the mistakes she had made at the age of twenty.

A very anxious-looking valet was waiting for them as they ascended the stairs to the castle. "My Heir," the young man said, darting forward and bowing, "your Lord Father is waiting for you in his study. He asks that Seer Arslan come with you."

That was interesting, the implication that Carys might have had the freedom to just return to her rooms. Lady Meliha had said she would be expected to be available at all times, but perhaps that simply meant accessible, not necessarily present. Carys followed Asil up the staircase to his father's study. It had only been two days, and already the Grand Staircase felt less intimidating than it had on that first night when she had been introduced to court. The way people watched her, however, had not become less unsettling.

At the top of the stairs, as they turned toward the office, Carys met the gaze of an older man. He did not hide his glare as she walked past. He was not very tall but had broad shoulders and looked like he still retained some of the strength of his youth. Very wealthy by his appearance—the man was as well-dressed as Asil, accented by rings on each hand and gold chains around his neck. The level of adornment bordered on gaudy. One of the Great Families, then. The noble houses were never so gauche in their displays of wealth.

"Who is that?" Carys murmured after they had passed the merchant.

"Hm? Oh, Pasha Muhan Kaplan." Asil didn't need to look back to see whom she meant. "House Kaplan is third in power within the Great Families. Pasha Kaplan does a fair trade in precious gems from Ropa."

"Ropa?" Carys fought the urge to look back at the pasha and see if he was still glaring.

"The northernmost kingdom on the Cliffs of Dawn," Asil answered. "It's mostly mountains, from what I understand." They reached the door to the study and Asil walked in without knocking. Carys hesitated, then followed.

Inside, Egemon was speaking with Lady Meliha Aydin and a man perhaps five or so years older than Carys who bore a familial resemblance to Lord Captain Kilic. This younger version of Lord Kilic had the same sharp gaze, but he kept his thick black hair shoulder length, and there were the beginnings of lines around his mouth, not quite hidden by his beard, that implied he smiled far more often. And smile he did as Asil and Carys came into the room.

Asil seemed surprised. "Hasim," he said, joy in his voice as he walked quickly up to the other man; they hugged rather than just clasping hands. "When did you get back?"

"Last night," Hasim said, setting his hands on Asil's shoulders. "Mother, look at you! A proper Heir!"

"Oblivion take you." Asil's continued smile said he didn't mean it. Carys had never seen Asil smile like that, free and exuberant.

"I am sorry to interrupt your reunion, but we're short on time," Egemon said, and the two men turned to face him. "Hasim, your father and his men should be here shortly along with our… guests, I suppose."

Asil arched an eyebrow. "Guests?"

"What else would you call them?" Meliha interjected. "They are foreign envoys who have arrived under a flag of peace."

"That brought an entire company of men with them," Hasim pointed out. Meliha sighed and Egemon gave a negligent wave.

"We must take them as they present themselves," Egemon said, rising up from his desk. "That does not mean we will not keep an eye on them. Asil, summon Baris, if you please. Carys?"

"Yes, my Lord." Carys stepped forward as Asil pulled back a tapestry and revealed an elaborate bell system. Hasim looked at her curiously.

Egemon pulled out a sheet of paper and picked up a pen. "Tell me how the meeting at the docks went."

Stepping aside, Meliha indicated that Carys could sit, and found a cup of tea for her. After taking a moment to gather and reflect, Carys described what took place, the impressions she had, her estimation of the character of the ambassador and the commander. Egemon took notes, and Meliha and Hasim occasionally asked clarifying questions.

"Is that all?" Egemon finally asked.

Carys turned a bit pink. "Yes, my Lord. I'm sorry, I've never… gone seeking in this manner before. I hope, in time—"

"Wait, is she apologizing?" Hasim asked, cutting Carys off. Meliha brought her hand to her mouth, Asil stifled a laugh, and even Egemon smiled despite himself.

"Um, yes?" Carys felt her blush growing deeper and felt very uncomfortable.

"My lady seer," Hasim said, coming around and crouching in front of Carys, "I have never heard of anyone doing what you just did."

It was hard not to find Hasim's closeness a little startling. It was not alarming—there was an earnest intensity to Hasim that spoke of a man with strong passions. Carys reached up and brushed a lock of hair back from her veil, trying not to fidget. He didn't immediately move, either, and something in his expression shifted slightly, as if he were seeing

Carys for the first time. He was a handsome man. Not as pretty as Asil, but what Carys assumed one might consider rugged.

"I saw her first, Hasim," Asil said behind her.

"You dare—" Carys's head snapped around to glare at Asil, ready to inform him that it didn't matter if he was high born, he had no claim to her. She was immediately stopped by the look on his face. It was the look of a man who knew exactly what he said and had managed to annoy two friends with one aside.

"Oh, you ass," Carys said, rumpled. She then gasped and put a hand to her mouth, remembering where she was and who she was with. She heard a rumble of laughter behind her and turned slowly.

Egemon was laughing. Hasim was glaring at Asil, but it was less effective as a smile played at the corners of his mouth. Meliha was just smiling fondly at Carys. Hasim stood and smoothed his pants, stepping away from Carys, and not-at-all-lightly punched Asil in the shoulder.

"Back to the matter at hand," Egemon said, composing himself and sitting forward. "Seer Arslan, you are comfortable interacting with people and have experience in your shop, yes?"

Not certain where this was going, Carys nodded slowly. "Yes, my Lord."

"Then I must ask you to liaise with our guests," Egemon said, making another note on the page before him. "Not over matters of state, of course, but you will be their contact and their guide while they remain in our city. I appreciate that this position is below your station, but you are uniquely suited to bring us insight we would otherwise lack. Be charming. Befriend them. Get them to talk to you."

Silence fell for a moment, and Carys was fairly certain everyone in the room heard her swallow. "As you wish, my Lord."

"And who will negotiate with them?" Asil asked, setting his hand lightly on Carys's shoulder. She fought the urge to reach for it.

Egemon looked at his son. "You will."

"By the waters," Asil muttered, but bowed his head to his father. "Of course, my Lord."

Nodding, Egemon stood. "Very good."

The door behind them opened, and Baris stepped in, bowing deeply. "I apologize for taking so long, my Highest Lord. What do you need of me?"

"Your timing is perfect, Baris." Egemon came around his desk and motioned for the others to follow. "It seems a foreign delegation from the Far South has arrived on our shores. Please prepare one of the cottages. The House of Flowers, I think."

Baris bowed once more. "Right away, my Lord."

As the castellan left, Egemon turned to Meliha. "They will need an attendant. I want your best in there."

The lady smiled. "Absolutely. I know just the one."

They all continued out of the room, heading across the broad hallway that led past the throne room to another heavy wooden door on the opposite side. Carys tried not to look around too curiously. Pasha Kaplan was still in the hall. He bowed deeply as Egemon passed but rose to once more glare daggers at Carys as she followed. When they began to follow Egemon through the other door, Pasha Kaplan became positively apoplectic.

"Welcome to the most exclusive salon in the kingdom," Hasim said quietly to Carys as they walked in the door, leaning close to murmur to her.

"Ah," Carys said, a bit weakly, and tried not to be nervous. She wondered if Hasim was flirting with her. He certainly didn't seem to have an issue with being close to her.

The room was larger than the study, containing a table that would easily seat eight, as well as couches, divans, and side tables clustered in comfortable groups for talking. The curtains were open, showing a lovely view of the gardens, and a lavish afternoon tea was set on the table. Already in the room was Lord Captain Kilic, and a man just a touch younger than Hasim who had the heavy black hair of the Kilic family but key differences in the face told Carys that this was not a sibling. Perhaps a cousin. A young man and a young woman were also sitting in the room, so close in age and feature that they had to be twins, with the same auburn hair and sharp gaze as Meliha Aydin, though the boy's eyes were more green and the girl's more hazel.

"What is she doing here?" Adnan asked sharply, looking at Carys.

"She is here because I bid her to follow, Adnan," Egemon said, with an edge to his voice that was clearly a warning. Adnan bristled, but stiffly bowed his head.

"Of course, my Lord," the Lord Captain said, sitting down, "though I'm sure you can appreciate my surprise. No one outside of the Three Families has entered the Salon since your Lord Grandfather died. May his rest be long."

Carys felt her stomach drop.

"Where is the party from the ship?" Egemon sat down at the head of the table, motioning for the pot of tea, which one of the twins swiftly picked up and began to pour for everyone. Asil sat to his right, Lord Captain Kilic to the left, and Meliha at the foot. The others fell into place as Carys set herself back, standing awkwardly behind Asil.

"Oh, Seer Arslan!" The other twin, the young man with the darker eyes, stood up with a smile. "Please, seer, take my seat. I'm Cemil Aydin; I'm delighted to finally meet you. This is my sister, Lale. Congratulations on your appointment to Lord's Seer!"

"Thank you," Carys murmured, bowing her head and hoping her voice wasn't shaking as badly as her hands were. She accepted the seat with a smile she didn't feel and clasped her hands in her lap. Cemil and Lale went about seeing that everyone was served, stepping about lightly with a grace that spoke of years of dance. Meliha watched her children with a gentle pride that shone from her eyes.

"The party from the southern lands is currently awaiting you in the South Parlor," Adnan said, looking irritated that he was interrupted for something as trivial as being nice to the commoner. "They have been the picture of decorum, though their ambassador comes across like he's selling something."

"We shouldn't keep them for too long, then," Meliha observed after taking a sip of her tea. "They surely know we don't entirely trust them, but the longer we let them sit, the more hostile they will assume we are."

"Does that matter?" the younger Kilic asked, looking down the table. "Surely we don't think they're a threat. I understand it's a company of men, but the guard alone outnumbers them three to one, even without including the irregulars."

"These strangers are soldiers, not guardsmen," Hasim said, looking over at his cousin with ill-concealed irritation.

The cousin wasn't getting it. "So?"

Sighing, Adnan leaned forward. "Okan, be quiet if you cannot add anything intelligent. Hasim is saying that they appear to be very well trained. While we have many fine warriors among the guard, we have just as many who know enough to break up a drunken brawl and not much more. And we don't know if another ship is just beyond the horizon."

"There is no other ship." Carys spoke clearly, with the certainty of her gift, and everyone else fell silent. Her eyes glowed softly behind the veil. "But this vessel holds one of their finest companies."

"So, they are confident that these men can take care of whatever they hope to accomplish here," Egemon said, tapping the side of his glass.

Blinking, the glow faded, and Carys bowed her head. That was happening more often, flashes of insight where it almost felt as if the spirits spoke through her rather than to her. "Yes, my Lord."

Egemon nodded and finished his tea, then set his cup down with a clink. "I have decided that the Heir will lead whatever negotiations and introductions these foreigners are hoping for. Seer Arslan will liaise with them, acting as go-between and arranging whatever entertainments and diversions they may require in the city. You will all defer to the Heir and Seer Arslan in these matters and know that they speak for me. Is that clear?"

"Yes, my Lord," was chorused by everyone at the table, though Adnan was a beat behind the others, looking a touch sour.

"Very well," Egemon said, and stood. "Let us go meet the enemy."

Chapter 9

AMBASSADOR CRIDDUBH, COMMANDER Bardha, and the three knights were stark and dark in the otherwise-vibrant South Parlor. The room was well lit, both with natural light and various lamps, the colors in the room clearly inspired by the roses planted just outside the windows. The dark, muted colors of their clothing gave them an air of solemnity that Carys wasn't sure was accurate. That suspicion was confirmed when she caught the ginger-haired knight exchanging looks with the older one and rolling his eyes as the negotiations played out.

The ambassador was as groveling as he had been at the port, though Carys noted that he was being more careful now that he was before the Lord of the Strait. Carys did not need her gift to tell that his every word was carefully weighed. Next to the ambassador sat a slight, quiet young woman whom Carys had heard addressed as Moira, her head down, her mousy hair bound back in tight braids. She was the ambassador's secretary and seemed very capable in her role. A scribe sat near Egemon Özdemir taking notes with the same efficiency. Carys suspected the scribe was also from House Aydin. Not from Meliha's immediate family, and not a first cousin either, but that auburn hair was hard to find outside the House.

A curse hung heavy over Moira, and it prickled Carys as she sat, quietly sipping her tea and watching the young woman swiftly notate anything said. It wasn't like what she felt from the commander and the three knights. This was something different. Something malevolent. It had distracted Carys from the moment she had come into the room, and she remained distracted as Asil and Egemon bantered with Peadar Criddubh.

"—Seer Arslan will be your primary liaison," Asil said, and Carys snapped out of her reverie, setting down her tea glass and hoping it didn't look like she hadn't been listening.

"You are too kind, my Heir," Peadar said, smiling that same patently false smile. Carys had to give him credit; he was keeping up with the room very well. He seemed more familiar with everyone's positions and titles than she was. Perhaps that was why he was chosen for this position.

"We shall retire for the afternoon," Egemon said, standing, and the room stood with him. "I have no doubt that you have had a long journey. The Heir and I look forward to seeing you at dinner and presenting you at court this evening."

"We are ever at your service, my Lord." Peadar bowed deeply, and Egemon nodded, making his way out of the room. Asil stepped up to Carys, a faintly apologetic smile on his lips.

"Baris has the cottage prepared," Asil murmured, his voice close to a whisper. "You need only accompany them to it, make sure they have no immediate questions or concerns, and then come meet me in my room when you are done. All right?"

"As you wish, my Heir." Carys's tone could not have been more irreverent.

It looked like it was taking all of Asil's self-control not to laugh. Instead, he just grinned at her and headed out. Hasim was right behind Asil, and he winked at Carys as he followed the heir out of the room. Taking a deep breath, Carys turned to face the ambassadorial party.

The ambassador nodded his head. It seemed that without the rulers in the room, Carys didn't merit a bow. Then again, the ambassador seemed very observant of power dynamics. Perhaps he understood that Carys was lacking in rank.

"I appreciate your assistance, Miss… I'm sorry, how should we address you?"

Carys arched a brow, though they couldn't see it. "Seer Arslan will do, Ambassador."

"Oh, that's a title!" The surprised statement came from one of the knights, the fiery one.

A variety of reactions filtered over the party before Carys. Peadar looked weary and irritated. The commander looked amused. The older bearded knight snickered quietly, and his icy compatriot glared at the firebrand.

"Áedh," the woman hissed, and the ginger knight just shrugged.

"Thank you, Seer Arslan," Peadar said, ignoring Áedh. "If it is not too presumptuous, could you explain your title to us?"

"I… well," Carys stumbled as her brow furrowed. "I apologize, I have never had to explain this before. A seer is a woman who has been gifted with the ability to… see the weave of life, the threads that connect us all. To look past the moment into the possibilities. To see beyond."

The small party looked fascinated and a touch confused. The exception was Moira, who was staring at Carys with wide eyes, holding her ledger in front of her as if it were a shield.

"Do… do you have another title for seers in the south?" Carys desperately wished Asil had not abandoned her.

Commander Bharda recovered first. "I'm afraid we do not have women with those capabilities in the south, my lady."

There was a long moment of quiet as Carys looked from the commander to the rest of the party. She saw agreement in all their faces, save for Moira, who just continued to stare with wide eyes. Carys had not thought the commander to be a liar. That was Peadar's job. It did not feel like he was lying, but he had to be. Five curses, which could only be the work of a seer, leered at her. It was beginning to give her a headache, like a faint buzz in the back of her skull.

"I see," was all Carys said on the matter. "Well then, allow me a proper introduction. I am Carys Arslan, the Lord's Seer. I hope what little guidance I can offer you during your stay in our city is helpful."

"I am sure you will be most helpful, Seer Arslan," Peadar said almost patronizingly.

"If you are to be our liaison, you should know us all." Tadhg Bharda motioned to the knights that followed him.

"Cillian ab Owain, Knight of the Field." The older man bowed his head to Carys, his sharp eyes seeming to bore through her.

"Generys Thomais, Knight of the Font." The snowy beauty bowed her head tersely.

"Áedh Ciar, Knight of the Fist." Áedh grinned shamelessly and winked. Actually winked. The corners of Carys's mouth quivered from the want to smile.

"A pleasure," Carys said, then turned and motioned toward the door. "You must be tired. Let us see you to the House of Flowers."

Turning away from the party to lead them, Carys took another steadying breath as they walked through the doors. She was certain she was failing at all of this. Peadar most certainly knew she was not a noble, from the way his regard shifted once Asil and Egemon had left the room. They had accepted her title and position, even if they didn't seem to understand it. That part was the most perplexing. Curses did not happen naturally. There were seers in the south. It seemed impossible for so many people to be cursed without any of them knowing about it. Moira knew something, but the girl was terrified. Was she afraid of Carys?

It was a relief to see Baris standing on the other side of the door. He did not speak, but simply bowed and walked next to Carys, leading the way to the guest cottages. They went out through the strolling gardens, over an elegant footbridge, and then across the cobbled road that circled Watcher Castle. As they approached the building, Carys's mouth twisted into a wry expression. "Cottage" was perhaps the most inaccurate term ever used for the lavish villas built on the north and south ends of Watcher Castle. The southern cottage was the House of Flowers. The northern was the House of Waves.

As they approached the cottage, the door opened and a young man with dark hair, dark eyes, and a slight frame stepped out and bowed deeply, his manner almost as obsequious as the ambassador's. Carys thought Meliha had done an outstanding job of finding the right valet for Peadar Criddubh's tastes.

"Ambassador, Commander, Sir Knights," Baris said, turning to them and bowing politely. "This is Halil. He will see to your needs during your stay."

"Thank you, Baris," Carys said, warmly and sincerely. They headed through the small courtyard into a gallery where the centerpiece was a large painting depicting the Divine Mother carrying two infants, a soft smile on her delicate face. Peadar bowed his head slightly, putting his fingertips to his forehead before the painting.

"It is a comfort to see a likeness of the Divine Mother here," Peadar said, his voice soft and earnest in a way that Carys suspected few ever heard. His words were something to ponder later.

"I am glad it gives you comfort," Carys said, stepping aside so that the rest of the party could make their way in. "Do you have any other questions at this time, or shall I leave you to be settled?"

"You may leave us for now, Seer Arslan." The moment of vulnerability had passed, and the ambassador was back to his old self. "Though I would like to send Sir Cillian and Sir Áedh back to retrieve the necessary belongings for our stay. I assume this is acceptable."

"Of course," Carys said, and looked to Baris, who nodded. He would see it done.

"Thank you for your time, Seer Arslan." The soft sincerity in Tadhg's voice startled Carys, and she looked up to see his bright eyes focused on her. "I am certain we will have more questions for you tomorrow."

"On the morrow, then." Carys nodded, then turned and saw herself out, Baris following her.

They were quiet as they crossed the road and went back over the footbridge. Carys chewed her lip and considered the interaction. A hand on her shoulder brought her up short. Baris held her shoulder gently and smiled at her.

"You did well," he said, giving her shoulder a squeeze before letting it go. "For someone still so new to everything, you are doing just fine."

"The ambassador knows that I'm… that I'm not…" Carys struggled with the words, with what she wanted to say.

"He knows you are an important person with a high position," Baris said, motioning that they should continue walking. "It does not matter if you do not have the mannerisms of the nobility. He will treat you with respect if he wants our Highest Lord or his Heir to take the southern nation seriously."

Another deep breath, and Carys nodded. Baris was right, and there was nothing to be done about it now, regardless of her fears or Peadar's judgment.

The two of them parted ways, and Carys continued up the grand staircase once more. It was quieter now. No one really gathered here at this time of day. She turned down the hall and made her way toward Asil's room. The servants she passed smiled and bowed to her, but also kept about their business. As she approached Asil's door, it was open just a crack, and she could hear laughter spilling out of it. Not just Asil's. She pushed open the door and was greeted by the sight of Asil and Hasim animatedly chatting as Hasim recounted… something. He was posed as if holding a sword, his other hand held aloft almost flamboyantly, legs situated in a long lunge.

"What in the Mother's name are you doing?" Carys found herself smiling as Asil and Hasim jumped, suddenly aware of her presence.

"I am simply demonstrating some of the fighting styles I studied in the north," Hasim said, smoothing his shirt and straightening his vest. "And perhaps telling amusing stories about the people I learned them from. Which would… not be appropriate in your presence, pale rose."

Carys arched an eyebrow. So that was how it was going to be.

Asil glanced between the two of them, amused. "So how did it go with the ambassador?"

With a quick turn, Carys closed the door behind her and then headed over to the table where meze and ale had been set out. Carys considered for a moment, then selected one of the two glasses and heard Asil laugh as Hasim made a sound of protest. Carys turned back to the two of them, sipping the beer, and sat down in one of the chairs.

"They appear to be happy with the accommodations," Carys said, and Hasim sighed in defeat and walked to the bells, ringing for Nazim. "The ambassador was reassured to see evidence that we revere the Divine Mother. The knights had titles: the Field, the Font, and the Fist. I'm sure these titles address their roles."

Asil looked intrigued. "Do you know their names?"

"Yes." Carys drank off a quarter of the beer and set the glass down with a sigh. "The older man is Cillian, Knight of the Field. The woman is Generys, Knight of the Font. The younger man is Áedh, Knight of the Fist."

Hasim stepped back from the bell system. "If you know their names, can't you try to seek the meaning?"

"I... I suppose I can try." Carys patted her hip reflexively and sighed. "I don't have my cards."

Hasim put his hands on his hips. "Why do you need them? You knew about the ship without them."

"The cards help me concentrate," Carys said, not liking the impatience in Hasim's voice. "They make it easier to guide what I'm looking for, a way for the spirits to fine-tune my vision."

"But you don't need them," Hasim continued, obstinately.

Clearing his throat, Asil smiled entreatingly at Carys. "Could you try? Please?"

Carys pursed her lips, irritated. "Fine."

Leaning back in the chair, Carys centered herself and ignored the somewhat-triumphant expression on Hasim's face. She folded her hands in her lap and let her gaze grow unfocused. Her eyes began to glow as she felt her awareness start to spread through the room and beyond. She could feel Asil happy with her, how she stepped up every time she was challenged. Hasim didn't know what to think of her, a pretty peasant girl with an extraordinary gift. He was confused by how Asil treated her. Nazim, coming down the hall, so young and proud of his position as the Heir's valet—

No, that wasn't what Carys wanted. She needed to find their guests. She tried to bring Peadar's face to mind, but he was aggravating and bland; it was difficult to build an image she could follow. Tadhge Bharda, then. His sharp blue eyes and heavy dark hair. She found the path she was seeking, following the thread to the House of Flowers. In the landscape of her mind the thread wove through stepping stones like chrysanthemums towards her goal.

"Ah!" The dissonance of the commander's curse was like hitting a literal wall, compounded by the other curses in the guest cottage. Carys put her hand to her head, reeling. A hand closed around the one that was still in her lap. She recognized Asil's touch.

"Carys, what happened?" he asked, soft concern in his voice.

Blinking, Carys's gaze focused once more on the room she was in, the two men before her. "Those damnable curses," she muttered, reaching for the beer and drinking another quarter of it.

Nazim entered the room before Carys could continue. "My lord? Er, lords?"

Hasim smiled wryly. "Another beer, young man."

With a nod, Nazim scampered off, and Hasim turned back to Carys. Asil continued to hold her hand. She gave Asil a light squeeze and let him go. She then finished the beer and set the glass down.

"I can't do it," Carys said, reaching up to rub the spot between her brows through the veil. "Four—no, five—cursed individuals in such a small space. It is hard to see past them. I need to… to do something about it!"

Folding his arms over his chest, Hasim tipped his head again. "Do what? What do you do about curses?"

"Break them, ideally," Carys said, dryly.

"Does this mean we are no longer assuming the curses might be benign?" Asil straightened up and stepped back to lean against the bedpost.

Sighing, Carys shook her head. "No, not after what I felt from Moira. It felt similar to what I sensed in the commander and the knights, but… more venomous. And, oh, this is strange: they insist that there are no seers in the south."

"There are seers everywhere," Hasim said, a certain derision in his tone. "I've been through half the Kingdoms of Dawn, and there are seers in every single one. The ones in Miterathea are ridiculous; they're practically worshiped."

The corner of Carys's mouth curled. "I should move to Miterathea."

Asil laughed. "You'd hate it."

"I would."

"So the southerners are lying or stupid," Hasim said, bringing them back to the subject. "I don't know them well enough to say if they're stupid, but it's easy to believe they might be liars."

Carys nodded. "The ambassador, certainly. The others, though… I'm not so sure."

"So, what do you need to banish the curses?" Hasim was persistent. It was probably for the best.

"More time," Carys said, pushing herself up out of the chair. "And I cannot unravel a curse from a distance. I need to be near—I need an opportunity to study it."

"Well, you'll get it," Asil said, standing up straight once more. "Your duties as liaison will no doubt begin tomorrow. Tonight, they will get settled, but they came here with an agenda, and I have no doubt they will begin implementing it as quickly as possible."

The two men laughed as Carys wrinkled up her nose and she made a moue of distaste. "I will try to contain my excitement. For now, I think I will take myself to my room. I can feel a headache coming on from the failed seeing."

Stepping forward, Asil set his hand on Carys's shoulder. "It wasn't failed; we learned something. Get some rest and remember to have Aylin bring you something to eat. You don't need to attend dinner, but you will need to be there at court tonight."

Somehow Carys managed not to groan, and simply nodded. "I shall see you then."

"See you tonight, my rose," Hasim added, with a grin. Carys arched an eyebrow at him again but nodded.

Heading down the hallway, Carys was just shy of the grand stair when Judex's voice whispered in her ear, "You are in very far over your head, 'pale rose.'"

Stumbling a little in surprise, Carys stopped and ran a hand over her face, skewing her veil just slightly. "I should have known you would put in an appearance soon," she muttered, and resumed her path to her rooms. "Well, thank you for saying hello, feel free to return to wherever it is you go when you're not bothering me."

Snickering, Judex floated up ahead of her. "So soon? Life in the castle is spoiling you. You used to have time for our chats."

Carys scowled. "Being a captive audience is not the same as making time for you." She pushed through the door into her room, wishing she could lock Judex on the other side of it.

"Do you wonder how you're going to deal with the foreigners' curses when you can't even get me to leave you alone?" Judex asked in a practically chipper tone as Carys took off her shawl and her veil, shaking out her hair.

"You might recall I've gotten much better since you came to plague me," Carys muttered, "and that I have banished more than one curse in the intervening years."

Judex gave a dismissive, wispy wave. "Trivialities. These are outsiders, the situation is tense, and you have no idea how this magic works. After all, they don't have seers in the south."

Snorting, Carys leveled a weary gaze at Judex. "You don't believe that any more than I do."

Laughing, Judex sat down on her table. "Well, that is true."

Carys rubbed her forehead. The headache was getting worse. Her eyes began to glow. "Judex, I cannot deal with you at this time."

The spirit regarded Carys for a moment, then nodded. "Very well. You're not any fun like this anyway." And he disappeared.

Stunned, Carys looked at the empty table, the glow fading from her eyes. Judex had never just left like that before. She almost wished he would come back so that she could ask him why. Instead, she rang for Aylin. Food would help, and then a nap. Then Aylin could come back in time to prepare Carys for court.

Chapter 10

THE EVENING AT court was significantly less nerve-wracking than Carys's first time had been. This was in part because she was no longer important. Not to the crowd. Nobles and merchant families clustered around the party from the south. While at least one knight always remained close to Peadar, they all seemed perfectly comfortable mingling with the assembly. Carys observed Hasim speaking with the commander and each of the knights in turn. The conversations seemed light and friendly, occasionally gesturing to one of their peace-tied swords. Tadhge rested his hand on the pommel with an ease that made it clear this was part of his daily ensemble.

Carys had snuck away from court as quickly as she could politely manage, after making certain that neither Asil nor the ambassadorial party had need of her. She noticed Cillian watching her as she left the throne room, something curious in his expression, but the persistent headache made it impossible for Carys to contemplate what he might be thinking. It was a scent to chase later, when she knew them better, and had an idea of how to unbind those horrid curses.

The evening was quiet once Carys made it back to her room. Asil did not come calling, no doubt catching up with his friend. That was fine; a long rest would help. By the time Aylin arrived in the morning with breakfast, the headache was gone. Carys rose and wrapped herself in a dressing gown as the maid set out breakfast and poured coffee.

"Thank you, Aylin," Carys murmured, accepting the coffee from the young woman. "What is expected of me today, can you tell me?"

"Yes, my la—seer," the girl corrected herself, trying to be mindful. Aylin wanted to please so badly it almost broke Carys's heart. "Ambassador Criddubh and Commander Bharda, as well as the commander's knights, have requested that you take them to a House of the Divine Mother."

Carys looked up from her coffee, surprised. "What, really? Why do they want to go there?"

"I do not know, seer," Aylin answered, and something in her tone suggested that there was not a circumstance in which she would have asked. "I only know that the ambassador expressed urgent interest in seeing one."

Sipping her coffee, Carys considered for a moment, then shrugged. "Very well. And then?"

"After that, the young Lord Özdemir will meet with the Ambassador," Aylin continued as she began to set out clothing for Carys. "Lord Özdemir has requested that you give the commander and his knights a tour of the city."

That got a quirked eyebrow. "A tour," Carys repeated. "Of what?"

"That is not for me to say, seer," Aylin answered, in that same tone of voice, the one that implied Cary was mad for asking. Carys found herself smiling; she liked seeing that Aylin had a little backbone.

"Very well," Carys said, setting the coffee down and looking over what Aylin had set out for clothing. Carys didn't particularly enjoy having her clothes chosen for her but was willing to concede until she learned more about court etiquette and fashion. She was surprised, however, to see that the ensemble included a matching veil. A new one.

"Where did this come from?" Carys asked curiously, picking up the bit of indigo mesh, its bottom edge dotted with the tiniest of seed pearls.

"The young Lord Özdemir had the seamstress use your gray-lace veil as a pattern, seer," Aylin explained, understanding what Carys was asking. "The young Lord Özdemir explained that it was not simply a sign of your office, but something that protected your eyes. That they were a need, not just an affectation. Pains were taken to make sure you had veils to match your wardrobe."

Another smile. "Of course he did," Carys murmured, setting the veil down. "Very well, Aylin, thank you."

"Ah, seer?"

Looking up, Carys found Aylin looking at her very curiously. A question burned in the young servant, and she was almost swaying as she shifted her weight from foot to foot in her anxiousness.

"Out with it, Aylin," Carys said, amused.

"Are you and young Lord Özdemir," Aylin began, looking up and then away, "that is… I mean, are you… will you be… um—"

"Asil Özdemir is not courting me, Aylin, and I was not brought here to be closer to his bed," Carys answered with a smirk, and Aylin grew scarlet. "He is my friend, and he is the Heir of the Strait. And that is all."

"Yes, of course, my lady! My seer!" The young woman was still vividly blushing and dropped a quick curtsey. "I will leave you to dress, I know you don't like it when I try to help and then I'll come back and get the dishes and I'm sorry, enjoy your coffee!"

Dashing from the room, Aylin didn't quite slam the door behind her, but it closed with a solid thud. Carys sighed and picked up her coffee again before looking over the clothing on her bed. Those questions were likely to come more frequently—and with less innocent curiosity—in the coming weeks. She would have to get used to it.

An hour later found Aylin, having regained her demeanor, returned to clean up as Carys made her way to the guest cottage that housed the ambassador and his company. There was a guardsman accompanying Carys, and he would apparently be following Carys throughout the day. The guard knocked and the valet answered quickly, ushering Carys into the gallery-like foyer. Ambassador Peadar Criddubh, Commander Tadhg Bharda, and the three knights were dressed and waiting.

"Good morning, Ambassador," Carys said with a nod, polite and civil. Peadar made her uncomfortable, but without allowing herself to read him, she couldn't pinpoint why. Something about the eyes. Well, and he was impossibly slimy. She continued to find it odd that he wasn't cursed like the rest of them, and wished she had the time and quiet to figure out why.

"Ah, Seer Arslan, how good of you to attend to us this day," the ambassador said with a smile and a bow, ever obsequious.

"Seer Arslan," Tadhg said, nodding as well, his smile considerably more genuine. His three knights behind him all bowed together.

"I understand that you all would like to see a House of the Divine Mother," Carys stated as she began to lead the party out of the cottage.

"Yes, yes," Peadar said, following, with the rest of the party just behind. "We are most curious to see your customs and rituals."

Brows creasing, Carys looked over at the ambassador. She was beginning to suspect that she was walking into a misunderstanding, perhaps an important one. Peadar didn't notice her expression, which would have been difficult to see through the thin veil, but then, Peadar wasn't looking at Carys. Tadhg, however, was, and the commander's gaze became curious as he sensed Carys's confusion.

A pair of carriages took them to the edge of the noble's district, Peadar and Carys in one, the general and his lieutenants in the other. They were open-air carriages, of course, as it was still lovely and balmy. At the edge of the noble's district, right as it blended with the immense merchant quarter, was the largest House of the Divine Mother in the whole of Vasi. It was an enormous stone building, half the size of Watcher Castle, lovingly and carefully carved from stones that came from farther up the coast and that had been brought there with great effort and expense. There was a soft blue cast to the pale stone, making it stand out from all the surrounding buildings, even from a distance.

Waiting outside the impressive building, with its enormous double doors, were two young sisters and one Revered Mother. The sisters fidgeted nervously, the white aprons over their blue dresses pristine, the white veils that covered their heads perfectly tucked in under their chins. The Revered Mother—in her deeper-blue dress, with no apron, and equally perfect white veil—appeared calm and easy, and greeted Carys with a smile.

"It is good to see you again, Seer Arslan," the Revered Mother said, nodding to the seer. "And greetings to our honored guests from across the sea. Welcome to the House of the Divine Mother. The children are up in the garden playing right now, so we have a moment to see everything before we are overrun."

As if cued by her words, the laughter of children rained down from the rooftop terrace above them. The commander and his knights looked a touch confused, but very curious. The ambassador just looked confused.

"Ambassador Criddubh," Carys began, "may I please present Revered Mother Azize, right hand to the High Revered Mother Bedia."

"I would ask how you knew about my recent position, my dear, but that would be silly," Azize said with a smile before turning to bow her head to the ambassador, who had begun to kneel before her. She was briefly taken aback, but Azize recovered quickly. "Ambassador, please, that is unnecessary."

The soldiers had begun to kneel as well, Carys realized, and they all looked quite confused again as they paused and straightened. "Thank you for making this time for us, Your Reverence," Ambassador Peadar stated, though his tone carried uncertainty.

"That is also unnecessary," Azize said, clearly perplexed but smiling. "Mother Azize is sufficient. But come, let us get this tour on the way before we are beset by small, curious people."

Seemingly at a loss, the ambassador and his party followed the Revered Mother and her acolytes through the building. Carys began to relax as they walked through. She had never lived at the House of the Divine Mother; her grandmother had taken her in after her mother's death. She had, however, found herself there frequently, seeking understanding and solace, and helping the acolytes with the younger children. Even as a child, Carys had understood how to help and how to take care of people. It was, ultimately, what a seer did.

They were shown the main assembly area where the children gathered in the mornings, the library, and the kitchens, and were preparing to see the classrooms when Ambassador Peadar abruptly stopped.

"This is an orphanage," Peadar said, his tone irritated, and he sounded as if he had only just realized it.

"Of course," Carys said, looking over at the ambassador, and then the commander.

"I asked your Lord Özdemir to see the temple to the Divine Mother," Peadar said, the irritation in his tone growing. He sounded almost petulant, and Carys frankly didn't care for it.

"Ahhhh," Mother Azize said, understanding what Carys was missing. "You were expecting to find a place of worship."

"Well, yes," Peadar stated. Behind him Áedh and Generys nodded, as if it were obvious. Tadhg continued to look curious and Cillian—was Cillian smiling?

"I understand," Mother Azize said, and began to lead the party back through the main hall. "I have made a study of how the Divine Mother is honored in other cultures. Here in Vasi, and in all of the kingdoms that make up the Cliffs of Dawn, you will find no temples to the Divine Mother."

"What?!" Ambassador Peadar looked horrified. His voice twanged in surprise.

"Seer Arslan, my dear, when we are done here, please take the ambassador and his entourage to the shrine," Mother Azize said, smiling at Carys, before looking back at the clearly offended ambassador. "Ambassador Peadar, we feel that we can best honor the Divine Mother by continuing her work. What does she who shepherds and nurtures our souls need of temples or grand ceremonies? That is not her endeavor. As the Divine Mother cares for us in the Cradle, and tenderly nurses each soul in her care, we care for the lost and abandoned babes of this world. All the people of Vasi honor and revere the Divine Mother, and you will not find a shrine without offerings in all the Kingdoms of Dawn, but you will also not find a single temple."

Carys let herself fall back as Mother Azize continued to soothe the ambassador, until she was close to Cillian. It was still a touch unnerving how Cillian looked like her. Of all strangers from across the sea that Carys had met, while she bore a surprising resemblance to them in general, Cillian looked like he could be a member of her family. She wondered sometimes if her father came from wherever Cillian's family was from.

"You are the only one that is not confused," Carys murmured, and Cillian looked over at her, surprised, but smiled again and nodded.

"It was once like this at home," Cillian said quietly, eyes darting carefully toward the ambassador. "Not in my lifetime, but I heard about it from my grandparents and my mother. The temples came when we joined the Empire."

"Interesting," Carys said, just as softly. She glanced forward as well and found that while the ambassador was still sufficiently distracted by Mother Azize, Tadhg was watching them. The general saw everything; that was beginning to be frustrating.

Drifting forward once more, Carys rejoined Peadar and Mother Azize as they turned to the door. Then, suddenly, they were surrounded—children of all ages, from those barely walking to those close to no longer being children, swarmed down the hallway, the older children trying to rein in the curious younger ones and ultimately failing. While many of them were curious about the soldiers, most of them were actually coming for Carys. She laughed and gave hugs and picked up a little girl grabbing at her sash.

"Is this how we behave in front of guests?" Carys asked, laughing a little but pitching her voice to carry.

"Sorry, Seer!" a chorus of voices answered, and the smaller children allowed their elders to line them up.

Turning to the little girl in her arms, who could not have been much older than three, Carys leaned in and pressed their noses together. "What have I told you about grabbing, Emine?"

The little girl—Emine—giggled and grabbed Carys's face, kissing the seer's nose. "I sorry!"

Sighing, Carys handed Emine off to one of the sisters that had been following Mother Azize, who took the girl and smiled at Carys almost adoringly. "They always love to see you, Seer Arslan," the sister said. "I know you have responsibilities, but if you could visit more…"

"I'll try," Carys said, somewhat sadly. She didn't know how she would. As the sister stepped away, Carys saw Tadhg watching her again while talking to one of the middling-aged boys, who seemed very interested in the commander's sword. She couldn't read the look on his face.

"Seer Arslan," a voice said, demanding her attention.

Carys turned to see another young woman, this one wearing a strange little hood that came down over her head like a voluminous hat, unattached from her clothing. The front of the hood cast a shadow over eyes that were so faint a gold that they were like the sunlight on the horizon at dawn.

"Hello, Ferah," Carys greeted the younger seer with a smile and a hug. "Good to see you. How goes your training? Do you like the cards I gave you?"

"Yes," the girl said shyly, shifting her weight from one foot to another. "I take them with me to my lessons with Seer Kaya. Kaya says she's not sure cards are the right focus for me, but they're very beautiful, and it's been good to try to practice with them!"

Still smiling, Carys cupped the girl's face. "I'm glad. Kaya is a good teacher; if she says your focus is elsewhere, listen and be willing to try everything. The cards are yours regardless."

"Thank you, Seer," Ferah murmured, looking at Carys with wide eyes as if the Lord of the Strait had come to praise her. "Oh, and I can make the sleeping tea now! Mother Azize says it tastes just like yours!"

Carys's smile grew even wider. "That's wonderful!"

Looking past Carys, Ferah's eyes flared for just a second, like tiny suns, and she murmured, "Your lover is looking at us."

Carys blinked, her smile falling in her surprise. "What?"

Blinking as well, Ferah looked back at Carys, and turned pink. "What did I say? Did I say the wrong word? I was trying to say that the man with blue eyes is watching us. What did I say?"

Glancing back over her shoulder, Carys met Tadhg's very blue eyes. He smiled disarmingly and looked away, still talking with a cluster of boys. She could also hear Judex snickering. Looking back to Ferah, Carys smiled reassuringly.

"I think you were dipping into the possibilities again," Carys said, hoping to convince Ferah that she had not just been shaken by the slip of the girl's talent. "That is Commander Tadhg Bharda, and around him are his knights. The redhead is Áedh, the woman is Generys, and the larger man with the beard is Cillian."

Convinced, Ferah relaxed and smiled. "It's very exciting, isn't it?" Ferah said. "People from the south! I hear the Mothers talking about it. They asked me if I had any dreams about it. I don't think I did. Did you?"

"I did," Carys confessed, quietly, "though I didn't entirely understand what they meant." That was true enough, at least.

There was a clap of hands, and the two sisters began to bustle the children away, back toward the main assembly. Carys hugged Ferah a final time and let the younger seer go. Turning back around, she wandered out into the street once more where the carriages still waited patiently. Ambassador Peadar seemed to have recovered himself and was giving his thanks to Mother Azize in the most florid manner possible.

"Thank you again for educating us on the idiosyncratic differences of religion between the Southern Empire and the Northern Kingdoms," Peadar was saying, bowing over Mother Azize's hand. "You are a learned woman with grace and patience, and we are ever grateful for your time today."

Mother Azize endured the praise admirably. "I am happy to have helped achieve understanding," the Revered Mother said, taking her hand back. "I hope you still enjoyed the tour, though it was not what you had anticipated."

"Oh, of course, of course," Peadar gushed, and Carys's brow twitched with the desire to roll her eyes.

"Seer Arslan," Mother Azize said, and Carys stepped forward quickly. "It is delightful to see you as always, my girl. I saw that young Ferah caught you. She seems to have a burgeoning raw talent, and she's studying hard and has the instincts to make a fine herbalist. I know you are busier now than ever you were, dear, but do come back again soon."

"I will try," Carys said, with another gently tinged smile.

Mother Azize nodded to the others and took her leave, the great doors of the orphanage closing behind her. Taking a breath, Carys turned to her charges.

"Before we depart, let me take you to the shrine of the Divine Mother," Carys said, motioning down the way. She nodded to the guard that had been shadowing them, sending him to the carriages. "It will be easier on foot from here; the carriages can go around to meet us there. If you'll follow me?"

The short walk was a quiet one, everyone absorbed in their own thoughts. The party from the south was presumably considering the strange differences in beliefs, and Carys was considering what Ferah had said. It couldn't be true, could it? Handsome as the commander was, that seemed to be horrifically ill advised at the very least. Though was that why the commander seemed to be watching her so intently? Carys had assumed that it was because she was the foreign representative, the unknown. She started to subconsciously reach, and immediately felt the twinge of the commander's curse, compounded by the curses of his knights. She needed to figure that out first, before any other possibility could be considered.

The shrine to the Divine Mother rested within a walled garden. Vines of all sorts, evergreen and blooming, covered the walls to soften the sounds from the city beyond. White roses rimmed the edge of the shrine, and Carys paused to remove her shoes, storing them in cubbies beneath stone benches that were clearly intended for this purpose. Barefoot, she walked across the grass to the large statue of a woman holding a swaddled child above an ornate cradle, the upper half of her face and her hair obscured by a long veil.

Around the base of the statue and in the cradle were offerings of all sorts. Coins, trinkets, flowers, sweets—anything dear and precious that someone might give to a loved one. The air in the garden was thick not only from the flowers but also from incense. Carys traded obols to a quiet merchant, and then handed each of her charges a small cone of incense. Lighting it from a nearby brazier, Carys blew out the flame and knelt before the statue, setting the smoldering cone down as the spicy, musky fragrance washed over her.

"From the Cradle we all come," Carys said quietly, and was joined by four voices as she intoned the rest of the refrain, "and to the Cradle we all return."

Carys closed her eyes for a moment, taking a breath, and silently hoped that her mother and her grandmother were enjoying their rest.

She then rose again and stepped out of the way. The ambassador, the commander, and each of the knights followed her lead, lighting the incense and taking a moment before rising to follow.

Generys came up to Carys and held out her hand. In it was a coin.

"For the offering," Generys said, something strangely vulnerable in her normally cold tone.

Carys brought up her hands and used them to fold Generys's fingers around the coin, clasping the closed hand as she did. "It was a gift and given freely. May all our ancestors rest in the Cradle as long as they need."

The pale knight looked down at Carys for a moment, and there was the faintest tremble in her lip. Carys realized with some surprise that Generys was on the verge of tears. There was also a moment of recognition. Both she and the knight had known loss, and that loss had been close and dear. Generys just nodded, however, and Carys released her hand before turning away to lead them through the garden, emerging on a different street. The carriages were there, the drivers knowing exactly where Carys had intended them to go.

"I understand that we shall now part ways," Carys said, turning back toward her charges. "Ambassador Peadar, the Heir of the Strait awaits you at Watcher Castle."

"Yes, yes, of course," the ambassador said, heading to the carriage. The garden had quieted him, quieted them all. "I thank you, Seer Arslan, for your time."

Chapter 11

ASIL DRUMMED HIS fingers against the table. The ambassador would be arriving shortly, and Asil wanted to get this done as quickly as possible. He didn't dislike the ambassador as much as Carys seemed to, but he did find the man to be a particularly weaselly example of his kind. But that was what ambassadors did: they ingratiate themselves to people in power, with the hopes of gaining something in return. Asil simply felt that the empire perhaps chose Peadar Criddubh for this mission in order to get rid of him for several months with the hope that he came back marginally successful.

The doors to the North Parlor opened, and Asil sat up straight, only to sink back into the chair as Hasim came in. "What are you doing here?"

"Good to see you too, my Heir," Hasim said with a smirk as he sat down in the empty chair to Asil's right. "I'm here because my father sent me. Presumably to see if these strangers inadvertently reveal anything interesting about their military capabilities. Your new pet isn't here?"

Asil bristled visibly. "You've certainly been talking to your father. You call her that again, and I'm kicking you out of the room, Lord Commander."

The smirk immediately fell from Hasim's face. "I'm sorry, Asil, truly. It was supposed to be a joke; I didn't realize you felt so strongly about it."

Sighing, Asil flipped his hand in a gesture very similar to his father and motioned for the attendant to come pour them each a glass of wine. "Carys's appointment has been met with mixed responses. The Great Families in particular seem to be of two minds about it. Your father thinks she's some low-born pet I picked up, elevated to her station to make it easier for me to pursue her."

"There are rumors," Hasim said, reluctantly, "as I am sure you know. She's beautiful; I don't blame you if a few of them are true."

"I probably wish some of them were," Asil admitted somewhat petulantly, and Hasim laughed. "The night we met, I invited her back to my room. She accepted the invitation but said she wouldn't sleep with me, because we were both too drunk."

Hasim gawked. "And you still took her with you?"

"I did." Asil picked up his wine and looked at it for a moment. "Have you ever had someone look at you and just… they neither wanted nor expected anything of you?"

"Other than you and I, you mean?" Hasim grinned.

That made Asil laugh. "Fair. She has a remarkable gift, Hasim. Father says she is the most powerful seer in the kingdom, and she has admitted this as well. If anyone in the kingdom should be the Lord's Seer, it is her. My interest in her should not detract from her qualifications." He took a long drink, and Hasim was quiet for a moment.

The doors opened again, and the two men sat straight once more. Ambassador Criddubh entered the room, accompanied by his slight, quiet secretary. The ambassador bowed deeply, and Asil nodded, gesturing for him to take a seat in the armchair across from him.

"I thank you for your time today, my Heir," Peadar said, settling in, the secretary sitting on a stool just behind him, drawn into herself and bent over her papers. It felt like she was hiding. "I understand that we are to discuss my proposed length of stay within your fair city."

"Among other things," Asil said, looking down at the agenda in front of him. It was odd to be doing this with someone new. While Asil had handled affairs of state before, all of the Kingdoms of Dawn were long-established allies. Asil had grown up around many of the men and women who typically sat across from him. In one or two cases, they had grown up together.

The attendant set wine in front of both Peadar and his secretary, which seemed to surprise them both. Specifically, it was that someone had served the secretary. In Vasi, the secretary to an ambassador was a position that still went to a person of rank. Asil suspected that Peadar saw the woman behind him as a servant, a tool, and she certainly acted like someone who was not used to being acknowledged or accommodated.

"So how long do you hope to stay, Ambassador Criddubh?" Asil said, and Hasim faintly snorted beside him. The ambassador was briefly poleaxed by Asil's bluntness.

"Well, I had hoped to speak with our captain and hear his recommendations," Peadar said after a moment. "It is the Council's plan that our vessel will return in the summer of next year with a full report of how the rest of the world has progressed. If possible, I am to open up trade negotiations wherever I am able. After we return once the year is out, I have no doubt you will see more-regular travel from our lands to yours."

Asil nodded. "I understand all that and understood it yesterday. What I would like to know today is how long you and your people will be staying in Vasi."

"A month, perhaps," Peadar answered, unsteady again. "I would like to resupply as much as possible. We have brought coin for supplies, of course. I would appreciate an opportunity to allow our soldiers off the ship. The ocean crossing was tense at times, and they would be grateful for the opportunity to… stretch their legs."

"I have no doubt," Hasim interjected, and Peadar looked at him curiously.

"Hm? Oh, yes—Ambassador Criddubh, this is Lord Commander Hasim Kilic." Asil made a brief notation on the paper in front of him, nodding to himself. "I hope you can appreciate that we will not allow you to bring an entire company of soldiers into the city at once."

"Oh, I of course understand the concern, my Heir," Peadar said in a stronger tone, more certain of himself now. He was prepared for this part. "I assure you that my men will be on their best behavior. And surely your guard could not be overwhelmed by our paltry force."

"They could not," Hasim answered, a little sharply.

Asil sighed. "That is not the point, Ambassador. You arrived without warning. We are not prepared to accommodate 150 men. I will discuss the matter with my father and Lord Kilic. We could perhaps allow a longboat of men to disembark for a few days, and you can decide on a system for how they might take turns." Hasim nodded, looking over at Asil. It seemed that plan was acceptable.

The ambassador bowed his head. "I thank you for the consideration, my Heir."

"As to the matter of supplies," Asil continued, making another note, "I assume your men are fine for the next few days? Are you in dire need?"

"Oh, no, my Heir, we were well equipped before we left." Peadar's tone was a touch too exuberant.

"Then I will arrange a meeting with the appropriate heads of the Great Families tomorrow, and we can see about refreshing your supplies." Asil made a few more notes and nodded to himself. "Now then, I—"

A firm knock on the door interrupted whatever it was Asil was about to say, and without waiting a guardsman let himself into the parlor. Asil raised an eyebrow as the guard walked up and bowed deeply.

"I apologize for interrupting, my Heir, Lord Commander," the guard said, his face red, chest rising and falling from the effort he made to get there. "There has been another altercation at the rivermouth. A disagreement with the wardens from Veli."

"And why are you coming to me about it?" Asil asked, glancing briefly from the guard to Peadar. The ambassador looked very curious, and it seemed his secretary was taking more notes.

The guard blinked for a moment, clearly confused, and Asil got the impression he wasn't the brightest of Adnan's recruits. "Be-because the Lord Captain told me to, my Heir. Or, he said to seek your Lord Father, but the Highest Lord is in a meeting with the pashas, so Lord Captain said—"

"Do you not appreciate that we are also in a meeting, guardsman?" Hasim asked, standing up as the guard continued to blink at him stupidly.

Sighing, Hasim bowed to Asil and Ambassador Criddubh. "Forgive me, gentlemen. I will take care of this."

Asil ran his hand over his face as Hasim practically hauled the guard out of the room. Glancing at the ambassador, Asil found Peadar looking at the door. Something in his expression was calculating. The expression made Asil very uncomfortable.

"Ambassador."

With a soft exclamation, Peadar's attention swung back to Asil, and he bowed his head. "Yes, my Heir, forgive me. I do hope everything is all right?"

"It is, Ambassador," Asil said, shuffling the papers before him, "thank you for your concern. As I was saying, let us reconvene for lunch tomorrow to discuss the matter of seeing your ship resupplied. I will pass on the length of your proposed stay to my Lord Father, and we will decide what the maximum number of men we can allow off the ship at once is. I will make sure to get an answer on that to you later today, as I imagine your men would very much like the reprieve. You could begin allowing them off tomorrow."

"Excellent! Thank you, my Heir." The ambassador stood, understanding the meeting was done. He bowed, his secretary bowed, and they both let themselves out.

Asil leaned back in the chair again and sighed. "Damn."

He was going to have words with Adnan about this.

☾ ☾ ☾

The tour had been a touch dull. Carys was unsure what was permitted, so she simply had the carriage driver take them through the city, pointing out the different districts. The commander and his knights were interested in a polite way, though she could see both Tadhg and Cillian making note of everywhere they went. Generys had been curious about the bath houses, and Carys had explained their function and purpose—apparently such a thing did not exist in the southern empire. Áedh had been interested in the port. No, that wasn't right—he had been interested in the drinking houses in the port. Carys had a suspicion that someone would request she take at least the knights if not the commander as well out drinking soon.

It became very apparent, though, that everyone understood no one in the entourage from the south went anywhere without Carys. She was their crown-appointed nanny, whether she or they liked it. It was difficult to relax into a real conversation, and entirely impossible to further explore the mystery of their curses. For now.

When Carys returned to Watcher Castle, a valet informed her that Asil was waiting for her. She found the Heir once more in his rooms, alone this time and glaring at a stack of papers on his desk. Smiling a little, Carys walked up and set her hand on Asil's shoulder. Without looking, he reached up and set his own hand over hers.

"You look as if your meeting with the ambassador did not go so well," Carys said softly.

"It did not go poorly, exactly." Asil sighed and let go of Carys's hand, turning in his chair to face her. "It did not go well, either. Adnan sent some fresh-faced dimwit up to inform us of a minor disagreement with the river wardens. It didn't look good."

"That sounds frustrating." Carys bit her lip, then reached up and gently ran her fingers through Asil's hair, which made him close his eyes and sigh. "Did Lord Captain Kilic have a reason? Were you able to figure out why?"

Asil nodded, but barely, clearly not wanting to move away from Carys's attentions. "The ship in question belonged to Pasha Yasuv."

"Ah." As the head of the Great Families, Pasha Yasuv was awarded a certain level of priority and attention in matters that might affect trade. They were both quiet for a moment as Carys continued to run her fingers through Asil's hair. He really was quite handsome. They had not been affectionate since she had been appointed. It was probably for the best, as rumors were already thick in the air like bees in climbing sweetrose. But right now, Carys was almost overwhelmed by the urge to kiss him.

The scrape of the door killed that desire, and Carys stepped away from Asil, turning to see who entered. Nazim came in bearing a tray for dinner, but a keen eye could see that it was too much food for two people. As Nazim set the table and Asil got to his feet, Hasim arrived as well.

The Lord Commander looked from Carys to Asil curiously, but apparently did not find what he was seeking, and turned his attention to the food with a shrug.

"Everything at the rivermouth dealt with?" Asil's tone was dry, a touch of the day's irritation lingering.

Hasim smiled in understanding at his friend and nodded. "Everything is fine. I also had a delightful bout of mutual yelling with Father, but he eventually conceded that he had overblown the situation and that he would send a less stupid guard next time."

Asil sighed and Carys giggled. Just a little. She enjoyed seeing Asil around Hasim, even if it felt like Hasim was still trying to determine how to interact with her. Asil sat down at the table, and Hasim pulled a chair out for Carys. Once they were all settled, Nazim poured tea and wine then made his way out. Dinner was friendly and light—conversation focused on such topics as new horses, some lovely, rare gems that Pasha Kaplan's people had brought back from Ropa, and plans for the upcoming festival to celebrate the late-summer harvest.

"So, my rose," Hasim said with a smile as they lingered over sweetcakes, "how was your time with the commander and his men today?"

Arching an eyebrow, Carys reached for her wine. "Why do you call me that?"

"What, pale rose?" Hasim asked, a little surprised. "Because you're beautiful and pale. Well, comparatively—I haven't seen a man as white as the southerners since I met those traders from Ropa. It must be cold down south."

"She just wants to make sure you're not courting her," Asil said, grinning impishly. "She hates that."

Rolling her eyes, Carys threw one of the extra rolls at Asil, who caught it laughing. Hasim also laughed. "I can stop if it bothers you," Hasim offered.

"No, it's all right." Carys took a sip of her wine and looked down into the glass. "I think I'm just not used to flattery that doesn't have an agenda."

"Who says I don't have an agenda?" Hasim grinned shamelessly, comedically so. Carys giggled again.

"So, back to the question," Carys said, still very amused by Hasim's antics. "The day was fine. I may have bored them a little; I wasn't sure what to do with them. We took a carriage tour of the city."

Asil nodded. "It's a good starting point. They are supposedly guests. They should know what is available to them."

"I would bet my shop that I get asked to take them drinking soon," Carys said wryly. The two men laughed.

"Did you learn anything new about the curses?" Hasim asked the question almost gently.

Sighing in frustration, Carys sat back with her wine. "No. I'm learning about the soldiers a little, though. It's no wonder Tadhg is in charge; he's sharp and sees everything. The older man, Cillian, is just as quick. It feels like he weighs everything I say, everything I do. Áedh's personality matches his hair. Generys is, I think, not as cold as she presents herself."

"Really, if you can befriend any of them, you should," Asil mused, tapping his fingers on the table.

Carys blinked. "That seems… reckless?"

Hasim waved his hand dismissively. "No, it makes sense. We're not saying form a deep friendship, but if you can get them to like you, it favors our position. Soldiers don't like to attack people they're fond of."

"I guess I'll try," Carys murmured into her glass before taking another drink. Ferah's words flitted through her mind again, but she pushed them away.

There was a chime, and Asil sighed. "We should get ready for court."

"I'll walk you to your room," Hasim said, standing up. Carys arched a brow, but Asil just nodded and headed into his own dressing room.

They were down the hall but before the first turn when Hasim spoke, his voice low, "I have been waiting for an opportunity to talk with you, truth be told. We are both busy people."

"That we are," Carys agreed, somewhat ruefully. Hasim laughed softly.

"I know a little bit more about you now," he said as they passed through the Lord's Hall on their way to Carys's wing. "I have of course heard the rumors, but I've also heard Asil speak of you. What… do you feel for him?"

"A bit of a dangerous question, isn't it?" Carys looked over at Hasim carefully. "You two are close, and clearly good friends. What if you don't like my answer? I… have heard that the Lord Captain is not pleased with my assignment."

Hasim made a tsking sound and waved his hand again. "My father's obsession with pedigree is not relevant to our conversation. I am asking how you feel about someone I love, Carys. I am speaking to you as Asil's dearest friend."

Carys let out a soft sound of surprise, an exhalation of breath. The threads moved with those words, twanging through Carys. The word had been spoken lightly, but a depth of emotion lay behind them. And it was… reciprocated. The bond between Hasim and Asil was complex, but it was not one-sided. Carys remembered Asil's comment when she had told him about the rumor that he liked men. I can see how people think that. Hasim looked over, brows drawn, then smiled softly.

"Let's step into your room for a moment," Hasim said with that same smile. "I'll explain as you freshen up."

"Of course," Carys said, blushing a little, and stepped into the room. She removed her veil as she did. The door clicked behind her, and she turned around to see Hasim paused just within the threshold of her room.

"I can't imagine this is going to help my already-questionable reputation," Carys said wryly, and she set the veil down and began to undo the fastenings on her jacket.

That got the loudest laugh out of Hasim yet. "No, it won't, and I'm sorry. I should have thought of that. I also have a bit of a reputation. And… well, you would not be the first woman that Asil and I shared."

Carys blushed again and drifted toward her own dressing room. "You would have a hard time sharing anything. Asil has not… had me, yet."

"Yes, I know." Hasim's voice was amused as it followed her through the open doorway. "The position is tenuous, isn't it? He is very taken with you, but if either of you give in to that desire before you've established yourself, it looks as if the rumors were right."

Sighing, Carys hung up her jacket. It appeared Aylin had already been here and had set out a fresh dress for court. Carys's wardrobe seemed to grow every day she was here. That was probably a correct assessment. Wiggling out of the linen underdress, she set it aside and began to put on a more silken one in a pale green.

"So, you said you would explain," Carys said after a minute, reaching for the short vest heavily embroidered and beaded with vines and blue-and-purple flowers.

"Ah, yes, I did." Hasim sounded almost sheepish now. "Asil and I… He is my dearest friend, as I said. He means a great deal to me. We mean a great deal to each other. We grew up together; we endured being our fathers' only sons together. There is a weight of expectation on me as Lord Commander that Asil understands as the Heir. No one else will ever understand me as Asil does."

Lacing the vest, Carys came back out into the room. "Hasim, I'm not trying to—"

"I know," Hasim said, smiling, and stepped up to Carys, taking the lacings from her and doing a better job of getting her secured. "We are not pining for each other; we will be friends until we die. I am not his true love, nor he mine. Truth is, I'm not sure Asil is capable of having one. His affection for you is the closest I've ever seen to a romantic inkling in him, and it is still very detached."

Laughing a little, Carys smiled up at Hasim. "Like how he kisses."

"Yes! You understand! It is attentive, it is practiced, and you have no doubt he means it. But…"

"But it's not passionate," Carys supplied, and Hasim nodded.

"So," Hasim said, reaching up to brush back Carys's hair. He paused, brows arched as if to be sure it was allowed, and Carys gave a faint nod. "Will you tell me what you feel for him?"

"I like him," Carys said honestly, eyes fluttering closed as Hasim ran a hand through her hair. It was a strange mirror to her and Asil earlier. "I have… begun to care for him. He is my friend. He is also very handsome, an excellent kisser, and I'm not dead." Hasim laughed again. "But as you said, the situation is delicate at best."

Nodding, Hasim looked into Carys's eyes and caressed her cheek. "You have the most fascinating eyes. I made assumptions about you when we met. About who you would be to Asil and, by extension, to me. I should not have, and I am sorry. I have something to ask, though, because as I said, you are beautiful, and I am also not dead. If you and Asil are able to navigate this situation, would it bother you very much if I join in? Eventually, I mean. Not the first time, of course."

"Mother, you two are impossible," Carys said with a faint laugh, cheeks glowing. "I… Hasim, you must know you are attractive. If this… friendship continues, I might be open to the idea. Though this is certainly a first for me."

Hasim grinned. "The experience, or the offer?"

"Yes."

Laughing, Hasim stepped back. "I'm glad you'll entertain the idea. I will say, however, that while I wouldn't call my relationship with Asil a secret, I think you can appreciate why I would rather you not discuss it with anyone else."

Carys nodded. The understanding for secrecy had come with the knowledge of their love for each other. "A substantiated rumor that the only sons of the heads of two noble families were romantically involved would cause uncertainty in the future of those houses."

"You are a bright one," Hasim said sincerely. "And both Asil and myself find women to be completely delightful, so there is no reason to arouse concern. Now! I'm going to head out before I've been in your rooms long enough to lend credence to any rumors. See you at court."

The door closed behind Hasim, and Carys took a deep breath. "Divine Mother forgive me, I don't think I have the strength to say no to any of this," she said, staring at the door in dazed wonder, trying to ignore the flush she felt through her body. She turned, picked the veil back up, and went to finish preparing for court.

Chapter 12

Three days passed.

Carys sat in the kitchen garden thumbing through the pages of notes and directives Asil had handed off to her that morning. She'd had the idea to take tea here because her presence had not been required anywhere this afternoon. It was rather nice. She felt a little bad that it meant Aylin had to cart the tea out to the garden, but she also found it very soothing to her ruffled spirit. Maybe Aylin wouldn't hold it against her if tea in the garden only happened once or twice a week.

The notes Asil had given Carys were meticulously organized, in a method that Carys never would have considered employing. It shed light on how Asil thought, how his mind shuffled the minutia necessary in being a leader. Carys smiled a little as she set aside a page explaining the different swords that Tadhg and his knights used, and what that likely said about their combat training. She wasn't sure why Asil thought she would need it, but she would make a point to read it eventually.

The last three days had been nothing if not educational. Further conversations had made Carys certain that for once the ambassador had not been lying when he insisted there were no seers in the south. Which, given the presence of the curses that plagued the southern soldiers, meant that secrets were kept at many different levels in the southern empire. She had learned they answer to a council, and that the council was revered both as rulers and as a divinely inspired guiding hand for temples of the Divine Mother (which were large and numerous in the south). The way they viewed the Divine Mother made Carys uncomfortable in ways she couldn't properly describe. It felt as if they were trying to turn the benevolent guardian of all souls into something at once greater and less than what she embodied. The Divine Mother had no use for the squabbles of government, the trappings of the nobility. Why did they try so hard to paint her as a queen rather than a mother? What purpose did it serve?

Carys was stirred from her thoughts by a gentle clearing of the throat from across the table, and she looked up to see Hasim standing there. He was in uniform, which Carys had never seen before. A crisp white collar peeked from the neck of his elaborately embroidered coat. The crest of Vasi, and of House Kilic, shone from his chest in the sunlight. The lines of his clothing were sharp and close to his body, lacking the movement that was so often preferred in Vasi fashion. He also wore a sword for the first time since Carys had met him, his hand resting on the pommel with the same ease that Carys had noted in Tadhg.

"That's a very flattering look for you," Carys said warmly, not bothering to hide her admiration for the figure Hasim cut.

Hasim grinned. "I did not know you were impressed by such a simple thing as a uniform, Seer Arslan."

"I am not." Carys picked up her tea and took a sip. "I am impressed by the man wearing it."

Something softened in Hasim's smile, and it became more genuine. "I thank you, seer. I'm here to tell you that I'm going to oversee the first deployment of soldiers from the southerners' ship. We've made arrangements to allow twenty-five off the ship at a time."

Setting down the cup, Carys arched an eyebrow. "That sounds like a lot, but I imagine you will tell me it isn't."

Hasim nodded. "It really isn't, unless every soldier on that ship is a trained assassin, but we are reasonably certain that's not the case. A side effect of this action, however, is that the commander and his knights will no longer be as necessary a presence at the ambassador's side. I understand that they are hoping for a night on the town. I came to warn you."

Carys blinked. "Are you implying that I have to accompany them even when they go carousing?"

Hasim grinned again. "Yes, seer."

Groaning, Carys reached up and rubbed the spot between her eyes through her veil. She had been ready for the demands of getting a drink, but not a full night's entertainment in the city. Hasim laughed and walked over, running a hand over Carys's hair.

"It can't be that bad, can it?" he asked, brushing her cheek with the back of his fingers. Carys flushed just a little and set her hand back down.

"No, it really isn't," she answered, looking back up at Hasim. "I am coming to find them to be mostly pleasant. Áedh needs a surprisingly firm hand, but Cillian treats him like a younger brother and keeps him in line. Tadhg is intelligent and perfectly willing to discuss almost any subject. Generys is… careful. I get the impression it was not easy for her to achieve her position. The three knights have an intense respect for Tadhg, like he is more than just their commanding officer."

Nodding, Hasim ran a hand over Carys's hair again. "He knows his men. I noticed very quickly that he doesn't set himself apart from them. He eats what they eat, sleeps where they sleep. Father is like that more often than not. It inspires loyalty. I've known commanders who see themselves as nobles first, and they don't get the same love from their men."

"You'll have to tell me about your travels someday," Carys said, doing her best not to lean into Hasim's hand. "If you can bring yourself to share your secrets in my company."

"Gladly." Hasim set his hand on Carys's shoulder for a moment, then stepped back. "Dinner, drinks, and war stories as soon as we all have a moment. We understand each other now; I don't feel the need to watch my tongue around you quite so much."

Carys smiled, touched. "Thank you, Hasim."

With a short bow and a wave, Hasim took himself off. Sighing, Carys set down the stack of notes and picked up her tea once more. Both Asil and Hasim had become more casually affectionate with her since her talk with Hasim, at least when they were away from wagging tongues and prying eyes. Carys had not been touched so much in a very long time.

The gentle pets, the innocent ruffle of hair, kisses on the cheek—there had been none of that since her grandmother died. It was lovely, and worrisome.

"My seer?"

Carys's head popped up. Aylin was standing where Hasim had been a moment before. The girl dropped a curtsey and smiled.

"Can I get you anything else, my seer?" Aylin asked.

"No, thank you, I'll be finished soon." Carys drank off what was in her cup and looked over at Aylin. "Do you know what my schedule for the evening is yet?"

Nodding, Aylin smiled brightly. "Yes, my seer! You will be accompanying the visiting party about town this evening. I have an outfit ready for you, as well as a purse of marks."

Carys furrowed her brow. "Marks?"

"Yes, my seer," Aylin said, looking back just as confused for a moment.

The urge to sigh was very strong. "And marks are…" Carys prompted.

"Oh!" Aylin turned pink. "Of course, you're not used to— I am sorry, my seer! A mark is used instead of obols. It's like a promissory note. You'll give one to every place you visit, and they'll send it back to the castle with a bill for your evening. You can leave extra marks at a single establishment as a sign that you well, that you spent a lot of money there, basically. Marks are safer than obols, because they're only useful to a business that has registered with the clerks."

"That's… very sensible," Carys said, gathering up the stack of papers once more. "All right, Aylin, can someone else gather this up so that you're free to help me prepare?"

Aylin looked like she was practically beside herself with excitement. "Yes, my seer! I'll have someone sent!" Carys wasn't sure whether or not she wanted to laugh or sigh, and so just smiled as she followed Aylin up the path and back to the castle.

As they left the kitchen garden, Carys saw Peadar climbing into a carriage along with Asil, Tadhg, and a young man who looked very familiar. Something about his face, the dour expression he turned toward Carys, the broad shoulders and too many necklaces.

"Aylin," Carys said, slowing her step, "the young man in the carriage with the others. Who is that?"

"Oh, that's Musa Kaplan," Aylin replied immediately, her voice low as if she feared it would carry. "He is Pasha Kaplan's heir, but he's also the second son. I guess it's a scandal, but no one will tell me about it; they say I'm too young." She sounded deeply disappointed by that last part.

"He has his father's cheerful disposition, I see," Carys noted, and Aylin giggled then clapped her hands over her mouth. "Though why is he heading into the city with them?"

"I don't know, my seer," Aylin said, clearing her throat and composing herself. Carys would have to ask Asil about that later.

Back in Carys's room, Aylin brought out what was purported to be a casual ensemble for the evening. It was similar to what Carys had worn to the garden party, though the colors were all pinks and violets of the wisteria blooming in the cliffside garden. The vest was heavily embroidered, the pants a silken material that draped over Carys's hips in a rather flattering manner, the fluttering blouse delightfully soft. Carys looked at herself in the mirror in surprise. Save for the veil, a delicate piece of embroidered work just sheer enough to see her expression through, she looked like any other noblewoman she had seen in her shop or down in the market on any given day.

"You look very lovely, my seer," Aylin said almost adoringly. She brought out some simple jewelry, including a brooch with the crest of Vasi that pinned to the crossfold of Carys's sash.

"I feel very much the pretender in this," Carys murmured.

Aylin just shook her head. "Everyone will think it suits you." Keeping further protests to herself, Carys let Aylin apply last touches.

The path to the House of Flowers was familiar by this point, and in another week, Carys imagined she would be able to walk it blindfolded. The butler opened the door and smiled at Carys, then went to fetch the others.

As Commander Tadhg and the knights emerged, Carys supposed that what they wore must be the less-formal version of their uniforms. There was still a great deal of gray leather, but they now wore vests instead of coats, sleeves loose with a gentle billow to them. Cillian wore his vest open, more similar to the Vasi style, while Generys's was laced tightly like a corset. They had left their crested hats behind as well, and the late-afternoon sun seemed to set Áedh's hair ablaze. They still had their swords, however.

"Seer Arslan," Tadhg said, bowing to her as they stepped out onto stones of the courtyard, "I thank you for making the time for us this evening."

"I am at your beck and call, Commander," Carys said dryly with a hint of a smile. "I understand you are hoping for an evening out."

"Absolutely," Áedh said, grinning and taking a step toward Carys. "All right, Seer Arslan. It's Carys, right? Do you mind if I call you Carys?"

"Not at all," Carys answered with a laugh, surprised at the sudden shift in demeanor. The others seemed to take it in stride. Apparently, this was just what Áedh was like.

"Fantastic," Áedh said. "So, for the rest of the night if not longer, I'm Áedh, she's Gen, he's still Cillian because Cill sounds like an order, and the commander is Tadhg. We have been on that ship for a very long time. We all need a drink, and that's just to get started." The others smirked, rolled eyes, and grinned as Áedh began outlining the rules for the evening.

Carys tipped her head to the side and put her hands on her hips. "All right, that narrows down our options a little, but not much," she said, smiling at Áedh. "And what else might you be hoping for this evening?"

"I'm hoping to relax," Áedh said with a grin, and took another step toward Carys. There was something about his tone, the way he approached her, that was heavy with implication. "Maybe with some company."

Generys made a sound of disgust and Cillian laughed. Tadhg smirked, though there was something about the way he was watching the whole exchange. Something measuring.

"Very well," Carys said, and let her hands fall to her sides. "Let's go to the Alchemist's Guild."

Áedh did not look impressed. "Please tell me that is the name of a tavern or something, and not the result of you misunderstanding the definition of the word fun."

"By the Mother, Áedh, be a little professional," Generys snapped at him, looking mortified. Cillian reached over and gently patted her shoulder sympathetically.

Carys just smiled, amused. "You're not far off," she said, and gestured to the carriage. It didn't quite have room for all of them, and Carys offered to sit up front with the driver, but Áedh took the seat ahead of her, forcing her to sit next to Tadhg. Generys and Cillian sat across, and Carys felt another pulling, a shifting of possibilities. She wanted to follow it, but she needed to resolve the curses first.

It was a winding path through Vasi to their destination. The merchant quarter was like a crescent through the city, and they followed it down almost to the docks. There were two sides to the port: the industrial side where the workers and fishermen did their business, and the side where the merchants traded and visitors came through. The latter was the side they found themselves on, standing before an impressively large building that had likely once served a different purpose before the city expanded. A carefully carved sign proclaimed it to be the Alchemist's Guild. There were sounds of music and plenty of drunken cheerfulness (though none of the brawling that might be found farther down the way) coming from within, and from the second-floor balcony waved a number of scantily dressed men and women beckoning people to come in.

"I will never doubt you again," Áedh said with a growing smile.

"Welcome to the Alchemist's Guild, dear guests," Carys said as she stepped down from the carriage, "the greatest house of entertainment in all of Vasi, and possibly the largest brothel in all the Kingdoms of Dawn. Whether you want to drink, to relax in the baths, to be pampered, or to be indulged in any manner as innocent or sensual as you wish, it can be done here."

"You're not bothered by this?" Tadhg asked curiously. He didn't sound shocked, and she clearly hadn't offended him.

Carys just shrugged. "I've been here. Though not often, and I've never tried their more-intimate services. The baths are amazing, and you cannot get a better massage."

Generys looked almost shy, though also very intrigued. Cillian was grinning nearly as much as Áedh. "Then why do they call it the Alchemist's Guild?" Cillian asked, looking over the offerings that beckoned from the second floor.

"Because they turn wood into gold."

Four heads snapped in Carys's direction, and then Áedh and Cillian started howling. Generys let out a shocked laugh, seeming to sway between being amused and scandalized, and Tadhg attempted not to smile but failed. Carys motioned for them to follow her toward the door. She knew the bouncer—had done a seeing for him, in fact—and he smiled as the little group approached.

"It has been a while, Seer Arslan," the bouncer said with a bow of his head. She remembered Tahir was his name. "I'm sure Mistress Seyda feared you'd lost interest in our offerings."

"I'm sure Mistress Seyda wouldn't know me if she tripped over me," Carys countered, but she smiled. "It's good to see you again, Tahir. You don't come to my shop anymore, so I assume things are well."

"Very well, Seer, and I thank you," the man said, genuinely. "Your guidance was very helpful. Who are your companions?"

"Guests of Watcher Castle," Carys answered, straightening up a little. She saw Tahir gesture subtly to the other doorman, who nodded and headed farther into the tavern. "I have been charged with keeping them entertained for the evening. And surely this was the best place to come."

"You know it is," Tahir said with a grin, and turned to the soldiers with a bow of the head. "Welcome, travelers, to the Alchemist's Guild. If you wish to keep your weapons, we ask that you allow us to tie them. Otherwise, we are happy to hold on to them until you leave."

The other three looked to Tadhg, who considered for a moment, then nodded. "We will surrender our weapons," Tadhg said, and Tahir looked relieved that it had been so simple.

Ushering them in, Tahir brought them up to a small counter where a young woman waited as each of the Southerners surrendered their swords. Cillian also had an axe, and Áedh had a surprising number of daggers on him. Each weapon was marked with a ribbon and a number, and a chit with the same number was handed back. Weapons deposited, they followed a host toward an alcove with a broad table, plushly padded chairs, and heavy curtains that could be drawn for privacy.

As they moved across the room, Carys felt the curses drift. She paused in her step and motioned for the others to continue, playing as if she were adjusting her slipper. She opened herself a little, just a little, more than she had dared in their presence since that painful first attempt. The curses were still there, but Carys realized with shock that they were not actually tied to the commander or the knights, but rather to the swords they had surrendered. This was her chance! If she could get the four of them sufficiently distracted, she could come back here to look at the swords. Of course, she also had to convince the proprietor to let her into the vault to do that, but surely her being a seer, and newly the Lord of the Strait's seer, had to count for something. She just had to find the right person to ask.

That, however, would have to wait. Adjusting her shoe, Carys smiled reassuringly and joined the others in the alcove. She found herself between Generys and Tadhg, with Cillian and Áedh nearest the curtained opening. Sweet wines and sour beers were brought, along with meats and flatbreads and other foods to keep the energy up as well as blunt the effects of the alcohol.

"So why do you wear that veil?" Áedh asked quite out of nowhere after they'd gotten settled. Generys hissed at him, but Carys gave a dismissive wave.

"It's all right," Carys said, and the other woman looked a touch surprised, but also smiled a little. "Most seers cover their eyes, and for two reasons: our eyes look strange, and they're sensitive to light. I can take it off if you wish; the lighting in here is soft enough. And if it bothers you, I can put it back on."

"I will admit to having been very curious," Tadhg said, and Cillian sort of nodded in agreement.

"You might be disappointed," Carys said with a laugh, but bowed her head and undid the veil. She set it in her lap and sighed in relief, gently running her fingers over her face. Then, with a bit of dramatic flair, she flipped her hair back as she brought her head back up and looked across the table.

"Oh, shit, that's different," Áedh said after a beat, looking surprised.

"Mother, you look like you could be my cousin," Cillian commented, amazed. "Your eyes are too pale, and the rest of you isn't pale enough, but if we hadn't met you here, I would have sworn you were from the archipelago."

"You're beautiful."

The last comment came from Tadhg, and Carys looked over at him in surprise. He was staring at her in that same studying way she had seen from him before. Now there was something more, though. He looked like a man enchanted. Carys found herself blushing.

"So do all seers have eyes like that?" Áedh asked, breaking the fragile tension. Generys made another disgusted sound in Áedh's direction, and he held up his hands, perplexed. "What, it's not a rude question; I'm curious!"

Taking a breath, and somewhat grateful, Carys nodded. "Ah, yes, the fading of our eyes is actually what warns us that the gift is coming. Within a few months, we start to... see things."

"What, like ghosts?" Cillian asked.

"What? No," Carys said, confused by the fact that they would speak of ghosts so casually. "Just spirits. What do they teach you in the south? There are spirits everywhere, the manifestations of energy, ideals, emotions. No one is certain where precisely they came from, but they exist everywhere. They are the tie to the beyond, and their presence is what allows a seer to, well, see."

"I've never heard of any of this," Generys said, perplexed.

"Well, according to what you've told me, you also have no seers," Carys said, and felt she managed to effectively keep the disbelief out of her voice. "You have to be able to look beyond to see them."

"I... feel like I've heard this before," Cillian said, brows drawn in thought. "Old stories from my gran. They're hard to remember, though."

Áedh finished his beer and set it down with a heavy thud. "All right, enough about that," he said with some authority. "We're here to have fun, not contemplate ghosts or spirits or whatever."

"Ghosts aren't— You know what, you don't care," Carys said, stopping herself. "Since intellectual conversation isn't what you were hoping for, let's get a host back over here. Ring the bell on the table."

The others looked like they might have been happy to pursue conversation a bit longer, but Áedh reached over and rang the bell.

Chapter 13

THE SILVER CHIME managed to cut above the music and the din, and in a moment a stunning woman with thick ebony hair that hung down past her backside and warm, inviting eyes appeared at the end of the table. Carys looked up in shock.

"Mistress Seyda," Carys said, slightly amazed.

"Welcome, Seer Arslan and honored guests," the statuesque woman said, bowing her head. Áedh looked positively spellbound, the others more just intrigued. "I am the proprietor of the Alchemist's Guild. We are delighted to have visitors from the south after so long. How can we entertain you this evening?"

"I have ideas," Áedh said, and Tadhg punched him in the shoulder. It wasn't a light tap, either. Mistress Seyda just laughed.

"I'm afraid I don't entertain anymore myself," the mistress said, reaching over and caressing the side of Áedh's face. "However, if you like the look of me and are hoping for companionship, I think I know who can best see to your needs. But what of your friends?"

There was a beat of silence, and then Generys looked up a touch shyly. "Carys said something about baths? And a massage? I have not had any kind of beauty treatment in months, and… well…"

"Of course," Seyda said with a warmer, more sympathetic smile. "I understand exactly what you mean; we will see to everything. And what of you?" Seyda gently set a hand on Cillian's shoulder, as he was closest to her.

Carys felt that tremble again and looked up to see Generys watching Cillian with barely concealed interest. This time Carys reached with her power—their swords were tucked away in the vault; it might be safer now. Her eyes shone for a moment as she felt along the connections between Generys and Cillian, and encountered the searing heat that was Generys's love for him. It was not the same for Cillian, but the possibilities were there. He had an affection for Generys that could easily be fanned into love. Both of their emotions were buried under a heavy weight of duty and obedience to their crown, which both frustrated and confused Carys. Neither of them were zealots, so where did the weight of the burden come from?

Letting go, Carys realized she had missed Cillian's answer. Generys looked a touch disappointed, but not crushed. Whatever the older warrior had chosen, she didn't see it as a betrayal. Carys also realized that Tadhg had been watching her the entire time, his gaze fixed on her faintly glowing eyes, lips parted slightly in surprise.

"Would you prefer to stay right here, Commander?" Áedh asked, smirking, and Tadhg punched him in the shoulder again without looking before turning to Mistress Seyda.

"I apologize, ma'am," Tadhg said. "I actually think a bath and a massage sound delightful. Though I do not wish to interfere with Gen's rest or to make her uncomfortable."

Seyda waved a hand negligibly. "I assure you, Commander, I have facilities to accommodate everyone. You will all be seen to, and I would never have anyone neglected in my house. Seer Arslan, my house is open to you as well, but I would speak with you first. Perhaps we shall see your guests taken care of?"

Nodding, Carys smiled. "Of course, Mistress," she said brightly, almost eagerly. A more-perfect opportunity could not have presented itself.

Seyda turned away and held up her hand, signaling to someone over by the bar. A moment later, a gathering of some of the most beautiful people in Vasi clustered around the edge of the alcove. Áedh was sent off with a young woman as dark and elegant as Seyda, though younger and with a fuller figure. The surprise, however, came in that along with the woman in question was a man of similar features and a slender but athletic build. Áedh blushed a little and looked almost shyly at the man, but the pair of them simply smiled and led Áedh away.

"How did she know?" Generys murmured to Carys.

"It is her job to know," was all Carys said in reply, though honestly Carys wondered that as well.

A considerably more buxom and cheerful woman took Cillian away, though it looked like they were heading toward the gaming tables, and an ale was in Cillian's hand before he could take three steps. A broad-shouldered man almost as large as Cillian was just behind, and he bowed to Generys, offering her a hand to lead her to the baths. Generys followed, pink-cheeked and charmed. Finally, a slender woman with chocolate curls and a spritely dancer's step came up to take Tadhg off. Carys thought it interesting that there was nothing flirty in the woman's approach, but Tadhg did not seem disappointed, and followed with a smile.

"You're confused about my last choice," Seyda said, smirking at Carys.

"She does not feel as if she matches his desires like the others did," Carys answered honestly, and shrugged a little.

Seyda shook her head and sighed. "I am not certain if you are being intentionally obtuse or not," the mistress said, and motioned for Carys to follow, "but there is only one woman in this building, perhaps in all the port, that Commander Bharda would like in his bed this evening. However, one does not just proposition the Lord's Seer, especially not a foreign officer."

Carys had the grace to blush, and the sense not to protest. Tadhg was fascinated with her, she had to accept that. But then Carys's eyes narrowed, and she looked up sharply at the mistress of the house.

"How do you know his name?"

Laughing softly, Seyda paused for a moment, and looked back at Carys. "We'll discuss it in my office."

Carys followed Mistress Seyda through the tavern, to a door tucked to the side and hidden underneath a tapestry. Carys had seen people come in and out of this door only a handful of times in past visits. Stepping through, she found herself in a well-lit hallway that went down a short ways and turned to the right. Mistress Seyda made sure the door behind them was securely shut, then led the way down the hall, taking the turn, and then to the end of the longer hall where there were two doors. The one on the right was noticeably heavier, and Carys realized it must lead to the vault. Seyda opened the door on the left, which turned out to be a rather comfortable office.

"Welcome to my quiet corner," Seyda said, smiling as she sat down at the desk and motioned for Carys to take one of the armchairs. "Very few patrons ever see this room, so I would appreciate you not discussing it with others."

"Of course," Carys said, settling in and looking around curiously. There was an elegant simplicity in here that was missing from the lush, almost gaudy tavern they had just left.

"I was surprised you were so willing to come speak with me," Seyda said, drawing Carys's attention back to her. "You must know I intend to ask a favor of you."

"I do," Carys answered with a wry smile, "and you must suspect that I intend to ask one in return."

Seyda laughed, and it felt as if she relaxed a little. "Of course," Seyda responded, and pulled a cord on the wall by her desk. "I appreciate your candor, Seer Arslan."

"I hope I will be able to appreciate yours as well," Carys commented, and Seyda let out another soft laugh.

The office door opened, and a pixie of a woman popped her head in. "Did you need something, ma'am?"

"A light wine, Rana," the mistress said with her perpetual smile. "Nothing too strong, something appropriate for conversation."

"Yes, ma'am," the pixie responded, and then the door closed again.

"Shall we lay out our cards, then?" Carys asked after she heard the door click.

"Interesting turn of phrase," Seyda said, folding her arms on the desk before her and leaning forward. "Because laying out your cards is precisely what I hope will happen. I need a reading, Seer Arslan, and I want it from the best. I also want it from someone I can trust. Your reputation precedes you, and you are now in the employ of the Lord of the Strait. I cannot imagine anyone more suited."

Nodding slowly, Carys tapped her lower lip in thought. "I can look beyond for you, but I cannot do it tonight. While I have traditionally made it a habit to always have my cards on me, having someone else dress you can disrupt your routine."

"And how is Watcher Castle treating you?" Seyda asked. "How are you enjoying being elevated from a fortune teller to the advisor of the Heir?"

Carys's eyes narrowed again. "I suppose next you're going to ask if I really did seduce the Heir, since I was apparently no more than a fortune teller. Though I'm not sure why you need my services if I'm so lacking in ability."

With a little push, Seyda sat back in her chair and held up her hands. "I apologize, Seer Arslan. You do not tell fortunes—you seek guidance from the spirits. I know you are not a charlatan. I was hoping to needle you into revealing something. Which I suppose you did. I take it you are not bedding the Heir of the Strait, then?"

"If I answer, will you tell me why you care, and why you know who Tadhg Bharda is?" Carys asked, also leaning back.

"Yes."

Sighing, Carys reached up and rubbed the spot between her brows. "No, I am not bedding the Heir of the Strait. We have a... flirtatious relationship, but it is currently nothing more than that."

Seyda nodded. "I suspected you were not. He has been here enough times since your appointment, and Asil Özdemir is not what I would describe as voracious."

"Oh, has he?"

"Yes, him and the Lord Commander," Seyda continued, looking amused at Carys's irritation. "They're a delightful pair to entertain. All the girls love them."

The threads shifted, and Carys looked at Seyda. "The boys, too, I would guess."

Seyda looked very surprised. "You know? That is privileged information, Carys. You took a risk revealing it to me."

Carys smiled a little. "I could see that you already knew."

"Ahhh, of course." Seyda nodded to herself, looking at Carys carefully. Seyda had perhaps another ten years on Carys, maybe even more; it didn't really show in her appearance, but it was in her eyes, a knowledge that came with experience. "I pay someone to feed me information from the castle. Several someones, in fact. I am not a member of the Great Families, though this business of mine is profitable enough that I should have one of the lower seats, but they would never allow it. Not a woman with no family. Not a whore who worked her way up. Yet, the decisions made in Watcher Castle, between the Lord of the Strait and the heads of the Great Families, affect me and mine. I need to know what is waiting around the corner."

That was a great deal more candid than Carys had anticipated. It seemed Seyda would be honest with her after all. "Thank you, Mistress. I will return to read the cards for you."

A smile lit Seyda's face. It did not bear much resemblance to the one she wore out on the tavern floor, and Carys suspected this might be Seyda's real smile, the one she saved for when she was being herself.

"Thank you, Seer," Seyda said genuinely. "What will you require of me in payment?"

"I need access to your vault," Carys said, and grew nervous as Seyda's eyes went wide in shock. "Tonight, before my charges are done with their pleasures. I will take nothing out, but I need to see their swords. The blades... there is something about them I need to know, but I cannot ask the knights to study them. I don't think Tadhg or the others would mind, but the ambassador cannot know that I looked at them, and I don't think they could keep from reporting it."

The mistress's face had moved from surprised to carefully neutral. "What do you hope to find?"

"I cannot entirely say," Carys said, frowning a little. She didn't want to have to explain how the weapons were cursed, or to give away the secrets of Asil's reading, but she also needed Seyda to trust her. "I do know, however, that someone in their chain of command is lying. About their intentions, about why they're here."

"And if you are worried, then the Lord of the Strait is worried," Seyda murmured, continuing to look at Carys carefully. There was a long quiet as the two women regarded each other. The tension was broken as Rana returned with the wine.

"Thank you, dear," Seyda murmured as Rana set down glasses and poured out a rosé into each glass, then bowed and took herself out. Seyda picked up her glass and looked over at Carys. "I will agree to it, with a condition."

Picking up the other glass, Carys looked over at Seyda. "Which is?"

"If I allow this," Seyda said carefully, her voice even, "you will let the Lord of the Strait know that I aided you."

An interesting request. "Why?"

"Because Pasha Kaplan wants to expand his warehouses," Seyda said matter-of-factly, "and because I had already petitioned for one of the buildings he hopes to annex. It needs to be approved by Watcher Castle. I need to make sure the Lord of the Strait sees me more favorably. Though given how often the nobles are here, you would think I shouldn't need to."

"They're a fickle bunch," Carys said sympathetically, and held up her glass, to toast and seal their arrangement. "I will be happy to inform the Lord of the Strait that you assisted me."

"Very well," Seyda said, and clinked her glass against Carys's. They both drank the entire contents of their glasses, the deal made.

"So," Seyda said, setting the glass down, "do you wish to go now?"

Standing, Carys nodded. "Yes. I don't know how long it will take."

Seyda nodded and rose as well. They went across the hall, and Seyda fished out a ring of keys to unlock the door to the vault.

"Whoever works the vault is locked in for the evening," Seyda explained as she began to undo the series of locks, "and you will be locked in as well, though I will stay in my office until they ring and I come to let you out. I am the only one who can. Worry not, I will have a drink sent in, and there is a latrine should you need it."

Carys nodded, and Seyda turned the lock. The door needed a good tug to open, it was so heavy, and by the time it was wide enough to allow Carys through, a young man was standing at the other side, looking confused. Seyda explained the situation as Carys drifted past, easily finding what she sought without direction. Curses twanged the air like discordant music; they were easy to follow. She pulled the swords down one at a time, careful not to disturb the ribbons that marked them. She distantly heard the heavy door close, and the young man set wine and a pitcher next to Carys with a mumbled "Pardon me, Seer," then stepped away.

Reaching over, Carys picked up the glass and poured herself more wine, taking a healthy swallow before setting it down and focusing on the first sword. She had unraveled curses before. The first time had been a bit of a mess, but each subsequent unraveling became easier. They tended to be tricky, like undoing a knot, and you needed to find the end. Her eyes began to glow as she turned the sword over in her hands. This was Tadhg's sword—she could tell by the wrap of the hilt, which matched the colored slashes and the more-elaborate crest on his uniform. It would have been commissioned for him, and just him, when he achieved his rank. She brought him to mind, the picture of him, his dark hair that looked almost black in shadow, and his eyes that rivaled the summer sky. Carys felt something in the sword begin to stir.

She followed that stirring, and let out a startled sound when, suddenly, the binding began to unravel. She could see the pattern now and was amazed at how simple it was. No seer worth their title would put so little work into a binding. Carys had gone in expecting a complex entangling of the spirit and its energies and found simply a child's bow that could be pulled loose by anyone who understood how and where to pull.

"Seer Arslan, are you all right?" the nervous young man from the desk asked, coming over.

"What—oh! Yes, I'm sorry, I'm fine," Carys said looking up, slightly annoyed at the interruption. The young man stepped back, startled by her glowing eyes, and she looked away quickly. "Sorry, sorry. You can return to the counter; I promise, all is well."

Turning back to the sword, Carys could feel where the bound spirit rested. She gently stroked the crest at the hilt. "Come on out," she murmured, coaxingly. "Come and let me see you."

There was a wriggling under her hand, and from the crest emerged… a bee. A honeybee, specifically, large and fuzzy. It was big, the size of a small bird, and it turned in place, looking at Carys with its unreadable eyes, before it began to clean its antennae.

Queen?

The word vibrated in her head with a buzzing. "I don't know," Carys murmured, looking at the creature. "Your Queen is gone. You can leave now too."

The spirit crawled off the sword, looking around. It didn't seem attached to the object, now that it was free. Carys checked the sword over, wanting to be certain that the binding was truly gone. It seemed impossible for a curse to be handled so negligently. The object was clean, though. Perhaps it was because it was an object. The sword would not have fought being bound. People fought bindings, whether they knew of them or not. It was the essence of freewill. Frowning and perplexed, but driven, Carys set the blade aside and picked up the next. This one appeared to be Generys's.

The process was simple, and even faster the second time. She brought an image of the lovely, cold knight to mind, the spirit started to stir, and she pulled the binding loose. Another bee wiggled out of the sword and looked up at her.

Queen?

That was bothersome, and the combined buzz was beginning to be jarring.

"No, no queen," Carys said as she set down Generys's blade and reached for Áedh's. "You can go."

The bee wandered off a little, finding the other spirit nearby. They seemed to greet each other. These were strange little spirits. Carys had seen nature spirits before in the world, even bee spirits, but these were different. They were larger by far, and they didn't ignore her the way most nature spirits ignored people. They still showed no attachment to the swords, though, so Carys continued. Áedh's sword went even faster, and another little bee spirit wriggled free.

Queen?

Sighing, Carys ignored the little spirit and shooed it away to greet the others. They seemed happy to be together. She picked up Cillian's blade, the last one. Once again, she brought an image of him to mind, and she felt wriggling. She followed the feeling and found slightly more of a binding than before. That was interesting. She looked at the binding again, trying to determine the purpose. What did these little bee spirits do? They didn't harass the bearers of the swords like spirits often did in a curse. And the only thing the bees seemed to care about was their Queen—

"The queen," Carys said out loud, eyes wide, as she pieced it together. "Duty, obedience. This is why their sense of duty is so abnormally strong. Your obedience bleeds off onto the swordbearers."

Reaching once more, Carys found the ties and pulled loose the curse on Cillian's sword. Not one but two bee spirits emerged from the crest, climbing over each other and looking up at her. Something in Cillian must fight harder against that sense of duty, and whoever did this took extra pains to make sure he toed the line.

Queen?

Thankfully, the double buzz was not worse than the individuals'. "No, the queen is gone; you are free now," Carys said, putting Cillian's sword back. The little bees really didn't seem to care about the weapons, as they didn't follow when the weapon was moved, the way a spirit would chase a person it had recently been unbound from. That was good, at least. Also, there did not seem to be anything residing in Áedh's daggers or Cillian's axe. That was even better.

Standing, Carys picked up her wine and finished it. She felt a little lightheaded and tired, but the process had been far less draining than she had feared. Now that the bees were unattached, they would likely disperse soon. There was nothing about the brothel that spoke to their purpose; they would see no reason to stick around. Now she just had to contemplate why on earth the Ealdorlang Empire would do this to their people.

"Are you finished, Seer?" the young man asked hopefully.

"Yes, thank you," Carys answered, and stifled a sigh as he didn't quite run over to pull the cord to summon Mistress Seyda. She had frightened him. The woman manning the counter (there were two people in here, one at the counter, one running things back and forth) giggled a little, amused by his discomfort.

It seemed only a minute passed before Carys heard the locks turning on the door. She left the vault and was greeted by a very curious Mistress Seyda. Carys stepped to the side while the mistress relocked the door, then turned back to the seer.

"Did you find what you were looking for?" Seyda asked, arching an eyebrow.

"Yes and no," Carys said, smoothing back a stray lock of hair. "Or rather, I did find answers, but they simply lead to more questions. As they often do."

Smirking, Seyda gestured back down the hallway. "There is truth in that," the woman said as they began to walk, "but did it help?"

"Yes," Carys answered honestly. "It has given me a deeper understanding of their magic, how they do things, and it also tells me that the lies begin higher up."

"That sounds very useful indeed," Seyda said as they approached the door behind the tapestry. She was quiet for a moment as they both got to the other side. "Well, you will be pleased to know that your activities took just shy of two hours in total, and that your companions are still very occupied. So how might we entertain you, Seer Arslan?"

Sighing, Carys considered. "A massage. And tea. With an extract for my oncoming headache."

"At once, Seer."

Chapter 14

ON THE WAY back to the castle, Áedh regaled the carriage with the highlights of his evening, which saw him punched twice by Tadhg, once by Cillian, and even once by Generys. Carys merely rolled her eyes, but the driver laughed so hard he had to stop the carriage a few times. By the time they'd reentered the grounds of Watcher Castle, however, everyone's sense of decorum had been restored. The carriage dropped the party off at the cottage, where Carys made a polite goodbye.

After, she allowed the carriage to bring her back around to the front of the castle rather than walking through the grounds as she had that morning. Up the right staircase, past the portraits of former Seers to the Lord of the Strait, then down the hall with the tapestries of flowers and unicorns. Stepping into her room, she let out a sigh and removed her veil.

"Long day?"

Looking up sharply, Carys found herself glaring not at Judex but at Asil. "Aren't you in the wrong wing?"

Laughing, Asil came over and held up a box. "I'm sorry, Carys; someone was supposed to have told you I was waiting for you," he said, presenting the box to her. "I promise I don't make a habit of lurking in your room. I have a gift for you. Will you accept it?"

Sighing again, Carys smiled at Asil and took the box. "Oh, I suppose I can't be upset if you have gifts," Carys said as she moved into the room, box in hand, and set down the veil. She saw that he had also called up a late supper, and that made her smile soften and grow fond. "You might be too good to me, Asil. How was dinner with the ambassador?"

"Oh, it was horribly tedious," Asil said cheerfully, and Carys snickered. "I still want to kidnap his secretary—the poor girl always looks so miserable. The ambassador has asked permission to stay in the city longer while he resupplies and becomes more familiar with the lands farther north before he chooses his next destination. Even without you there, I'm confident he's lying about his intentions to move north. He has been granted permission by my father and the other noble houses to rent an old barracks that has sat unused in the Eastern Port. They'll use it as a base of operation, a place to conduct trade and store the goods they buy for their journey, and also somewhere to house the soldiers on the ship and potentially allow even more of them off at a time. It won't house everyone on that ship, but it will allow more than a quarter of the combined company and crew to offload, and it sounds like he'll let them trade out every week or so. As of right now, he insists they will not remain more than two months."

Arching an eyebrow, Carys sat down at the table and poured herself some tea. "I suppose they could still travel even after summer ends; the farther north they go, the warmer it will become, unless they travel all the way to the Frozen Coast," Carys mused, thinking. "They could spend the winter near Miterathea if they wanted to avoid icy seas. Though let's perhaps get back to the fact that we are giving them a barracks? So that's, what, fifty or more soldiers can move freely through our city?"

Sighing, Asil sat across from her and picked up a peach. "I know," he whined before taking a bite, "and I tried to point that out as diplomatically as possible. For as much as he's clearly a weasel, Peadar is good at what he does. The representatives all cleared it, and it would have made Father look paranoid not to. It would have also implied Father was not confident in Lord Kilic's guardsmen, which would have been a different problem."

Carys frowned. "How?"

"The guard outnumbers those soldiers, by about four to one," Asil explained between bites. "And that does not include any Irregulars in the countryside. An outright assault would fail. Should fail."

Carys's frown deepened. "I seriously doubt anyone as perfidious as the ambassador would rely on an outright assault."

Asil nodded and tossed the pit of the finished peach lightly onto a dish. "He certainly will not," Asil agreed, "but you can't just accuse someone of being duplicitous without proof. So, they get the barracks, and we have fifty more problems."

Sighing, Carys picked up the other peach and ate as she looked out the window into the deepening twilight. Asil watched her for a moment and started to grin.

"A little bird told me you took the soldiers to the Alchemist's Guild," Asil said after a moment, and Carys glanced up as if caught. "I'm guessing you didn't make your way to the second floor, based on how you looked when you came in."

Carys almost choked on the peach, and Asil laughed. After a moment she managed to swallow, and then set the rest of the fruit down.

"And how would you know that?" she asked.

"You were flushed," Asil answered with that same grin. "Like you were the night we met. You need to indulge more often, Carys; that kind of tension isn't good for a person."

"Ass," Carys muttered, and sipped her tea to further clear her throat. "I hear you've been down there multiple times."

Asil had the grace to look a little sheepish. "Yes, well."

"Well, why don't you come with me next time?" Carys took another bite. "You can make a recommendation, and I'll do my best to take it."

Laughing again, Asil winked at her. "Deal. Though if I'm paying, do I get to watch?"

Carys snickered. "Isn't your father paying?"

"Semantics."

"I'll think about it."

Even more laughter, louder and echoing. "This is why I like you, Carys," Asil said. "Open your gift."

"Oh, right," Carys murmured as she looked down at the box she'd set on the table. Undoing the simple latch, she opened it and gasped, stunned. Inside was a necklace and matching earrings, pearls interspersed with violet stones set in silver. It was old, likely an antique, and it would have bought her grandmother's shop twice over.

"Asil," Carys began, wide eyes, "I can't… I mean—"

Asil held up a hand. "You can, and you will. There is a precedent," he explained, retrieving a small cookie off the tray of sweets. "Calm down, it's not my grandmother's or anything; I promise I'm still not courting you."

Shock gave way to irritation. "I pity the woman you do marry," Carys said blandly.

"The entire kingdom will weep for her," Asil agreed without a blink. "But this set actually belonged to one of your predecessors, a former Seer of the castle. She was a woman who seemed very fond of jewelry. I'm having most of what we found redone into something more modern, but this set had a timelessness to it that I thought you would appreciate."

Closing the lid carefully, Carys looked at Asil with a quirked brow. "I feel like you're implying the other jewelry will also be mine. Asil, I don't need this."

Sighing, he looked up at her. "You're being obtuse," he said, and shrugged when she glared. "You are! Carys, you accepted the position as the Lord's Seer. Technically you're the Heir's Seer, but since that title doesn't exist, you're the Lord's Seer. Which means you dress for court and formal events. Which includes jewelry. Carys, I know this wasn't what you had in mind; the Mother knows it wasn't what I had in mind either. But if I have to play nice with the other families and jump through their hoops, then so do you."

Letting out a long sigh, Carys leaned back in her chair. "Fine, you're right," she said, looking down at the box. "I'm sorry, Asil. Thank you, it is beautiful. And you were right, I do like it. I am simply still… adjusting."

Asil rose up from his chair with a smile, this one softer and sympathetic. "I know it's a lot," he said, coming around and dropping a kiss on the top of Carys's head. "It's a lot for me sometimes, and I was born into it. You're doing fantastically."

Smiling a little, Carys reached out and squeezed Asil's hand. "Thank you," she said, then brightened up. "Oh, I almost forgot! I figured out the curses, the ones I could feel when we greeted them!"

Asil looked at her, excited, and then the clock chimed, and he cursed under his breath. "I very much want to hear about this," Asil said, almost pouting, "but it will have to wait until tomorrow."

Carys blinked. "It's early."

"I know," Asil said with a bit of a glare. "I'm meeting with more representatives from the Great Families this evening, and there will be drinking and attempts at negotiations and more drinking. You will not see me again until tomorrow, where I will likely be hung over."

"I know how to make something for that," Carys commented dryly. "Maybe I'll risk the wrath of the kitchens and see if they have what I need."

"I would be in your debt." Asil leaned down and kissed Carys softly, then pulled away and headed for the door. "Tomorrow! Breakfast!"

Exhaling sharply, Carys watched him go and shook her head, then turned back to her food.

☾ ☾ ☾

"…Good thing it's impossible to make it in less than five doses. Can you fetch another of the bottles from my room?"

"Of course, seer."

"And send Aylin for more food should you pass her. I hadn't anticipated an additional guest."

Asil groaned and slowly opened his eyes, then closed them again as the sunlight drove daggers into his skull. "Nazim, the curtains," he muttered, putting a hand over his face.

"I've got it. Please do what I asked of you." Carys's voice was not harsh, but it was commanding in a way that Asil felt he would admire if everything wasn't awful. The room grew darker, and he tried to open his eyes again.

"Did you have water before bed?" Carys appeared next to the bed, bending over and brushing Asil's hair back from his face.

Asil made soft, happy sounds and set his head back on the pillow as Carys's fingertips ran through his hair. She had such a gentle touch.

"No," Asil murmured, and he heard Carys sigh.

"Well, that is definitely part of the problem," Carys muttered. "Can I assume Hasim is in the same shape?"

"How would I know?" Asil had closed his eyes again. When the petting abruptly stopped, Asil opened them again. "Why did you stop?"

Blinking, Asil looked up and focused on Carys's face. She had not yet put her veil on, so her hair was still down, a wry smile on her lips and amusement in her mist-gray eyes. She gestured with her head to the other side of the bed. Still blinking, Asil rolled onto his back, and he could see Hasim fast asleep beside him. They were both still mostly in their underclothes, though Hasim had managed to remove his pants. Both Asil and Carys stared at Hasim's bare ass for a moment, with no small amount of admiration.

"Mother, we were very drunk last night," Asil murmured, a little astounded.

"I'm noticing that." Carys sounded like she wanted to laugh. "Let me help you up; I've got something to make you feel better."

Strong hands lifted Asil into a sitting position, and he looked at Carys in some amazement as she got him up and put some pillows behind him. He wasn't enormous, but he also was not a delicate man, and he was too busy struggling to wake up and shake off his hangover to help much. Once she had him settled, Carys looked up at Asil and tipped her head to the side.

"Why are you looking at me like that?" she asked, and stepped away to retrieve a bottle on the table that contained a deeply red tincture.

"You continue to surprise me," Asil said honestly, settling back against the pillows and getting comfortable once more.

"It sounds as if you mean that as a compliment," Carys said, smiling. She uncorked the bottle, then presented it to Asil. "I add as much cherry and raspberry syrup as I can, but it will have a bitter finish. Better to just drink it all in one go if you can."

Accepting the bottle, Asil looked at it for a moment then took a deep breath, let it out, and drank down the whole thing. It tasted fine at first— berries, faintly herbal. As he finished, however, the aftertaste struck him, and it was vile. Carys presented a glass of water to Asil as he tried not to retch. The water helped.

"That's the best you can do with that?" Asil asked grumpily, and Carys smirked, taking the glass away.

"You're lucky I made it, and not my grandmother," Carys said as she set the cup down. "She thought the vile taste was a fitting punishment for people stupid enough to get that drunk. I at least try to make it better."

Asil was not amused. "Your grandmother sounds surprisingly petty."

It was quiet for a moment, and even hungover, Asil sensed he might have crossed a line. He watched Carys pour out tea and place a dollop of honey and a slice of lemon in it, just like Asil liked it. When she turned back toward him, however, she looked thoughtful, not angry.

"You may actually be right," Carys said, handing the short glass to Asil. "I remember her being very angry fairly often. Never at me. She was bitter that neither your father nor your grandfather had appointed a Lord's Seer. Most likely because it would have been her. And she grew sharper toward the world after my mother died."

Asil took a careful sip, and leaned back with a sigh, already starting to feel better. "How old were you?"

"Ten," Carys said, understanding. She poured another cup of tea, this one for herself. "I remember her being… frail. She had always had a hard time with winters, and I understand giving birth to me was very trying for her. She was too sick for even my grandmother to help. I… I knew she was dying months before she did. The spirits showed me. I think Grandmother knew as well. We still tried."

"I don't know how you couldn't have," Asil said, watching as the shadow of sorrow that passed over Carys's face lifted. "I was two. I don't remember my mother. Hasim does, and we've talked of it before, but even his memories aren't clear. He would have been six. He says he remembers her giving him sweets when his own mother had told him no."

Carys smiled. "A charming memory, then."

The door opened again, and Nazim came in with another tray, a smaller one. He set out the additional food and extra pot of coffee, as well as two more red bottles. "Is there anything else, my Heir?"

"Tell the baths to be ready in an hour," Asil said, sitting up. "Thank you, Nazim."

The young man bowed, then looked cautiously at Carys. "My lady seer?"

"Just seer is fine, Nazim," Carys said, and Asil tried not to smile at the slightly weary look on her face.

"Yes, my seer," Nazim said, shifting a little. "I… was asked if I knew where you were, my seer. It seems your presence has been requested. The party from the south will be taking lunch with Pasha Koc, and the pasha was very insistent that you also be there."

"Oh, Mother." Carys ran a hand over her face. "Of course he was."

"Timur Koc?" Asil asked and started to smile. "He was the one gushing over you at the party. Called you Sundrop, yes?"

Carys sighed. "Yes."

"You'd better hurry; it's rather close to lunch," Asil said, and was rewarded by the glare Carys shot in his direction.

"Next time I'm not going to help you," she said, and grabbed a cheese roll and a fresh coffee before heading toward the door. "Make some time for me! I still need to talk to you—it's important!" And then she was down the hall, the door closing behind her.

On the bed next to Asil, Hasim stirred and picked up his head. "Was that Carys?" Hasim blinked and looked over at Asil. "This… is not my room. Mother, how much did we drink last night?"

"Enough to forget," Asil said as he climbed out of bed and stretched. "How are you feeling? Carys left a remedy. The taste leaves something to be desired, but it seems to be remarkably effective."

"I'll take it."

Asil dragged Hasim into a sitting position, significantly less kindly than Carys had for him, and handed over the bottle. "Drink it down, and don't pause until the end if you can manage. It's fine going down, but the aftertaste is dreadful."

It was somehow unsurprising that Hasim had less trouble getting down the concoction than Asil had, and likewise seemed less bothered by the taste. It didn't take long after that for the two of them to get moving, have breakfast, and be about their days. For Asil, this largely meant a bath and returning to his rooms to pore over the notes on his desk. It seemed that he'd had the foresight to document what had been discussed before he, Hasim, and the heirs of the Great Families drank themselves into stupors.

In his stack of notes, however, was a letter. Specifically, it was a letter from Serhat Yasuv. Serhat had not been there yesterday—something about an engagement negotiation. Asil could distantly remember the letter being delivered by a retainer of Pasha Yasuv's household. Asil cracked the violet wax of the seal and unfolded the paper.

The letter began very cordially and full of regrets, about what Asil expected. The second page, however, was more intriguing:

...should be brought to your attention, my Heir, that your guests have made a point of becoming acquainted with each of the Great Families. My father himself entertained Ambassador Criddubh just yesterday, though my father did not care much for the man's company and I would be most surprised to see your guests darken our doorway again. Perhaps most remarkable, however, is the fact that Pasha Kaplan has seemed to have become great friends with Ambassador Criddubh. Given how little Pasha Kaplan cares for any company, let alone that of someone outside of his exceptionally small inner circle, it is something to remark upon, is it not?

With a furrowed brow, Asil set the letter down. Muhan Kaplan was self-serving and motivated by money, power, and little else. What did he think he could gain from an alliance with the Ealdorlang Empire? And why was the ambassador calling on the Great Families? Asil had arranged the first meeting for the purposes of Peadar's claim for trade, but Muhan Kaplan traded in gemstones and jewelry. Why was he interested? For that matter, what was today's lunch with Timur Koc about? Pasha Koc dealt in books and antiquities.

Sighing, Asil folded the letter back up and locked it away in the top drawer of his desk. As he had told Carys last night, he could not accuse Peadar of being duplicitous without proof. This was very interesting information to have, but it was a small piece and not terribly actionable. Yet. Opening another drawer, Asil penned a response to Serhat, thanking him for the letter, congratulating him on his engagement, and expressing a desire to meet and discuss matters of the kingdom soon. There was little else he could do.

Chapter 15

LUNCH WITH TIMUR KOC had been, while not precisely humiliating, possibly counterproductive. The food had been quite lovely, and had included a thin, heavily spiced soup that was so flavorful Carys had requested the recipe. The problem was the conversation. Carys had found herself the subject of discussion for most of lunch, as Timur went on about her beauty, her kindness, and her talent. He spoke of her grandmother, of Carys's little shop in the merchant district, and about how proud he was to have known Carys before she "ascended to her rightful place in the castle!" Peadar had grown weary of the conversation early into lunch and had tried to steer it toward other topics several times. But Pasha Koc was in his cups, as was his wont, and the man could be quite difficult to steer under even ideal circumstances. Timur addressed Carys more often than not, tried to get Generys to eat more, and tried to get everyone to drink more. Áedh had been happy to oblige.

Deviating from the schedule, a visibly aggravated Peadar returned to Watcher Castle immediately after lunch, tasking Tadhg and Áedh with escorting Carys on her brief tour of the cleaning and resupply of the barracks, after which Carys was to oversee another evening out. Cillian had returned to the ship to oversee the transition. Generys had landed the unfortunate task of escorting Peadar back to the castle. Now that their curses had been lifted, Carys no longer held herself tight around the soldiers of the south, and she could feel the disgust that hovered beneath

Generys's very careful, cold veneer. She was a loyal soldier of the Empire, but she had no respect for Peadar.

As the carriage pulled up before the almost squat, stolid building in the port, Áedh all but leapt from the carriage and offered a hand to Carys. He smiled at her as she accepted and stepped down.

"It's nice to know you're one of us," Áedh said brightly, and Carys blinked in surprise.

"One of you?" Carys wasn't offended by the comparison, simply confused.

"A commoner," Áedh said, still smiling. "Or, you were one. You're a normal person under your station. One of us."

"Áedh," Tadhg said, a warning in his voice.

Áedh ignored it. "So how did you get a position in the castle?"

"Oh." Carys turned pink, matching the deep rose of her veil. "I… well, as Pasha Koc said an unfortunate number of times, I am very good at what I do. My abilities came to the attention of the Lord of the Strait, and I was given my position and place in Watcher Castle."

"Yes, a position under the prince." The implication in the tone was impossible to miss. Carys's head popped up, and her veil hid her eyes widening in shock, but not the clenching of her teeth.

Áedh looked surprised. "Is something wrong?"

"You—" Carys stopped as she saw the indigo wisps behind Áedh. Judex had been drawn by Carys's discomfort, no doubt. The shade stepped away from Áedh, grinning. Carys took a deep breath and managed a polite, apologetic smile.

"I'm sorry, I thought I heard you say something," Carys said as the two soldiers regarded her curiously. "Obviously I was mistaken."

"About so many things," Judex interjected.

Thankfully, Áedh's smile returned. "Glad it was nothing." Tadhg looked less convinced, but otherwise didn't comment.

The doors of the barracks were open wide, and soldiers from the ship were busily and cheerfully straightening things up, bringing in fresh bedding from crates in the small courtyard. It looked as if they had missed most of the cleaning process. The soldiers saluted Tadhg and greeted Áedh less formally. The lack of beards was strangely off-putting, as it made many of them look younger than Carys could sense they were. The ones that did have beards reminded her of Cillian—they were brushed and either braided or banded, not kept short like she was used to. There were two women out of the twenty or so people running about, both more-solidly built than the fair knight back at the castle.

Stepping into the barracks themselves from the courtyard, Carys immediately felt the shrill vibration of more curses. She set her teeth and took another steadying breath. Maybe she would have an opportunity to do something about it.

"Everyone seems happy to be off the ship," Carys remarked as they walked.

"Well, aren't you a riveting conversationalist," Judex remarked as he floated ahead of her.

Oblivious to the spirit, Tadhg turned to Carys and nodded. "We all are, Seer Arslan. The voyage was trying in many ways. We are fortunate to have found not only a populated region, but such a hospitable one. In truth, we weren't certain what to expect, and feared we'd find nothing but ruins and remains."

"That is true farther inland," Carys remarked. "It is said that the once-great cities were abandoned in the calamity that created the Cliffs of Dawn; with trade collapsed and ships destroyed, the surviving populations migrated back to the coasts."

"The what?" Áedh looked confused.

Judex sighed. "Oh, joy, another bright one." Carys felt bad, but it was nice to have Judex's ire pointed elsewhere for once.

"The Cliffs of Dawn is what we call the eastern coast," Carys explained, stepping around a couple of soldiers fixing one of the old beds. "Vasi is a member of the Kingdoms of Dawn."

"That is interesting," Tadhg remarked, brows furrowed. "I was under the impression that you didn't have a central government, that you were all disparate kingdoms."

"We are allied," Carys explained, "but you're right that we don't have a central government that rules all the different kingdoms. I understand that your empire is different in this."

Áedh nodded. "Yup! The Empire has taken many of the neighboring lands in the south under their wing, uniting us into a greater country."

"I wonder if Cillian thinks so." The words were out before Carys could stop them, and Tadhg looked at her sharply. Judex simply laughed, entertained by her bumbling.

The conversation was halted as a young soldier, likely barely in his seventeenth year, timidly approached with a question for the commander. Carys motioned for him to see to it as she roamed the building. She began to follow the discordance, moving slowly to make it seem as if she were taking everything in, nodding to the people setting things up. She stepped through a door and found the armory.

Racks of swords shone in the room, and a wave of nausea passed over Carys as the curses rattled through her brain and down her spine. So many! Not every sword, though. A small mercy. Carys summoned her power as she headed toward the first rack. She needed to be quick, and it would be a little dirty as a result, but if these swords held the same bee spirits, she didn't need to worry about having the time and finesse to see to a proper banishment. Reaching forward, she pulled, and she felt the unraveling.

"Come out!" Her voice was a harsh whisper in the small stone room. As expected, a bee came forth, large and fuzzy, and flew around her almost joyfully.

Queen!

Sighing, Carys concentrated and pulled again. Another unraveling, another bee. This was taking too long; she'd barely get through any of them before Tadhg or Áedh returned, and there were ten in this room. She held up her hand and concentrated, trying to pull power the way she did when she was angry sometimes. She saw it coalesce at her fingertips, like frost gathering on a window in the winter. She reached, and this time instead of pulling loose the binding, she sliced through it with ephemeral claws.

Queen! Queen!

Gasping, Carys took a step back and put a hand to her head. It had worked! But it had been exhausting. Her hand tingled as if it were covered in actual frost, and she flexed her fingers, trying to get rid of the sensation.

"Seer Arslan?"

Turning around, Carys looked up to see Tadhg regarding her with concern and perhaps some suspicion. She knew her eyes were glowing— she hadn't had enough time, so there was nothing to do about it. She took a step forward but had to pause to steady herself. In a breath, Tadhg was next to her, gently holding her up.

"Carys, are you all right?" The suspicion was gone from Tadhg's voice, only concern left in its wake.

"Yes." Carys took a breath and felt herself calm, the power retreating. She became aware of the fact that Tadhg was still holding on to her. She looked up at him and smiled softly. "I think I can stand now, Commander."

"Of course." Tadhg stepped back, though Carys thought his hand might have lingered a moment as he pulled away. "Should we return you to the castle?"

"And ruin your evening? No, I'll make it." Carys smiled again. "Perhaps food will improve my bearing."

Not entirely convinced, Tadhg simply nodded, and Carys let herself be escorted out of the barracks and back to the carriage. Even though she hadn't had time to dispel all the curses, she was feeling fairly elated. She had done something she didn't know was possible. Had her grandmother known? In all their time together, Carys had never seen her grandmother wield her power in such a way. Tracing the threads of fate had been hard when Carys was younger, but now it was almost like breathing. Perhaps this skill could also be developed. Furthermore, Judex seemed to have disappeared about the time Carys had begun trying to break the curses, so clearly the evening could only get better from here.

As they left the barracks, they were intercepted by Generys, who had been sent down with a message for Tadhg. Whatever the message was, it didn't stop the commander from climbing into the carriage with Carys, Áedh, and now Generys. It was generally accepted that they would be returning to the Alchemist's Guild, and Áedh excitedly urged the driver to go faster. It was a short trip from the new barracks to the Guild. As they disembarked in front of the entertainment house, music drifted out the windows, louder and more lively than their last visit.

"That's different," Generys remarked, though she looked hopeful, perhaps even excited.

They made their way through the doors, and the others surrendered their weapons as they had the last time. They were shown to a table, not a private curtained one like before, but a more-central table with comfortable chairs that allowed them to see the animated trio playing music as people danced. A young woman in a short vest and loose pants spun as she fiddled, while a man sat next to her playing a tambur and another kept the beat on a set of nakkare drums. Drinks were brought, and they had barely settled when a smiling man approached and asked Generys to dance. Generys looked as if she wanted to, but blushed and shook her head. Undeterred, the man turned and asked Carys. Carys considered, then nodded and allowed herself to be pulled out onto the small dance floor.

When Carys returned to the table, flushed but smiling, Mistress Seyda was chatting amicably with her three charges. The mistress of the house smiled as Carys approached, and Carys was grateful that she had remembered to bring her cards. She still owed Seyda a reading, and she imagined tonight would be the night that debt was paid.

"It is nice to see you dance, Seer Arslan," Mistress Seyda said as Carys retook her seat. "I hope the rest of you will find your ways onto the floor before you retire to your pleasures. Alara is one of the best fiddlers in the kingdom, if not the entire coast, and we are delighted to have her here this evening."

"It does look like fun," Generys said, still a touch pink. "Though, it… doesn't mean anything, does it? Accepting a dance."

Carys looked at Generys in surprise, but Seyda simply smiled. "No, lovely," the mistress said, "a dance is simply a dance. Here, especially."

The music changed, and a cheer went up from the room as women flocked to the floor. "Ah, *The Rain on Water*," Seyda said, looking over to Carys. "Seer Arslan, while I would normally never presume, might you be willing to show this dance to our dear knight? To help her warm up?"

Stifling a sigh, Carys stood and smiled. "Of course!"

As Carys came around the table, Generys stood and leaned in to murmur to Carys. "But… we're both women."

"Not that it much matters, but *The Rain on Water* is a folk dance," Carys explained, and took Generys's hand. "While anyone can dance it, it's mostly taught to girls, so we usually just dance with each other. You'll like it."

As Carys pulled Generys out onto the floor, she remembered the Midsummer party and Emiri Bulut dragging her over to dance. Carys couldn't help but be amused that she was now in the role of instigator. She held Generys's hands, guided her through the steps, and attempted to ignore the fact that Tadhg appeared to be watching her raptly. It was distracting having the dedicated admiration of a handsome, intelligent man. Oh, certainly Asil's attraction was flattering, as was Hasim's flirtation, but neither of them wanted Carys the way Tadhg did. She could feel it when she let herself think about it too long. Carys wasn't sure anyone had ever wanted her so much. It was… rather stimulating, if she were forced to admit it.

The dance ended, and the two women returned to the table, Generys smiling in a way Carys had never seen in the short time she'd known the other woman. Carys drank half a glass of cold apple wine as Generys let herself be taken back out for another dance, the hurdle effectively crossed. Tadhg and Áedh discussed the music and food and compared them to things back home as Carys sat quietly and let them relax. Before too long, Áedh disappeared with the same pair of beauties as last time, and Tadhg turned to Carys.

"Would you favor me with a dance, Seer Arslan?" Tadhg asked, his smile easy and pleasant, though there was a tension coiling between his shoulders.

Carys smiled and stood. "I would be happy to, but please, call me Carys while we're dancing. This place is too lively for formalities."

Laughing, Tadhg also stood. "Of course."

While Tadhg took Carys's hand and led her out to the floor, he was careful not to let his eyes linger on her for too long, often looking around rather than at her. As he turned his head, Carys saw a scar running along his collarbone, visible now that he was just in his shirtsleeves with the collar of his shirt open. His hand at her waist felt warm, and he held her close—not inappropriately so, but closer than might have been considered proper given their positions. Carys, relaxed and just a touch intoxicated, bit her lip. Then against all logic, she slid her hand up his shoulder so that she could brush her thumb against that scar.

"Where did this come from?" Carys asked, tracing over the jagged line. Tadhg drew a ragged breath as she did.

"A skirmish, when I was still a man-at-arms," Tadhg said, finding his voice. He lost his step for a moment but recovered. "Carys, what are you doing?"

"Testing you," Carys said simply. That caused Tadhg to look at her in confusion and irritation, but at least he was looking at her.

"And what, exactly, are you testing?" Tadhg asked.

"I know you desire me, Tadhg," Carys answered, and the irritation left Tadhg's expression. Carys smiled a little, and her fingertips danced lightly over the exposed skin. "But I'm not sure how much."

The commander let out a soft laugh. "It hardly seems professional to tell you."

Carys slid her hand back down his shoulder. "Not that much, then, it seems."

"Oh, I see," Tadhg said, beginning to grin. He pushed her away a moment for a spin, then pulled her back against him, more tightly than before. "It's not that you don't think I want you, but you want to know if I'm willing to do something about it. Carys, if we were alone, I would kiss you until neither of us could breathe, and then I would remove that dress and do everything I could think of to make you cry out for me. I want to hear you say my name as you tremble. I would not stop until we were both completely spent. Is that what you wish to hear?"

"Yes," Carys breathed, eyes wide and cheeks lightly flushed. "There is a garden behind the guest villa. You are the only dignitaries visiting at this time. Will you meet me there? Tonight?"

"Yes."

It was only one word, but it was spoken firmly and without hesitation. Carys felt the tension coiling in herself as well. This was foolish, but his want was like a sweet wine and she was thirsty for it. She wanted him, now, but this was not the place, and she had just enough sense to know that she should probably not be seen being overly familiar with the commander of what was, potentially, an invading army. Her chest rose and fell as she took a deep breath.

"There is an arbor, heavy with vines that bear night-blooming lilies," Carys said, her voice just loud enough to carry to Tadhg's ears. "I will go there at 10, after the court is dismissed. I will stay until midnight. If you are not there by then, I will leave, and never speak of this again."

"I understand," Tadhg said, his voice sounding almost strained.

They did not speak again. The song ended and they returned to the table, after which Tadhg left almost immediately for the baths. Carys had another glass of wine as Generys danced a bit longer, finally returning to ring the silver bell and have herself taken to the baths as well. It was then that Mistress Seyda returned.

"You look like you enjoyed yourself this evening," Seyda said with her perpetual stage smile. "Are you ready for me, Seer Arslan?"

"Do I get to boast that the mistress of the house makes time for me and me alone?" Carys rose from her seat and smoothed the front of her dress.

With a wave of her hand, Seyda motioned for Carys to follow her back over to the tapestry, ducking down into the quiet hall. "You could, if you wished," Seyda said after a moment, "but I would bet you 10 gold obols that you don't enjoy the company of women."

"Not in the manner you're implying, but no one else knows that," Carys said with a bit of a smile. "I doubt I can make my reputation much worse in the castle at this point, and this might make it better."

Mistress Seyda smiled sympathetically, and unlocked her office, ushering Carys inside. "Wine?"

"Coffee actually," Carys said, fishing into the folds of her dress to unhook the pouch that held her cards. "I've had enough wine already this evening."

"Of course." Seyda pulled the cord and walked back to her desk. As she sat down, she looked pensive, and Carys's brow furrowed. The possibilities shifted, and Carys tipped her head to the side.

"I'm not here to read for you," Carys said, and Seyda looked up in surprise and chagrin.

"I'm sorry." The mistress of the house sighed and leaned back in her chair. "I did not mean to bargain with you under false pretense. I thought that was what I needed. As I said last time we spoke, I pay many people for information, but none of those sources could find the answers that I sought."

The conversation was halted as Rana opened the door and stuck her head in. "Did you need something, Mistress?"

Seyda pulled up her stage smile. "A glass of wine for myself, and coffee for Seer Arslan." She considered for a moment. "Make it the way the young Lord Özdemir likes it. Also, please tell Havva I need her."

Rana looked surprised but nodded. "Of course, Mistress."

The door closed, and Seyda looked back to Carys. "Havva will inherit this place someday," she said, expression still. "She is not my daughter by blood, but she is my daughter by law, and by my heart. She has not been well. I've been to every herbalist and physician in the city, save yourself. However, something new has come to light. I no longer think there is anything natural about her illness."

Carys's eyes glowed, and she saw what Mistress Seyda was trying to say. "You think she's cursed."

Seyda nodded. "Is she?"

The light behind Carys's veil flared. "Yes."

Chapter 16

RANA RETURNED WITH a tray and a young woman. She was tall but too thin, her skin sallow, the luster gone from her hair. She looked like she hadn't slept or eaten in days. Rana set the tray down, and the young woman made her way to the other chair before Seyda's desk, nodding to Carys politely and folding her hands in her lap after she sat down. She shivered, and Seyda was immediately there with a blanket, wrapping it around the ailing woman.

"Havva, this is Seer Arslan," Seyda said, her voice soft. Havva looked up.

"A pleasure to meet you, Seer Arslan," the woman said, in the most beautiful voice Carys had ever heard. It was quavering and weak, but it was like a harp being played, even in this state. Carys was stunned.

"Hello, Havva," Carys managed after a moment. "I hope that I can help you today."

Havva let out a short, bitter laugh. "So many have tried, Seer Arslan. I have a hard time discovering hope. I have asked Seyda to let me die, though she won't hear of it."

"I'm so sorry," Seyda said, pain in her voice, "but… Havva, I can't! While there is still a chance that we can help you, I cannot let you do that! You are the only daughter I will ever have, I cannot just—" The mistress of the house broke off, voice full of emotion.

"I know," Havva murmured, closing her eyes, and tears streaked down her cheeks. She opened her eyes and looked back to Carys. "I am starving, but I can barely eat. I cannot sleep, and what little sleep I have is plagued with nightmares. Every day I grow weaker, and sometimes I feel like I'm losing my mind! I don't know what day it is anymore—I just lay in my room and cry! Poppy tea helped in the beginning, but Seyda won't let me have it anymore."

"No, I understand why," Carys said, wincing. Poppy tea was something used in emergencies, not daily. Carys's grandmother had told her about how people became dependent on it.

Whimpering, Havva put her hands to her face. "I just want it to end. I don't... I don't really want to die; I just want it to end!"

"I'm so sorry," Carys said, feeling tears in her own eyes. "Once... once we begin, if I do not address you directly by name, know that I am not talking to you, and you should refrain from answering anything you hear from me. Do you understand?"

Both women nodded. "What do you need, Seer?" Seyda asked.

"Dim your lamps, please, and bring me a table to cast my cards upon."

Seyda waved, and Rana immediately began to move through the room turning down the lamps. Carys reached up and removed her veil. It didn't interfere while doing readings, but this was different. She let her eyes relax and soften, and slowly she was able to see the spirit behind Havva's curse.

A serpent the color of bile with strange markings was wrapped around Havva. It constricted at her throat and under her ribs, and its head hovered over Havva's shoulder. It had the face of a woman, almost, though still with the fangs and wide mouth of a snake. It was nightmarish, far more so than Carys's own persistent spirit. She took a deep breath, and then pulled her cards out of her pouch. Standing up, she approached Havva.

"Here, Havva," Carys said, handing over the deck. "Hold these for a moment, and if it is not too uncomfortable, hold them to your body... here." Carys gently brushed her fingertips along Havva's neck, her hand passing through where the snake was wrapped. Havva nodded and did as instructed, and Seyda brought over one of the side tables for Carys. It was a little small, but it would do.

"Why are you here?" Carys murmured, looking at the spirit. Havva looked up but remained silent.

"Puniiiiishhhhh," the spirit hissed, a black forked tongue flickering from its mouth.

Carys's brow furrowed. "Why?"

"Sssssssssssssslut. Puniiiiiiiiiiishhhhhhhhhhhhhhh."

Tsking, Carys gently took the cards from Havva. Spirits existed along a spectrum. This appeared to be an ideal spirit, like Judex, but less sophisticated. Noxious, vile. Someone was very unhappy with Havva for something. Carys flipped over four cards in a cross shape. She would find out.

As Carys's eyes began to glow, Seyda stepped up behind Havva, adjusting the blanket around the younger woman's shoulders and holding her lightly. The spirit hissed, unhappy. It didn't care for Seyda's love. It didn't want Havva to have it.

"The caster is from Veli," Carys said, eyes focused on the cards before her, "but the person who commissioned the curse…"

"You can see who cast it?" Seyda asked, surprised.

Carys didn't answer, her hands drifting over the cards. One stood out. She picked up the card depicting an infant swaddled in a cradle. "Havva, you had a child? No… no you rid yourself of one. Recently?"

"A few months ago," Havva said, brows furrowed.

"With silphium," Seyda offered, unsure where Carys was leading. "But these aren't the side effects of silphium!"

"No," Carys murmured, "these are the side effects of a scorned lover. A scorned lover who thinks he was cheated out of a son, not even understanding that the child was never his."

Havva gasped. "Tabeeb. He knew I had refused clients, due to the morning sickness. When I saw him again, after I had been purged, he was angry, accusatory."

The light in Carys's eyes flared. "Yes. Did he give you something? Something just before you fell ill? I need it."

Havva's brow furrowed. "Yes, as an apology for the fight. A tourmaline necklace."

"Rana, can you get it?" Seyda asked, and the girl nodded before darting from the room.

The spirit hissed, angry, and tightened. Havva gagged, but cleared her throat and took a breath. Carys set her teeth, her eyes still aglow. It did not surprise her that the caster was from Veli. There was a time when no seer would curse for money, but something had changed among the seers of the River. It was particularly rare to see a curse come so close to killing the afflicted. Most curses were meant to be a long-term burden, the afflicted never quite aware of it. This Tabeeb had wanted Havva to suffer and die.

A moment later Rana returned with the necklace. Carys accepted it, and turned it in her hands, examining it. It was very lovely, a string of tourmaline beads that shaded from pink to green. The curse was woven into the string, and cleverly done. It wasn't like the bees and the swords. This curse wasn't actually attached to the string; instead, the necklace merely made it easier for the spirit to find Havva. Carys grimaced. The first curse she'd ever unraveled had also been anchored in a necklace.

"Seyda, a knife," Carys said, and Seyda had one for her in an instant. Carys held the blade, considering, then concentrated on the tip. When it began to glow with the same light as her eyes, Carys sliced through the string.

The spirit shrieked, angry, and Havva gagged again, but Carys got to her feet and approached with the glowing blade. Seyda watched, silent and confused, tears in her eyes as Havva suffered, but she seemed to trust that Carys knew her business. Carys could feel the bindings that wrapped around the girl and the spirit, and pulled at them even as she stepped up and set the blade against the coil around Havva's throat. "Let go."

The snake spirit hissed. "PUNIIIISSHHHHH!"

Carys pressed the blade into the coil, and the spirit screamed. "Let go," Carys repeated, undeterred.

Another angry shriek, and the snake spirit uncoiled from Havva, dropping to the ground. Havva's eyes grew large in surprise, and she gasped, taking a full breath like a swimmer just breaching the surface of the water. She then started to cry again, relieved and amazed. Carys, however, was still advancing on the snake spirit, who thrashed angrily, spitting, not content to be torn away from its task.

"SSSSSSSLUT!" The spirit shrieked, but continued to back away from Carys, afraid of the knife. "PUNIIIIIISHHHHHHH!"

Darting forward, Carys drove the knife into the coils again, which parted before the empowered blade. The spirit screamed, thrashed, and then dispersed, becoming nothing but a mist that only Carys could see.

With shaky breaths, Carys looked at the knife in her hand. With the anchor broken, the spirit shouldn't be able to find Havva again, and would hopefully fear another encounter. Carys had never banished a spirit like this before, calling on the power to manifest the way she did, but it had worked, and it had been a damn sight faster than any banishment she had done in the past. Standing back up, Carys returned to the table, set down the knife—which no longer glowed—and began to gather up her cards. Havva sobbed into Seyda's arms. Seyda was also crying, stroking Havva's hair and comforting her.

"Rana," Carys said softly, and the girl startled, looking at Carys in surprise. "Bring Havva something to eat. Perhaps a thick broth to start; she will need to go slowly."

A smile lit Rana's face, and she darted forward to hug Carys before running off. Carys put everything away and sat back down again, picking up her coffee. It wasn't quite hot anymore, but it would do, both to keep her awake and to stem the potential oncoming headache.

Rana returned with the broth, setting it on the table Carys had been using a moment ago, and skipped out of the room. Havva had cried herself out, and Seyda was looking at Carys once more.

"What you have done for me is worth so much more than what little I gave you," Seyda said, her eyes still shining from the tears. "I will find a way to make this up to you, Seer Arslan. You will never pay for anything in my establishment ever again, but that is not enough. That is not enough for restoring my daughter and my legacy."

It seemed impossible to respond to such a thing. Telling Seyda that she needn't worry would be considered insulting, and Carys could not say that it had been a simple task. She could feel the strain and fatigue from the banishing settle into her. She simply smiled and bowed her head, drinking the rest of her coffee.

It took a bit of intervention to keep Havva from gulping down the contents of the bowl, but she finished the soup and briefly teared up once more in happiness and gratitude. Rana was sent for more, and both Seyda and Carys helped Havva eat until she was drowsy, then sent her off with Rana to be bathed and put to bed. Seyda also teared up many times throughout the process and kept looking at Carys as if she were the Divine Mother herself.

"Is there nothing you can think of, nothing I can give you?" Seyda asked after Rana and Havva had left. Carys just shook her head.

"I am sorry, but I want for nothing," Carys said, spreading her hands helplessly. "Or rather, nothing that can be just given."

Sighing, Seyda nodded. "I understand. I will consider, and we will see what the future brings. But I owe you, and I pay my debts."

Carys tipped her head to the side. "I suppose you won't let me say that you do not, and that I was happy to help someone who so dearly needed it?"

"You are correct." Seyda smiled a little.

Carys spread her hands again. "As I suspected."

Rana returned to take Carys back to the main room, and Carys was left comfortably at the table with another cup of coffee, this one fresh and hot. She sipped contentedly, listening to the music and gently refusing further dances. The coffee was starting to help. By the time her charges began to return from their activities, Carys was feeling bright and perky enough to at least make it back to the castle without falling asleep in the carriage.

As they disembarked, Tadhg looked back at Carys with a fire in his eyes that made her faintly blush. Generys was relaxed and unobservant, but Áedh arched an eyebrow in Carys's direction and grinned as if he understood what might be happening. Carys hoped the bland expression she met him with was convincing.

Returning to the castle proper, Carys immediately sent Aylin to ready the baths, and reflected that for all of the frustrations related to living in the castle, having someone draw the hot water and make everything ready was a rather pleasant perk.

Chapter 17

CARYS DOZED IN the baths as the heat penetrated her limbs, and the warm, still quiet allowed her to relax. It wasn't until Aylin came back to check on Carys that she woke up and climbed out of the water that was now moving from warm to cool. Looking down at her pruned fingers, Carys sighed at herself. It was still almost two hours until she was to meet Tadhg in the gardens. It would go away by then.

"Shall I bring you some tea, my seer?" Aylin asked as they returned to Carys's rooms. "Something soothing before bed?"

"Actually, I have some things to attend to," Carys said, smiling gently at her maid. "If you could bring me some coffee and a light snack, I would appreciate it. Where is the Heir?"

Aylin looked apologetic. "The Heir is at a dinner at his aunt's estate this evening, my seer. I believe his cousin has been betrothed and will be leaving for Fas in the morning."

Asil had mentioned an aunt before, the day that the ship had arrived. For some reason Carys had assumed she lived elsewhere. "Where is his aunt's estate?"

"It's actually outside the city," Aylin said, perking up, happy to have answers, "down the Mendicant's Road along the southern cliffs, about an hour away by carriage, from what I understand. Lady Elif Özdemir married Lord Dimitris Chrysos, but when the lord died, Lady Elif returned to Vasi and had her great-grandmother's summer retreat restored. I understand our High Lord did not approve, though no one will speak of it!" The girl giggled and turned pink, enjoying the breath of scandal.

Nodding, Carys smiled at her maid; she always enjoyed seeing Aylin open up a little. "So, he will not be back at a reasonable time this evening. Unfortunate. Can you please tell Nazim to let Asil know that I need to speak to him in the morning?"

"Of course, my seer." Aylin curtsied and ran off.

Carys wandered over to the window, looking out at the lights sparkling across the darkening city. She wasn't certain Asil would want to hear about what she was intending with the commander. Part of her was fairly convinced she shouldn't be doing this at all. But she kept thinking about what Tadhg had said, and how immediately he agreed to her proposal. Asil was her friend, but she couldn't see how they would take the step into being lovers. They were attracted to each other, true, but pursuing each other seemed impossible. She thought about what she and Hasim had discussed, how Asil was caring but not passionate. She cared for Asil. More than she had for anyone since her grandmother died, if she were being honest. And yet, there were so many complications. He was the Heir of the Strait. Half the castle already thought Carys had slept her way into her position. They were both so busy. Tonight, what she intended with Tadhg—he wanted her so desperately. It was intoxicating. She was in no danger of losing her heart to him. The corner of her mouth quirked up. They had told her to befriend the commander and his knights, hadn't they?

The click of the door brought Carys out of her musings as Aylin returned, setting down a tray with coffee, a few biscuits, and a small plate of fruit. "Will there be anything else, my seer?"

"No, thank you," Carys said smiling. "I will review the notes I wished to share with the Heir, and then perhaps walk the gardens. You needn't worry about me tonight, though I will wish some time in the baths tomorrow morning and I will need a generous breakfast."

"Of course, seer," Aylin said, practically glowing, and Carys internally sighed. She highly suspected that it wasn't the free evening but rather the fact that Carys had actually given Aylin so many instructions that made the girl so happy.

As the clock struck 9, Carys tried to read. After she'd reread the same page three times, she gave up. Heading over to her closet, she considered her ensemble. What she was currently wearing would be more difficult to slip back into, and the blouse would show dirt. Something different, then. Flipping through the closet, she came across a simple dress of a knit material, though the neckline was daringly low. She had heard about these dresses—it was a fashion that came from Veli. They were for lounging and entertaining casually, typically among friends and lovers. She wasn't sure why one had been included in her wardrobe, other than being fashionable because it was new. It would do for tonight.

A little before the agreed upon time, Carys descended the south staircase and headed out into the grounds. Guards nodded to her and smiled but left her about her business. She wore the soft gown, wrapped in a voluminous but lightweight shawl, and her gray lace veil over her eyes. Her hair was down and had curled up almost into ringlets after the bath without any further brushing or styling. She reflected with some amusement that no one would think she was meeting someone. No makeup, not enough jewelry—a noblewoman would never have left for a tryst in so little.

Laughing at herself, Carys headed down the stone path between the peach trees, still heavy with late fruits. The smell was divine. She crossed a small footbridge and then passed over the lane that separated the guest cottages from the castle proper. Rather than heading toward where the guests from the South were staying, she skirted the building and found the path that led back into the ornamental gardens. She smiled to herself as she walked down it, remembering the party that had started it all, so to speak. The blossoms were already fading from many of the branches, though the late-summer lilies were just beginning to open.

It wasn't long before Carys passed under the arbor, which led to the balconies that oversaw the sea. As she approached, she saw movement and was more than a little surprised to see that Tadhg was already there. He had foregone his armor, wearing only the lighter undershirt and leather breeches. As his eyes landed on Carys, he smiled like a child at a sweetshop with a pocket full of obols.

"You came," Tadhg said softly, as if he couldn't entirely believe it, stepping forward and holding out a hand to her.

"Of course I did," Carys responded with a laugh and took his hand. "It was my idea. How long have you been waiting?"

"Since the day we met," Tadhg answered, and pulled her in against him.

In all of Carys's life, she had never been kissed the way Tadhg kissed her. There was such hunger, a desperate desire. His hands moved into her hair, finding the ties for her veil, which he undid and pulled away. He kissed across her cheek, tasted the nape of her neck, and breathed her in as if he were a man drowning. Carys melted against him, overwhelmed. It seemed like ages since she had last been touched like this. She could feel his want; it vibrated the possibilities around her and consumed everything. Other thoughts and considerations fell to nothing—there was only this man, his hungry mouth, his strong hands holding her against him, and the fragrance of lilies. No further words were spoken as Tadhg continued to kiss her with fervor and pulled away her shawl, his surprisingly nimble fingers undoing the buttons of her gown. Every inch of skin revealed was covered with kisses, tasted, and touched. Tadhg kept the promise he made when they danced, and it wasn't until Carys cried out his name, quaking with pleasure, that he finally sought to relieve the want that had been burning in him.

Afterward, as they rested on a padded chaise with Carys's shawl laid loosely across them, Tadhg smiled almost sheepishly as he looked over the woman he held.

"You are perfect," he said softly, adoringly. Carys lifted her head and smiled at him, brushing his hair back from his face.

"Was it everything you imagined?" Carys asked, her smile playful.

"And more," Tadhg responded, shifting positions so that Carys was lying atop him, and he could look up into her strange eyes. "It wasn't too much in the beginning, was it? You seemed so surprised, but also so… responsive."

"No." Carys settled against him and folded her arms on his chest. "It was not too much. You were not too much. You were glorious."

Tadhg's hands slid down her sides, settling on her hips. "Never in my life would I have thought you would agree to this. Do you think you would agree to it again?"

With a giggle, Carys shifted slightly in his lap. "What, now?"

That got a laugh, but Tadhg's hands on her hips tightened. "Absolutely now, but I was also hoping for the future."

Something twanged through Carys at those words, and her smile fell a little. "I… you mean in a few days, but you want… you want more than that. And I can't give it."

"I'm not stupid," he said softly. "I am aware of who we both are. I know this won't last. I'm just trying to see how long we can continue to dance."

That felt true. Carys hoped it wasn't just because she wanted it to be. Leaning in, she kissed Tadhg once more and let him take the lead. One more dance.

When Carys returned to her room, she was beyond exhausted. She had exercised her gift too many times that day, and then had a very energetic evening with a man in peak physical condition. She didn't quite stumble into bed, but it was a near thing. She lay there, warm and more relaxed than she had been since before she'd come to the castle. She hoped there would be another opportunity with the commander soon.

And yet, she couldn't stop herself from wistfully thinking of Asil as she drifted into sleep.

(((

"My Heir?"

Stepping down from the carriage, Asil looked at the nervous guardsman standing before him. The same guard that had barged in on his meeting with Peadar, if he wasn't mistaken. It was well after midnight, Asil had lost count of how many toasts there had been, and all he wanted was his bed.

"If you're here to tell me Adnan is upset about something happening in the harbor again, I will run you through with your own blade." Asil was probably going to hear about this later, but he didn't care. The guard winced.

"No, my Heir," the guard said, looking to the side. "Your father has requested your presence, with urgency. He is in the North Parlor."

That was very odd. Asil nodded and followed the guard down the hallway. "Can you tell me what this is about?"

The guardsman lowered his voice. "I have been instructed not to speak of the matter in the halls, my Heir, but to tell you only that an emissary came to retrieve the satchel taken off one of their scouts."

"Satchel..." Asil's brows furrowed, then smoothed as his face went still with realization. The party that had been attacked by the guards on the western border. Carys had said that many things in the satchel were expensive. It must have represented more of an investment than he realized if they sent someone to parlay for it.

The guard darted ahead and opened the door to the North Parlor, and Asil strode in, head up and mindful of the impression he might make, drunk or not. Within the parlor Asil saw his father seated in a high-backed chair, Adnan at his side and Hasim standing just behind the two of them. Lale Aydin sat a little behind, off to Egemon's left, pretending to be a scribe and doing an admirable job in the role—her mother would be proud. There was an empty chair next to Egemon, and Asil nodded to the room and took the seat that was clearly his without a word.

Across from them were two of the most fascinating people Asil had ever seen. A woman of middling years sat in a chair, her hands folded in her lap, her expression almost eerily still. She didn't look relaxed—she looked like she was waiting, hovering in a moment as the rest of the room moved around her. Most of her clothing was leather, as exquisitely tooled as the satchel that had brought her to the castle, over undyed linen that hung in a manner which implied their weavers were as talented as their leatherworkers. Behind her stood a man Asil would prefer not to fight, large and well-muscled, his bare arms covered in elaborate tattoos. They all seemed to be of a piece, a pattern that flowed together, and were surprisingly colorful. Tattoos in Vasi and Veli were most often in a deep indigo ink, sometimes a deep red, but there was little variation. He likewise was mostly clad in leather, painstakingly tooled, and the two curved swords strapped to his back were dutifully tied. From the way the man held himself, Asil doubted he needed them.

"Elder Cehsa," Egemon said after Asil sat, "this is my son. He was attending a family gathering this evening, hence his late arrival."

The still woman gave a small nod. She had been looking down, but her gaze lifted as she briefly regarded Asil. Her eyes were pale, green-blue like the shallow sea, and an even-more-striking contrast to her deep sepia skin. They were not as pale as Carys's eyes, but they reminded Asil of her gaze so strongly that he would have bet his rings that this woman was also a seer. Perhaps that was what "elder" meant to these people?

"Greetings, young prince," Cehsa said, her accent lending a lilting quality to her speech. It was almost musical. "I hope our presence did not pull you away from your family. We came unannounced, and we would be aggrieved to have caused any inconvenience."

"No, Elder, I just arrived home of my own accord," Asil said, hoping he didn't sound drunk. He didn't think he did.

Egemon cleared his throat. "Elder, if we could return to what you had mentioned. You say you are here to retrieve the satchel but also to negotiate safe passage?"

"Yes." The woman's movements were so minimal it was difficult not to wonder if she were some sort of strange, magical puppet. Asil would have to ask Carys if that was possible. The guard behind her was not so still, shifting his weight regularly, looking like he would pace if it wouldn't be considered rude or aggressive. He was obviously uncomfortable, and he glared at Adnan and Hasim in their uniforms.

"We recognize that we can no longer come to the shore in secret," Elder Cehsa continued, "and we would prefer to avoid any further skirmishes with your men."

"And why should we allow this?" Adnan was clearly aggravated by the idea, based not only on his question but how he spoke out of turn.

One eyebrow lifted, but otherwise the elder's face did not change. "Well, to begin, we would stop killing your men."

Adnan drew himself up, ready to roar, but Hasim set his hand on his father's shoulder, and Egemon took in a deep, audible breath through his nose. Somehow, this was enough to make the old warhorse quiet himself. Egemon raised his eyes to Cehsa, who in turn looked down.

"I apologize," the elder said. "That was tactless. It is, however, true. We do not suffer casualties from these encounters, though we have taken many injuries and lost some amount of items and coin. Despite my rudeness, we do not wish to fight with you or injure your people. However, we need items that come from the shore. Traders no longer follow the river as far north as they once did. As your people have built their kingdoms along the coasts, the forests continue to lay forgotten. We would have met each other eventually. It is better that it happens now, before either of our cities came for the other in force."

A flicker of emotion entered Cehsa's voice toward the end. There was something plaintive there, hiding behind her stillness. This was important to the elder. This was personal, on some level.

"You are right," Egemon said at last. "As our people grow, we would have found each other in time. Better that it happen now, when there is still an opportunity for a peaceful alliance."

"Yes." Asil could hear just the barest tremble of relief. The enormous guard behind her relaxed as well. He seemed surprised that Egemon had agreed so readily.

"Do you have the authority to agree to the terms of a treaty?" Egemon asked, and Cehsa grew still for another breath before giving a slight nod.

"I speak for the guardians of our borders," Cehsa said, choosing her words carefully, "and I can bring a treaty to our... I think you would call her our queen."

"Understood." Egemon rose to his feet, and the rest of the room rose with him, Cehsa included. "Let us retire to my study and discuss the terms of this agreement. Lord Captain, if you will come with me. My Heir, Lord Commander, you are released for the evening, though I thank you both for joining us on such short notice."

Asil bowed his head. "Of course, Father."

Everyone was quickly bustled from the room, Lale following close behind in her role as scribe, though she did turn and wink at Asil and Hasim before she left. Asil sighed once the doors closed and ran a hand through his hair.

"You're holding it together damn well," Hasim said with a grin. "Pretty sure I only know how drunk you are because of how often I've seen it."

"By the Mother's tits." Asil almost collapsed back into the chair. "I just want my fucking bed."

Laughing, Hasim came up, put an arm around Asil, and began to steer him out of the parlor. "So, the mysterious people from the forest have faces now. What did you think of the elder?"

"She's a seer." Asil put his arm over Hasim's shoulder and let out a relieved sigh, even as they started up the servant's staircase. "I'd bet on it. Her eyes aren't as pale as Carys's, but they have the same gaze."

"Huh," Hasim said, looking over at Asil and almost tripping over the strange stone lip on the top stair. "That's very interesting." Hasim let go of Asil long enough to push open a door behind a tapestry and let Asil shuffle past.

There was another relieved sigh as they stumbled to Asil's door and pushed through. "Where was Carys, anyway? I feel like she should have been there for this."

"Asleep," Hasim answered, pulling Asil's jacket off his shoulders. "I tried to send someone for her, but all I got in return was a very apologetic note from her maid saying that Seer Arslan had exhausted herself today but that she needed to speak with the Heir at his convenience in the morning."

Asil pulled off his shirt. "It will have to wait. She's accompanying Peadar to another meeting with Muhan Kaplan in the morning. That'll be fun for her."

Hasim tsked. "Why is that weasel seeing Pasha Kaplan again?"

Kicking off his shoes, Asil shrugged. "Trade, ostensibly. They did bring some rather pretty gems that look like the water in the harbor, even in a relatively rough cut. I'm sure Muhan could sell them throughout the Kingdoms of Dawn. I don't trust it, but what am I going to do?"

Hasim's hands slid up Asil's back to his shoulders, and Asil sighed as Hasim worked at the tense muscles. "You'll need to find time to talk to her soon. Isn't this the second time she's asked for you?"

"It might be the third," Asil admitted, simultaneously sheepish and frustrated.

The hands on Asil's shoulders let go for a moment, and then Hasim's arms came around him, his friend's skin warm against his own. It seemed Hasim had also managed to get his jacket and shirt off.

"We can't do anything about it tonight," Hasim murmured in his ear, "and you've had a long day. Maybe we should relax?"

Asil let out a small laugh. "Will you get mad at me if I admit that I wish Carys was also here?"

"No," Hasim said, sounding amused. He let go long enough to turn Asil toward him. "I wish she could be, too. Not just because you want her. She looks… adventurous."

Laughing harder, Asil nodded. "I suspect she might be. She has a strength I've never encountered in a woman. Not just in her character, but also physically."

"Hopefully someday she'll let you or the both of us test her endurance," Hasim said with a shameless grin. Asil laughed again and pulled his friend in for a kiss.

Chapter 18

IT SEEMED ALMOST as if the spirits were working against Carys. She knew that spirits didn't work that way, and she knew her craft well enough to know that she was not cursed or battling someone's petty vengeance, but she was starting to become frustrated. Getting time with Asil was proving to be impossible. She rose in the morning with the intention to go seek him but was immediately dressed and bundled off to Muhan Kaplan's estate. There she endured the most uncomfortable breakfast imaginable; Pasha Kaplan seated her at the opposite end of the very long table, making it almost impossible to participate in or listen to the conversation. During the tour of the pasha's workshops and stores, she was forced to ride in a separate carriage, and Muhan glared if she came within ten feet of him. By the time she returned to the castle, Asil was off on some errand for his father.

The following two days were remarkably similar. Pasha Nacar, who was assisting with the renovations of the barracks, was initially more civil toward Carys than Pasha Kaplan had been but found every possible way to make backhand comments about her birth and her "simple little shop," and almost outright asked her if she was having an amorous affair with the heir. Twice. Returning to the castle, Carys learned that Asil had been sent to Veli and would not return until the following evening.

On the next morning, when the ambassador met with Pasha Reis, the pasha was a great deal kinder, and treated Carys with the respect due her office. The meeting with Esin Reis ended surprisingly abruptly, however, with the pasha almost throwing Peadar out of his house. Pasha Reis hollered about loyalty to the Lord of the Strait while Peadar bowed and scraped and stammered about misunderstanding the question. Carys felt something tingle up the back of her neck and heard Judex laughing as she quietly followed the sullen ambassador back to the carriage. She did pause long enough to thank Pasha Reis for his hospitality.

"Be careful, Seer Arslan," Esin said, looking past her at Peadar. "Men like him plot. It's all they know."

The carriage ride back was miserable, Peadar too embarrassed to hide his disdain of the low-born woman shadowing him. Carys was fighting her own battle maintaining her civility. She needed to talk to Asil. She needed one day without having to speak with Peadar or endure a condescending glare. When they returned to the guest cottage, Peadar tromped out of the carriage without a word and headed inside, yelling for his secretary as the door swung behind him. Carys sat in the carriage for one more moment, sighed, then moved to climb out, only to find Tadhg waiting to offer her a hand down.

"It seems the day's meeting didn't go well," Tadhg said in a low voice, something faintly apologetic in his expression. "I won't keep you, seer, though I wondered if perhaps you might be available for a tour of the gardens this evening?"

Thankfully, Carys was not so irritated as to misunderstand what Tadhg was requesting. "Yes, of course," she said, hoping she wasn't blushing. "The same time, then?"

With a smile too happy to be professional, Tadhg nodded, then headed back into the villa. Carys ran a hand over her face and turned to walk back to the castle. At least there would be something to look forward to this evening. Something to take her mind off of the last few days. Perhaps even lift her spirit, unwind this knot of stress that had been building between her shoulders. With luck, Asil would also be back this evening, and she would corner him in the morning whether he liked it or not.

"This continues to be one of the worst ideas you've ever had," Judex pointed out as Carys headed up the grand staircase toward her wing. It was still early in the day, and the Lord's Hall was quiet.

"Well, fortunately for us all, it can't possibly continue for much longer," Carys commented dryly. "In the meantime, like everything else in my life, it does not actually affect you, so I don't see how it is your business."

"Someone has to remind you to stop embarrassing yourself," Judex countered, and Carys clenched her teeth. She was too frustrated to deal with Judex right now, which was likely why he was there. He sought her still moments and her times of weakness.

Carys turned down the hallway and glanced around. "I don't know why you can't just shut up and leave me alone," she murmured, keeping her voice low. The hall was thinly populated, but people were still there.

"Make me," Judex said, an unexpected edge to the words. Carys stopped in the hall and looked over at him. She was used to derision from Judex, but not aggression. Not a challenge.

Taking a breath, Carys continued toward her room. "You know I can't."

She heard a derisive snort over her shoulder, and then nothing. When she glanced back, Judex was gone. She was under the clear impression that she had disgusted him, and it made her uncomfortable in a manner she didn't completely understand.

Sighing, Carys headed through the door and rang for Aylin. Tea would help. Tea held civilizations together; it would get Carys through to the evening.

☾ ☾ ☾

As Asil stepped out of the carriage, tired and smelling faintly of brine, he reflected that he was growing weary of guards with pensive expressions awaiting his return home. At least he wasn't drunk this time. Asil stepped up to the guard in question and arched an eyebrow.

"Well?"

"Welcome home, my Heir," the guard said, and bowed his head. "Lady Aydin has bid me to await your return and request your presence. She says it is a matter both delicate and somewhat urgent."

Asil arched an eyebrow. "Is this a new trend where I leave the castle for more than a span of hours and come home to increasingly unusual requests?"

The corner of the guard's mouth quirked as if he were trying very hard not to smile. "That is not for me to say, my Heir. Can you attend Lady Aydin now, or should I deliver to her a message about when you will be available?"

"Let's just get this over with." Asil motioned for the guard to proceed, and followed him into the main hall, past the grand staircase, and into the library. Watcher Castle's library was not actually that large; House Aydin's library was far more impressive, though as the founders of the university, that was unsurprising. Still, it was a grand room with tall stacks of books, and ladders on wheels and rails.

Entering the room, the guard bowed. "My lady, the Heir has returned."

"I see that, Rami," Meliha said, amused. She sat in one of the many wingback chairs, a book in her lap, and a teapot with two glasses on the table next to her. "Please step back into the hall and close the doors behind you. Do not allow anyone to enter short of the Lord of the Strait himself."

"Of course, my lady." The guard retreated after another bow, and Asil watched him go with curiosity. This was beginning to look serious.

"Would you like some tea, my Heir?" Meliha asked, motioning to the table next to her and the chair beyond it. "It is still hot."

Asil considered for a moment, then decided that the tea was welcome and there was nothing wrong with being civil. "Yes, thank you."

"This is one of my favorites," Meliha said as she poured him a cup and topped off her own. Asil sat down and picked up the glass, admiring the deep color and the nutty yet slightly floral fragrance. He took a sip and could see why she enjoyed it.

Picking up her own glass, Meliha leaned back in her chair. "You're being patient. I appreciate that. I know it frustrates you at times."

"Which is why you're drawing this out?" Asil looked at Meliha expectantly, and she sighed.

"I am sorry, my Heir," she said, and paused to sip her own tea. "I am uncertain of your reaction to what I need to tell you. It involves Carys. I know you have a great deal of affection for her. I also know that despite this, the rumors of how she came into her position continue to be quite untrue."

"You're spying on me," Asil said, a little incredulous.

Meliha waved her hand. "I spy on everyone, my Heir. More accurately, I have people throughout the castle that keep track of the comings and goings of everyone here, for the safety of the House and the kingdom, and that means I often learn things about you."

Drinking more of the tea, Asil relaxed back into the chair. "Well, that I knew. So, what does this have to do with Carys?"

Looking down into the depths of her glass, Meliha considered. "Seer Arslan has been thrust into a situation she finds uncomfortable and has done an admirable job. The position as liaison to the strangers from the south has been trying for her, and we have all seen it. However, she has made an error in judgment, and I am bringing my concerns to you first. Only Halil and I know this. I haven't even told your father."

Asil's brows drew down. "Who is Halil?"

"The young man currently posing as butler in the House of Flowers." Meliha set her glass on the table, then looked at Asil carefully.

There was another sigh and a clink as Asil set his own tea on the table. "Lady Meliha, I appreciate that you are concerned for my feelings, but I have been on a ship for most of the afternoon and I am desperate for a bath. Where are we going with this?"

Meliha closed the book in her lap and leaned forward. "Carys has met privately with Commander Tadhg Bharda. They headed to the gardens at approximately the same time and returned hours later. Halil is certain they are having an affair."

There was silence as Asil stared at Meliha in disbelief. He felt something wrap around his chest like a vice.

"She is not being flagrant," Meliha continued, eyes on Asil's face. "I have to give her credit, actually. If Halil had not noted the commander leaving at the same time, or his state upon his return, I'm not certain we would have put it together."

The commander's state… Asil's jaw clenched, and his hand curled around the arm of the chair, but he still said nothing. Meliha's watchful gaze took in his reactions, and Asil was able to rise out of his discomfort and anger just long enough to wonder why it interested her so much. Carys and Tadhg. The vice around his chest grew tighter.

"She clearly knows that this is ill-advised," Meliha said after a long moment, "but I don't think she understands just how badly this could go if she were discovered by the wrong parties. There are already many among the Three Houses and the Great Families that are uncomfortable with how much time she spends with the southerners."

"That's hardly her fault," Asil snapped, taking out some of his anger on Meliha. "We thrust her into that position!"

"I understand that, my Heir," Meliha said, her own voice firming up slightly. "And I know you and Hasim told her to befriend the commander and his knights, to earn their sympathy. But she has taken it a step too far. Many of the Great Families protested her appointment. I'm fairly certain Muhan Kaplan hates her. They will see her tried for treason if this gets out."

Those words knocked the breath out of Asil. Treason was dealt with by exile or death. Of course, they would have to convict her, which would be harder, but Asil still did not enjoy the idea. It seemed to only make the tightness in his chest worse.

"No one else knows?" Asil finally managed to ask.

Meliha shook her head. "Correct, my Heir."

"Tell no one else," Asil said firmly, and Meliha nodded. "Not even my father. She… she is in over her head; she does not understand the implications."

Meliha nodded again. "I know, my Heir. I have spoken with her before, and while she is a powerful and skilled woman, she is neither an actress nor a saboteur."

Leaning back in the chair, Asil propped his elbow on the arm of the chair and put his head in his hand. "I will talk to her. Where is she now?"

"Ah… she is in the garden."

The way Meliha said it, the tension in her words, spoke volumes to Asil. "She's with the commander again," Asil said, his voice tight.

"Yes, my Heir," Meliha answered. She looked at him with a sympathy he didn't understand. He wasn't sure he wanted to understand.

Standing up, Asil smoothed his vest and nodded to Lady Aydin. "I will wait for her in her rooms, then. Thank you for the information."

Meliha looked pained. "Asil…"

"We'll speak tomorrow," Asil said, and left the library without another word.

Chapter 19

"YOU'RE IN TROUBLE," Judex said as Carys walked down the hall, her steps surprisingly loud despite the carpeted floors. Probably due to the late hour and the emptiness of the hallway.

"And who, pray tell, am I in trouble with?" Carys asked, unconcerned. Her body still hummed from her time with Tadhg.

Judex floated up beside her, smirking. "Your pet prince has been waiting for you," Judex said smugly.

Carys sighed. "He is my friend, not my pet, and I didn't think I would see him before the morning," Carys said, brow furrowing. Judex laughed mockingly as she reached her door and went in.

As the spirit had said, Asil was waiting inside, sitting at her table, reading one of the books she had borrowed from him. He looked up as the door opened, and watched Carys silently as she came inside. He appeared as if he were trying not to scowl and failing.

"Where have you been, Carys?" Asil asked, his tone even and cold.

"Good evening to you too," Carys answered, looking at Asil carefully, not at all understanding what was going on. "I was out. I met with someone. I knew you were returning home from Veli today; I didn't think you would have time for me tonight."

"Were you with Commander Bharda?" Asil asked in the same cold tone.

Carys removed her shawl, draping it over the back of the other chair, and followed it with her veil. "Yes," she said, surprised by his surety but seeing no reason to deny it.

Asil closed the book with a snap and slammed it down onto the table. Carys stepped back, eyes wide.

"Damn it," Asil said, standing up, shoving the chair back as he did. "Damn it! By the Mother, Carys, are you mad?! I know you said he was handsome, but you're not some thoughtless wisp of a girl! I never thought you'd be stupid enough to fuck him!"

"Language," Carys said, her eyes narrowing. "I appreciate that the tryst is ill-advised, but I fail to see how it makes me stupid, and I'll thank you to watch what you call me in the future."

"He's the enemy," Asil shouted, frustrated.

"His superiors are the enemy," Carys countered. "They're all being manipulated by something, as I've been trying to tell you for days, though you couldn't fit me into your schedule long enough to talk privately."

Asil sneered. "Are you sleeping with the other three as well?"

Eyes wide again, Carys took another step back, stung. "Not that it's any of your business, but no," she said, bewildered. "Asil, what is wrong with you? Why do you even care?"

With a growl Asil picked up the book and hurled it across the room. "Because I changed my mind!"

Carys fell silent, startled and confused. Asil looked up at her, and his angry demeanor cracked, eyes wide as if he were surprised at his own words. Then his brow softened as his eyes filled with pain. He ran a hand through his hair and turned away from her, drawing a deep breath.

"I changed my mind," Asil said again, staring out the window into the dark night. His voice was softer now, vulnerable. "I said I wouldn't court you, but Carys, I… You're everything I could hope for in a woman, in a partner. You make me laugh, you are unbothered by my curtness, and it doesn't matter to you that I'm Egemen Özdemir's son. Being with you is like being with Hasim: you see me and all you care about is the person before you. No woman speaks to me the way you do. No woman ever will."

"Oh, Asil," Carys murmured, her heart going out to him. She crossed the room and set a hand gently on his back. When he didn't pull away, she wrapped her arms around him.

"I'm sorry," Asil said quietly, still staring out the window. "I'm sorry I yelled, I'm sorry I—I'm sorry. I'm not trying to tell you this is true love, or that we are destined, but I… I can't imagine it being anyone other than you."

Turning in Carys's arms, Asil cupped her face and looked down at her for a moment, then leaned in to kiss her. She allowed it, returning the kiss with tenderness and affection. His kiss was exactly like she remembered it, thorough and seeking. Focused, but not passionate.

"Asil," Carys murmured as their lips parted, "I… I do care for you, so much. Even if you dismiss me, even if I lose my post, I will always consider you my friend. You will not lose me, but I cannot… I cannot be more than your friend."

"Why?" he asked, searching her eyes.

"Because while I may not care about your title, I can't forget it," Carys said sadly. "You are the Heir of the Strait. I am no one, save by your grace. A seer, yes, but the bastard daughter of a sailor and a witch. I have no place in the Three Houses."

"I don't care," Asil growled, almost petulant.

Carys sighed. "You should," she said, pulling out of his arms. "The Great Families are baying for an excuse to unseat the Three Houses. They have their own courts now, their own machinations, but Vasi is a place of tradition, and they won't fight that. Unless you break first. If you marry a commoner, how long before they decide House Özdemir is no longer pure enough to lead?"

With a sigh Asil sank back into the chair and ran his hands through his hair again. "You don't have to be right all the time, you know," he said wearily, defeated.

Carys said nothing, but she walked to the chair and leaned against it, drawing her fingers through Asil's hair. He closed his eyes, and for a moment they stayed like that, calm and quiet. Carys wanted to say more, wanted to tell him that he haunted her thoughts and that she adored him, but what good would it do?

"Come back to my room with me tonight," Asil said after a moment, catching Carys's hand and turning to look up at her. "Or allow me to stay here."

"You want me like this," Carys asked, brows arching, "covered in another man?"

"I don't care," Asil said, and she could feel the truth of it resonate in her. "Nothing… nothing needs to happen. Just… stay with me."

"I will," Carys agreed, and he kissed her hand. She then smiled a little. "Though I will follow you to your room. Nazim has already been horrified; I would prefer to spare Aylin."

Asil blinked, then laughed. "I won't let this go, Carys."

"And I won't agree to anything that could hurt you or your father," Carys countered with that same small smile. "So, you will have to."

Asil laughed again, sadly. "Obstinate."

"Apparently that is part of my charm," Carys said, reaching down to caress his face. She felt like more needed to be said, but maybe not just yet. "Come along, my brooding prince. Let's wake someone up for some tea and rice pudding, and then we'll sleep."

Asil allowed Carys to pull him from the chair. He picked up the book he had thrown and set it carefully back on the table. Carys grabbed her robe, laying it over one arm, and they walked hand in hand down the empty hallways to Asil's room.

❨❨❨

Sunbeams and a gentle knock woke Carys. She was in Asil's bed, though this time Asil was not on the distant side of it. He had one arm wrapped around her, his cheek pressed to her shoulder. She was in one of his shirts again, her smallclothes underneath. The gentle knock came once more, and Carys nudged Asil a little before calling out, "Come in."

As Asil yawned and let go of Carys, Nazim came inside bearing a tray. "Ah, Aylin said you were not in your rooms last night, my lady, so I made an assumption," the valet said, keeping his head down as he set breakfast on the table. "Will you require anything else? Should I have Aylin bring clothes?"

"No, Nazim, I had the foresight to bring a robe, thank you," Carys said with a wry smile as she sat up and scooted to the end of the bed. "I'm sure Lord Asil will require a bath when we're done. You may inform Aylin that I need to make a trip into town and that she should plan my ensemble accordingly."

"Yes, my lady," Nazim said, bowing his head, and took off without actually checking in with his lord.

"You're going into town today?" Asil asked as he also climbed out of the bed and padded toward where breakfast waited.

Carys picked up her coffee and sat at the table. "Yes, to my shop," she said, looking out the window at the sunny morning. "I have plants to check on, and I should see if I've received mail. And… well, I should make more-long-term arrangements. I'll be honest, when you first summoned me, I thought I would be here a week, maybe two. Clearly it is going to be awhile."

Hiding a smile in his coffee, Asil simply nodded. "Very well, though please have Aylin arrange a carriage to take you and don't just walk the whole way."

"I wasn't going to!"

"Yes, you were."

Carys glared at Asil for a moment, then they both laughed, and Carys shook her head. "I won't be long," Carys said, "or at least I don't intend to be. I understand that our guests are returning back to their ship today to check in on their men and rotate who is in the barracks."

Nodding, Asil reached for a pastry. "You said last night that they were being manipulated," he said, his gaze growing thoughtful. "What did you mean by that?"

"It has to do with the curses I sensed," Carys said, leaning back with her cup. "I've never seen anything like it before. I don't know how they attracted so many of the same spirit to one spot. Their curses press them into obedience to their rulers, probably by instilling doubt and fear anytime they start to question. And, for example, Cillian had two spirits bound to him, not one. From what I understand, Cillian is from a group of islands that fought joining the Empire for generations. They must have feared he still harbored divisive beliefs."

"That's… monstrous," Asil said, his brows drawing down as he considered it. "And they just do that to everyone?"

Carys shook her head. "No," she said, "not everyone. The ambassador isn't cursed, but he's an obsequious weasel who craves wealth and power; he'll do whatever their Council wants. The lower-ranked soldiers I've seen don't seem to be cursed either, because they're more likely to just follow their commanders. Anyone with any rank, however, is."

"Monstrous," Asil repeated, making a face. "The Great Families may be pests, but I would never rob them of their autonomy just for smoother bureaucracy. What are we going to do about it?"

That earned a smile from Carys. She knew Asil was a good man but was pleased to see it in action.

"I've already begun removing curses where I can," Carys explained. "The binding is almost insultingly simple. Then again, if they do this to all naysayers, maybe they're confident that no one would ever dare reverse it. The spirits seem to disperse. They're strange little creatures, look like large bees. Once unbound they seem harmless enough. Even friendly."

"Bees?" Asil asked, laughing a little. "No, that makes sense— obedience to a queen. Presumably the queen is just whoever the seer binding them says is in charge. And that would be reinforced among them if they were all in a group. It's obnoxiously clever."

Smiling, almost wearily, Carys nodded. "It makes sense. I still don't understand how they summoned so many. Or maybe they found the hive of bee spirits first and devised their experiment from there."

"Hive?" Asil asked, quirking a brow.

Carys just shrugged. "Spirits that resemble animals often mirror their traits," she said, spreading soft cheese on a slice of apple. "The bee spirits would probably create a hive if enough of them congregated in one place."

They ate quietly for a moment before Asil cleared his throat. "Carys," he began, "about the commander…"

Carys set down her coffee and looked embarrassed. "Asil, I never meant to hurt you with this. I truly didn't think it would bother you so much."

Asil gave a small, dismissive wave. "We talked enough about my feelings last night. You need to be careful. If you are caught, it could be considered an act of treason."

"What… treason?" Carys stared at Asil with wide eyes, the color leaving her cheeks.

"You are the Lord's Seer," Asil pointed out. "Tadhg is the commander of a foreign army. You have access to the castle, to information that few others have, and you are in the confidence of the Highest Lord and the Heir."

Carys went from white to red, cheeks burning as she looked down. "I didn't think of it that way. I understood his position, but… I did not consider it in relation to mine. I tried to be careful. How… how did you know?"

"Lady Aydin," Asil said, and Carys' blush grew even darker. "Halil, the butler, put it together. No one else knows, and I have ordered her to keep it that way."

The rest of breakfast was quiet as Carys wallowed in her embarrassment and Asil let her be. In short order, however, they were both off to their separate responsibilities: Asil preparing to head down to oversee the trading out of soldiers from the rented barracks, and Carys to manage the life that felt as if it were slipping further from her every day.

Mindful of Asil's request, Carys had Aylin arrange for a carriage as she bathed and dressed, and in no time, she was riding through streets she hadn't seen in weeks, though it felt like far longer. Neighbors peered from doorways as Carys alighted from the carriage and unlocked her door. Messages were piled just inside, having been fed through the slot in the door. She gathered them up with a sigh and headed back to the counter. She had only just set the bundles of paper down when the bell on the door chimed, indicating someone had entered.

"I am not open," Carys said, turning around to see who had entered. Coming into the shop was Oya, the woman who sold flowers next door.

"I didn't figure you were, dear," Oya said as she not-quite waddled up to the counter. Carys was genuinely surprised she hadn't given birth yet. "I wanted to tell you that your herbs are doing just fine, though I'm honestly a touch surprised I hadn't heard from you. You said a few days, Carys. What happened?"

Sighing, Carys put a hand to her face. "I never sent that letter to you. I kept thinking of it, but— It doesn't matter," Carys said, and brought the hand down to smile apologetically. "Oya, I'm sorry, I thought this was a small thing that would blow over quickly. I didn't realize… Well. I will need you to keep watering my herbs."

Leaning against the counter, Oya tipped her head to the side and smiled at Carys with the soft, concerned gaze of a mother. "Of course I'll keep watering them, my dear," Oya said, reaching over and patting Carys's hand. "But can you tell me what's going on, so I won't worry? Maybe just a little?"

Carys looked over at Oya a bit sheepishly. "I… I have been given the position of the Lord's Seer."

Oya blinked, and then started laughing, holding on to the counter for balance. "Oh, by the Mother! I thought you were in trouble," Oya exclaimed, cackling. "But of course you're not! You just don't like the attention! You didn't want people to know!" The woman was holding her side with one arm, wheezing a little, while the other gripped the counter as if she'd collapse if she let go.

Wrinkling up her nose, Carys glared at Oya. "You're going to go into labor if you keep that up," Carys muttered.

"Ah, I would welcome it," Oya said, still giggling as she composed herself. "It's been long enough. Carys, my dear, congratulations. I never knew your grandmother, but my mum has told me about her, and I'm sure she would be proud."

Blinking in surprise, Carys smiled at Oya. "Thank you," she said genuinely, "that was kind. I think she might be."

"I'm happy to keep everything watered," Oya said, "though your mint is due for a harvest. The yarrow isn't far behind."

"I could pay you to harvest it and set it on the drying racks," Carys said, moving around the counter and rummaging for her coin box. "And then I can… Oh, I know, I'll contact Mother Azize and see if they could send Ferah to pick it up. She's getting very good, you know. She made sleeping tea for Mother Azize, and the Revered Mother said she has the recipe down."

"Maybe Ferah could take over for you," Oya suggested, with a little uncertainty. "She must be getting to the age where she will leave the House soon, yes?"

Carys set the box on the counter and paused, considering. "I… yes, I suppose she is," she said, as she absently pulled out the key to unlock the little box. "I know she's been taking lessons with Kaya, but Kaya has her own children, and at least one daughter with the gift; she probably won't want to take on a full-time apprentice. I… I'll have to think about it."

Fishing in the box, Carys pulled out two gold obols and set them down on the counter in front of Oya. "There," Carys said, pushing them forward, "to harvest and dry whatever is ready for the rest of the month."

"The month?" Oya repeated, and her brows rose. "Oh, Carys, I thought you were going to say for the year! That's too much!'

Carys looked pointedly at Oya's very round belly and then back up at the woman. "For the month. Consider it compensation for your inconvenience. If I have not made other arrangements by next month, we can discuss payment again at that point if you like."

Oya looked at the coins, at Carys, and at her belly, then nodded and reached across to take the coins. "Thank you, seer."

"Thank you for helping me," Carys said sincerely, and relocked the box, tucking it away. "Though I'm surprised the yarrow is ready; I thought I'd gotten the last blooms of the year from it."

Oya shook her head. "No, everything is doing just fine. We even had bees come through! I didn't see them, but I've heard them buzzing away almost every day. Looks to be a late summer this year; everything is still bright and blooming, and the days have yet to cool."

Nodding, Carys began to gather up the mail again. "Well, thank you very much, Oya. And I suppose you can tell people where I am, since they will see that you came in while I was here, and I'm sure they'll ask. If anyone needs herbs, you can sell for me and keep a bit for yourself. Here, I'll leave the key with you. Just don't let people into the shop. Tell them to come back the next day and then come in and gather what you need, all right?"

"Thank you, my dear," Oya said, accepting the key that the seer held out. "That's a generous offer, and I'll be happy to. Let me know if you decide on something with young Ferah, all right?"

"I will," Carys promised, and gave Oya a quick hug before the woman made her way back out of the shop. Carys stared at the pile of messages again, then just gathered them up and tossed them into her satchel. She would look at them later.

Chapter 20

MOVING THROUGH THE shop, Carys took a quick inventory, made some notes about what was low, and gathered up a few items from the alcove where she gave readings. Cards were not her only focus, they were just her best, but it might not hurt to have other items. She gathered up a pouch of stones carved with symbols from Miterathea, and a pendulum carved from lapis lazuli. As she packed things up, she heard buzzing. Oya had said that bees had been in the garden. Maybe a window had been left open.

Climbing the narrow stairs, Carys reached the second floor and froze. Over a dozen bee spirits buzzed and flitted around her room, moving through the walls to the garden and back again. If she focused hard enough, she could just barely see ethereal honeycomb structures forming in the corners. As she stood there, one of the bees noticed her.

Queen!

Before Carys could respond, she was swarmed. The bee spirits flew around her, excited and happy, like puppies whose master had just come home.

Queen!

Queen!

Queen queen queen!

Eyes wide, Carys put her hands over her ears, though she knew it wouldn't make a difference. The bees were a buzzy, cheerful chorus.

They nuzzled at her, and she was shocked to realize she could feel them, feel their tiny velvety bodies as they pushed at her hands and cheeks. If she moved, she passed through them as she would any spirit, but the fact that she could feel them at all shouldn't be.

"Oh, Mother, I'm an idiot," Carys said as her heart beat faster and her skin prickled in panic.

"I'm glad you said it first," Judex chimed in, materializing beside her, looking disgusted. "You didn't even try to banish them."

"Because they didn't care," Carys exclaimed, her voice becoming more shrill, "Once they were unbound, they just began to wander off! They should have returned to the wild!"

"They're from across the sea, child," Judex pointed out, his voice dripping with scorn, as Carys stared at the swarming bees. "Where is a wild they would recognize?"

"But I… I didn't command them!"

Now fully formed, Judex turned toward Carys and looked down at her. He seemed bigger now, looming over the seer in the small room.

"You broke their binding and told them their queen was gone," Judex said with cold derision. "You are the most powerful seer in Vasi, even if you are the most incompetent. A beacon of spiritual energy. What other queen would they have sought?"

One step forward, two, and then Carys fell to her knees. This was too much—she didn't know what to do. Her heart was hammering and it was hard to breathe. Judex stood behind her, his presence overwhelming, oppressive. The bee spirits scattered, frightened, and flew to their honeycomb corners.

"Your grandmother would have done it right," Judex said, sneering. "She would have cared more about breaking the curse than bedding the man afflicted. Are you good for anything other than being pretty, Carys? Would you even be the Lord's Seer if the prince wasn't so determined to have you in his bed?"

"Stop it," Carys said, her voice quavering. Her hands shook as her heart pounded. "Stop! I didn't… It was a mistake…"

"That's putting it mildly," Judex snapped as he moved to the other side of her to stand at her head. He seemed to fill the small room, the plumes of smoke that formed him wisping out farther, like a corona. "You're pathetic. Too busy begging at Tadhg's door and then feeding Asil scraps of affection so he'll keep you around. The greatest gift in generations, and as usual you're throwing it away!"

Carys pressed her hands against the floor, setting her teeth. "Stop it," she said again, and her hands began to curl, her nails dragging like claws against the old rug. If Judex had been paying attention, he would have seen her eyes begin to glow.

"It's a small favor everyone who ever loved you is already dead," Judex continued, his mouth twisting cruelly. "At least now no one is left to be shamed when you're banished from the castle for being a useless whore—"

"I said STOP!"

Blinding light flared from Carys's eyes and she flailed at Judex in rage as power lashed out from her hands. The spirit cried out in shock and pain, and immediately dispersed, the magenta and purple smoke becoming fine mist and then nothing. Carys collapsed again, crying, and lay on the floor sobbing into the carpet as her head throbbed with the power she had channeled. She cried until she was exhausted and her vision blurred, and eventually fell into unconsciousness.

"Miss? Seer Arslan? Miss, are you all right?"

Carys woke with a start. She was on the floor of her bedroom, in her shop, with a concerned and slightly panicked carriage driver looking down at her. She was tired, her head hurt from the power she had channeled, and her face was still wet from her tears.

"I… I'm sorry," Carys said quietly, and allowed the driver to pick her up. She could see the bee spirits skittering around nervously. They were all around her; they had been worried. It was strangely touching.

Looking at Carys's face, the driver's brows drew down. "Seer Arslan, are you sure you're all right? I'm sorry I came in, but you've been in here for almost two hours, you see, and when I opened the door to check on you, you didn't answer, and so I came looking and I… well, I found you like this, miss."

Nodding, Carys managed a soft, reassuring smile. "I'm all right. Again, I am sorry to have worried you. Let me… let me just gather a few things, and then we can return."

The driver did not look convinced, but he also didn't look like he was about to argue with the Lord's Seer. He simply nodded and then headed back down the narrow stairs. Carys stumbled to the basin and washed her face. The water was stale, but still clear and unsullied. She pushed open a window to pour everything out into the garden.

The bee spirits continued buzzing around Carys, rubbing up against her. There was something almost soothing about it. She had no idea what to do about them, and there was no one to ask. She closed her eyes and tried not to cry again. She missed her grandmother. After a breath, she opened her eyes once more and gathered what she had wanted from the room, changing her veil for one that was not soaked through with her tears.

"Stay," she said quietly, and found that if she concentrated, she could give the bees tiny pets with her fingertips. "I'll come back soon. Please stay."

Queen!

"I hope that's a yes," Carys murmured to herself as she walked down the stairs, turning down the lamps once more. She went ahead and emptied her coin bank—it seemed silly to leave the obols here if she wouldn't be back for a month. She found her extra key, grabbed her satchel, and locked the door behind her as she headed out.

"Back to Watcher Castle, miss?" the driver asked almost hopefully. He still looked concerned.

Carys nodded and settled herself in the back of the carriage. She was quiet for the ride back, looking out over the city in the late afternoon light. When they returned to the castle, she said nothing, simply drifted inside with her things. Aylin greeted Carys in the hall on her way to her room, and Carys sent the girl to ready the baths. She said nothing else to anyone, communicating with nods and shakes of the head to the bath attendants, and was left to soak in peace.

The quiet was eventually broken by two gentle words in a concerned tone. "What's wrong?" Asil asked.

Opening her eyes slowly, Carys looked up at the Heir, who had come into the room still in his formal clothing. "Would I be here at all if you did not desire me? Would I be the Lord's Seer if you had not wished me to stay that first night?"

"Assuming that in this theoretical setting you were still the strongest seer in Vasi, then yes," Asil said, his expression showing his confusion. "It might have taken longer, because I probably would not have approached you at the party if I didn't find you interesting, but you're not here because you're attractive, Carys. I very much hate to be the one to say this, but there are prettier women in the city, and most of them would require far less effort in wooing."

Carys was stunned into silence for a moment, and then laughed. It was a bit of a shocked, gasping laugh, quiet at first, but it grew louder. Asil watched her as if she were mad but waited as Carys pulled herself together and calmed down.

"I can always trust you to be yourself with me, can't I?" Carys said. "You'll be candid with me, because it's what you want in return."

"Well, yes," Asil agreed, looking a touch uncomfortable, as if he didn't appreciate how well she read him.

Carys closed her eyes and took a breath. "Can… I tell you something? Something I have never told anyone?"

"Of course," Asil answered immediately, then looked around. "Though… could it not be in the bath? I haven't changed yet, it's very humid and hot in here, and I'm not going to strip down and climb in without being scrubbed first."

Laughing again, Carys opened her eyes and nodded. "It can, yes. If you just got back, I imagine you haven't eaten. Have someone arrange food and meet me in my room."

"Yes, my lady seer," Asil said with a teasing smile, then disappeared. Carys climbed out of the bath and slid into her robe, then headed back to her quarters.

By the time Carys arrived, Aylin was there setting up a respectable afternoon tea, though the eager handmaid paused the task long enough to help Carys into a soft knit dress under a sheer open front jacket embroidered in roses. As Aylin returned to the food, Asil arrived, having shed his jacket and sash but still wearing his crisp, high-collar shirt and the heavier formal pants and boots. Tea was laid out, Aylin disappeared, and the two of them settled in.

"How did you know to come looking for me?" Carys asked, curious.

"Aylin told Nazim that you were despondent," Asil answered with a bit of a smirk. "Nazim informed me of this as I returned from my trip. I suspect he may have exaggerated a touch, as you were hardly weeping and inconsolable when I came into the baths, though you did seem upset."

"Ah."

Asil poured them both tea. "So, what were you going to tell me?"

Picking up her cup, Carys was quiet for a moment, considering how to start. "I was cursed when I was 20," she said finally, having decided to just jump in, her voice soft. "It was miscast. I learned much later that the target had been my grandmother, but the person casting the curse didn't realize she had died. As my grandmother's heir, the item that had been used to anchor the binding then belonged to me."

Asil sat frozen, a biscuit in one hand and his tea in the other, watching Carys in shock. "Are you still?"

"Technically, no," Carys answered, ruefully. "There are two steps to undoing a curse. Unraveling the binding, and then banishing the spirit. Most seers aren't powerful enough to actually banish a spirit, so they negotiate with it in some way, get it to leave. I didn't know this at the time. I barely knew anything about curses; my grandmother didn't like them and had only begun to explain how to unravel them. I… unraveled my own curse. Which I understand is unheard of. But I didn't have the knowledge or strength to banish the spirit."

Brow furrowed, Asil set the uneaten biscuit down. "What does that mean?"

"It means I'm haunted," Carys said, not knowing how else to put it. "I call him Judex. He's a spirit of judgment or scorn. He's… grandmother would have called him an ideal spirit, meaning that he was born of a human ideal or emotion. Spirits, as we understand them, fall into three categories: ideal, natural, and ethereal."

"What are ethereal spirits?" Asil asked, intrigued.

"Really hard to explain."

"Oh, very funny," Asil returned, glaring.

Carys let out a sad little laugh and spread her hands helplessly. "They are, though. They're the hardest to explain and the least understood, but they also seem to carry the most raw power. Ethereal spirits are, I believe, how seers see beyond. I don't know this and it's not exactly testable, but that is my intuition, anyway."

"Very well," Asil said, letting it go. "So, what is, or who is Judex? You called it a 'he'. Do spirits have a gender of any sort?"

Carys shook her head. "No," she said, "I call Judex 'he' because that is how he appears to me: as a human-like creature of mist and smoke, vaguely shaped like a man and with a man's voice, though also with horns, and his features are too sharp."

Asil's eyes flicked briefly across the room. "Is he here now?"

Another shake of the head. "No, he comes and goes," Carys explained, pausing to sip her tea. "He's capricious and shows up when he wants to, typically when he can criticize me. We… we are not friends, but when someone is part of your life for so long, you become friendly. Today, though—in a moment of panic and overwhelm, I gave in to my doubts. That feeds him. It was like that in the beginning, before I understood what he was and was able to unbind him. When he makes me angry enough, my power… manifests in response, and he… usually stops. Today, he made me so angry, I lashed out at him. It seemed to hurt him. It will probably be days before he can manifest again."

"Mother's mercy," Asil murmured. "Is that… is that why you asked me those things? Did he say them to you?"

A tear slid down Carys's cheek, and she dropped her gaze, then nodded. "It is, and he did. And also called me a useless whore and said my grandmother would have better known how to banish the bee spirits, and how she wouldn't even have entertained the idea of an affair with the commander. He's ri—"

"Stop," Asil said firmly, setting down his tea, and Carys looked up in surprise. "You will not say this spirit was right after what it said to you. You are not useless, and you are certainly not a whore. And your grandmother would be twice Tadhg's age; the affair wouldn't have even been an option. You cannot guess at what she would have done if she were actually in your place."

Asil rose from his chair and crossed to Carys, kneeling before her. "I should not have said the things I said to you about Tadhg," he said, looking faintly embarrassed. "Maybe the affair is ill-advised, or maybe it actually makes a great deal of sense to win the affection of the general of the opposition. I know you are not calculating in that manner—you would not have done it for those reasons—but for all we know this will benefit us in the end. I… I said what I did out of jealousy, not out of any tactical knowledge. And my warning about treason is actually Meliha's warning; she fears for you. But you are not failing, Carys."

A rose the shade of her jacket spread over Carys's cheeks. "Thank you, Asil," she murmured.

Reaching up, Asil took Carys's hand, and gently kissed the back of it. "I will see about getting you a day or two away from Peadar. I know it's trying on you. Hasim or I will go with him if he visits one of the Great Families again."

"Really?" Carys said, eyes wide and hopeful. "Oh, Mother, I would be so grateful! He's awful, and I cannot take the rudeness or the condescending comments anymore, I just… Pasha Kaplan made me ride in a separate carriage! If he could have left me outside during breakfast, he would have!"

Asil's jaw fell open in shock. "He did not!"

"He most certainly did!" Carys felt a little like a child telling on someone, but she also felt it was merited.

"The unmitigated gall of that man," Asil muttered, astounded. He shook his head and rose to his feet, still holding Carys's hand. "At least two days, I promise. It will give you a chance to recover."

Carys smiled. "Thank you, Asil." Two days away from Peadar would also be two days away from Tadhg, but perhaps that was for the best. "You still might be too good to me."

Asil leaned in to kiss her forehead. "Not possible."

Chapter 21

AFTER TEA, ASIL returned to his rooms. He was preoccupied with the pain he had seen in Carys today, and the signs of the strain of her position. He was beginning to suspect they had asked too much of her too soon. The knowledge of her affair with Tadhg still made Asil uncomfortable and angry, but they had brought her into the castle only to shove her at the commander and his knights the moment they arrived. He stewed as he headed to his desk and pulled out paper and wax. They couldn't ask less of her at this point. There was not a way to step back. But he could try to give her a small reprieve and find a way to make it up to her when all of this was over.

Smoothing the paper out onto the desk, Asil considered for a moment then picked up his pen. He began with a letter to Hasim, explaining how certain heads of the Great Families were taking pains to keep Carys out of the room during their talks with the southern ambassador. While Asil had no doubt that Muhan Kaplan despised Carys, he also understood that this was strategic. They knew Carys was inexperienced, that she wasn't accustomed to asserting herself in these situations. Hasim, however, wouldn't stand for it, and was strong enough to push his way into a room or a carriage if someone tried to bar the way. While Hasim had duties as Lord Commander, he also had a certain flexibility in his role. He should be able to help.

The letter was freshly sealed when Nazim entered Asil's room and cleared his throat. "I'm sorry to bother you, my lord, but your Lord Father has requested your presence."

"Of course." Asil rose and handed the letter to Nazim. "See that this gets to the Lord Commander. Instruct the courier to wait for a reply unless Lord Kilic is occupied."

Nazim bowed and took the letter, opening the door for Asil before heading in the opposite direction as Asil walked down the hall toward his father's study. Egemon wouldn't be anywhere else this time of day.

As Asil approached the study, the door was slightly open and Asil could hear people arguing. That was unusual. Brows furrowed, Asil pushed the door open and stepped inside. He was greeted initially by a wave of warmth, as there was a small fire going in the fireplace. That seemed odd for later summer. His father was on the couch, going over paperwork and being yelled at by the court physician.

"With all due respect, my Highest Lord, the fact that you are not in bed does not speak to your intelligence," the woman said sharply, and Asil's brows rose. Asil had not been attended by the court physician much, and was more often seen by the woman's apprentice, who was not as bold. "Taking a day of rest now will help you more than pushing yourself until you are bedridden."

"Yes, you have been making your thoughts on the subject very clear for the last several minutes," Egemon commented dryly, seemingly unbothered by the physician's tone. He also sounded exhausted.

Asil cleared his throat. "A bit warm for a fire. Father, are you feeling unwell?"

As Egemon looked over at his son, Asil schooled himself to remain neutral. The Lord of the Strait had circles under his eyes, and he was noticeably paler. The physician turned and bowed her head to Asil with a look of exasperation.

"My Heir," she said, clasping her hands before her, "your father has at best caught a late summer cold, but these could be the symptoms of something much worse yet to come. Please, if you are at all able to, convince him to go to bed!" She nodded once more, then headed for the door to the study, pausing only long enough to shout, "And take your medicine!" over her shoulder before heading off.

The door closed with a heavy thud. "Well, she must have a delightful bedside manner," Asil commented, and Egemon laughed, wheezing slightly. Looking around the room, Asil saw a bottle on Egemon's desk and brought it over. "Father, while I would never presume to tell you what to do, would you perhaps consider taking the physician's advice?"

Sighing, Edgemon eyed the green glass bottle with distaste. "I haven't taken anything yet because I know it will make me sleep."

"You've been tired," Asil said gently, sitting down next to his father. "I did wonder if you had caught something small, but this… I wouldn't go to court, if I were you."

Egemon raised a brow. "Do I look that bad?"

Asil nodded and let some of his concern show. "You should find an excuse, any excuse, to avoid court this evening and head to bed early."

A wry smile turned up the corners of Egemon's mouth. "You would have to go in my stead."

Somehow Asil managed not to wince. "I understand that it is my duty as the Heir."

"I must look very poor indeed for you to agree so readily," Egemon said, reaching over and setting his hand on his son's knee. "Very well. Let me finish these letters, then I'll take Maris's concoction and head to my bed. Tell people I am unexpectedly attending to my sister. Your aunt is insufferably demanding—I have no doubt people will believe it. And have Meliha send a runner to inform your aunt of the ruse."

Asil nodded. "Of course, Father."

Rising, Asil rang for tea, but he stayed with Egemon until his father finally declared himself finished and headed to his rooms. Asil straightened up his father's desk, made sure the letters were handed off to a courier, and scattered the fire as well as he could before tossing ashes on it. Meliha arrived as he was setting down the ash pail.

"Is everything all right?" Meliha asked after the door closed. "Did you have a chance to speak with Carys about her… activities?"

Blinking, Asil looked up. "What—oh, yes. We discussed it; she understands. I did not ask what her next steps would be, but I trust her. That's not what this is about, however."

Nodding, the spymistress moved to one of the chairs and sat. "Your father's illness, then? I find myself concerned. It seems to have come upon him rather suddenly. I know he has been tired, but today he looks as if he's been combating ague for weeks."

Asil couldn't help but smile ruefully. Of course, Meliha already knew. Asil sat down across from Meliha and topped off his tea before leaning back with the glass.

"I need you to send someone to Aunt Elif," Asil said, before taking a healthy swallow of the cooled tea. "Use my father's carriage. We do not want people to know he's ill, so we will be telling everyone that he had to head up to attend to her. She knows what she's like; she'll understand."

Meliha smiled. "Elif does take a certain pride in the amount of effort she can require. She's always been that way. Honestly, I think your grandfather was relieved when she married and left for Miterathea."

"I have no doubt." Asil set his glass down and sighed. He might not be able to keep his promise to Carys afterall. Not if he was needed to stand in for his father.

"You'll survive a few days in your father's shoes," Meliha said, smiling reassuringly and not understanding what had prompted the sigh. Asil just smiled back and nodded.

"We should be about it, then," he said, standing up, and Meliha followed. "Oh, and can you have someone clean the study? Air it out properly, all that? He was in here for some time today, and I don't want anything lingering when he returns."

Nodding, Meliha set a hand on Asil's shoulder. "Of course, my Heir. If there is anything else I can do, just let me know."

ↄↄↄ

"Seer?"

Looking up, Carys saw one of the many pages of the castle standing before her. She had fled to the kitchen garden with her pile of letters, along with a pot of tea and a sampling of desserts. The page wasn't all that surprising, almost expected, but her mouth fell open as she saw that just behind the page was Cillian, looking a touch unsettled but determined.

"It seems I will have company for my reading this evening," Carys said with a polite smile, motioning to the empty seat across from her. "Knight ab Owain, please join me. Deniz, dove, can you fetch a cup and a larger pot of the black for sir knight?"

The page smiled and dropped a quick bow. "Yes, seer," he said, then took off without another word. Cillian stood for one more moment, then dropped into the chair across from her. He was in uniform, but not in armor, and had left his sword behind.

"Thank you, my lady," Cillian said as he attempted to get comfortable. "I am sorry to interrupt you, but I had been meaning to speak with you. While you have done an admirable and lovely job of showing us the city and keeping us entertained, there is not often time for quiet conversation."

"No, I suppose not," Carys remarked, tipping her head to the side. "What did you wish to converse about, Cillian?"

The gloomy soldier was quiet for a moment, his perpetually knitted brow more tangled than usual as he looked out on the growing twilight beyond the lanterns of the garden. Carys was also quiet, happy to sip her tea and wait for him to find his words. The valet returned, poured Cillian a cup of tea, and was off again.

"I wished to talk to you about seers," Cillian said at last, carefully picking up the delicate tea glass. "Every time Tadhg or Ambassador Peadar said there are no seers in the south, you would get this look on your face. Like you wouldn't dare accuse us of lying, but you were fairly certain someone was."

Carys turned faintly pink. "I had hoped I was hiding it better than that."

That made Cillian chuckle. "No, you've been fine," he reassured her. "I notice a lot that others miss. It's how I am—I'm quiet, I observe, I calculate. I have been thinking about what we've learned here, and I find myself... well, ruminating on things for the first time in years."

The knight sounded surprised as he confessed his wandering thoughts, and Carys did her best to contain her excitement. If Cillian was admitting that he had just now begun to think about things after ignoring them for who knows how long, then that was a good indication that lifting the curse had worked. Cillian was apparently intelligent or willful enough that whoever in the south monitored such things had deemed it necessary to tie two spirits to him. It made sense that he would be the first to start questioning.

"I'm happy to tell you anything you want to know," Carys said genuinely. "What is it you would like to know about seers?"

Cillian considered. "How does the gift come upon you? I know you spoke of this before, but if you don't mind."

Carys sipped her own tea and considered. "As I said before, with warning, thankfully. It starts with the fading of the eyes," she explained, motioning to her own veiled face. "Over the span of, oh, a season, typically. The severity of the fade marks the strength of the gift. There are many theories as to why the color bleeds away, but in the end, no one really understands it."

"So, there is an implication, then, in the fact that your eyes are almost colorless," Cillian said, arching an eyebrow.

Carys blinked. "Ah, the implication is that I am a woman with a great deal of raw talent that wishes her teacher had lived long enough to see that talent turned into useful skill."

That prompted a soft, almost sympathetic smile from Cillian. "I have also lost a mentor," he said, looking at her with kindness. "I'm sorry for your loss."

Again, Carys was surprised, but smiled in return. "Thank you. And I for yours."

"So, the fading of the eyes," Cillian said, ready to move on. "What comes next?"

"You start to see things," Carys said with a bit of a shrug. "Especially in areas where the barrier between our existence and what lies beyond is thinner. Which, despite fanciful tales otherwise, is not often cemeteries. Battle sites, great halls, untouched forests—those are the places spirits congregate, places where a concept in its ideal form can manifest."

"So, spirits are not ghosts," Cillian said carefully, and Carys nodded. "That was why you looked offended at the Guild."

Sighing, Carys laughed at herself a little. "I really thought I was better at hiding my reactions."

Cillian smiled again. "You are fine, really," he reassured her. "This is just something that I do. It runs in the family."

Nodding, Carys moved on. "Ghosts are not spirits. Ghosts are far less common than stories would have you believe. Sometimes spirits who embody negative emotions can play that part, but," Carys paused and looked into her tea, "ghosts are the greatest tragedy that can befall a human soul. They are a manifestation of will, bound to the earth through great emotion, and they have removed themselves from the order of the world. Seers are particularly at risk for such a fate—we are already so attuned with the spirits; it would be easy to stay with them rather than move on."

Cillian's brow furrowed as he drank his tea, considering what she had said. "What do you mean by that, exactly?"

"I mean a ghost never returns to the Cradle," Carys said, looking back up. "And when their will falters, as is inevitable because mortal creatures are not capable of immortal will, they will simply end. I've seen it happen. Mother willing, it will never happen to me."

Quiet fell for a moment as Cillian considered what Carys had said. They drank tea, and Carys nibbled on a piece of fruit while Cillian helped himself to a couple biscuits. He looked at her speculatively a few times, as if weighing something in his mind.

"All right," Cillian said at last, "so what can seers do?"

"Well," Carys began, looking off to the side for a moment as she considered where to start, "as we just discussed, we can see spirits. We interact with them, connect with them. Something about that interaction also allows us to see the whole of the world; we call it seeing beyond. It shows us things, sometimes secrets, sometimes things that just sit outside of our grasp. Sometimes flickers of what is to come, but that can't be trusted. Fate is not fixed, and most seers won't try to look into the future—it's a fool's gamble. If you are smart, you learn to look at the now, and from there you can extrapolate."

The stormcloud lifted a little, and Cillian looked interested, even curious. "Can you give me an example?"

Head tipped to the side, Carys looked at him for a second, then grinned. "All right," she said, sitting forward. "I had a young woman come to me because she had been chasing one of the merchant princes but was afraid things had changed. She wanted me to reassure her that she hadn't lost her chance with him. So, I looked into the possibilities and followed the threads. I could see the shape of him, his heart, and what he desired. I could see that the girl could meet that desire, was happy to. Then, from my understanding of their characters, I could predict the most likely play of events if the young woman were to follow through with my advice."

Cillian's eyes grew wide. "And? Were you right?"

Smirking, Carys picked up the brilliant magenta envelope that had been sitting by her on the table. "I think this invitation to their engagement party answers that well enough."

There was a long silence as Cillian looked at her, his eyes narrowing again. Carys set down the envelope and met his gaze, wondering what he was thinking. The nightbirds chirped in the garden as darkness fell.

"You knew we were coming," Cillian said at last, quietly.

"Yes," Carys answered, her voice soft but even. She was not going to lie to this man, not when he had come to her on his own seeking answers. "I could see change coming from the south, with an ancient weight behind it. I did not know what to expect, but I knew it was coming."

Sighing, Cillian dropped his head into his hands. "You said you can see the shape of people, their character," he said, something akin to despair in his voice. "Then you know what the ambassador intends."

"Not precisely, but I know he has… ambitions," Carys agreed, her voice even and calm. "Though honestly, Cillian, the ambassador is a weasel even by the standards of his office. I think everyone knew what he intended from the moment he set foot in the port. The question is, how will it come?"

"I don't know," Cillian said, picking his head up and sitting back in his chair. "Truly, my lady, I don't know. I don't even think the commander knows." The knight sighed, frustrated. "The Empire. My father was a child when they took the archipelago, though I—I haven't thought about it in ages. I used to be so angry, even when I joined the military. I used to always question. I don't understand why I stopped."

Carys was silent, pensive, and struggled with what to say. She wasn't sure how to explain it, how to even broach the subject. As it turned out, she didn't need to. Cillian looked up suddenly, eyes bright as if he had just figured something out.

"But you know," Cillian said, looking at her. "You know something. You held yourself distant from us all at first, but after that first night when you took us to the tavern you were warmer, more friendly. Something changed that night."

Drawing in a deep breath, Carys let it out slowly. "Yes," she said, still a touch nervous.

The stormy brows sank again. "You won't tell me."

"No, I just—," Carys broke off, leaning back. "I'm not sure how. I'm not sure how you'll believe me. Why would you trust anything I said?"

"My lady," Cillian began, then stopped, looking away, considering again. Finally, when he looked back at Carys, his expression was uncomfortable but determined. "I know about you and the commander. I know he's gone to meet someone at night. I have seen his face when he returns, and I have seen how he's looked at you since the day we arrived. And your face has just gone white, so if I wasn't entirely certain before, I am now."

Carys was, indeed, paler, and doing her best not to panic. "And?"

"Tadhg Bharda is a good man," Cillian said with a conviction that resonated. "I would say he is the best man I know. I would follow him anywhere. He saw potential in me. He didn't care that I was from the archipelago. He didn't care that I had little taste for bloodshed."

"An unfortunate trait for a soldier," Carys said quietly.

Cillian let out a short, bitter laugh. "It is," he agreed, "and it would have seen me die a man-at-arms. But Tadhg believed in me. He believes in everyone under him. Any of us would die for him. I tell you this, my lady, because if such a man could love you, as it is clear to me he does, then I would believe anything you told me."

Silence again, save for Carys's heavier, almost-panicked breaths. She wanted to argue with Cillian. Surely Tadhg did not love her; he enjoyed her; he was fascinated with her. She wanted to insist that it was a passing fancy, and nothing more. But she couldn't ignore how the possibilities aligned with Cillian's words, how she felt the truth in it. Taking a shaky breath, Carys looked away.

"There is something else seers can do," Carys said at last, her gaze focused on the now-cold tea in front of her. "Spirits can be bound to a person. We call it cursing. When you curse someone, you give the bound spirit instructions. These can be simple, but more-sophisticated spirits can be given more-complex directions. Many of those cursed will never know that they are—the spirit is an influence, a pressure that guides, inciting emotions that match the instructions and intended results."

"And what does this have to do with us?" Cillian asked, something dangerous in his eyes. Carys could see him connecting the dots between her words and the anger he used to have toward the empire.

"I know that you have seers in the empire because out of everyone who greeted us that first day when you left the ship, only the ambassador was not cursed."

Silence again. Cillian was angry, but he wrestled with it silently and did not shout or lash out. Either too upset to speak, or simply not knowing what to say, he continued to stare in silence. After a moment, Carys decided to continue.

"The first night we went to the Alchemist's Guild," Carys said, starting to look a touch sheepish, "there was a point when you all left me with the mistress of the house. By then I had realized that your curses weren't actually tied to you, but to your weapons. I'd never seen anything like it. Physical objects can be used to anchor a curse, but usually it is the person who is cursed, not the object. So, I made a deal, and in exchange I was allowed into the vault to look at your swords."

"And?" Cillian asked. It was like a stone hitting a glacier.

Carys swallowed and shifted in her seat. "I lifted the curse from each of your swords. The spirits… they were to encourage you to obey. To keep you focused on duty."

Cillian pushed himself to his feet with force, the chair falling behind him as he did. He seemed to tremble for a moment with the want to lash out at something, anything. And then it passed. The older soldier took a breath and closed his eyes for a moment. He then came around and knelt before Carys.

"I thank you, my lady," he said, head down.

"Cillian, don't," Carys said, reaching down and tipping up his chin. "Please, stand back up; retake your chair."

Looking up at Carys, Cillian gently took her hand from the side of his face and held it in his hands, kissing the back of it. He looked up at her again and smiled, though there was a touch of sadness to it.

"You did this for us, when we were still nothing more than foreign soldiers," he said quietly. "It is no wonder he loves you. I find myself charmed as well. I might also try for your favor if he wasn't my commander."

Carys giggled—the words had surprised her, but she could feel the shape of him, and knew that "charmed" was where it ended. "Generys would never forgive me," was all Carys said, with a bit of a wry smile.

It took a moment, but Cillian's eyes brightened again as he understood her words, his smile growing wider even if it was a touch disbelieving. "My lady, just what might you be insinuating?"

"If you can't figure that out, you don't deserve your rank, Knight of the Field."

Laughing, Cillian let go of Carys's hand and stood, retrieving the chair and setting it back in place. He looked at her for another moment, still smiling.

"You really do look like you come from the archipelago," he said after a moment. "The flash of fire in you makes me feel at home. Carys is one of our names, did you know that?"

Carys's mouth fell open in shock. "I... did not. My father was a sailor. I never knew him."

Cillian just nodded. "I thank you for your time, my lady. I shall not trouble you further."

Carys smiled gently. "I am here if you need me."

With another nod, Cillian stepped back, and then bowed deeply before turning and heading out of the gardens. Carys watched him go for a moment, then gathered her letters and hurried back inside.

Chapter 22

A PARTICULARLY UNREMARKABLE night at court was coming to a close, and Ambassador Peadar made his way to the dais just as Asil was beginning to descend. Asil somehow managed not to make a face; he had done an admirable job of avoiding the ambassador through most of the evening, but it seemed Peadar would not be denied.

"My Heir," Peadar said, bowing, "what a surprise to see you presiding over the assembly this evening. I had hoped to speak with your father, though you did a masterful job."

"Fortunately for me it was such an uneventful evening," Asil replied dryly. He slowed his step to converse with Peadar, but did not actually stop, forcing the ambassador to follow. "Is there something you would like me to relay to my father?"

"Oh, no, my Heir, not as such," Peadar said, smiling his faintly condescending smile. "I had just hoped to share my impressions of the city! I have been learning so much about it these past weeks."

Glancing at Peadar, Asil kept his expression neutral. His eyes flicked up briefly to the guard accompanying the ambassador—neither the commander nor any of his knights had attended court this evening. Peadar was followed by some soldier from the ship of middling rank.

"Yes, I understand you have met with every head of the Great Families," Asil said evenly. "I hope you have also taken the time to see what the city is like outside of the homes of our most prosperous."

223

The ambassador bowed his head. "We have made time for what we could, my Heir. Seer Arslan gave us a… charming tour of the Divine Mother's orphanage. How very charitable of your kingdom to devote the temples to such a cause. I do hope your citizens have not felt a lack of guidance as a result. I am not certain the Empire would be the shining beacon that it is without direction from the temples."

They passed the door into the Lord's Hall, and Asil paused to regard Peadar fully. "The people of Vasi seem content with the level of guidance they experience. I will be sure to express to my father your hopes to speak with him soon."

Peadar bowed more deeply, understanding a dismissal when he heard one. "Thank you, my Heir, you are too kind. I do hope your father is in better health soon."

"My father's health is exemplary, as it always is, Ambassador." Asil felt his pulse quicken, but kept up his cold, featureless expression. "He is gone this evening attending to my aunt, the Lady Elif Chrysos, who has an estate on the outskirts."

"Oh!" For the first time since Asil had met Peadar, the ambassador looked embarrassed. He also looked surprised. Asil had given him an answer he hadn't expected. "My apologies, my Heir! I had assumed. Forgive me."

Asil gave a dismissive wave. "There is nothing to forgive. It was simply a misunderstanding. Now, if you'll excuse me, I do have matters to attend to."

Another obsequious bow. "Of course, my Heir. Have a lovely evening."

Jaw set, Asil headed down the Lord's Hall to his father's study, motioning for one of the guards always stationed outside to follow him in. The study had been cleaned, as Meliha had promised, and it smelled faintly astringent. She had taken his request seriously. Good.

"Is something wrong, my Heir?" the guard asked. Asil gave a terse nod and rang for a servant.

"I need someone to fetch the Lord Commander for me, immediately," Asil said, and the guard straightened. "And tell Lord Captain Killic to increase the guard at the port and the gate. Subtly, if you please—he shouldn't double it, just add a few extra men. Go at once, and tell no one other than the Lord Commander and Lord Captain Killic. Do you understand?"

"Of course, my Heir." The guard's demeanor was somber, and he bowed and left with haste. He was an older guard, not one of the young recruits. The guardians of Egemon Özdemir were often veterans—too old for long patrols in the forests, but still hale enough to take out an assassin or quell an upstart nobel.

A page entered just a breath after the guard left. "My Heir?"

"Find Maris, the physician," Asil said, walking around to the other side of his father's desk. "Tell her it is urgent that she check on the Lord of the Strait, and that I will meet her in the Lord's apartments shortly. Then find Lady Meliha Aydin and have her attend to me immediately."

The page nodded and took off. Asil flipped through the papers his father had been reviewing that day. He didn't even know what he was looking for. All he knew was that Peadar Criddubh had known that the Lord of the Strait was ill, had been expecting to hear it from Asil's mouth, and had been so shocked to hear otherwise that it had actually rattled him.

Hasim was the first to arrive. He looked tired, and as if he had been hunting; his hair was tied back, he wore leather pants made to take the abuses of the wood, and his sword hung from his side. "You're lucky I arrived when I did. I understand you needed to see me immediately?"

Confused, Asil wrinkled his brow and regarded Hasim for a moment, then sighed. "Right. You were at the border, overseeing the return of the Elder and her guard."

"Yes." Hasim stepped forward and set an ornate sealed scroll case in front of Asil. "I also brought back a missive from their queen. But I assume that's not why you rushed me back here. What is going on?"

Briefly, Asil explained the day's developments, and Lord Egemon's worsening condition. "I cannot prove it, but I think the ambassador has… I don't know, poisoned him or something. He knew."

"Mother's tits," Hasim swore, expression pinched. Before he could say more, Meliha Aydin entered the room.

"My Heir." Meliha bowed her head quickly but did not fully enter the room. "I understand you sent Maris to your father's quarters. I assume we are going there now. Is everything all right?"

The papers on the desk revealed nothing. Asil set them down and headed toward the door. "I fear something may be very wrong. Let us go to my father's rooms."

They hurried down the hall in the same direction as Asil's wing, but then turned into a narrow hallway just before where the wing joined the Lord's Hall. At the end of this narrow hallway was a heavy door, which the three of them passed through quickly. Asil briefly worried over the fact that the door was unlocked, before remembering that he had sent Maris ahead. The door revealed a stair, which made three turns before opening to the expansive apartments above the throne room that were the Lord of the Strait's chambers. They walked swiftly through the seating area to the double doors that marked Egemon's bedroom. One of the doors was already pushed open, and inside was Maris and her assistant, examining a clearly unconscious Egemon.

"Is he poisoned?" Asil asked without preamble. Looking up, Maris just shook her head, visibly frustrated.

"If it is poison, it is not one I have ever seen," she said, straightening up. Her assistant, Nasrin, blushed and bowed her head before so much assembled royalty. "He appears to be suffering from exhaustion, but I cannot tell what is exhausting him."

Asil set his hands on the foot of the bed, leaning on the wood frame while swearing under his breath. Meliha came around the other side and reached out, gently setting a hand against Egemon's wrist.

"A steady pulse," Meliha said, and Maris nodded in agreement. "A touch slow, perhaps, but then, he is sleeping."

"It is a touch slow," Maris said, nodding, "and he does not respond to sound. He still flinches away from pain. That is promising, but no less vexing."

"So we know nothing," Asil said sharply.

Sighing, Hasim set a hand on his friend's shoulder. "We know he is still alive. We just need to seek an answer."

Asil nodded, staring at his father for a moment longer, then suddenly pushed off the bed, standing up straight. "Carys! We need Carys. She should be in her rooms. Hasim, can you bring her here?"

"Wait." Meliha came back around the bed, concern on her face. "I am sorry for saying this, my Heir, but Carys is already under some suspicion. If… if your father's condition were to worsen after she visited his rooms, it would only fan those flames. Let us return to the study. Send Hasim to retrieve her and bring her there."

The urge to argue with Meliha was overwhelming, but Asil choked it back. "Very well. Let's be on our way. Maris, stay with him. I want you or Nasrin in here until he wakes."

"Of course, my Heir." Maris spoke with such a firm surety that, for the moment at least, Asil felt comforted.

They left the Lord's chambers and headed back into the hall, Asil and Meliha returning to the study while Hasim turned in the opposite direction to find Carys. Meliha beckoned a young woman who had appeared to just be milling about in the hall and spoke to her in quiet tones before sending her off. Asil let out a bitter laugh.

"My Heir?" Meliha asked, concerned.

"It seems we have found a circumstance in which I do not notice all of your people," Asil said as they stepped into the office.

Sighing, Meliha shook her head. "This is not how I wanted to achieve this victory. I wanted my people to get better, not for you to be so distracted with worry that you didn't notice."

For a period, there was little to do but wait. The young woman returned with a stack of letters; Meliha thanked her and then sent her off again. Shortly after, a page arrived with wine. Asil was briefly confused until Meliha indicated that she had arranged that as well. Asil allowed himself to have a glass. The idea that it might soothe his nerves, even a touch, was very appealing. Finally, Hasim returned with Carys. It seemed Carys had been in the baths—she wore a dress intended for lounging, and her hair was still damp, spiraling into curls as it dried. She wore a jacket with a hood, which was pulled up over her eyes, but beneath it Asil saw that she had skipped the veil. Hasim looked slightly pink cheeked, and Asil wondered briefly about what state of dress Carys had been in when Hasim had burst into her rooms looking for her.

"What's going on?" Carys asked, pulling back her hood before shrugging the short jacket off entirely. "Hasim would tell me nothing, simply that it was urgent and that I needed my cards."

Meliha approached Carys and presented a glass of wine. "We are sorry to disturb your rest, Seer Arslan. The Lord of the Strait has fallen ill. We need you to see if the cards can tell us why."

Taking the glass, Carys looked at Asil with wide eyes. Asil found himself reaching for her, then stopped and pulled his hand back. He found comfort in Carys, and he longed for that now. But he wasn't sure that this was the time. Hasim would understand, but what would Meliha infer from those actions? Instead, he just nodded to Carys and refilled his glass as Meliha further explained the situation. When it was done, Carys looked back to Asil with such empathy and compassion that Asil lost the battle against his better judgment. He set his glass down and pulled Carys into his arms. Meliha made a slight sound of surprise, but Hasim said nothing, and Carys just held him and brushed back his hair.

After a long moment, Asil let go and stepped back. "Can you do this?"

Carys nodded. "Of course. Clear the table."

The wine service was moved to Egemon's desk, the low table before the fireplace was quickly cleared, and Meliha even used the napkin by the wine pitcher to give it a quick dust. Carys settled on the chair before the table, sitting where Egemon would normally have sat, and drew out her cards. She breathed deeply and evenly as she shuffled the cards. They hovered for a moment, watching her; then first Meliha, then Asil, and finally Hasim found seats on the settees flanking the table.

As Carys began to lay out the cards, Asil sat forward. He had seen her set down three before, but this time she kept going. Nine cards in total ended up on the table, some crossed over others. Her eyes began to glow, and this time Asil watched it without her veil in the way. The glow began in the center, in the ring almost devoid of color save for the faintest gray of a morning mist, and then it spread as the light grew brighter.

"Mother!" Hasim gasped, staring at Carys's face. The glow from her eyes illuminated the cards before her.

"An affliction," Carys said after a moment, "not born of Vasi. An illness of spirit. Like a curse, but not. It came from Peadar." Her hovering fingertips set briefly on one of the cards, an image of a man in dark clothes, a dagger in one hand and a coin pouch in the other, the lower half of his face covered. "It brings dreams, heavy and taxing, that will slowly take away all remaining strength. To see it undone…"

Carys's hand drifted again, and touched lightly on a card that depicted a young woman reading a large book. "A student… a scribe… Moira! Moira knows how it works, knows the key to turning it off! She…"

Abruptly, Carys yelped in pain and put her hands to her face, covering her eyes. Asil and the others looked up sharply in surprise. Before Asil could collect his thoughts, Hasim was on his feet, gently checking Carys for injury.

"What happened?" Asil asked after a moment, and Carys took a shuddering breath.

"Moira's curse." Carys let Hasim finish his examination, then smiled as reassuringly as she could manage. Asil could tell by how she kept her eyes down that she had a headache at the very least. "It's a nasty piece of work. I was following the thread and ran into it."

"So now what do we do?" Hasim asked, frustrated. "We don't dare tip our hand until we can figure out how to wake your father. For all we know, they can make it worse."

The urge to punch or break something was intense. Asil put his hand up to his face and sighed. "I hadn't thought of that, but you're right."

"Wait." Meliha stood and walked back to Egemon's desk, where she had set the stack of letters that the young woman had brought her. "Halil says Moira suffers from intense headaches and went to bed with a particularly awful one this evening. Carys, you have to be next to someone to break a curse, correct?"

Carys nodded, retrieving her glass of wine. "Yes, my lady."

"Hasim, go check with Maris and confirm that Lord Özdemir is stable enough that we needn't be concerned about his health through the night," Meliha ordered. Hasim arched a brow but got up and headed out into the hall. "Carys, you are one of the better witches in our kingdom. Go in the morning and tell Peadar that you heard Moira was ill and as a healer you are there to help. Get yourself alone with the girl and lift her curse. Either you can convince her to tell you what is wrong, or with the curse gone you can complete your reading."

Both Asil and Carys just looked at Meliha in surprise for a long moment. "You have a surprising grasp of how the curse impedes me," Carys said, looking up at Meliha's eyes as if she expected to see something there.

Meliha just smiled. "It is my job, darling. I am House Aydin; we are the Keepers of Knowledge."

"I'll have to have some longer talks with you when this is all over," Asil murmured, and Meliha continued to smile, though she was beginning to look more smug about it. He turned back to Carys. "Are you all right? How bad is the headache?"

"Pretty bad." Carys reached up and rubbed the spot between her brows. "Moira's curse is… malevolent. I wonder if it is also the cause of her headaches."

Asil frowned. "Will you be able to deal with it?"

"I should be," Carys said, straightening up. "The pain I'm experiencing is not from interacting with the curse, but rather from running into it. Imagine… imagine you were walking along, following a trail, and you were so focused on the trail that you didn't see a low tree branch until you hit your head on it. Now imagine the tree branch is also covered in spikes. That is effectively what I did."

"Oh." Asil considered for a moment, then nodded. That was a very understandable metaphor.

The door opened, and Hasim came back inside. "Maris says that his condition is stable, and she is not worried about the evening," he reported, and Asil felt himself relax just a little. "She says the danger is more long term, if he does not wake up for several days."

Nodding, Meliha folded up the letters. "Then, by your leave my Heir, I suggest we retire for the night. Carys can recover, and we can begin to take steps in the morning after she returns from seeing Moira."

"Yes," Asil said, smoothing his clothing. "Thank you, Lady Aydin. I will have Hasim explain the situation to Lord Kilic. He has a gift for convincing his father to take a more-nuanced approach. We shall all reconvene at lunch tomorrow unless Carys says the situation requires more urgency."

After a quick bow, Meliha took her letters and headed out of the study. Hasim looked at Asil with arched brows.

"I can lead my father to nuance?" Hasim folded his arms over your chest. "Surely you're joking. He'll be storming the castle in a breath."

"We can't let that happen," Asil said, reaching up to rub his temple. "We don't know if Peadar has any way of accelerating whatever it is he's done. And we don't know the whole of his plans. Peadar has taken pains to curry favor with the heads of the Great Families. Who knows what deals he might have made."

Hasim's arms dropped. "Surely you don't think the Great Families would conspire against the throne?!"

"Wouldn't they?" Asil stared at Hasim for a long moment, and Hasim eventually backed down.

"Some might," Hasim said begrudgingly.

"Muhan Kaplan," Carys said as she gathered up her cards. She held one in her hand, staring at it; it was an image of coins falling through the air.

Hasim grunted. "If anyone would, it would certainly be him."

There was quiet for a moment, then Asil cleared his throat. "Did your father increase the guard as I asked?"

"Yes." Hasim turned back to look at Asil. "He assumes, for now, that it is a precaution related to the Highest Lord's current condition."

Asil nodded. "Good. Wait until morning, and then tell your father our concerns, that the ambassador may be fomenting a coup. He may be itching for a fight, but he is still the Lord Captain and a master tactician. Convince him not to fly off in a rage and see what he suggests."

Hasim bowed his head and smiled softly at his friend. "Yes, my Heir."

"Carys," Asil began, and she stood up and stepped toward him, "you will need to rest. I had originally intended to persuade you back to my room this evening, but given our plans for tomorrow, you should probably be allowed to retire in peace."

Carys gave Asil a teasing smile. "Always a reason."

"I could stay here and go back in the morning," Hasim pointed out, grinning. "And are you sure Carys couldn't come by for, say, a few hours?"

Carys laughed, then winced, and put a hand to her head. "You are both delightful and awful at the same time. But I'm afraid I am in too much pain to call your bluff, Lord Commander."

"A shame," Hasim said, looking genuinely disappointed.

Asil stepped forward and embraced Carys once more, holding her tight. "Rest, recover," he said softly. "I believe much of tomorrow will hinge on you."

"I will find the answer," Carys said, a soft quaver of emotion in her voice. Then she let go, bowed, and took herself from the room.

There was a moment of quiet as the door closed behind Carys, then Hasim stepped up and put his arm over Asil's shoulder. "Come on, then. Let's go back to your room and exhaust ourselves so that we get some sleep."

Asil snorted. "She's right, you are awful."

"Perhaps, but I'm fairly certain you love that in me," Hasim said, retrieving the decanter of wine and motioning for Asil to lead the way. "Also, I can't help but notice that she didn't say no, just 'not right now.' That's promising."

"Shut up, Hasim."

"Also not a no."

Chapter 23

CARYS WAS ALREADY awake when Aylin arrived in the morning with breakfast. She had awoken a little before dawn, plagued by uncomfortable dreams, and had wandered out onto the balcony to watch the sun rise. She felt a strange tension within her, like she'd had before the garden party just weeks ago, only stronger this time.

Before starting breakfast, Carys allowed the girl to help her choose a dress, and she even let Aylin style her hair. The young maid was practically beside herself, and Carys once more felt slightly guilty for all the times she had balked at Aylin's attempts to serve. Carys drank her coffee but otherwise picked at breakfast, her appetite off as anticipation roiled within her.

Finally, Carys slung her satchel over her shoulder and headed out, down the south stairs, and once more toward the House of Flowers. She was now quite familiar with this route, and immediately noticed that guards were patrolling the perimeter of the main castle. It seemed that perhaps Hasim had managed a successful conversation with his father after all.

"I hope it makes a difference," she muttered as she crossed the footbridge. She smiled and nodded to the guard on the other side, who nodded back without an answering smile.

Stepping lightly across the lane, Carys came to the door of the villa and knocked twice. Halil answered swiftly and ushered Carys inside, where the ambassador looked up from his desk with some surprise.

"My lady Seer," the ambassador said, standing up and coming around. "It is, of course, delightful to see you, but I was not expecting you today. I have no appointments, and the commander and his knights are down at the barracks, overseeing the next exchange of soldiers."

"I am not here for them, Ambassador," Carys said, her polite smile fixed. "I believe they know the city well enough without me at this point. And I am sorry to arrive without sending word. I came because I heard that your secretary is suffering from a particularly severe headache. I wanted to offer my assistance."

"Oh, I see," Peadar said, and Carys noted something in him relax a bit. "She has suffered from them for some time, the poor thing. I'm not sure what you could do."

Carys simply smiled again. "With respect, Ambassador, while I am a woman with strange and specific talents, I was also trained by the greatest witch Vasi has ever had the pleasure to know," she said evenly. "I may have something new in my bag. I promise I won't make anything worse, and I may help."

The ambassador looked at Carys for a moment, ever calculating, then nodded. "Very well, Seer Arslan, right this way."

They walked down a short hall to a small room—servant's quarters, close to the main bedroom but not adjoined to it. That was a relief, as it implied that the secretary really was just that; Moira was not expected to perform any further duties for Peadar. Carys would not have wished the ambassador on anyone. Inside, Moira lay on the bed, the lamps dimmed and the curtains drawn.

"The light makes it worse, you see," Peadar explained, speaking a touch quieter than he usually did. "As does sound, so keep your voice low."

Nodding, Carys approached the bed, and Moira winced and whimpered as Carys drew close. Reaching out, Carys gently petted the back of the young woman's hand and made a soft hushing noise, and Moira relaxed. Turning back around, Carys nodded to Peadar.

"Thank you, Ambassador, you may go."

"Oh, I thought I might stay and answer questions if you needed," Peadar said, with that slightly smug and completely awful smile of his.

Sighing, Carys set down her bag and took a few steps toward the ambassador so that she could keep her voice low. "Tension in the neck and shoulders can often add to pain in the head," Carys explained, "so I will need to open her blouse to treat her. I would ask, for her privacy, that you leave."

There was a small flash of irritation in Peadar's eyes, and Carys knew she had won. "Oh, of course, Seer," the ambassador said, bowing. "I simply didn't understand your quaint and strange methods. I shall be at my desk if you have need. Please be certain to take every care and precaution; I am hobbled without Moira's aid."

"Of course," Carys said with a smile as the ambassador made his way out. The door closed, and the smile dropped. "You disgusting weasel."

Turning back to the bed, Carys approached carefully. Moira was awake and aware now, breathing through her pain as she looked at Carys. With the most reassuring smile possible, Carys gave Moira's hand a light squeeze, and pulled down the blanket enough to see a heavy necklace with no clasp around her neck. Carys examined it for a moment, and shortly confirmed that it was fused together. It would take a file and a few hours to remove.

"You know what it does," Moira said very quietly.

Carys looked up at Moira in surprise. "Yes," she said, "and so do you?"

Moira nodded, once.

"But you're the only one?" Carys asked, and Moira nodded again, though she winced as she did. "And... you can't speak of it."

Another nod and wince.

"Right, no more questions," Carys said, and opened up her satchel.

First, Carys set a small brazier by the bed, then retrieved a coal from the banked fireplace. Blowing on the coal a bit to give it life, she set it in the brazier and dropped a handful of carefully-selected herbs onto it. Fragrant smoke plumed forth and Carys fanned it towards Moira, who relaxed as she breathed it in. Next, she set out a tincture she had prepared earlier. That would be for after. Finally, she turned back to the necklace. The light was dim enough in the room, so Carys removed her veil and let her eyes relax. A soft glow overtook them as she stroked the large locket, calling forth what hid within.

The expected bee came first, wriggling out, looking around, and followed by a second.

Queen!

Sighing a little, Carys let them crawl up her hand and onto her arm. The bees were not alone, though, and as Carys watched, a thorned vine began to manifest. It looped through and around the necklace and also wrapped up around Moira's head, the long thorns passing through Moira's flesh.

"Oh, you are a nasty piece of work," Carys muttered, brows drawn down.

Focusing, she unraveled the bee spirits with the same ease as the rest of them. The vine, however, was harder—whoever had designed this had seen Moira as a bigger risk than Cillian, which seemed strange when comparing this delicate young woman who had to be the same age as Emiri Bulut, to the massive veteran soldier that Cillian was. But eventually, the binding gave. In the end it wasn't more complex, just more layered—the same binding as with the bees but applied over and over. There was a utilitarian quality to the bindings from the empire, but a distinct lack of finesse.

The vine spirit, however, was another problem. It did not move of its own, and it could not be persuaded to simply leave. It would have to be physically removed, a difficult task for an incorporeal object anchored to a necklace that could not be removed. The process would surely hurt Moira, but leaving it there wasn't an option.

"Moira," Carys murmured, "I… I can help you, but it will hurt first. I'm sorry, I don't know of another way. I need you to do everything you can not to cry out."

The woman's eyes opened, and she looked up at Carys for a moment, searching. Finally, Moira nodded, closing her eyes once more and setting her teeth. Taking a deep breath, Carys opened herself to the possibilities, and reached for that energy that sprang from her hands when Judex had pushed her too far, the energy she had channeled to rake through the bindings of the swords and to drive away the snake killing Havva. She brought a hand up over the locket and trembled with uncertainty, then pushed the power out toward the vine.

Moira squeaked in pain and whimpered as Carys heard an inhuman shriek in her mind, but the vine began to burn. Not disperse, burn. The light traveled over Moira, the vine falling into insubstantial ash as the power Carys channeled passed over it. And then, abruptly, the pain and tension completely left Moira, and she collapsed against the bed with a sob.

Moving quickly, Carys retrieved a cloth from the basin and bathed Moira's face and neck, the cool water soothing the poor girl, who continued to cry quietly with relief. Carys then brought out an oil and coated the locket in it; while she didn't necessarily think there was anything dangerous about the object itself, a touch of rose oil—sacred to the Divine Mother—couldn't hurt and would at the very least be calming. Carys fanned smoke over Moira again, who breathed it in and calmed further; she also cleaned Moira's face once more, wiping away the tears. Then she sat on the edge of the bed and waited.

It felt like a long time, but Moira finally turned her head toward Carys. "You're like me," Moira said in a quiet voice. "You're Defiled."

Carys blinked. "I'm what?"

"Defiled," Moira said again, breathing deeply. "That's what they call it. We try to steal the Divine Mother's sight, her ability to see and shepherd souls, and so we are Defiled. That's what they teach us in the temples. It's very rare in the south, but more common in the archipelago. They took me when I was 10. My eyes got lighter, and they said that was how it started."

Carys went cold. That was it, that was what she had been missing. That was the reason why the soldiers thought there were no seers.

"But they lied," Moira said, and tears began to fill her eyes again. These tears were angry. "They didn't fix me. They don't fix any of us. They chain us and use us to chain others. I wasn't strong enough—I can't make the magic work. I can only see. That's why they sent me, so I could find the magic, point it out."

Tears began to prick Carys's eyes as well. "Moira, I'm so sorry," she said, clasping the other woman's hand. "You're not Defiled, and you stole nothing. You're a seer. If you had been raised here, we would have been kind to you. And yes, I am like you, but… I am stronger. The magic answers me."

Nodding, Moira squeezed Carys's hand. "You're the one that started breaking the chains," Moira said, and Carys nodded. "I saw the magic fading, saw that it was gone. I… I didn't tell the Ambassador. He doesn't really understand, anyway. But… but I was supposed to, and the longer I didn't tell him, the more it hurt."

"It's gone now," Carys said. "It's broken, and I will make sure you do not go back with them. I can teach you. To understand what you see. You will have to pretend to be the same, just for a few days, but I promise I will not leave you with them."

With another sob, Moira reached out for Carys, and Carys took the girl in her arms and held her as she cried, as they both cried. The rage that surged through Carys made the light come to her eyes again. How dare they. How dare they! Carys would have gone out into the hall that instant and hurled her power into Peadar if she thought it would do anything to him at all. Instead, she stroked Moira's hair and let the girl cry herself out. When the sobs had reduced to sniffles, Carys laid Moira back down.

"You need to know something," Moira said quietly as Carys gently cleaned her again. "The Ambassador gave your king a gift. It also contains chains. I don't… I don't completely understand how it works, but it's been activated. The ambassador knows that the prince lied. I… I told him that the prince lied. I had to! If the ambassador asks me a direct question, I have to answer—it hurts too much!"

"It's all right, Moira, it isn't your fault," Carys said softly. "How do I stop it? Can I stop it without hurting Lord Özdemir?"

"Yes." Moira smiled, happy that she had an answer. "Find the statue, break it, and get it as far away from the king as possible. Otherwise he won't wake, and eventually he'll just… fade away. They'll arrange an accident for the Heir, soon, maybe even today. In the chaos, the

Ambassador will take over. The soldiers will take the castle. He'll promise the merchant families power if they stand aside."

Carys's eyes grew wide, and her face went pale. "And they'll do it," she murmured. Not all of the Great Families, but enough of them would. She remembered holding the Coin, and how Muhan Kaplan rose with a swiftness in her mind. With a trembling hand, Carys set the cloth down. "I understand," she said, and picked up the tincture. "Moira, this is a valerian draught, mixed with other herbs. It will put you to sleep for the rest of the day and into tomorrow. When you wake, you will be groggy for a while longer, but at that point you can declare your headaches cured. I prepared this so that no one could question you about what I did until I had time to… well, until I had more time. Will you take it? I won't force you."

"I will," Moira said without hesitation, and Carys helped her sit up. The draught was not the most pleasant tasting, though Carys had been sure to add mint and honey to help, but Moira got it down and Carys helped her get comfortable.

"Not long now," Carys said as she watched Moira drift, and gave her hand one more squeeze.

In minutes the girl was out, and the Divine Mother herself would have had to come down to wake her. Standing, Carys buried the empty tincture bottle in the bottom of her satchel and refreshed the herb mixture on the brazier. With any luck, Peadar would think that was the majority of what she had done. She also rinsed out the cloth and washed her own face, composing herself. She would have to interact with Peadar when she left, and without revealing her anger or disgust.

After another moment, Carys donned her veil once more and slung her satchel back over her shoulder, then headed out into the hall. It seemed impossibly bright after the darkened room, and Carys brought her hood up to further shield her eyes. As she headed down the hallway, she almost ran into Ambassador Peadar.

"Ah, Seer Arslan," the ambassador said, smiling as always. "I was just about to come check on you; it seemed you were taking so long! How is Moira?"

"Sleeping," Carys answered honestly, and Peadar looked surprised, but he also relaxed again. "I worked on the tension in her shoulders and neck, and had prepared herbs, which I left smoldering in a brazier by her bedside—the butler can return the brazier later. I set down a fresh bundle as I was heading out, so that should burn for a while. I find the fact that she fell asleep very reassuring. She must have been in quite a lot of pain."

"Yes," Peadar agreed, nodding. "I had not appreciated how great a hindrance her headaches were when she was assigned to this voyage, but she's very competent, and one trusts the Council in all things."

"Well then," Carys said, bowing her head to the ambassador, "if she worsens, do send someone for me immediately, but I am extremely confident that she will sleep, probably through the night, as she seemed utterly spent, and then wake up feeling better. I will see you this evening at court, Ambassador."

The ambassador bowed, then returned to his desk. "I shall look forward to seeing you, Seer Arslan."

Carys left the villa as quickly as she politely could, nodding to the guard again as she passed over the footbridge. He watched her curiously, as if there were something remarkable about her comings and goings. Heading back into the castle, she quickened her step up the south staircase, not quite sprinting to her room, and set everything down before ringing for Aylin.

Chapter 24

CARYS POURED THE contents of her satchel out onto the table and sent Aylin to fetch her another coffee and something light to make up for the breakfast she had largely skipped. As she sorted and put away the items on the table, she considered what to do next. Was it safe to wait until their agreed-upon meeting at lunch? It might not be, not if Peadar intended to move quickly. Hasim was probably still down at the guard house. It occurred to Carys that she didn't actually know where Asil was. How careful did she need to be about finding him? How closely was she being watched by Peadar's allies?

Pausing, Carys removed her jacket and hung it in the dressing room. It was heavy with the scent of the herbs she had used on Moira, and while there was nothing wrong with the fragrance, they were herbs meant to soothe and relax. Carys needed her mind clear. She returned to the table in her underdress and continued to sort and stew.

She was still putting things away when she heard Aylin clear her throat. That was odd—Aylin normally waited or called her name. Looking up, Carys saw Aylin coming in with a tray, but also saw that she was followed by Pasha Kaplan and two of the pasha's personal guards. Carys wrapped herself in her shawl to cover her half-dressed state and narrowed her eyes as she came around the large bed to face the intruders.

"I'm sorry, seer," Aylin said quietly, looking afraid.

"It's all right," Carys replied quietly, eyes on the men by the door, "this is not your fault. Though if they let you leave, you should try to speak to Nazim about this."

With a timid nod, Aylin set down the tray on the table, scooting aside the herbs and empty phials, and left it still covered as she moved to leave. The pasha looked Aylin over, measuring, but let the girl go with a dismissive sniff before turning toward Carys.

"I am here to speak with you on a very grave matter, Seer Arslan," Pasha Kaplan said, drawing himself up and looking down his nose at Carys. "We of the Great Families are prepared to see you tried for treason. You have been seen spending time in the company of foreign soldiers. The Commander, as well as his knights, have sought you out for private conversations. You were in the House of Flowers for hours this morning. You seduced the Heir to secure your position but knowing that he will not wed outside of the Three Families, you have made a deal with this foreign entity for power."

The shock on Carys's face was almost comical. She blinked, just staring at the pasha for a moment. "Do you have any idea how utterly absurd you sound right now?" Carys asked, arching an eyebrow.

That caused Pasha Kaplan to pause, and the guards flicked their eyes at each other. Whatever response they had been anticipating, that was not it. The pasha recovered quickly.

"We have witnesses," the pasha began, but Carys cut him off.

"Of course you do," Carys said, with a weary tone reminiscent of a mother chastising her rebellious child. "You have witnesses because at no point have I tried to hide my actions. Because, as the Lord's Seer, I have been assigned the task of liaison to the party from the Ealdorlang Empire."

"How convenient, then, that you achieved the position of Lord's Seer shortly before they arrived," Pasha Kaplan returned, walking toward the table.

Sighing, Carys reached up and rubbed the bridge of her nose through the veil. "Either I failed to seduce the Heir, or I succeeded in placing myself in line to benefit from an unknown entity. Which is it?"

Ignoring Carys's challenge, Pasha Kaplan picked up the empty cobalt-blue bottle. "And what is this, then, if not poisons used to incapacitate the Lord of the Strait?"

"That, Pasha, was a tincture of valerian, mint, honey, and wine," Carys explained, growing more weary of the conversation by the moment. "And a few other herbs. If I recall correctly, a runner from your own household came to my shop for the same tincture four or five times last winter. For one of your sons, I believe."

Lip curled in disgust, Pasha Kaplan pocketed the bottle. "I only have one son. And that's a convenient excuse. We all know you are a low-born witch, Seer Arslan. Your sad attempt at securing a spot here will not save you."

Narrowing her eyes, Carys took a step forward. "I know why you are here, Muhan, and I'm not going to answer your insane accusations anymore," Carys said, her voice firm. She glanced at the guards, and saw them look between themselves again, uncertain. "I answer to the Lord of the Strait and his Heir. And that galls you, doesn't it? That a low-born bastard sleeps in a castle that will never house a single member of your family."

Pasha Kaplan's eyes grew wide, and Carys sensed she had come to the heart of it but had also gone too far. The pasha was a large man, and while he had grown fatter with age and success, he had not yet lost the strength of his youth. He took two steps and his arm came up, swinging quickly and landing a blow to the side of Carys's face with the back of his hand.

The blow brought Carys down, and she collapsed onto the rug, dazed. She had never been struck before—she found that she didn't care for the sensation. Pain throbbed from the side of her face, and she brought up a hand to touch her cheek. Feeling something wet on her fingers, she brought her hand away and saw blood. The skin of her cheek had split between the pasha's rings. She heard one of the guards make a small sound of surprise, as if he couldn't believe what had just happened. Pasha Kaplan said nothing else to Carys, just swore under his breath and stormed out.

"One inside, one outside," she heard the pasha yell as he left. "You will make sure she stays put!"

For another minute Carys stayed on the floor, breathing through the pain. Then the guard that had been left inside came over and gently helped her to her feet, guiding her into the chair by her table.

"Seer Arslan, I am sorry," the guard said, brow furrowed and eyes slightly panicked.

"If you must stay here," Carys said, her voice calmer than she felt, "you will stand by the door and you will not speak to me."

The guard looked struck, but he nodded and did as she commanded. There was a reasonable chance that Carys would feel bad about this later, but for now all she knew was pain and anger. Gathering herself, she walked unsteadily into her dressing room and closed the door behind her. The guards wouldn't concern themselves—the dressing room led to nowhere, other than the balcony that connected around her entire room.

"The balcony," Carys murmured, and looked at the small keyhole door that led out from the dressing room.

Taking a breath, Carys began to get dressed. She pulled out her clothes from before the castle. Most of them were gone, but she still had the sea-colored ensemble she had met Asil in, and it was infinitely more practical than anything else that had been added to her wardrobes since. She hooked the pouch with her cards to her belt, and also picked up the pendulum she had brought from her shop. Something in it sang to her, told her she would need it. Sitting down at the vanity, she removed her veil and looked at her face. The cut was small, but her eye was starting to blacken and swell. It would ache and throb, but she would be all right. Should be all right. She cleaned the cut, hissing quietly as she did, and found a new veil that did not have blood staining the edge.

Walking to the little door, Carys opened it carefully. The room had been freshly turned for her use, just weeks ago, which had thankfully included oiling the doors. It opened without a squeak, only the lightest of scrapes. Stepping carefully outside, she pulled the door closed and moved down along the castle.

When Carys came to the noble quarter that first night, the night that started this mad journey, she had thought the balconies impractical and risky. Now they were her path. She just needed to find a way back in. She began trying doors, following the balcony around the edge of the building. Each one was locked.

"Damn it all," Carys said through clenched teeth. She had come to the end of the balcony. Walking up to the balustrade, she looked over the edge. The next balcony was not that far down. She might be able to make it.

She undid her sash and looped it around the support pillar of the balustrade, letting the ends hang free. She then climbed over, holding on to the smooth, pale stone. Her heart beat fast, and she tried not to look farther down than the balcony below. She would not survive a fall to the ground. She needed to not think about it. Crouching down, she took hold of either side of the sash, and wrapped it around each hand. As carefully as she could, she started to lower herself, letting her legs drop down, dangling over the edge.

Legs above the lower balcony, Carys tried to lower herself farther. The controlled descent she had pictured in her head failed, however, and she suddenly dropped, her grip on the sash keeping her from falling too far, but the wrenching in her arms made her cry out in pain. Breathing hard, she began to swing herself a little, and as she swung in toward the balcony, she let go of one side of the sash, falling forward. She landed, thankfully, with bent knees, and while she ended up on her backside, it wasn't that bad of a fall. She'd have bruises, but after a minute she was able to push herself up, wincing as she did.

"Remember when you wanted a life of adventure as a child?" Judex asked, materializing beside her.

"You were not there then, and now is not the time!"

Panting through pain, Carys got to her knees and then back onto her feet. Her body ached, her hands were scuffed, and the Mother only knew how many bruises now adorned her hips and legs. She wound her sash back around her waist and tried to smooth her hair. If she was about to walk through the castle, she had to look like everything was fine. Lunch was soon, and afterward the anticipatory hours before court, when the halls would fill with nobles and merchants.

With deepening breaths, Carys calmed herself and began to walk. It hurt, but it wasn't the worst pain she had experienced, and in a way the movement made it better, pulling out the muscles that had seized when she hit the floor of the balcony. She found an open door easily and slipped back into the north wing, heading toward the main hall. She felt almost as if she were being led, and thought she heard the buzz of bees. There, waiting by the grand stair—the ambassador, and two ensigns that Carys didn't recognize. The ambassador didn't see her; his focus was on the other side of the room, where Pasha Yasuv was having a heated conversation with Pasha Kaplan's heir. The ambassador looked nervous. Did that mean Pasha Yasuv didn't approve of this action against the Lord of the Strait? Had Peadar played his gambit before making sure all the Great Families were in accord?

Carys turned sharply, ducking behind a column and making her way toward the main doors while drawing up her hood to hide her features.

"The hood gives you away as much as the veil does," Judex commented with dry disapproval, "but they're too tied up in their machinations to notice the obvious regardless. They really don't deserve to succeed."

A slightly bitter smile quirked the corners of Carys's mouth. "For once we agree," she said. She turned again and stepped out through the smaller servant's door at the edge of the great hall, following the edge of the building and slipping into the private garden that surrounded the North Parlor. Blessedly, the parlor was empty.

Carys reached into her jacket and pulled out the pendulum. She wasn't sure where to go, where she was needed. She didn't use the pendulum often, but today it would guide her. The lapis lazuli weight spun, and then pulled sharply toward the east. Carys tucked it away, then began to run through the gardens.

☾☾☾

There were only three gates into Watcher Castle. There was the Petitioner's Gate, also called the Main Gate, which was typically open but well guarded. Then there was Veli's Gate, or the Sea Gate. It was believed that, many centuries ago, there was a great bridge of land that connected Veli and Vasi over the strait. This belief was rooted in the fact that there was a gate that opened to a sheer cliffside, and historians had no other explanation for it. Then there was the Merchant's Gate. Smaller, the closest entrance to the east wing, and jointly guarded by Killic's men and the Great Families. When Carys reached the gate, she could see Pasha Kaplan on the other side, speaking with his guards, as well as Tadhg, his knights, and more than a dozen soldiers from the ship. There were no guards on the castle side.

Carys slowed to a walk and drew in deep breaths, even as her heart hammered in her chest. This was where she needed to be. This was where the spirits had led her. Not to find Asil, but to confront the people set on destroying her home.

"Seer Arslan," Cillian said, bewildered, as he spotted her first. Tadhg turned around at her name, eyes wide in surprise, and Pasha Kaplan looked toward her and glared.

"How did you get out of your chambers?" the pasha demanded and did not notice the curious looks that slowly came to bear on him. "You two, take her back, and find out how they lost her," he said, gesturing to his own men on the far side of the gate.

Their path was abruptly blocked by Cillian, with one hand on his sword and his axe drawn. "You will not lay a hand on her," Cillian said with cold surety. Kaplan's guards looked surprised and glanced from Pasha Kaplan to Cillian and back.

The pasha's face grew red without outrage. "What?!" he nearly shrieked and was prepared to continue when Tadhg's heavy hand came down on the pasha's shoulder. The pasha spun his head so quickly that his jowls quivered, but he fell silent.

"Carys, what are you doing here?" Tadhg asked, his voice even and calm.

For a moment, Carys just looked at him, her heart breaking. She had hoped… she wasn't sure what she had hoped. That it wouldn't be him, that he wouldn't know, that he at least would not be leading the charge. That this man who made her body sing wouldn't be here to kill her dearest friend. Tadhg couldn't see her eyes but still seemed to feel the pain of her gaze, looking away for a moment.

Taking a breath, Carys let out a slightly manic laugh and straightened, lifting her head. "I am here to hold the gate," she said. She could just barely hear the buzzing in the soldiers beyond. The bees were waking up. Their queen was near.

There was quiet for a moment as they all considered her words, and Tadhg's hand fell from Kaplan's shoulder in the shock. Áedh looked bewildered. Generys's face was impassive, but she did not move to take action either. Kaplan recovered first and began laughing.

"Have you taken leave of your senses?" Pasha Kaplan asked, looking at Carys as if she were mad. "By the Mother, child, did I rattle your brain? I didn't hit you that hard!"

Cillian growled, and the pasha stepped back, startled. Áedh retrieved a dagger from wherever he hid them and spun it slowly between his fingers. Generys remained cold, though her hand tightened on the grip of her hilt. Tadhg, however, just continued to gaze at Carys.

"Carys, the prince is unfit," Tadhg said evenly, his voice calm as he tried to explain. "The merchant families have said they will support us. The Empire has helped many countries unify, find purpose. We can help you."

"You have been lied to," Carys said quietly, her hands grasping the metal bars of the gate. Her eyes began to glow beneath her veil. "The Great Families have not reached an agreement. Even now the head of the Great Families argues with this one's son in the hall, as Peadar quakes with nervousness. Asil is not unfit, and even if he were, it would fall to the Three Families to decide who took his place. You will start a civil war. You will burn Vasi to the ground for Peadar's lies and Kaplan's greed."

Áedh looked to Tadhg, uncertain. Kaplan began to try to reassure Tadhg, but the general held up his hand for silence. Carys could not see Cillian's face, but the warrior didn't move, still standing between the pasha's guards and the gate. Generys's cold countenance began to fray.

"How will you alone stop us?" Tadhg asked.

Carys blinked as tears filled her eyes, and they streaked down her cheeks. "Not alone," she said. She opened herself to the threads. She gave the bees a command.

Buzzing filled the air around Carys, and she realized quickly that everyone could hear it, not just her. Heads swiveled, expecting to see a swarm, save for Tadhg who continued to stare at her, and Cillian who continued to stand between Carys and Pasha Kaplan's guards. The bee spirits she had already gathered swarmed around her, dancing and ecstatic. Tadhg and his knights stared in bewilderment as every soldier with them stepped back, drew their swords, and joined Cillian in a line before the gate.

"What did you do to them?" Generys demanded, angry and terrified.

"I took over their curse—the curse your Council set on them, set on all of you," Carys explained, still crying quietly. It felt wrong, and she did not want to endanger them, but she didn't know what else to do. "Because in your land, I am not a seer. In your land, I am Defiled. Your Council did horrible things to Moira, to who knows how many children, and I will not let them do that to me or to anyone else. I will die first."

They could all see the bees now, flying around Carys and buzzing in tight circles around the swords of the soldiers. The pain in Carys's body became all the greater as she channeled more energy than she ever had before. She clenched her teeth on a cry of pain but held fast. Tadhg's eyes grew wide, and Carys could see the chain of calculations coming together for him. He had always been so curious, so quick. Having the missing piece made the puzzle whole, instantly.

"No, that can't be," Generys said, taking her hand from her sword and stepping forward. "Carys, you can't be Defiled—they're monsters! They defy the Divine Mother! They… they…" The words fell away as Generys couldn't find any arguments. She didn't know why the Defiled were wrong; she just knew that she had always been told they were.

"Carys told me of the curses," Cillian said, and his companions looked at him, startled. "I am sorry, Commander. I meant to speak with you about it, but there was never a quiet moment. You have found yourself questioning, haven't you? All of you, for the first time in years. Carys said the spirits kept us obedient, kept us docile."

"I couldn't… couldn't get rid of the spirits after I freed them," Carys said, and spasmed with pain. It was getting harder to talk, to do anything other than hold the soldiers before her. "They s-started to collect around me. A sympathy f-formed, between the ones still b-bound and the ones unbound. I never… I never m-meant for this to happen, but while they are still bound, your men will answer to me. I can f-force them. You will have to k-kill me if you want through this gate."

"Done," Pasha Kaplan said, disgusted, and motioned to the guard on his left, who drew a dagger and brought his arm back to fling it.

The guard never finished the motion. Blood blossomed from his neck, the dagger Áedh had been holding now buried almost to the hilt in the soft hollow of the guard's throat. Cillian drew his sword, and the second guard fell just as quickly. Pasha Kaplan stumbled back and turned to run, but instead impaled himself on Generys's blade; she had taken up position behind him to stop a possible retreat. The four turned and regarded Carys, still shaking as she held the gate with her hands and with the line of soldiers.

"Carys, stop, it is done," Tadhg said, stepping forward. "You're hurting yourself."

"I need your w-word," Carys managed to get out. Mother, it hurt so much! She felt like she was burning.

"You have it," Tadhg said, and went down on one knee. Only a beat behind, the others followed. "I am a soldier. I must serve—it is who I am. Carys, Lady Arslan, you have shown yourself to be a woman of principle and honor. If the Council is unworthy, I will serve you."

Carys let out another manic laugh that ended in a whimper of pain. Then she let go—of the bees, of the soldiers, and finally of the gate. The relief that flooded her senses overwhelmed her, and she slumped to the ground, falling into a velvet darkness as Tadhg called her name.

Chapter 25

THE DOOR BURST open, and a panicked guard moved quickly into the room. "My Heir!"

Asil was in his father's study, reviewing the letters and notes from the last few days, struggling to get a sense of what he might need to take care of as his father recovered. The nervous twang in the guard's voice immediately set him on edge.

"What is it?" Asil asked, standing up and fearing the worst.

"In the Hall, my Heir! The commander from the south has Seer Arslan!" The guard looked fearful and somewhat bewildered, as if he didn't understand what was going on. Asil was beginning to share that emotion, but simply nodded and headed toward the door, almost colliding with Hasim as he reached it.

"I don't know that you'll believe this," Hasim said, speaking quickly as he turned about to walk with Asil. "I don't entirely believe it myself."

"What is going on? The guard said Tadhg had Carys?" Asil was not in the mood to deal with the emotions that brought forth in him.

"Yes. Nasrin says she is stable, just exhausted, and possibly dealing with some form of backlash from her abilities," Hasim said, looking around. "Maris is still… indisposed. I have moved them into the South Parlor, but— Asil, stop for a moment!"

Growling in frustration, Asil stopped. He had pulled ahead of Hasim, panic lending him speed when he understood that Carys had been injured. "What?!"

Sighing, Hasim took Asil by the shoulders and turned the other man to face him, keeping his voice low. "The commander, and all of his soldiers, have surrendered. They subdued Peadar and handed him over to the guard, admitting that they had been prepared to seize the castle today, on the orders of the ambassador and Pasha Muhan Kaplan."

Frustration gave way to shock, and Asil stared at Hasim for a moment. "Where is Pasha Kaplan now?"

"Dead," Hasim answered, his voice even quieter, "along with a handful of his guards. The bodies are just outside the Merchant's Gate; I have sent the guards to take care of it."

Asil nodded. "Where is Carys?"

"In her rooms. Nasrin is with her."

Another nod. "What have you done with Peadar?"

"He is sitting in a carriage, in shackles, waiting to be taken to the garrison."

Closing his eyes, Asil took a deep breath, then let it out slowly. Hasim took his hands from Asil's shoulders but did not step away. Asil opened his eyes again, regarding his friend.

"Go and find the secretary, Moira," Asil said, calmer and more certain now. "Have her brought to the South Parlor. If Carys was right, she will know how to wake my father."

Hasim bowed and took himself off swiftly. Asil resumed his journey to the parlor, his panic gone, ready to deal with the mess that awaited him.

C C C

Light and the sound of birds brought Carys to wakefulness. Eyes fluttering open slowly, Carys looked up at the canopy above her for a moment. She was back in the castle, then, in her room. Tucked into bed, wearing one of those ridiculous nightgowns that Aylin kept laying out for her. Shifting in the bed, Carys started to push herself up and then stopped. She felt horrifically weak. Blinking, she saw a man on the far side of the room setting down a book he had been reading. His back was to her, and his dark hair curled to just past his shoulders.

"Asil?"

Upon Carys's words, the man turned around. "No, not Asil," Egemen Özdemir said with a gentle smile, coming out of the shadow to stand by Carys's bedside. "Though my son has been here many times in the past two days. However, the physician said you would wake soon, and I wanted to speak with you first. How are you feeling?"

"You have recovered, my lord," Carys said, a touch embarrassed. She never seemed to be at her best around the Lord of the Strait. "I am… tired. How long have I been in bed?"

"Just the two days," Egemen said, pulling up a chair and sitting down so that he wasn't looming over her. "Tadhg Bharda, former commander of the Empire, brought you into the castle and then abruptly surrendered, along with all of his men. The young woman, Moira, explained that I could be revived simply by breaking the statue in my quarters, and so I was. And now I have four officers under house arrest in the House of Flowers, an ambassador in the garrison, and a barracks overly full of foreign soldiers, also under house arrest."

"I missed a lot, then," Carys murmured, and looked back up at Egemen. "I am grateful you are revived, and that Asil is all right. What… what will you do with them?"

"I have been thinking about that quite a lot," the lord said, watching Carys's face. "I find myself in a difficult position. I would prefer not to put almost 200 men to death for following poor orders, particularly when their commander saw reason and surrendered peacefully."

Wincing, Carys glanced away. "I would prefer you not as well. They are good people who have been misused."

Egemen nodded. "I am beginning to understand that," he said, "but it does make the situation more complicated. The matter is further twisted because, as I understand it, they have sworn fealty to you. Not to me or to Vasi. The commander and his men follow Seer Arslan."

"What?" Carys said and struggled to sit up. Egemen rose from the chair and helped her, adjusting her pillows as if he were her servant or nurse, then adjusted the blanket and carefully brushed her hair back from her face. The caring gesture left Carys quietly stunned.

"Do you think you could eat?" Egemen asked, moving toward the bellpulls. "It would probably help the feeling of weakness. You have not had food in three days, if I understand how events fell out."

"I… yes, I think so, thank you," Carys said, still looking a touch confused. "My lord, what do you mean they swore fealty to me? I… I asked Tadhg… ah, I asked the commander to give his word, but—"

Carys was cut off as the door opened. Aylin must have been waiting for the summons, as the young woman came into the room quickly and practically ran toward the bed. "My lady!"

However, it seemed Aylin had not known who else was with the seer, and upon seeing the Lord of the Strait, the young woman froze, bowing deeply and not moving. Egemen chuckled quietly, almost soundlessly, and shook his head.

"Maid, will you please fetch some food and tea for Seer Arslan," Egemen said, and Aylin nodded without coming out of the bow. "Something suitable for convalescence. I'm sure the cooks will know what to do. And quickly, if you please."

"Yes, my lord," Aylin said, backing away and almost tripping over the rug as she did. "Of course, my lord, immediately! I'm sorry! I'll be back as soon as I can!"

With another little stumble, Aylin was out the door and down the hall in a flash. They could hear the steady drum of her steps as the door slowly swung closed behind her. Egemen chuckled again and turned back to Carys.

"I can't remember ever being that young, though I'm sure I was," the lord said with a wry smile, and Carys found herself smiling in return. "As we were discussing—Tadhg Bharda informed first the guard, then the Lord Commander, and finally Asil, that he would abide by any decision our courts made, but that he and his men no longer served the Empire, but rather served your will."

"I don't… really understand what that means," Carys said helplessly.

Egemen nodded, his expression thoughtful. "I'm still determining that myself. I do believe you, Carys—I think they are good people.

However, I cannot harbor a threat in my own city. Then there is the matter of the killing of Pasha Kaplan. I understand it likely saved my life, and certainly saved yours, but as the head of one of the Great Families, it has also made many people very upset."

Closing her eyes, Carys leaned her head back against the headboard and sighed. Then she felt a hand on her head, gently brushing back her hair again. She looked up to see Egemen smiling at her sympathetically.

"It is exhausting, isn't it," the lord said, "having the weight of so many lives on your shoulders."

"My lord, I never meant to—"

"I know," Egemen said, and gently touched her cheek. "Asil is infatuated with you, do you know that? I'm sure you do—you're too knowledgeable a woman. And now you have a battalion at your command, one that is better trained and outfitted than any guard in Vasi. I know you mean no harm to my family or my city, Seer Arslan. It is your city, too, after all. And I am sure I owe you my life, and my son's life, for your actions. It is… a predicament."

There didn't seem to be any way Carys could answer or assuage the lord's concerns, and Egemen did not seem to be expecting it. He brushed back Carys's hair a final time, a comforting and fatherly gesture, and stepped away from the bedside.

"You should rest, Seer Arslan," Egemen said, heading toward the door. "I'm sure Aylin will be back shortly to see you fed and cared for. I thank you for all you have done for Vasi, for my son, and for me. I will weigh all of it in my decisions."

There was that same sympathetic smile, and then the Lord of the Strait left the room, leaving Carys in bed feeling helpless in more ways than one. Aylin appeared moments later, helped Carys eat, then helped the seer to lie back once more, cleaning up the tray and heading out. With nothing else to keep her up, Carys slept.

ℂ ℂ ℂ

Asil paced in his father's study as Egemen composed a letter, though Asil was not sure to whom. Neither man spoke, but Asil continued his restless pacing, his gaze far away as he contemplated what his father had said. There was no simple way out of this situation. Imprisoning the commander and his knights might mollify the Great Families, but it felt wrong, and Asil imagined there was a good chance Carys would never forgive either of them. Not to mention that they would still have a company of soldiers to deal with. Executions were absolutely out of the question. The only man who actually committed a crime was Ambassador Criddubh, and he would rot away in the garrison for the rest of his days. The death of Pasha Kaplan and his two guards had been unfortunate, but a trial would likely see Tadhg absolved of all guilt, particularly with Carys's testimony. The trial wouldn't satisfy the Great Families, however. It was possible that the Lord of the Strait could just exile the remaining southerners, but Tadhg would probably refuse to leave Carys, and… Asil honestly didn't want to know if Carys would agree to go with them.

"You don't have to stay," Egemen said, rousing Asil from his thoughts and bringing an end to the pacing. "If you wish to see if she is still awake, or to wait for her to wake once more, you may go. Honestly, the pacing is distracting."

Sensing the rebuke, Asil turned toward his father and straightened his shoulders. "We still have not resolved the situation," Asil pointed out.

"Nor will we today," Egemen said, not looking up from his task. When Asil still didn't leave, Egemen sighed and set down his pen, looking up at his son. "This is not a simple situation, and there is no simple answer, but you must know that things are going to change. Spend time with your friend while you can, Asil."

The implication was impossible to miss, and Asil wanted to argue, but he also knew his father well enough to know it wouldn't do any good. After a moment, he gave a curt nod and left the room, heading to the west wing at what he hoped did not appear to be too hurried of a pace. When he arrived at Carys's door, he encountered Aylin quietly slipping out.

"Oh! My lord!" The young maid almost dropped her tray, though thankfully it was empty. "The seer is still sleeping, my lord. The physician sent me with a draught and a salve for her scrapes, but I left them by her bedside along with some juice. And… and, well, I just wanted to check on her, my lord."

Asil smiled at the nervous young woman. "It's all right, Aylin. I know Carys trusts you; I'm not worried about you being here."

"She does?" Aylin asked, her eyes growing wide and hopeful, and Asil found himself charmed.

"Of course she does," he said. "I believe I will stay and wait for her to wake. Could you be so kind as to bring me tea, and perhaps some cheese rolls?"

"Of course, my lord," Aylin said, bobbing a curtsey and taking off.

Watching her go, Asil shook his head. Aylin's devotion was touching. Another shake of the head, and Asil went into Carys's room.

As expected, Carys was in bed, her breathing deep and even, sound asleep. The bruise that stretched under her eye to her cheekbone was a vivid purple, and the cut beneath it had scabbed over and darkened. It still filled Asil with anger to think that Muhan Kaplan had laid a hand on her; he would be clamoring for vengeance if the pasha had not already died on Generys's blade. Carys looked paler than usual, young and vulnerable. Asil had never thought of her as being either of those things.

"I couldn't protect you," Asil murmured into the quiet room, and felt his heart ache. "You were in my own house, and they still hurt you. But you… you protected me."

There was no answer, save for Carys's continued breathing. Asil shook his head, and sat down in the high-backed chair, plucking one of the many books off the table and leafing through it for something to distract himself with.

Tea and more arrived in short order, with Aylin bringing up a tray and setting everything out. It was more food than Asil had asked for—not just cheese rolls, but slices of apricot and a couple small cakes. As Aylin picked up the tray to leave, she paused and looked pensively at Asil. Asil decided to take pity on her.

"Did you want to ask me something, Aylin?" he asked, doing his best not to smirk.

"Y-yes, my lord," Aylin said, eyes downcast. "I just… I wondered if… has anyone told Commander Bharda that Seer Arslan is all right? I know… I heard what he did, but… well, I know he cared for her. I asked Nazim, but he didn't know."

That was not the question Asil had been expecting. "No, I don't imagine anyone has," he said coldly.

"Well… shouldn't someone?" Aylin asked, and looked up, her eyes imploring.

A muscle in Asil's jaw twitched. "Thank you for the tea, Aylin. That will be all."

Aylin dropped a quick curtsey and left immediately. Asil sighed after the door shut. It was not the young woman's fault that Asil did not wish to be reminded of Carys's affection for the general. It was not precisely Aylin's place to question the Heir of the Strait on the matter, or any matter, but he had given her permission to. It was also hardly a secret at this point, as no one in the castle could imagine what would have prompted the general's declaration of fealty aside from love. Asil scowled at the door for another moment, and then felt… uncomfortable. As if someone were glaring at him. Carys was still asleep, and there was no one else in the room, but Asil felt the weight of judgment settle on his shoulders.

"All right," he said at last, loud enough that Carys shifted in her sleep and murmured but did not wake. Asil walked over to Carys's desk and sat down, pulling out a paper and pen. With a sigh, he began to compose a letter to the commander while Carys continued to sleep. The strange weight began to lift, and Asil begrudgingly admitted to himself that it was probably the noble thing to do. After the letter had been finished, sealed, and sent off, Asil finally settled in for tea. It was more warm than hot by then, but it would do.

The tea was reduced to dregs and crumbs, and Asil was beginning to drift while attempting to read when he heard a quiet groan on the bed. Looking over, he saw Carys slowly open her eyes, yawning, and eventually focus on him.

"It is you this time," Carys said with a soft smile.

Asil smiled in return. "Who else would I be?"

"Last time it was your father," Carys said, and tried to push herself up. She was unsteady, and Asil set down the book, coming over to help.

"The two of you look very similar from behind. Your hair is the same length, it curls into those perfect ringlets, and you both have magnificent shoulders."

Asil's brows flew up in surprise. "I didn't realize you had looked at me often enough to have such a clear image of me," he said as he adjusted the pillows and then sat on the edge of the bed.

With a bit of a wry smile, Carys just shook her head. "Of course I have, you idiot. We spend almost every day together. And you know you're handsome. Why wouldn't I look?"

Taking Carys's hand, Asil lifted it up and kissed it softly. "I suppose we have spent quite a bit of time together," he said, and felt his heart ache again. "How are you feeling?"

"Still tired, and it hurts a bit," Carys said honestly. "All through my body, but particularly my face."

Asil's eyes darted to the table. "Oh, right," he said, letting go and standing up. "Aylin brought this in from the physician while you were sleeping. A draught for pain, and a salve for the cut and your scrapes."

A soft, warm smile lit up Carys's face as Asil played nurse, helping her drink the tincture and then applying the salve. She continued to just watch him, her eyes full of affection. In a way, that made the ache even worse. What would he do without her wit, her calm, and her smile?

Sensing that something was wrong, Carys considered what it might be. Asil would have told her if the Lord of the Strait had come to a decision, so it wasn't that. Perhaps it was just the same uncertainty that held all of them. She looked up at the clock, and back at Asil, then reached out to grab his hand.

Asil stopped. "What is it?"

"It's a little late," Carys said, smiling again, "and I'm still very sleepy. Come to bed with me. I'm sure Nazim will know where you are."

For a moment Asil considered, then sighed and smiled back. "We should really try this someday when one of us isn't physically or emotionally broken," he commented, but began to remove his sash.

Carys just giggled. "Someday."

As Asil undressed, Carys just watched him quietly, with that same affectionate smile, and yawned now and then. It didn't take long to disrobe and turn down the lights, and in moments he was climbing into Carys's bed, which, being smaller than his own, meant they were closer together by necessity. Reaching out, Asil took her hand, and Carys laced their fingers together.

"I'm not letting this go, Carys," he said quietly, and she murmured something unintelligible in response. He laughed quietly at himself, and then settled in to sleep.

Chapter 26

IT WAS TWO more days before Carys was able to get out of bed and begin moving about on her own. Once on her feet again, however, she seemed to recover very quickly. Maris had feared a longer convalescence, but the same day Carys managed to get out of bed also saw her taking a leisurely walk around the balcony. She was not permitted to leave her room, and though it galled her, she obeyed Maris's orders. Carys read, visited with Asil, and endured Judex manifesting long enough to inform her that she was a terrible patient. She considered reading the cards but decided against it. She wanted to inquire about Tadhg and the others but was not certain it would be well received.

Five days after the attempt on the castle, three days after Carys had come back to consciousness, Aylin entered Carys's room earlier than usual bearing an exquisite dress. It was the blue-green of the shallow waters in the harbor, painstakingly embroidered with seed pearls and lapis, over an underdress of the palest misty gray. The sleeves were tight to the elbows, then the full, gauzy sleeves of the underdress spilled out. Carys simply stared at it for a moment.

"Aylin, what is going on?" Carys asked, looking over at the girl.

Looking a touch uncomfortable, Aylin hung up the dress. "You are expected in the court in a little over an hour, seer," Aylin said, not looking up. "I... I will need to help you dress. The baths are already warmed, and we have a litter to take you down if you cannot walk that far. The

Lord of the Strait has made his decision and will pass judgment today. He says that it is necessary that you be in attendance."

"Oh," Carys said, standing up carefully. "Did he say anything else? Or did Asil say anything?"

Eyes still downcast, Aylin just shook her head and brought Carys her robe. It seemed that the maid was not saying something, possibly not saying many things, but Carys didn't have the energy to question her. Instead, she pulled on her robe and took the litter down to the baths, where the attendants saw her scrubbed and her hair done, and then returned to let Aylin dress her. It was a lengthy process, and she understood why Aylin had insisted Carys would need help. She would have needed a second pair of hands even if she were not still in recovery. There were the smallclothes, then a slip, then the underdress, then the dress itself, and finally a heavy sash. It fit Carys perfectly, which was really no surprise—everything from the seamstresses in the castle had been perfect.

"It suits you, seer," Aylin said, with a soft and shy smile. "You look very lovely."

"I'm pretty sure I could buy my shop with this dress," Carys muttered, looking at herself in the mirror. She couldn't argue with Aylin, though. It did look lovely.

Stepping over to the wardrobe, Aylin returned a moment later with a small case. It was the jewelry Asil had given Carys, the pieces that he'd said had once belonged to the Lord's Seer. She had the sense to sit so that Aylin could put the necklace on her. With the final touches in place, Aylin stepped back and positively glowed at Carys.

"My la—ah, seer, you look like a princess," Aylin said, something softly adoring in her gaze. Carys looked into the maid's eyes and didn't have the heart to argue.

There was a knock at the door, and Aylin's smile fell. "Oh, it's time," the maid said. She just stood for a moment as Carys rose to her feet, then impulsively stepped forward and took Carys's hand. "I know a little about what is going to happen, and I can't tell you, but please know that no one will abandon you."

Startled, Carys just looked back at Aylin for a moment, then slowly nodded. "Thank you, Aylin. You will help me out of this dress when all this is done, yes?"

"Of course, my lady," Aylin said, not bothering to correct this time, and stepped out of the way.

At the door, Asil waited with a guardsman. The Heir was also dressed formally, resplendent in his jacket and long vest, and possibly wearing more layers than Carys. He just stared at Carys for a moment, slightly stunned as she stood in the doorway, then smiled.

"You look exceptional," Asil said, taking her hand and kissing the back of it. "I wish it was for a happier occasion. My father and the prisoners await us. We should not keep them waiting."

The walk to the throne room was surprisingly quiet. There were no extra servants in the hall, no retainers mingling at the grand stair. As they reached the throne room, however, Carys understood why. She had never seen so many people attending court. The remaining heads of the Great Families were there, as were their sons. No one from the Kaplan family was in attendance, but Carys suspected that was a problem that was still being solved.

A herald announced their arrival, and all eyes turned to Carys and Asil as they walked toward the throne, an excited murmur building in the crowd. All eyes except those of the four who stood in chains before the Lord of the Strait. Carys felt her heart lurch. Generys looked cold and detached, as she had the day the ship had arrived. Cillian looked shamed and resigned, his gaze downcast. Áedh appeared agitated, his gaze flicking from the Lord of the Strait to Tadhg. And Tadhg—the commander looked ahead at the Lord of the Strait. Not with anger—he accepted his possible fate—but wherever his gaze fell, it was absolutely not on Carys.

The Lord of the Strait stood, and the excited murmur hushed, though did not disappear entirely. "Nobles of Vasi," Egemen began, his voice clear and resonant, carrying through the hall, "representatives of the Great Families, and honored guests. We are here this morning to decide a serious matter. It has been eight days since the attempt on my life, and five days since the failed attempt on my son's life. The vile outsider who devised these plans is in custody and will remain so as we question him about the intentions of the nation to the south. Before us stand the commanders of the battalion which sits under guard in the harbor. They surrendered themselves to us of their own accord, with no resistance."

"They murdered Pasha Kaplan," a voice cried out, and the murmur in the room rose and fell again. The voice belonged to an older man, surely someone's grandfather, standing next to a somewhat nervous but determined-looking man close to Asil's age.

"Have a care, Pasha Köse," Egemen said, turning toward the protester with a dry countenance. "Muhan Kaplan, by all evidence, was a traitor to Vasi and came close to igniting a chain of events that would have not only destroyed House Özdemir but also much of the city. We have not yet determined how many members of his family were complicit in his actions. There is also evidence to suggest that other members of the Great Families may have been prepared to aid and assist with his treason."

The murmur quieted again as the implication in the lord's words filtered through the crowd. The Great Families were still under suspicion. The representatives of the other noble houses, standing to the right and left of Egemen, were quiet and unaffected. Carys suspected that Egemen had already briefed them on his plans. That, or they were both consummate actors.

Pasha Köse drew himself up, indignant. "I am a proud and loyal citizen of Vasi," he said, and the man next to him—his grandson, if Carys recalled, now that she knew the family name—was beginning to look more nervous and less resolute. "I would never commit actions that weakened our city. But I cannot accept that a man of the Great Families was cut down like a dog by these southern snakes!"

"Then maybe he shouldn't have tried to run," Generys said, her icy voice cutting through the crowd.

There was a moment of shocked silence, and then the room was in a roar. Cillian hissed at Generys, who continued to stare impassively forward. The pashas were shouting, and Pasha Köse, in particular, looked as if he were about to collapse as his face grew red and he hurled insults at the four in chains, and Generys in particular. Carys made out the word "whore" several times and was unable to keep from glaring at the man. Pasha Yasuv and his son, Serhat, were silent, as was Pasha Bulut. They were looking at the other families, seeing which ones were frothing in rage, and coming to conclusions.

"Enough," Egemen shouted, and the room fell into silence. "Pasha Köse, if you speak out again, you will be cast from the room along with your grandson. Do I make myself clear?"

Still red in the face, and not trusting his voice, Pasha Köse simply bowed his head. Egemen then looked to Generys and said no words, but the woman's eyes drifted down under the weight of the lord's stare.

"Seer Carys Arslan."

With a start, Carys's eyes snapped to the Lord of the Strait. She had honestly not expected to be addressed in all this. She thought she was there to witness, not participate.

"Please step forward," Egemen commanded, and Carys did so without hesitation, hands clasped before her. "Seer Arslan, you were assigned as liaison to the prisoners while they were guests of the castle. You spent time with them, studied them. My son tells me you found that the soldiers of the battalion and their commanders were bound and cursed, and many still are. Is that correct?"

"Yes, my lord," Carys answered, her head up, and the murmur in the room rose again. "When I discovered the curses, I began lifting them, but I have had very little contact with the greater number of soldiers. From what I have been able to deduce, the leaders in the south keep their soldiers fettered so that they will not question orders."

The shocked gasps and growing current of outrage in the crowd was satisfying. Say what one might about Vasi with its tensions and the merchants with their fake court, it was a place that took pride in the sense of individuality that shone through the city, from its mismatched neighborhoods to its vibrant and opinionated peoples.

"Seer Arslan, you were instrumental in discovering this plot and stopping the attempt on my son's life," Egemen said, and there was a strange mix of both gratitude and sorrow in his voice. "We understand that the prisoners turned their blades because you demanded it, and that

Pasha Kaplan forced their hands to the actions that ended in his death. We also understand, however, that they have sworn themselves to your service, and that those men still cursed in the barracks have taken this to mean that you are now their liege. Is that correct?"

Carys was certain she could have heard a pin drop in that moment. It felt as if the entire room were holding its breath. "I—" she began, wanting to explain, but suddenly understood that the details didn't matter. "Yes, my lord."

The room exploded again. It wasn't angry, per se, but there was more shock, and the chatter was intensely animated. It was the scandal of a generation when laid out in its bare bones this way, without any of the details or an understanding of how the spirits worked.

"Oh, they'll be talking about you for ages," Judex murmured from behind her, and Carys twitched with the want to punch him.

"Silence," Egemen roared, and the room once again hushed. He sighed and looked back to Carys. Everyone looked at Carys. For the first time that morning, even Tadhg looked at Carys. She realized quite suddenly that he was afraid of what he would see in her gaze. Not that it mattered, as her eyes were veiled as usual.

"Seer Arslan, we are grateful for all you have done," Egemen said, his voice firm and carrying. "You saved House Özdemir from demise, and you saved Vasi from being seized by opportunists and vultures. And you now command a battalion of the most finely trained soldiers I have ever witnessed. I have conferred with House Killic and House Aydin, as well as the Lord of the River. Approach."

Eyes wide, and now a touch frightened, Carys obeyed and approached the throne. Her eyes flicked briefly to Asil as she passed him, and she saw that Asil's eyes were growing wide in realization. Whatever this was, Asil had not been a part of it, but he was bright enough to piece something together. Looking back to the throne, Carys saw that Lady Meliha Aydin had also stepped forward, and was holding something. Carys felt the threads tug at her, and intuition told her to only go to the second step, not ascend completely. That got a faint smile of approval from Lady Aydin.

"Seer Carys Arslan," Egemen said, turning to Lady Aydin and taking the object from her. It was a coronet. "For your service to House Özdemir, the people of Vasi, and all of the Strait, we have seen fit to award you peerage. The abandoned city of Adalar shall be granted to you, along with its titles and rights within the Kingdoms of Dawn."

The color drained from Carys's face, and Egemen looked at her with that sad, sympathetic smile she had seen when she first woke after the attack. He lifted the coronet, and Carys had enough sense left to bow her head as he placed it upon her brow. She felt a shifting of the threads and remembered her vision with the ring of fire circling her brow. This was it. This was what the spirit had been showing her.

"You and your men will have a chance to reclaim Adalar from the wilds," Egemen said quietly, his voice not reaching past the throne and dais. "We will assist you in all possible ways to prepare you for your departure. I will not leave you to the wolves, but I cannot continue to harbor a potential threat. Face the room, child."

Gathering her resolve, Carys turned and faced the elite of Vasi. Tadhg and Generys both looked shocked, though not confused. They understood what was happening. Cillian also understood, and smiled sadly, bowing his head to Carys. Áedh was actually starting to grin. The merchant families were a mix of surprised and outraged, though Pasha Bulut just smiled, lifting his hands in a pantomime of a clap as Carys looked his way. The different members of the noble houses, however, seemed strangely at peace and pleased—even Adnan Kilic smiled gently at Carys. Asil…

Asil looked as if his heart had just been broken.

"Citizens of Vasi, I present to you," Egemen called out, his voice ringing in Carys's ears, "the Lady of the Bridges!"

There was no quieting the crowd after that. Carys took unsteady steps down as a guard came forward and unlocked the chains binding Tadhg and the others. Asil glared at his father, who just looked back at his son with that same regretful sympathy. As Carys drew close, Tadhg bowed deeply, the others just a beat behind, and Áedh was grinning like a fiend. Carys nodded and then turned back to face the throne, the four falling in formation behind her. She looked up at Egemon and inclined her head respectfully but did not bow. She was no longer his subject. She then turned and took herself from the room, her reserves depleted, and the commander and his knights followed her.

As the doors of the throne room closed behind them, shutting out the sound of the crowd, Carys's legs started to give out. Tadhg was at her side immediately, holding her up. She silenced her pride and let him help her to a bench. Her heart was hammering in her chest, and tears had started to fill her eyes. She half-expected Judex to start demeaning her, but the spirit was silent and absent.

"Are you all right, my lady?" Tadhg asked carefully, his tone cautious.

"No," Carys whispered, closing her eyes.

"Really?" Áedh asked, surprised. "You were just given a title and land, if I caught what's going on. And us! You should be fine!"

"By the Mother, Áedh, shut up!" Generys smacked him in the back of the head, then turned toward Carys. "My lady, I'm sorry."

Eyes still closed, Carys took a shuddering breath. She wanted to correct them, as she had corrected Aylin almost daily since she'd come to the castle, but it was no longer a mistake. She reached up carefully and took the coronet from her head so that she could examine it. It was a simple and beautiful piece. She wanted to hurl it across the hallway, but she didn't dare.

The sound of someone clearing their throat brought Carys and the others out of their reverie. Baris was there, and clearly had been for some time.

"My lady," the castellan said, bowing. "Congratulations on your ascension. I am here to oversee moving you and your belongings to the House of Flowers until you are ready to depart for Adalar."

Looking up at Basil, Carys wilted. "I don't even get to return to my own room?"

Baris looked pained but shook his head. "It is not your room anymore, my lady. The ruler of another kingdom cannot be the Lord's Seer."

Carys couldn't keep the tears from falling.

"I hope you burned the sheets if she gets Peadar's room," Áedh muttered, and Cillian punched him.

"I have a litter ready to take you to the House of Flowers, my lady, and a fresh lunch will be waiting for you and your men," Baris said, gently pushing the conversation forward. "Lady Aydin will be visiting you after lunch to discuss the future. You are expected to sail in two weeks, my lady."

Carys had almost gone catatonic. She simply nodded and said nothing else, as Tadhg helped her into the litter and she was taken from the Lord's Hall.

Chapter 27

ASIL HAD LEFT the throne room as quickly as he reasonably could, but Carys was gone, and the hall was mostly empty by the time he stepped out. He paced for a moment, then headed down the hall to her room, only to find it also empty, the bed stripped, the dressing room barren. He stood there for a moment in shock, then slowly drifted over to the bed, sliding a hand over the coverlet waiting to be washed.

"This is a nightmare," Asil murmured, clutching the fabric.

"My Heir," the voice of Meliha Aydin caused Asil to turn and let go, "the Lady of the Bridges has been moved to the House of Flowers." Meliha looked at Asil with the same sad sympathy he had been seeing from her since she told him about the affair.

"I assume my father ordered it," Asil said, his voice sounding hollow even to himself. "How long before they send her away?"

"Two weeks," Meliha said, and walked up to Asil, setting a hand on his shoulder. "Asil, I'm so sorry. We need to keep the southerners out of the castle, but as the newly crowned ruler of Adalar, Carys needs to be with her retinue. It was the best solution."

Asil ran his hands over his face. "How are we just sending her off in two weeks? We're perilously close to fall. How is she going to survive the winter in the ruins of a city? With a bunch of soldiers?"

"You should give your father more credit than that," Meliha said, gently admonishing. "There are funds available to those who would retake one of the cities, from a purse that all the Kingdoms of Dawn have contributed to. It has been done before, up near Ropa. There are people from the castle who have volunteered to go with her and be part of her new household. Aylin practically leapt at the chance. The ship that brought the soldiers was also fully crewed. The Lord of the River has promised to send builders to repair the docks surrounding Adalar, and they should already be on their way. And finally, she will have the benefit of our new allies from the interior. They respect those with a seer's abilities. They may look more kindly upon Carys than they did your father."

"That is…something," Asil said, begrudgingly.

"Asil…" Meliha considered for a moment. "Your father did not do this to punish you. He didn't do it to punish anyone. And this is not the nightmare you think it is. Asil, he knows… we all know you love her. You just need time to see—"

Turning, Asil held up his hand. "I cannot discuss this right now." He stormed out of the room, leaving Meliha behind, the sound of her sigh following him out. Did he love her? Perhaps. It wasn't a love like the storybooks. She was important to him, like Hasim was important to him. His dear friend. If it was easy to admit he loved Hasim, perhaps he did love Carys. Perhaps that explained the pain he felt at losing her.

Two weeks. Asil knew there was no changing his father's mind. He had two weeks with his friend. Then it would all end.

☾ ☾ ☾

The days seemed to pass in a blur. It was another two days before Carys felt like herself again, able to move about as she pleased without needing a litter for longer trips. She learned more about Tadhg, Cillian, Generys, and Áedh. She considered how she might need to alter their established hierarchy. Áedh needed a hand to guide him, but Cillian and Generys less so. Carys felt like she should restructure things out of necessity, to make it less like the Empire, but she also had no idea what a better way would look like.

The shifting in their positions had also seemed to curb Tadhg's desire for her. In a way it was a relief. Her heart still hurt from their meeting at the gate, when she realized they likely would have murdered Asil had she not been there to stop them.

As for Asil, the two of them spent every moment they could together, though there weren't many. It was no longer appropriate for either of them to stow away for a night in the other's room. Technically it never had been, but now Carys could not enter the castle without a guard, and similarly Asil could not come to the House of Flowers without one. They would laugh, a touch bitterly, about how despite all the rumors, Carys had never actually succeeded in seducing the Heir.

There were meetings. Carys met the Lord of the River, Boldizsar Nagy, and his sons, Farkas and Elek. Carys had been seated between Farkas and Elek during dinner, and both had been competitively flirtatious, attempting to outdo the other. Long hours were spent speaking with Meliha Aydin. Lady Aydin was sending a small contingent from her house with Carys, to help start another university, and to continue to be the keepers of all knowledge. Carys met her new spymaster, a young man who barely seemed old enough for the position, but who came with every recommendation Lady Aydin could give.

The ship in the harbor was scrubbed down, the crest of the empire painted over with a coronet tangled in vines against a silver circle that represented the moon. This was to be the crest of Carys's house. She had chosen the symbols from her cards, her shop, the things that had mattered most to her. The heraldry artist had done a fine job combining them.

Ferah was now running the shop. She had sobbed in gratitude when Carys visited her and offered her the shop and the practice. Ferah would still need lessons, but there were people here who could teach her. Carys had left Ferah everything, save for her grandmother's cane and the great carved chair from the alcove.

The sun rose bright and clear on the morning Carys was to depart. Aylin brought in breakfast, excited and happy for the voyage. Carys had tried to dissuade her from the journey, but the young maid had been insistent. That was when Carys learned that Aylin's parents lived and worked in Ropa, that Aylin had lived with an aunt before coming to work in the castle, and that there was very little keeping her here.

"I have your traveling clothes, my lady," Aylin said, coming in the room with a bundle as Carys finished her breakfast. "Will you need any help dressing?"

"Not today," Carys murmured, looking out the window at the gardens beyond. The view from the master suite in the House of Flowers was quite lovely. "Is everyone waiting on me?"

"Ah, well," Aylin squirmed a little and blushed. "Yes, my lady. But that doesn't mean you need to hurry! You are the Lady of the Bridges—you can take your time if you please!"

Carys looked down into her coffee. The title still did not feel real. There were times when all of this felt like a farce, and she kept waiting for a curtain to go up and to see an audience laughing at her.

"We will be ready when you are, my lady," Aylin said, and took herself out of the room.

"You really ought to stop feeling so sorry for yourself," Judex chimed in after the door shut. "I appreciate that you never wanted this, but you still managed to go from a nothing shop girl to a peer of the realm. As much as it completely pains me to say it, your grandmother would likely be proud. Aside from how disgustingly sullen you are about the whole thing."

Blinking, Carys looked up from her drink. "Did you just… compliment me?"

Judex sighed. "No, I made an observation while criticizing your demeanor. I'm not here to discuss your general ingratitude. I am here to say goodbye."

Carys's mouth fell open. "I would ask if you were joking, but that isn't something you do. You are sarcastic and biting, but… you're leaving?"

"There is someone who requires my oversight more than you," Judex said simply. "I have followed you for ten years, and while you're fairly stupid, there are others who are more stupid. It is time for me to move on."

"This day could not feel more uncanny," Carys murmured, "and I'm having some trouble believing you."

"Because you're being stupid again," Judex pointed out acidly. His expression softened, just for a moment, and he bowed his head. "Goodbye, Seer."

"Goodbye," Carys returned, and watched the plumes of smoke fade into nothing. She didn't completely understand the churning combination of relief and sorrow that flooded her. She just continued to stand there for another moment, then finally moved to get dressed.

By the time Carys emerged from her room, the main hall of the House of Flowers was empty, save for Halil and Tadhg. The butler smiled at Carys and bowed. "It has been an honor to serve you, my lady. I do hope you will return to Vasi soon."

"I suppose we will see," Carys said, still feeling unsettled and a touch helpless.

Tadhg also bowed. "Are you ready, my lady?"

"No," Carys said with a small laugh, "but I never will be. Let us go."

Tadhg led the way out of the villa to a waiting carriage. It was an open carriage, the days still warm, though the faintest chill in the breeze promised that fall was coming. Carys rode with Tadhg across from her, the knights and Aylin in another carriage. They circled the castle and Carys looked for Asil. He was nowhere to be seen. Perhaps he was at the dock.

The journey through the city was melancholy, and Carys fought the urge to cry. This was her home. The home of her mother, her grandmother, generations of her family. They passed through the merchant quarter, and Carys looked down the street where her shop sat, now in the hands of someone new. Tears fell as they headed past the House of the Divine Mother, children giggling and waving from the second floor.

The tears were stilled by the shock of what awaited Carys in the port. It seemed as if half the city were there, and cheers went up as her carriage rumbled down the cobblestone toward the docks. People screamed and waved, jubilant, and Carys waved back almost in a daze. Asil, Hasim, Lady Aydin, and Lord Özdemir were all waiting on the docks as the carriage pulled to a stop. Hasim ran up with a smile, offering Carys a hand down. Moira was just behind him, her writing board in hand.

"What is all this?" Carys asked, bewildered, as Hasim's smile grew wider.

"You are a legend in your own time, Lady Arslan," Hasim said. "The seer who saved the Lord of the Strait and won herself a crown in the process."

Carys simply looked around, stupefied, as people continued to cheer and wave. Moira giggled a little. Carys was pretty sure she had never heard Moira giggle before.

"Wave back, my lady," the secretary said. Carys did, and the crowd grew louder.

Hasim escorted Carys to where the nobles of Vasi waited. Egemon set his hands on her shoulders and smiled down at her. "I hope you do not hate me for this, Lady Arslan. I hope in time you will understand."

"I do not hate you, Lord Özdemir," Carys said, looking embarrassed. "I..it hurts too much right now, and I don't completely understand yet, but I do not hate you."

Egemon nodded. "Thank you, my lady."

Stepping in, Meliha took Carys's hands and squeezed them. "You have everyone you need, Lady Arslan. I am sorry that it is terrifying and that it hurts, but you can come back to the city soon. You will have a new home, but you are not abandoning this one forever."

Tears stung her eyes once more, but Carys managed a smile and nodded. She stepped away from Meliha and turned to Asil. He looked miserable, but he stepped forward and took Carys's hands, his thumbs gently brushing the back of them.

"When I came for you that night, at your shop, I never thought it would lead us here," Asil said ruefully.

"Nor I." Carys looked up at Asil, and her head tipped slightly as she considered. "I have something I have to tell you before I step onto that ship, and I hope you can forgive me for it."

Taking a breath, Asil nodded. "Anything, Carys."

"I love you, Asil."

Tears streaked Carys's cheeks again as Asil stared at her in wide-eyed shock. She took her hands away and let herself be ushered to the ship, Moira and Tadhg just behind her. She stood at the railing, staring down at everyone she had come to care for, everyone who had filled the life she hadn't realized was empty.

"Wave again, my lady," Moira said gently. "No one can see that you're crying from here."

☽☽

"Are you all right?" Hasim asked as they watched the ship pull away from the dock.

"I most certainly am not," Asil answered, and ran a hand through his hair. "Do you know what she had the gall to tell me before she boarded?"

A smile quirked the corner of Hasim's mouth. "Based on how utterly poleaxed you looked at the time, I would guess that she said she loved you."

"I hate you for knowing that," Asil muttered, still watching the ship.

The playful smile softened. "You do not. I am sorry, Asil. I know it hurts. I know you feel lost right now."

Closing his eyes for a moment, Asil just nodded. "So now what do we do?"

"Get drunk," Hasim suggested, "go visit the Alchemist's Guild, see if there are any bets on how long Carys has before the suitors start arriving? I understand Fardas and Elek were quite insistent at that dinner last week."

Asil looked at Hasim in confusion. "Suitors? Why?"

"Carys is the only unmarried woman in a ruling family between the ages of 16 and 40," Hasim pointed out, amused. "It makes her very popular."

Asil's eyes grew very wide. "My father is a conniving bastard, and I am an idiot. She's the head of a noble house now. She is my peer."

Laughing, Hasim clapped Asil on the back. "Yes. On all counts."